ROADS
NOT
TAKEN

Books published by The Ballantine Publishing Group are available at quantity discounts on bulk purchases for premium, educational, fund-raising, and special sales use. For details, please call 1-800-733-3000.

ROADS NOT TAKEN

Tales of Alternate History

Edited by
Gardner Dozois
and
Stanley Schmidt

A Del Rey® Book
THE BALLANTINE PUBLISHING GROUP • NEW YORK

A Del Rey® Book
Published by The Ballantine Publishing Group
Compilation and introductions to the stories copyright © 1998 by Penny Marketing Limited Partnership

All rights reserved under International and Pan-American Copyright Conventions. Published in the United States by The Ballantine Publishing Group, a division of Random House, Inc., New York, and simultaneously in Canada by Random House of Canada Limited, Toronto.

Permission acknowledgments can be found on pages v–vi, which constitute an extension of this copyright page.

http://www.randomhouse.com
http://www.asimovs.com
http://www.analogsf.com

Library of Congress Catalog Card Number: 98-92821

ISBN 0-345-42194-9

Manufactured in the United States of America

First Edition: July 1998

10   9   8   7   6   5

Dedicated to
L. Sprague de Camp

Contents

What Is
Alternate History?

What if ... things had been different? What if ...
someone had made a different choice? How would history have progressed from that point on? The past can be
a signpost to the future. The exciting questions are:
which past ... and which future?

Alternate History is exactly what it sounds like: an
alternative to the history we know and have always
thought of as untouchable. It is the ultimate in "What
might have been?" in which an author takes a pivotal
turning point in history, spins it on its axis, and examines
what path events might have taken as a result. Another
name for this concept, used increasingly by historians, is
"counterfactual history." It is, without a doubt, fiction.
Yet it is so solidly based in fact that the best of it reads as
if it really happened.

One could, of course, describe any historical fiction as
alternate history, in that the fictional elements never actually occurred. What distinguishes true Alternate History is
its exploration of the *ramifications* of the author's machina-
tions. The initial change—often, but not always, centered
on a crucial turning point in history—can be achieved by
science-fictional means, such as time travel, or by taking
actual events and engineering slight but utterly plausible

twists. One example of the latter is Stephen Baxter's *Voyage* (1966), which uses the survival of John F. Kennedy to allow the development of a more ambitious—and very different—space program. Another is Harry Turtledove's *How Few Remain* (1997), which posits a Civil War in which the famed Confederate orders were *not* lost, so that the U.S.A. and the C.S.A. would have to learn to live alongside each other—albeit *very* unhappily.

Harry Turtledove has also used science-fictional devices to examine alternate histories: in his *The Guns of the South* (1992), it is the meddling of time travelers that brings on the victory of the South in the Civil War, and in his *Worldwar* series (1994–1996), an alien invasion of Earth right in the middle of World War II forces mortal foes, such as the Nazis and the Polish Jews, to unite in a common cause, thus drastically changing the course of history from that point on.

The urge to change history isn't new. The earliest Alternate History dates back to Louis Napoléon Geoffrey-Château's French nationalist tale *Napoléon et la conquête du monde, 1812–1823* (1836). In this book, Geoffrey-Château had Napoléon turn away from Moscow *before* the disastrous winter of 1812. Without the severe losses he would otherwise have suffered (and indeed, in real history, did suffer), Napoléon was able to conquer the world.

The first English-language Alternate History novel published was Castello Holford's *Aristopia* (1895). This one used a more fantastical premise to tweak history: *Aristopia* posited that the earliest European settlers of Virginia discovered a reef made of solid gold, which gave them the wealth to build a utopian society in North America.

The next major work of note was actually an anthology, published in 1931, assembled by British historian Sir John

Squire and titled *If It Had Happened Otherwise*. These stories, by Oxford and Cambridge scholars—some of the leading historians of their time—wrestled with questions such as "If the Moors in Spain Had Won" and "If Louis XVI Had Had an Atom of Firmness." In fact, four of the fourteen pieces comprising the book examined what have remained two of the most popular themes in the Alternate History genre: Napoléon's victory and the American Civil War. The authors included such luminaries as Hilaire Belloc, André Maurois, and Winston Churchill.

In 1933, Alternate History burst on the popular marketplace with the publication, in the December issue of *Astounding* magazine, of Nat Schachner's story "Ancestral Voices." This was followed quickly by Murray Leinster's "Sidewise in Time." William Sell's "Other Tracks" (*Astounding,* October 1938) tossed time travel into the mix for the first time, and a couple of years later L. Sprague de Camp's classic *Lest Darkness Fall* and "The Wheels of If" solidly established Alternate History as a viable and popular concept.

One of the most popular change points explored in Alternate History is World War II and the possibility of a Nazi victory. The first book to examine this was *When the Bells Rang* (1943), by Anthony Armstrong and Bruce Graeme. These authors postulated a Nazi invasion of England in 1940. Phillip K. Dick's *The Man in the High Castle* (1962) looks at a world in which North America was divided between the victorious Nazis and Japanese. And in what may be the most successful Alternate History to date, Robert Harris's *Fatherland*, Hitler's final solution was successful, and the postwar Nazi government actually managed to erase all knowledge of the death camps.

The other most popular historical change point is that of the American Civil War. One of the most famous of these examples is Ward Moore's *Bring the Jubilee* (1953), in which the reader spends much of the story in a third-world United States that never recovered from its defeat at the hands of the Confederacy. Harry Turtledove has since examined this same concept—executed quite differently, of course—in *The Guns of the South* and *How Few Remain*. And in *Stars and Stripes Forever* (1998), famed science fiction author Harry Harrison takes a different approach, postulating a British attack on America at the height of the Civil War that forces the United States and the Confederates to unite against a single enemy.

Alternate History can make great entertainment—especially as it so often involves fascinating political and military strategies and exciting battle scenes. But it can be more than that. Alternate History can encourage historical research, spark lively political debate, and, by examining how things *didn't* happen, shed light on the reason things *did* happen the way history says they did. It can be a wonderful teaching tool—a great way to incite curiosity in students and history buffs alike. And it's just plain fun.

We at Del Rey Books love Alternate History and believe you will, too. The following stories were collected to provide a taste of the genre for both neophytes and converts alike. They've been culled from *Asimov's Science Fiction* magazine and *Analog Science Fiction and Fact* by the editors of those two publications. Give them a try: I think you'll find they'll change not only the way you think about history but your own future reading history as well!

Enjoy!

Shelly Shapiro
Executive Editor
Del Rey Books

Must and Shall

Harry Turtledove

"Must and Shall" appeared in the November 1995 issue of Asimov's, *with an illustration by Steve Cavallo. Harry Turtledove publishes with us less frequently than we'd like, but he has had a string of stories in the magazine over the years, many of them Alternate History stories, including the Basil Argyros series, detailing the adventures of a "magistrianoi" in an alternate Byzantine Empire (collected in the book* Agent of Byzantium), *and the Sim series, which ran concurrently in both* Asimov's *and* Analog, *and which takes place in an alternate world in which European explorers find North America inhabited by hominids—Sims—instead of Indians (collected in the book* A Different Flesh). Asimov's *also published his chilling look at a Jewish family struggling to survive in a world where the Nazis won World War II, "In the Presence of Mine Enemies."*

Although he writes other kinds of science fiction as well, Turtledove has, in fact, become one of the most prominent writers of Alternate History stories in the business today, and probably the most popular and influential writer to work that territory since L. Sprague de Camp. In addition to the series mentioned above, Turtledove has published Alternate History novels such as The Guns of the South, *dealing with a time line in which the American Civil War turns out very differently, thanks to time-traveling gunrunners; the best-selling Worldwar series, in which the course of World War II is altered by attacking aliens; and, most recently, a look at a world where the Revolutionary War didn't happen, written with actor Richard Dreyfuss,* The Two Georges. *Turtledove is also the author of two multivolume Alternate History fantasy series, the multivolume Videssos Cycle and the Krispos Sequence. His other books include the novels* Wereblood, Werenight, Earthgrip, Noninterference, *and* A World of Difference, *and the collection* Kaleidoscope. *He won a Hugo Award in 1994 for his story "Down in the Bottomlands." A native Californian, Turtledove has a Ph.D. in Byzantine history from U.C.L.A., and has published a scholarly translation of a ninth-century Byzantine chronicle. He lives in Canoga Park, California, with his wife and family.*

The usual Alternate History take on the American Civil War is to postulate a world where the South won. In the unsettling story that follows, Turtledove instead paints a picture of a world where the North won—it just won a bit more decisively, with disastrous long-term results.

12 July 1864—Fort Stevens, north of Washington, D.C.

General Horatio Wright stood up on the earthen parapet to watch the men of the Sixth Corps, hastily recalled from Petersburg, drive Jubal Early's Confederates away from the capital of the United States. Down below the parapet, a tall, thin man in a black frock coat and a stovepipe hat asked, "How do we fare, General?"

"Splendidly." Wright's voice was full of relief. Had Early chosen to attack the line of forts around Washington the day before, he'd have faced only militiamen and clerks with muskets, and might well have broken through to the city. But Early had been late, and now the veterans from the Sixth Corps were pushing his troopers back. Washington City was surely saved. Perhaps because he was so relieved, Wright said, "Would you care to come up with me and see how we drive them?"

"I should like that very much, thank you," Abraham Lincoln said, and climbed the ladder to stand beside him.

Never in his wildest nightmares had Wright imagined the president accepting. Lincoln had peered over the parapet several times already, and drawn fire from the Confederates. They were surely too far from Fort Stevens to recognize him, but with his height and the hat he made a fine target.

Not far away, a man was wounded and fell back with a cry. General Wright interposed his body between President Lincoln and the Confederates. Lincoln spoiled that by stepping away from him. "Mr. President, I really must insist that you retire to a position of safety," Wright said. "This is no place for you; you must step down at once!"

Lincoln took no notice of him, but continued to watch the fighting north of the fort. A captain behind the parapet, perhaps not recognizing his commander-in-chief, shouted, "Get down, you damn fool, before you get shot!"

When Lincoln did not move, Wright said, "If you do not get down, sir, I shall summon a body of soldiers to

*remove you by force." He gulped at his own temerity in
threatening the President of the United States.*

*Lincoln seemed more amused than anything else. He
started to turn away, to walk back toward the ladder.
Instead, after half a step, he crumpled bonelessly. Wright
had thought of nightmares before. Now one came to life
in front of his horrified eyes. Careless of his own safety,
he crouched by the president, whose blood poured from a
massive head wound into the muddy dirt atop the
parapet. Lincoln's face wore an expression of mild surprise. His chest hitched a couple of times, then was still.*

*The captain who'd shouted at Lincoln to get down
mounted the parapet. His eyes widened. "Dear God," he
groaned. "It is the president."*

*Wright thought he recognized him. "You're Holmes,
aren't you?" he said. Somehow it was comforting to
know the man you were addressing when the world
seemed to crumble around you.*

*"Yes, sir, Oliver W. Holmes, 20th Massachusetts," the
young captain answered.*

*"Well, Captain Holmes, fetch a physician here at
once," Wright said. Holmes nodded and hurried away.
Wright wondered at his industry—surely he could see
Lincoln was dead. Who, then, was the more foolish, himself for sending Holmes away, or the captain for going?*

21 July 1864—Washington, D.C.

*From the hastily erected wooden rostrum on the east
portico of the capitol, Hannibal Hamlin stared out at the
crowd waiting for him to deliver his inaugural address.
The rostrum was draped with black, as was the capitol,*

as had been the route his carriage took to reach it. Many of the faces in the crowd were still stunned, disbelieving. The United States had never lost a president to a bullet, not in the eighty-eight years since the nation freed itself from British rule.

In the front row of dignitaries, Senator Andrew Johnson of Tennessee glared up at Hamlin. He had displaced the man from Maine on Lincoln's reelection ticket; had this dreadful event taken place a year later (assuming Lincoln's triumph), he now would be president. But no time for might-have-beens.

Hamlin had been polishing his speech since the telegram announcing Lincoln's death reached him up in Bangor, where, feeling useless and rejected, he had withdrawn after failing of renomination for the vice presidency. Now, though, his country needed him once more. He squared his broad shoulders, ready to bear up under the great burden so suddenly thrust upon him.

"Stand fast!" he cried. "That has ever been my watchword, and at no time in all the history of our great and glorious republic has our heeding it been more urgent. Abraham Lincoln's body may lie in the grave, but we shall go marching on—to victory!"

Applause rose from the crowd at the allusion to "John Brown's Body"—and not just from the crowd, but also from the soldiers posted on the roof of the capitol and at intervals around the building to keep the accursed rebels from murdering two presidents, not just one. Hamlin went on, "The responsibility for this great war, in which our leader gave his last full measure of devotion, lies solely at the feet of the Southern slaveocrats who conspired to take their states out of our grand Union for their own evil ends. I promise you, my friends—Abraham

Lincoln shall be avenged, and those who caused his death punished in full."

More applause, not least from the Republican senators who proudly called themselves Radical: from Thaddeus Stevens of Pennsylvania, Benjamin Wade of Ohio, Zachariah Chandler of Michigan, and bespectacled John Andrew of Massachusetts. Hamlin had been counted among their number when he sat in the Senate before assuming the duties, such as they were, of the vice president.

"Henceforward," Hamlin declared, "I say this: let us use every means recognized by the Laws of War which God has put in our hands to crush out the wickedest rebellion the world has ever witnessed. This conflict is become a radical revolution—yes, gentlemen, I openly employ the word, and, what is more, I revel in it— involving the desolation of the South as well as the emancipation of the bondsmen it vilely keeps in chains."

The cheers grew louder still. Lincoln had been more conciliatory, but what had conciliation gotten him? Only a coffin and a funeral and a grieving nation ready, no, eager for harsher measures.

"They have sowed the wind; let them reap the whirlwind. We are in earnest now, and have awakened to the stern duty upon us. Let that duty be disregarded or haltingly or halfway performed, and God only in His wisdom can know what will be the end. This lawless monster of a Political Slave Power shall forevermore be shorn of its power to ruin a government it no longer has the strength to rule.

"The rebels proudly proclaim they have left the Union. Very well: we shall take them at their word and, once having gained the victory Providence will surely grant

us, we shall treat their lands as they deserve: not as the states they no longer desire to be, but as conquered provinces, won by our sword. I say we shall hang Jefferson Davis, and hang Robert E. Lee, and hang Joe Johnston, yes, hang them higher than Haman, and the other rebel generals and colonels and governors and members of their false Congress. The living God is merciful, true, but He is also just and vengeful, and we, the people of the United States, we shall be His instrument in advancing the right."

Now great waves of cheering, led by grim Thaddeus Stevens himself, washed over Hamlin. The fierce sound reminded him of wolves baying in the backwoods of Maine. He stood tall atop the rostrum. He would lead these wolves, and with them pull the rebel Confederacy down in ruin.

11 August 1942—New Orleans, Louisiana

Air brakes chuffing, the Illinois Central train pulled to a stop at Union Station on Rampart Street. "New Orleans!" the conductor bawled unnecessarily. "All out for New Orleans!"

Along with the rest of the people in the car, Neil Michaels filed toward the exit. He was a middle-sized man in his late thirties, most of his dark-blond hair covered by a snap-brim fedora. The round, thick, gold-framed spectacles he wore helped give him the mild appearance of an accountant.

As soon as he stepped from the air-conditioned comfort of the railroad car out into the steamy heat of New

Orleans summer, those glasses fogged up. Shaking his head in bemusement, Michaels drew a handkerchief from his trouser pocket and wiped away the moisture.

He got his bags and headed for the cab stand, passing on the way a horde of men and boys hawking newspapers and rank upon rank of shoeshine stands. A fat Negro man sat on one of those, gold watch chain running from one pocket of his vest to the other. At his feet, an Irish-looking fellow plied the rag until his customer's black oxfords gleamed.

"There y'are, sir," the shoeshine man said, his half-Brooklyn, half-Southern accent testifying he was a New Orleans native. The Negro looked down at his shoes, nodded, and, with an air of great magnanimity, flipped the shoeshine man a dime. "Oh, thank you very much, sir," the fellow exclaimed. The insincere servility in his voice grated on Michaels' ears.

More paperboys plied their trade outside the station. Michaels bought a *Times-Picayune* to read while he waited in line for a taxi. The war news wasn't good. The Germans were still pushing east in Russia and sinking ship after ship off the American coast. In the South Pacific, Americans and Japanese were slugging away at each other, and God only knew how that would turn out.

Across the street from Union Station, somebody had painted a message: YANKS OUT! Michaels sighed. He'd seen that slogan painted on barns and bridges and embankments ever since his train crossed into Tennessee—and, now that he thought about it, in Kentucky as well, though Kentucky had stayed with the Union during the Great Rebellion.

When he got to the front of the line at the cab stand, a

hack man heaved his bags into the trunk of an Oldsmobile and said, "Where to, sir?"

"The New Orleans Hotel, on Canal Street," Michaels answered.

The cabbie touched the brim of his cap. "Yes, sir," he said, his voice suddenly empty. He opened the back door for Michaels, slammed it shut after him, then climbed into the cab himself. It took off with a grinding of gears that said the transmission had seen better days.

On the short ride to the hotel, Michaels counted five more scrawls of YANKS OUT, along with a couple of patches of whitewash that probably masked others. Servicemen on the street walked along in groups of at least four; several corners sported squads of soldiers in full combat gear, including, in one case, a machine-gun nest built of sandbags. "Nice quiet little town," Michaels remarked.

"Isn't it?" the cabbie answered, deadpan. He hesitated, his jaw working as if he were chewing his cud. After a moment, he decided to go on: "Mister, with an accent like yours, you want to be careful where you let people hear it. For a damnyankee, you don't seem like a bad fellow, an' I wouldn't want nothin' to happen to you."

"Thanks. I'll bear that in mind," Michaels said. He wished the Bureau had sent somebody who could put on a convincing drawl. Of course the last man the FBS had sent ended up floating in the Mississippi, so evidently his drawl hadn't been convincing enough.

The cab wheezed to a stop in front of the New Orleans Hotel. "That'll be forty cents, sir," the driver said.

Michaels reached into his trouser pocket, pulled out a half-dollar. "Here you go. I don't need any change."

"That's right kind of you, sir, but—you wouldn't

happen to have two quarters instead?" the cabbie said. He handed the big silver coin back to his passenger.

"What's wrong with it?" Michaels demanded, though he thought he knew the answer. "It's legal tender of the United States of America."

"Yes, sir, reckon it is, but there's no place hereabouts I'd care to try and spend it even so," the driver answered, "not with *his* picture on it." The obverse of the fifty-cent piece bore an image of the martyred Lincoln, the reverse a Negro with his manacles broken and the legend SIC SEMPER TYRANNIS. Michaels had known it was an unpopular coin with white men in the South, but he hadn't realized how unpopular it was.

He got out of the cab, rummaged in his pocket, and came up with a quarter and a couple of dimes. The cabbie didn't object to Washington's profile, or to that of the god Mercury. He also didn't object to seeing his tip cut in half. That told Michaels all he needed to know about how much the half-dollar was hated.

Lazily spinning ceiling fans inside the hotel lobby stirred the air without doing much to cool it. The colored clerk behind the front desk smiled to hear Michaels' accent. "Yes, sir, we do have your reservation," she said after shuffling through papers. By the way she talked, she'd been educated up in the Loyal States herself. She handed him a brass key. "That's room 429, sir. Three dollars and twenty-five cents a night."

"Very good," Michaels said. The clerk clanged the bell on the front desk. A white bellboy in a pillbox hat and uniform that made him look like a Philip Morris advertisement picked up Michaels' bags and carried them to the elevator.

When they got to room 429, Michaels opened the door.

The bellboy put down the bags inside the room and stood waiting for his tip. By way of experiment, Michaels gave him the fifty-cent piece the cabbie had rejected. The bellboy took the coin and put it in his pocket. His lips shaped a silent word. Michaels thought it was *damn-yankee*, but he wasn't quite sure. He left in a hurry.

A couple of hours later, Michaels went downstairs to supper. Something shiny was lying on the carpet in the hall. He looked down at the half-dollar he'd given the bellboy. It had lain here in plain sight while people walked back and forth; he'd heard them. Nobody had taken it. Thoughtfully, he picked it up and stuck it in his pocket.

A walk through the French Quarter made fears about New Orleans seem foolish. Jazz blasted out of every other doorway. Neon signs pulsed above ginmills. Spasm bands, some white, some Negro, played on streetcorners. No one paid attention to blackout regulations—that held true North and South. Clog-dancers shuffled, overturned caps beside them inviting coins. Streetwalkers in tawdry finery swung their hips and flashed knowing smiles.

Neil Michaels moved through the crowds of soldiers and sailors and gawking civilians like a halfback evading tacklers and heading downfield. He glanced at his watch, partly to check the time and partly to make sure nobody had stolen it. Half past eleven. Didn't this place ever slow down? Maybe not.

He turned right off Royal Street onto St. Peter and walked southeast toward the Mississippi and Jackson Square. The din of the Vieux Carré faded behind him. He strode past the Cabildo, the old Spanish building of stuc-coed brick that now housed the Louisiana State Museum, including a fine collection of artifacts and documents on the career of the first military governor of New Orleans, Benjamin Butler. Johnny Rebs kept threatening to dynamite the Cabildo, but it hadn't happened yet.

Two great bronze statues dominated Jackson Square. One showed the square's namesake on horseback. The other, even taller, faced that equestrian statue. Michaels thought Ben Butler's bald head and rotund, sagging physique less than ideal for being immortalized in bronze, but no one had asked his opinion.

He strolled down the paved lane in the formal garden toward the statue of Jackson. Lights were dimmer here in the square, but not too dim to keep Michaels from reading the words Butler had had carved into the pedestal of the statue: *The Union Must and Shall Be Preserved,* an adaptation of Jackson's famous toast, "Our Federal Union, it must be preserved."

Michaels' mouth stretched out in a thin hard line that was not a smile. By force and fear, with cannon and noose, bayonet and prison term, the United States Army had preserved the Union. And now, more than three quarters of a century after the collapse of the Great Rebellion, U.S. forces still occupied the states of the rebel Confederacy, still skirmished in hills and forests and sometimes city streets against men who put on gray shirts and yowled like catamounts when they fought. Hatred bred hatred, reprisal bred reprisal, and so it went on and on. He sometimes wondered if the Union wouldn't have done better to let the Johnny Rebs get the hell out, if that was what they'd wanted so badly.

He'd never spoken that thought aloud; it wasn't one he could share. Too late to worry about such things anyhow, generations too late. He had to deal with the consequences of what vengeful Hamlin and his likeminded successors had done.

The man he was supposed to meet would be waiting behind Butler's statue. Michaels was slightly surprised the statue had no guards around it; the Johnny Rebs had blown it up in the 1880s and again in the 1920s. If New Orleans today was reconciled to rule from Washington, it concealed the fact very well.

Michaels ducked around into the darkness behind the statue. "Fourscore and seven," he whispered, the recognition signal he'd been given.

Someone should have answered, "New birth of freedom." No one said anything. As his eyes adapted to the darkness, he made out a body sprawled in the narrow space between the base of the statue and the shrubbery that bordered Jackson Square. He stooped beside it. If this was the man he was supposed to meet, the fellow would never give him a recognition signal, not till Judgment Day. His throat had been cut.

Running feet on the walkways of the square, flashlight beams probing like spears. One of them found Michaels. He threw up an arm against the blinding glare. A hard Northern voice shouted, "Come out of there right now, you damned murdering Reb, or you'll never get a second chance!"

Michaels raised his hands high in surrender and came out.

Outside Antoine's, the rain came down in buckets. Inside, with oysters Rockefeller and a whiskey and soda in front of him and the prospect of an excellent lunch ahead, Neil Michaels was willing to forgive the weather.

He was less inclined to forgive the soldiers from the night before. Stubbing out his Camel, he said in a low but furious voice, "Those great thundering galoots couldn't have done a better job of blowing my cover if they'd rehearsed for six weeks, God damn them."

His companion, a dark, lanky man named Morrie Harris, sipped his own drink and said, "It may even work out for the best. Anybody the MPs arrest is going to look good to the Johnny Rebs around here." His New York accent seemed less out of place in New Orleans than Michaels' flat, midwestern tones.

Michaels started to answer, then shut up as the waiter came over and asked, "You gentlemen are ready to order?"

"Let me have the *pompano en papillote*," Harris said. "You can't get it any better than here."

The waiter wrote down the order, looked a question at Michaels. He said, "I'll take the *poulet chanteclair*." The waiter nodded, scribbled, and went away.

Glancing around to make sure no one else was paying undue attention to him or his conversation, Michaels resumed: "Yeah, that may be true now. But Ducange is dead now. What if those stupid dogfaces had busted in on us while we were dickering? That would have queered the deal for sure, and it might have got me shot." As it hadn't the night before, his smile did not reach his eyes. "I'm fond of my neck. It's the only one I've got."

"Even without Ducange, we've still got to get a line on the underground," Harris said. "Those weapons are somewhere. We'd better find 'em before the whole city goes up." He rolled his eyes. "The whole city, hell! If what we've been hearing is true, the Nazis have shipped enough guns and God knows what all else into New

Orleans to touch off four or five states. And wouldn't that do wonders for the war effort?" He slapped on irony with a heavy trowel.

"God damn the Germans," Michaels said, still quietly but with savage venom. "They played this game during the last war, too. But you're right. If what we've heard is the straight goods, the blowup they have in mind will make the Thanksgiving Revolt look like a kiss on the cheek."

"It shouldn't be this way," Harris said, scowling. "We've got more GIs and swabbies in New Orleans than you can shake a stick at, and none of 'em worth a damn when it comes to tracking this crap down. Nope, for that they need the FBS, no matter how understaffed we are."

The waiter came then. Michaels dug into the chicken marinated in red wine. It was as good as it was supposed to be. Morrie Harris made ecstatic noises about the sauce on his pompano.

After a while, Michaels said, "The longer we try, the harder it gets for us to keep things under control down here. One of these days—"

"It'll all go up," Harris said matter-of-factly. "Yeah, but not now. Now is what we gotta worry about. We're fighting a civil war here, we ain't gonna have much luck with the Germans and the Japs. That's what Hitler has in mind."

"Maybe Hamlin and Stevens should have done something different—God knows what—back then. It might have kept us out of—this," Michaels said. He knew that was heresy for an FBS man, but everything that had happened to him since he got to New Orleans left him depressed with the state of things as they were.

"What were they supposed to do?" Harris snapped.

"I already said I didn't know," Michaels answered, wishing he'd kept his mouth shut. What did the posters say?—LOOSE LIPS SINK SHIPS. His loose lips were liable to sink him.

Sure enough, Morrie Harris went on as if he hadn't spoken: "The Johnnies rebelled, killed a few hundred thousand American boys, and shot a president dead. What should we do, give 'em a nice pat on the back? We beat 'em and we made 'em pay. Far as I can see, they deserved it."

"Yeah, and they've been making us pay ever since." Michaels raised a weary hand. "The hell with it. Like you said, now is what we've got to worry about. But with Ducange dead, what sort of channels do we have into the rebel underground?"

Morrie Harris' mouth twisted, as if he'd bitten down on something rotten. "No good ones that I know of. We've relied too much on the Negroes down here over the years. It's made the whites trust us even less than they would have otherwise. Maybe, though, just maybe, Ducange talked to somebody before he got killed, and that somebody will try to get hold of you."

"So what do you want me to do, then? Hang around my hotel room hoping the phone rings, like a girl waiting to see if a boy will call. Hell of a way to spend my time in romantic New Orleans."

"Listen, the kind of romance you can get here, you'll flunk a shortarm inspection three days later," Harris answered, chasing the last bits of pompano around his plate. "They'll take a damnyankee's money, but they'll skin you every chance they get. They must be laughing their asses off at the fortune they're making off our boys in uniform."

"Sometimes they won't even take your money." Michaels told of the trouble he'd had unloading the Lincoln half-dollar.

"Yeah, I've seen that," Harris said. "If they want to cut off their nose to spite their face, by me it's all right." He set a five and a couple of singles on the table. "This one's on me. Whatever else you say about this damn town, the food is hellacious, no two ways about it."

"No arguments." Michaels got up with Harris. They went out of Antoine's separately, a couple of minutes apart. As he walked back to the New Orleans Hotel, Michaels kept checking to make sure nobody was following him. He didn't spot anyone, but he didn't know how much that proved. If anybody wanted to put multiple tails on him, he wouldn't twig, not in crowded streets like these.

The crowds got worse when a funeral procession tied up traffic on Rampart Street. Two black horses pulled the hearse; their driver was a skinny, sleepy-looking white man who looked grotesquely out of place in top hat and tails. More coaches and buggies followed, and a couple of cars as well. "All right, let's get it moving!" an MP shouted when the procession finally passed.

"They keep us here any longer, we all go in the ovens from old age," a local said, and several other people laughed as they crossed the street. Michaels wanted to ask what the ovens were, but kept quiet since he exposed himself as one of the hated occupiers every time he opened his mouth.

When he got back to the hotel, he stopped at the front

desk to ask if he had any messages. The clerk there today was a Negro man in a sharp suit and tie, with a brass name badge on his right lapel that read THADDEUS JENKINS. He checked and came back shaking his head. "Rest assured, sir, we shall make sure you receive any that do come in," he said—a Northern accent bothered him not in the least.

"Thank you very much, Mr. Jenkins," Michaels said.

"Our pleasure to serve you, sir," the clerk replied. "Anything we can do to make your stay more pleasant, you have but to ask."

"You're very kind," Michaels said. Jenkins had reason to be kind to Northerners. The power of the federal government maintained Negroes at the top of the heap in the old Confederacy. With the Sixteenth Amendment disenfranchising most Rebel soldiers and their descendants, blacks had a comfortable majority among those eligible to vote—and used it, unsurprisingly, in their own interest.

Michaels mused on that as he walked to the elevator. The operator, a white man, tipped his cap with more of the insincere obsequiousness Michaels had already noted. He wondered how the fellow liked taking orders from a man whose ancestors his great-grandfather might have owned. Actually, he didn't need to wonder. The voting South was as reliably Republican as could be, for the blacks had no illusions about how long their power would last if the Sixteenth were ever to be discarded.

Suddenly curious, he asked the elevator man, "Why don't I see 'Repeal the Sixteenth' written on walls along with 'Yanks Out'?"

The man measured him with his eyes—measured him for a coffin, if his expression meant anything. At last, as if speaking to a moron, he answered, "You don't see that on account of askin' you to repeal it'd mean you damn-yankees got some kind o' business bein' down here and lordin' it over us in the first place. And you *ain't*."

So there, Michaels thought. The rest of the ride passed in silence.

With a soft whir, the ceiling fan stirred the air in his room. That improved things, but only slightly. He looked out the window. Ferns had sprouted from the mortar between bricks of the building across the street. Even without the rain—which had now let up—it was plenty humid enough for the plants to flourish.

Sitting around waiting for the phone to ring gave Michaels plenty of time to watch the ferns. As Morrie Harris had instructed, he spent most of his time in his room. He sallied forth primarily to eat. Not even the resolute hostility of most of white New Orleans put a damper on the food.

He ate boiled beef at Maylié's, crab meat *au gratin* at Galatoire's, crayfish bisque at La Louisiane, *langouste* Sarah Bernhardt at Arnaud's, and, for variety, pig knuckles and sauerkraut at Kolb's. When he didn't feel like traveling, he ate at the hotel's own excellent restaurant. He began to fancy his trousers and collars getting tighter than they had been before he came South.

One night, he woke to the sound of rifle fire not far away. Panic shot through him, panic and shame. Had the uprising he'd come here to check broken out? How would that look on his FBS personnel record? Then he realized that, if the uprising had broken out, any damnyankee the Johnnies caught was likely to end up too dead to worry about what his personnel record looked like.

After about fifteen minutes, the gunfire petered out. Michaels took a couple of hours falling asleep again, though. He went from one radio station to another the next morning, and checked the afternoon newspapers, too. No one said a word about the firefight. Had anybody tried, prosecutors armed with the Sedition Act would have landed on him like a ton of bricks.

Back in the Loyal States, they smugly said the Sedition Act kept the lid on things down South. Michaels had believed it, too. Now he was getting a feeling for how much pressure pushed against that lid. When it blew, if it blew . . .

A little past eleven the next night, the phone rang. He jumped, then ran to it. "Hello?" he said sharply.

The voice on the other end was so muffled, he wasn't sure whether it belonged to a man or a woman. It said, "Be at the Original Absinthe House for the three A.M. show." The line went dead.

Michaels let out a martyred sigh. "The three A.M. show," he muttered, wondering why conspirators couldn't keep civilized hours like anyone else. He went down to the restaurant and had a couple of cups of strong coffee laced with brandy. Thus fortified, he headed out into the steaming night.

He soon concluded New Orleans' idea of civilized hours had nothing to do with those kept by the rest of the world, or possibly that New Orleans defined civilization as unending revelry. The French Quarter was as packed as it had been when he went through it toward Jackson Square, though that had been in the relatively early evening, close to civilized even by Midwestern standards.

The Original Absinthe House, a shabby two-story building with an iron railing around the balcony to the second floor, stood on the corner of Bourbon and Bienville. Each of the four doors leading in had a semicircular window above it. Alongside one of the doors, someone had scrawled, *Absinthe makes the heart grow fonder*. Michaels thought that a distinct improvement on *Yanks Out!* You weren't supposed to be able to get real absinthe any more, but in the Vieux Carré nothing would have surprised him.

He didn't want absinthe, anyway. He didn't particularly want the whiskey and soda he ordered, either, but you couldn't go into a place like this without doing some drinking. The booze was overpriced and not very good. The mysterious voice on the telephone hadn't told him there was a five-buck charge to go up to the second story and watch the floor show. Assuming he got out of here alive, he'd have a devil of a time justifying that on his expense account. And if the call had been a Johnny Reb setup, were they trying to kill him or just to bilk him out of money for the cause?

Michaels felt he was treading in history's footsteps as he went up the stairs. If the plaque on the wall didn't lie for the benefit of tourists, that stairway had been there since the Original Absinthe House was built in the early nineteenth century. Andrew Jackson and Jean Lafitte had gone up it to plan the defense of New Orleans against the British in 1814, and Ben Butler for carefully undescribed purposes half a century later. It was made with wooden pegs: not a nail anywhere. If the stairs weren't as old as the plaque claimed, they sure as hell were a long way from new.

A jazz band blared away in the big upstairs room. Michaels went in, found a chair, ordered a drink from a waitress whose costume would have been too skimpy for a burly queen most places up North, and leaned back to enjoy the music. The band was about half black, half white. Jazz was one of the few things the two races shared in the South. Not all Negroes had made it to the top of the heap after the North crushed the Great Rebellion; many still lived in the shadow of the fear and degradation of the days of slavery and keenly felt the resentment of the white majority. That came out in the way they played. And the whites, as conquered people will, found liberation in their music that they could not have in life.

Michaels looked at his watch. It was a quarter to three. The jazz men were just keeping loose between shows, then. As he sipped his whiskey, the room began filling up in spite of the five-dollar cover charge. He didn't know what the show would be, but he figured it had to be pretty hot to pack 'em in at those prices.

The lights went out. For a moment, only a few glowing cigarette coals showed in the blackness. The band didn't miss a beat. From right behind Michaels' head, a spotlight came on, bathing the stage in harsh white light.

Saxophone and trumpets wailed lasciviously. When the girls paraded onto the stage, Michaels felt his jaw drop. A vice cop in Cleveland, say, might have put the cuffs on his waitress because she wasn't wearing enough. The girls up there had on high-heeled shoes, headdresses with dyed ostrich plumes and glittering rhinestones, and nothing between the one and the other but big, wide smiles.

He wondered how they got themselves case-hardened enough to go on display like that night after night, show after show. They were all young and pretty and built, no doubt about that. Was it enough? His sister was young and pretty and built, too. He wouldn't have wanted her up there, flaunting it for horny soldiers on leave.

He wondered how much the owners had to pay to keep the local vice squad off their backs. Then he wondered if New Orleans bothered with a vice squad. He hadn't seen any signs of one.

He also wondered who the devil had called him over here and how that person would make contact. Sitting around gaping at naked women was not something he could put in his report unless it had some sort of connection with the business for which he'd come down here.

Soldiers and sailors whooped at the girls, whose skins soon grew slick and shiny with sweat. Waitresses moved back and forth, getting in the way as little as possible while they took drink orders. To fit in, Michaels ordered another whiskey and soda, and discovered it cost more than twice as much here as it had downstairs. He didn't figure the Original Absinthe House would go out of business any time soon.

The music got even hotter than it had been. The dancers stepped off the edge of the stage and started prancing among the tables. Michaels' jaw dropped all over again. This wasn't just a floor show. This was a— He didn't quite know what it was, and found himself too flustered to grope for *le mot juste*.

Then a very pretty naked brunette sat down in his lap and twined her arms around his neck.

"Is that a gun in your pocket, dearie, or are you just glad to see me?" she said loudly. Men at the nearest table guffawed. Since it was a gun in his pocket, Michaels kept his mouth shut. The girl smelled of sweat and whiskey and makeup. What her clammy hide was doing to his shirt and trousers did not bear thinking about. He wanted to drop her on the floor and get the hell out of there.

She was holding him too tight for that, though. She lowered her head to nuzzle his neck; the plumes from her headdress got in his eyes and tickled his nose. But under the cover of that frantic scene, her voice went low and urgent: "You got to talk with Colquit the hearse driver, Mister. Tell him Lucy says Pierre says he can talk, an' maybe he will."

Before he could ask her any questions, she kissed him on the lips. The kiss wasn't faked; her tongue slid into his mouth. He'd had enough whiskey and enough shocks by then that he didn't care what he did. His hand closed over her breast—and she sprang to her feet and twisted away, all in perfect time to the music. A moment later, she was in somebody else's lap.

Michaels discovered he'd spilled most of his over-priced drink. He downed what was left with one big swig. When he wiped his mouth with a napkin, it came away red from the girl's—Lucy's—lipstick.

Some of the naked dancers had more trouble than Lucy disentangling themselves from the men they'd chosen. Some of them didn't even try to disentangle. Michaels found himself staring, bug-eyed. You couldn't lo *that* in public . . . could you? Hell and breakfast, it was illegal in private, most places.

Eventually, all the girls were back on stage. They gave it all they had for the finale. Then they trooped off and the lights came back up. Only after they were gone did Michaels understand the knowing look most of them had had all through the performance: they knew more about men than men, most often, cared to know about themselves.

In the palm of his hand, he could still feel the memory of the soft, firm flesh of Lucy's breast. Unlike the others in the room, he'd had to be here. He hadn't had to grab her, though. Sometimes, facetiously, you called a place like this educational. He'd learned something, all right, and rather wished he hadn't.

Morrie Harris pursed his lips. "Lucy says Pierre says Colquit can talk? That's not much to go on. For all we know, it could be a trap."

"Yeah, it could be," Michaels said. He and the other FBS man walked along in front of the St. Louis Cathedral, across the street from Jackson Square. They might have been businessmen, they might have been sightseers—though neither businessmen nor sightseers were particularly common in the states that had tried to throw off the Union's yoke. Michaels went on, "I don't think it's a trap, though. Ducange's first name is—was—Pierre, and we've found out he did go to the Original Absinthe House. He could have gotten to know Lucy there."

He could have done anything with Lucy there. The feel of her would not leave Michaels' mind. He knew going back to the upstairs room would be dangerous, for him and for her, but the temptation lingered like a bit of food between the teeth that keeps tempting back the tongue.

Harris said, "Maybe we ought to just haul her in and grill her till she cracks."

"We risk alerting the Rebs if we do that," Michaels said.

"Yeah, I know." Harris slammed his fist into his palm. "I hate sitting around doing nothing, though. If they get everything they need before we find out where they're squirreling it away, they start their damn uprising and the war effort goes straight out the window." He scowled, a man in deep and knowing it. "And Colquit the hearse driver? You don't know his last name? You don't know which mortuary he works for? Naked little Lucy didn't whisper those into your pink and shell-like ear?"

"I told you what she told me." Michaels stared down at the pavement in dull embarrassment. He could feel his dubiously shell-like ears turning red, not pink.

"All right, all right." Harris threw his hands in the air. Most FBS men made a point of not showing what they were thinking—Gary Cooper might have been the Bureau's ideal. Not Morrie Harris. He wore his feelings on his sleeve. *New York City,* Michaels thought, with scorn he nearly didn't notice himself. Harris went on, "We try and find him, that's all. How many guys are there named Colquit, even in New Orleans? And yeah, you don't have to tell me we got to be careful. If he knows anything, we don't want him riding in a hearse instead of driving one."

A bit of investigation—if checking the phone book and getting somebody with the proper accent to call the Chamber of Commerce could be dignified as such—soon proved funerals were big business in New Orleans, bigger than most other places, maybe. There were mortuaries and cemeteries for Jews, for Negroes, for French-speakers, for Protestants, for this group, for that one, and for the other. Because New Orleans was mostly below sea level (Michaels heartily wished the town were underwater, too), burying people was more complicated than digging a hole and putting a coffin down in it, too. Some intrepid sightseers made special pilgrimages just to see the funeral vaults, which struck Michaels as downright macabre.

Once they had a complete list of funeral establishments, Morrie Harris started calling them one by one. His New York accent was close enough to the local one for him to ask, "Is Colquit there?" without giving himself away as a damnyankee. Time after time, people denied ever hearing of Colquit. At one establishment, though, the receptionist asked whether he meant Colquit the embalmer or Colquit the bookkeeper. He hung up in a hurry.

Repeated failure left Michaels frustrated. He was about to suggest knocking off for the day when Harris suddenly jerked in his chair as if he'd sat on a tack. He put his hand over the receiver and mouthed, "Said he just got back from a funeral. She's going out to get him." He handed the telephone to Michaels.

After just over a minute, a man's voice said, "Hello? Who's this?"

"Colquit?" Michaels asked.

"Yeah," the hearse driver said.

Maybe it was Michaels' imagination, but he thought he heard suspicion even in one slurred word. Sounding like someone from the Loyal States got you nowhere around here (of course, a Johnny Reb who managed to get permission to travel to Wisconsin also raised eyebrows up there, but Michaels wasn't in Wisconsin now). He spoke quickly: "Lucy told me Pierre told her that I should tell you it was okay for you to talk with me."

He waited for Colquit to ask what the hell he was talking about, or else to hang up. It would figure if the only steer he'd got was a bum one. But the hearse driver, after a long pause, said, "Yeah?" again.

Michaels waited for more, but there wasn't any more. It was up to him, then. "You do know what I'm talking about?" he asked, rather desperately.

"Yeah," Colquit repeated: a man of few words.

"You can't talk where you are?"

"Nope," Colquit said—variety.

"Will you meet me for supper outside Galatoire's tonight at seven, then?" Michaels said. With a good meal and some booze in him, Colquit was more likely to spill his guts.

"Make it tomorrow," Colquit said.

"All right, tomorrow," Michaels said unhappily. More delay was the last thing he wanted. No, not quite: he didn't want to spook Colquit, either. He started to say something more, but the hearse driver did hang up on him then.

"What does he know?" Morrie Harris demanded after Michaels hung up, too.

"I'll find out tomorrow," Michaels answered. "The way things have gone since I got down here, that's progress." Harris nodded solemnly.

* * *

The wail of police sirens woke Neil Michaels from a sound sleep. The portable alarm clock he'd brought with him was ticking away on the table by his bed. Its radium dial announced the hour: 3:05. He groaned and sat up.

Along with the sirens came the clanging bells and roaring motors of fire engines. Michaels bounced out of bed, ice running down his back. Had the Rebs started their revolt? In that kind of chaos, the pistol he'd brought down from the North felt very small and useless.

He cocked his head. He didn't hear any gunfire. If the Southern men were using whatever the Nazis had shipped them, that would be the biggest part of the racket outside. Okay, it wasn't the big revolt. That meant walking to the window and looking out was likely to be safe. What the devil *was* going on?

Michaels pushed aside the thick curtain shielding the inside of his room from the neon glare that was New Orleans by night. Even as he watched, a couple of fire engines tore down Canal Street toward the Vieux Carré. Their flashing red lights warned the few cars and many pedestrians to get the hell out of the way.

Raising his head, Michaels spotted the fire. Whatever was burning was burning to beat the band. Flames leaped into the night sky, seeming to dance as they flung themselves high above the building that fueled them. A column of thick black smoke marked that building's funeral pyre.

"Might as well find out what it is," Michaels said out loud. He turned on the lamp by the bed and then the radio. The little light behind the dial came on. He waited impatiently for the tubes to get warm enough to bring in a signal.

The first station he got was playing one of Benny Goodman's records. Michaels wondered if playing a damnyankee's music was enough to get you in trouble with some of the fire-eating Johnny Rebs. But he didn't want to hear jazz, not now. He spun the dial.

"—Terrible fire on Bourbon Street," an announcer was saying. That had to be the blaze Michaels had seen. The fellow went on, "One of New Orleans' longstanding landmarks, the Original Absinthe House, is going up in flames even as I speak. The Absinthe House presents shows all through the night, and many are feared dead inside. The building was erected well over a hundred years ago, and has seen—"

Michaels turned off the radio, almost hard enough to break the knob. He didn't believe in coincidence, not even a little bit. Somewhere in the wreckage of the Original Absinthe House would lie whatever mortal fragments remained of Lucy the dancer, and that was just how someone wanted it to be.

He shivered like a man with the grippe. He'd thought about asking Colquit to meet him there instead of at Galatoire's, so Lucy could help persuade the hearse driver to tell whatever he knew—and so he could get another look at her. But going to a place twice running ... That let the opposition get a line on you. Training had saved his life and, he hoped, Colquit's. It hadn't done poor Lucy one damn bit of good.

He called down to room service and asked for a bottle of whiskey. If the man to whom he gave the order found anything unusual about such a request at twenty past three, he didn't show it. The booze arrived in short order. After three or four good belts, Michaels was able to get back to sleep.

Colquit didn't show up for dinner at Galatoire's that night.

When Morrie Harris phoned the mortuary the next day, the receptionist said Colquit had called in sick. "That's a relief," Michaels said when Harris reported the news. "I was afraid he'd call in dead."

"Yeah." Harris ran a hand through his curly hair. "I didn't want to try and get a phone number and address out of the gal. I didn't even like making the phone call. The less attention we draw to the guy, the better."

"You said it." Michaels took off his glasses, blew a speck from the left lens, set them back on his nose. "Now we know where he works. We can find out where he lives. Just a matter of digging through the papers."

"A lot of papers to dig through," Harris said with a grimace, "but yeah, that ought to do the job. Shall we head on over to the Hall of Records?"

Machine-gun nests surrounded the big marble building on Thalia Street. If the Johnny Rebs ever got their revolt off the ground, it would be one of the first places to burn. The Federal army and bureaucrats who controlled the conquered provinces of the old Confederacy ruled not only by force but also by keeping tabs on their resentful, rebellious subjects. Every white man who worked had to fill out a card each year listing his place of employment. Every firm had to list its employees. Most of the clerks who checked one set of forms against the other were Negroes. They had a vested interest in making sure nobody put one over on the government.

Tough, unsmiling guards meticulously checked Harris' and Michaels' identification papers, comparing photographs to faces and making them give samples of their signatures, before admitting them to the hall. They feared sabotage as well as out-and-out assault. The records stored here helped down all of Louisiana.

Hannibal Dupuy was a large, round black man with some of the thickest glasses Michaels had ever seen. "Mortuary establishments," he said, holding up one finger as he thought. "Yes, those would be in the Wade Room, in the cases against the east wall." Michaels got the feeling that, had they asked him about anything from taverns to taxidermists, he would have known exactly where the files hid. Such men were indispensable in navigating the sea of papers before them.

Going through the papers stored in the cases against the east wall of the Wade Room took a couple of hours. Michaels finally found the requisite record. "Colquit D. Reynolds, hearse driver—yeah, he works for LeBlanc and Peters," he said. "Okay, here's address and phone number and a notation that they've been verified as correct. People are on the ball here, no two ways about it."

"People have to be on the ball here," Morrie Harris answered. "How'd you like to be a Negro in the South if the whites you've been sitting on for years grab hold of the reins? Especially if they grab hold of the reins with help from the Nazis? The first thing they'd do after they threw us damnyankees out is to start hanging Negroes from lampposts."

"You're right. Let's go track down Mr. Reynolds, so we don't have to find out just how right you are."

Colquit Reynolds' documents said he lived on Carondelet, out past St. Joseph: west and south of the French Quarter. Harris had a car, a wheezy Blasingame that delivered him and Michaels to the requisite address. Michaels knocked on the door of the house, which, like the rest of the neighborhood, was only a small step up from the shotgun shack level.

No one answered. Michaels glanced over at Morrie Harris. FBS men didn't need a warrant, not to search a house in Johnny Reb country. That wasn't the issue. Both of them, though, feared they'd find nothing but a corpse when they got inside.

Just as Michaels was about to break down the front door, an old woman stuck her head out a side window of the house next door and said, "If you lookin' for Colquit, gents, you ain't gonna find him in there."

Morrie Harris swept off his hat and gave a nod that was almost a bow. "Where's he at, then, ma'am?" he asked, doing his best to sound like a local and speaking to the old woman as if she were the military governor's wife.

She cackled like a laying hen; she must have liked that. "Same place you always find him when he wants to drink 'stead of workin': the Old Days Saloon round the co'ner." She jerked a gnarled thumb to show which way.

The Old Days Saloon was painted in gaudy stripes of red, white, and blue. Those were the national colors, and so unexceptionable, but, when taken with the name of the place, were probably meant to suggest the days of the Great Rebellion and the traitors who had used them on a different flag. Michaels would have bet a good deal that the owner of the place had a thick FBS dossier.

He and Harris walked in. The place was dim and quiet. Ceiling fans created the illusion of coolness. The bruiser behind the bar gave the newcomers the dubious stare he obviously hauled out for any stranger: certainly the four or five men in the place had the look of longtime regulars. Asking which one was Colquit was liable to be asking for trouble.

One of the regulars, though, looked somehow familiar. After a moment, Michaels realized why: that old man soaking up a beer off in a corner had driven the horse-drawn hearse that had slowed him up on his way back to the hotel a few days before. He nudged Morrie Harris, nodded toward the old fellow. Together, they went over to him. "How you doin' today, Colquit?" Harris asked in friendly tones. The bartender relaxed.

Colquit looked up at them with eyes that didn't quite focus. "Don't think I know you folks," he said, "but I could be wrong."

"Sure you do," Harris said, expansive still. "We're friends of Pierre and Lucy."

"Oh, Lord help me." Colquit started to get up. Michaels didn't want a scene. Anything at all could make New Orleans go off—hauling a man out of a bar very much included. But Colquit Reynolds slumped back onto his chair, as if his legs didn't want to hold him. "Wish I never told Pierre about none o' that stuff," he muttered, and finished his beer with a convulsive gulp.

Michaels raised a forefinger and called out to the bartender: "Three more High Lifes here." He tried to slur his words into a Southern pattern. Maybe he succeeded, or maybe the dollar bill he tossed down on the table was enough to take the edge off suspicions. The Rebs had revered George Washington even during the Great Rebellion, misguided though they were in other ways.

Colquit Reynolds took a long pull at the new beer.

Michaels and Harris drank more moderately. If they were going to get anything out of the hearse driver, they needed to be able to remember it once they had it. Besides, Michaels didn't much like beer. Quietly, so the bartender and the other locals wouldn't hear, he asked, "What do you wish you hadn't told Pierre, Mr. Reynolds?"

Reynolds looked up at the ceiling, as if the answer were written there. Michaels wondered if he was able to remember; he'd been drinking for a while. Finally, he said, "Wish I hadn't told him 'bout this here coffin I took for layin' to rest."

"Oh? Why's that?" Michaels asked casually. He lit a Camel, offered the pack to Colquit Reynolds. When Reynolds took one, he used his Zippo to give the hearse driver a light.

Reynolds sucked in smoke. He held it longer than Michaels thought humanly possible, then exhaled a foggy cloud. After he knocked the coal into an ash tray, he drained his Miller High Life and looked expectantly at the FBS men. Michaels ordered him another one. Only after he'd drunk part of that did he answer, "On account of they needed a block and tackle to get it onto my hearse an' another one to get it off again. Ain't no six men in the world could have lifted that there coffin, not if they was Samson an' five o' his brothers. An' it *clanked*, too."

"Weapons," Morrie Harris whispered, "or maybe ammunition." He looked joyous, transfigured, likely even more so than he would have if a naked dancing girl had plopped herself down in his lap. *Poor Lucy,* Michaels thought.

He said, "Even in a coffin, even greased, I wouldn't

want to bury anything in this ground—not for long, that's for damn sure. Water's liable to seep in and ruin things."

Colquit Reynolds sent him a withering, scornful look. "Damnyankees," he muttered under his breath—and he was helping Michaels. "Lot of the times here, you don't bury your dead, you put 'em in a tomb up above ground, just so as coffins don't get flooded out o' the ground come the big rains."

"Jesus," Morrie Harris said hoarsely, wiping his forehead with a sleeve, and then again: "Jesus." Now he was the one to drain his beer and signal for another. Once the bartender had come and gone, he went on, "All the above-ground tombs New Orleans has, you could hide enough guns and ammo to fight a big war. Goddamn sneaky Rebs." He made himself stop. "What cemetery was this at, Mr. Reynolds?"

"Old Girod, out on South Liberty Street," Colquit Reynolds replied. "Don' know how much is there, but one coffinload, anyways."

"Thank God some Southern men don't want to see the Great Rebellion start up again," Michaels said.

"Yeah." Harris drank from his new High Life. "But a hell of a lot of 'em *do*."

Girod Cemetery was hidden away in the railroad yards. A plaque on the stone fence surrounding it proclaimed it to be the oldest Protestant cemetery in New Orleans. Neil Michaels was willing to believe that. The place didn't seem to have received much in the way of legitimate business in recent years, and had a haunted look to it. It was overgrown with vines and shrubs. Gray-barked fig trees pushed up through the sides of some of the old tombs. Moss was everywhere, on trees and tombs alike. Maidenhair ferns sprouted from the sides of the above-ground vaults; as Michaels had seen, anything would grow anywhere around here.

That included conspiracies. If Colquit Reynolds was right, the ghost of the Great Rebellion haunted this cemetery, too, and the Johnnies were trying to bring it back to unwholesome life.

"He'd better be right," Michaels muttered as the jeep he was riding pulled to a stop before the front entrance to the cemetery.

Morrie Harris understood him without trouble. "Who, that damn hearse driver? You bet he'd better be right. We bring all this stuff here"—he waved behind him—"and start tearin' up a graveyard, then don't find anything . . . hell, that could touch off a revolt all by itself."

Michaels shivered, though the day was hot and muggy. "Couldn't it just?" Had Reynolds been leading them down the path, setting them up to create an incident that would make the South rise up in righteous fury? They'd have to respond to a story like the one he'd told; for the sake of the Union, they didn't dare not respond.

They'd find out. Behind the jeep, Harris' *all this stuff* rattled and clanked: not just bulldozers, but also light M3 Stoneman tanks and heavy M3 Grants with a small gun in a rotating turret and a big one in a sponson at the right front of the hull. Soldiers—all of them men from the Loyal States—scrambled down from Chevy trucks and set up a perimeter around the wall. If anybody was going to try to interfere with this operation, he'd regret it.

Against the assembled might of the Federal Union (*it must and shall be preserved,* Michaels thought), Girod Cemetery mustered a stout metal gate and one elderly watchman. "Who the devil are y'all, and what d'you want?" he demanded, though the *who* part, at least, should have been pretty obvious.

Michaels displayed his FBS badge. "We are on the business of the federal government of the United States of America," he said. "Open the gate and let us in." Again, no talk of warrants, not in Reb country, not on FBS business.

"Fuck the federal government of the United States of America, and the horse it rode in on," the watchman said. "You ain't got no call to come to no cemetery with tanks."

Michaels didn't waste time arguing with him. He tapped the jeep driver on the shoulder. The fellow backed the jeep out of the way. Michaels waved to the driver of the nearest Grant tank. The tank man had his head out of the hatch. He grinned and nodded. The tank clattered forward, chewing up the pavement and spewing noxious exhaust into the air. The wrought-iron gate was sturdy, but not sturdy enough to withstand thirty-one tons of insistent armor. It flew open with a scream of metal; one side ripped loose from the stone to which it was fixed. The Grant ran over it, and would have run over the watchman, too, had he not skipped aside with a shouted curse.

Outside the cemetery, people began gathering. Most of the people were white men of military age or a bit younger. To Michaels, they had the look of men who'd paint slogans on walls or shoot at a truck or from behind a fence under cover of darkness. He was glad he'd brought overwhelming force. Against bayonets, guns, and armor, the crowd couldn't do much but stare sullenly.

If the cemetery was empty of contraband, what this

crowd did wouldn't matter. There'd be similar angry crowds all over the South, and at one of them . . .

The watchman let out an anguished howl as tanks and bulldozers clanked toward the walls of above-ground vaults that ran up and down the length of the cemetery. "You can't go smashin' up the ovens!" he screamed.

"Last warning, Johnny Reb," Michaels said coldly. "Don't you try telling officers of the United States what we can and can't do. We have places to put people whose mouths get out in front of their brains."

"Yeah, I just bet you do," the watchman muttered, but after that he kept his mouth shut.

A dozer blade bit into the side of one of the mortuary vaults—an oven, the old man had called it. Concrete and stone flew. So did chunks of a wooden coffin and the bones it had held. The watchman shot Michaels a look of unadulterated hatred and scorn. He didn't say a word, but he might as well have screamed, *See? I told you so.* A lot of times, that look alone would have been plenty to get him on the inside of a prison camp, but Michaels had bigger things to worry about today.

He and Harris hadn't ordered enough bulldozers to take on all the rows of ovens at once. The tanks joined in the job, too, knocking them down as the first big snorting Grant had wrecked the gate into Girod. Their treads ground more coffins and bones into dust.

"That goddamn hearse driver better not have been lying to us," Morris Harris said, his voice clogged with worry. "If he was, he'll never see a camp or a jail. We'll give the son of a bitch a blindfold; I wouldn't waste a cigarette on him."

Then, from somewhere near the center of Girod Cemetery, a tank crew let out a shout of triumph. Michaels had never heard sweeter music, not from Benny Goodman or Tommy Dorsey. He sprinted toward the Grant. Sweat poured off him, but it wasn't the sweat of fear, not anymore.

The tank driver pointed to wooden boxes inside a funeral vault he'd just broken into. They weren't coffins. Each had *1 Maschinengewehr 34* stenciled on its side in neat black letter script, with the Nazi eagle-and-swastika emblem right next to the legend.

Michaels stared at the machine-gun crates as if one of them held the Holy Grail. "He wasn't lying," he breathed. "Thank you, God."

"Omayn," Morrie Harris agreed. "Now let's find out how much truth he was telling."

The final haul, by the time the last oven was cracked the next day, astonished even Michaels and Harris. Michaels read from the list he'd been keeping: "Machine guns, submachine guns, mortars, rifles—including anti-tank rifles—ammo for all of them, grenades . . . Jesus, what a close call."

"I talked with one of the radio men," Harris said. "He's sent out a call for more trucks to haul all this stuff away." He wiped his forehead with the back of his hand, a gesture that had little to do with heat or humidity. "If they'd managed to smuggle all of this out of New Orleans, spread it around through the South . . . well, hell, I don't have to draw you a picture."

"You sure don't. We'd have been so busy down here, the Germans and the Japs would have had a field day over the rest of the world." Michaels let out a heartfelt sigh of relief, then went on, "Next thing we've got to do is try and find out who was caching weapons. If we can do that, then maybe, just maybe, we can keep the Rebs leaderless for a generation or so and get ahead of the game."

"Maybe." But Harris didn't sound convinced. "We can't afford to think in terms of a generation from now, anyhow. It's what we were talking about when you first got into town: as long as we can hold the lid on the South till we've won the damn war, that'll do the trick. If we catch the guys running guns with the Nazis, great. If we don't, I don't give a damn about them sneaking around painting YANKS OUT on every blank wall they find. We can deal with that. We've been dealing with it since 1865. As long as they don't have the toys they need to really hurt us, we'll get by."

"Yeah, that's true—if no other subs drop off loads of goodies someplace else." Michaels sighed again. "No rest for the weary. If that happens, we'll just have to try and track 'em down."

A growing rumble of diesel engines made Morrie Harris grin. "Here come the trucks," he said, and trotted out toward the ruined entryway to Girod Cemetery. Michaels followed him. Harris pointed. "Ah, good, they're smart enough to have jeeps riding shotgun for 'em. We don't want any trouble around here till we get the weapons away safe."

There were still a lot of people outside the cemetery walls. They booed and hissed the newly arrived vehicles, but didn't try anything more than booing and hissing. They might hate the damnyankees—they *did* hate the damnyankees—but it was the damnyankees who had the firepower here. Close to eighty years of bitter experience had taught that they weren't shy about using it, either.

Captured German weapons and ammunition filled all

the new trucks to overflowing. Some of the ones that had brought in troops also got loaded with lethal hardware. The displaced soldiers either piled into jeeps or clambered up on tops of tanks for the ride back to their barracks, where the captured arms would be as safe as they could be anywhere in the endlessly rebellious South.

Michaels and Harris had led the convoy to the cemetery; now they'd lead it away. When their jeep driver started up the engine, a few young Rebs bolder than the rest made as if to block the road.

The corporal in charge of the pintle-mounted .50-caliber machine gun in the jeep turned to Michaels and asked, "Shall I mow 'em down, sir?" He sounded quiveringly eager to do just that.

"We'll give 'em one chance first," Michaels said, feeling generous. He stood up in the jeep and shouted to the Johnnies obstructing his path: "You are interfering with the lawful business of the Federal Bureau of Suppression. Disperse at once or you will be shot. First, last, and only warning, people." He sat back down, telling the driver, "Put it in gear, but go slow. If they don't move—" He made hand-washing gestures.

Sullenly, the young men gave way as the jeep moved forward. The gunner swung the muzzle of his weapon back and forth, back and forth, encouraging them to fall back further. The expression on his face, which frightened even Michaels, might have been an even stronger persuader.

The convoy rattled away from the cemetery. The Johnnies hooted and jeered, but did no more than that, not here, not now. Had they got Nazi guns in their hands . . . but they hadn't.

"We won this one," Morrie Harris said.

"We sure did," Michaels agreed. "Now we can get on with the business of getting rid of tyrants around the world." He spoke altogether without irony.

An Outpost of the Empire

Robert Silverberg

"An Outpost of the Empire" appeared in the November 1991 issue of Asimov's, *with an illustration by Robert Walters. It was one of a long series of distinguished pieces by Silverberg, including three Hugo Award winners, that have appeared in the magazine since its inception, under four different editors. Silverberg is one of the most famous SF writers of modern times, with dozens of novels, anthologies, and collections to his credit. He has won five Nebula Awards and four Hugo Awards. His novels include* Dying Inside, Lord Valentine's Castle, The Book of Skulls, Downward to the Earth, Tower of Glass, The World Inside, Born with the Dead, Shadrack in the Furnace, Tom O'Bedlam, Star of Gypsies, At Winter's End, *and two novel-length expansions of famous Isaac Asimov stories,* Nightfall *and* The Ugly Little Boy. *His collections include* Unfamiliar Territory, Capricorn Games, Majipoor Chronicles, The Best of Robert Silverberg, At the Conglomeroid Cocktail Party, Beyond the Safe Zone, *and a massive retrospective collection,* The Collected Stories of Robert Silverberg, Volume One: Secret Sharers. *His most recent books are the novels* The Face of the Waters, Kingdoms of the Wall, Hot Sky at Morning, *and* Mountains of Majipoor.

He lives with his wife, writer Karen Haber, in Oakland, California.

Silverberg has been important to the Alternate History subgenre, publishing a novel about a world where the Black Death kept Europeans from discovering the New World, The Gate of Worlds. *He's also edited an Alternate History anthology,* Worlds of Maybe: Seven Stories of Science Fiction, *and his Hugo-winning story "Enter A Soldier. Later, Enter Another," an* Asimov's *story in which Pizzaro and Socrates meet in a battle of wits and wills in a computer simulation, has much the flavor of Alternate History as well. His most substantial and intriguing contribution, though, has been his Roma series, a series to which the story that follows belongs: an evocative and vividly drawn alternate world, one where the Roman Empire never fell and the Pax Romana has continued even to the present, creating a society half-strange and half-familiar, full of haunting echoes of our own time line, yet also very different. Here he takes us to a border town on the edges of the great empire of Roma, for a sensuous tale of palace politics, sexual intrigue, and the making—and breaking—of allegiances.*

You know your enemy from the first moment you see him. I saw mine on a gleaming spring day almost a year ago, when I had gone down to the Grand Canal as I usually do in the morning to enjoy the breezes. A flotilla of ornate Roman barges was moving along the water, shouldering our gondolas aside as though they were so much flotsam. In the prow of the foremost barge stood a sturdy dark-bearded young imperial proconsul, grinning in the morning sunshine, looking for all the world like some new Alexander taking possession of his most recently conquered domain.

I was watching from the steps of the little Temple of Apollo, just by the Rialto. The proconsul's barge bore three poles from which the eagle-standard fluttered, and they were too tall to pass. The drawbridge, for some reason, was slow to open. As he looked impatiently around his gaze fell on me and his bright, insolent eyes met mine. They rested there a moment, comfortably, presumptuously. Then he winked and waved, and cupped his hand to his lips and called something to me that I could not make out.

"What?" I said automatically, speaking in Greek.

"Falco! Quintus Pompeius Falco!"

Then the bridge opened and his barge passed through and was gone, swiftly heading down the canal. His destination, I soon would learn, was the Palace of the Doges on the great plaza, where he was going to take up residence in the house where the princes of Venetia formerly had dwelled.

I glanced at Sophia, my waiting-maid. "Did you hear him?" I asked. "What was that he said?"

"His name, lady. He is Pompeius Falco, our new master."

"Ah. Of course. Our new master."

How I hated him in that first moment! This hairy-faced garlic-eating Italian boy, making his swaggering way into our serene and lovely city to be our overlord—how could I not detest him? Some crude soldier from Neapolis or Calabria, jumped up out of sweaty obscurity to become proconsul of Venetia as a reward, no doubt, for his bloodthirstiness on the battlefield, who now would fill our ears with his grating Latin crudities and desecrate the elegance of our banquets with his coarse

Roman ways—I loathed him on sight. I felt soiled by the cool, casual glance he had bestowed on me in that moment before his barge passed under the drawbridge. Quintus Pompeius Falco, indeed! What could that ugly name possibly mean to me? I, a highborn woman of Venetia, Byzantine to the core, who could trace her ancestry to the princes of Constantinopolis, who had mingled since childhood with the great ones of the Greek world?

It was no surprise that the Romans were here. For months I had felt the Empire seeping into our city the way the bitter ocean tides slip past our barrier islands into our quiet lagoon. That is the way it is in Venetia: we shelter ourselves as best we can from the sea, but in time of storm it prevails over everything and comes surging in upon us, engulfing us and flooding us. There is no sea in all the world more powerful than the Empire of Roma; and now it was about to sweep us over at last.

We were a defeated race, after all. Five, eight, ten years had passed, already, since the Basileus Leo VII and the Emperor Flavius Romulus had signed the Treaty of Ravenna by which the Eastern and Western Empires were reunited under Roman rule and all was as it had been so many centuries ago in the time of the earliest Caesars. The great Greek moment was over. We had had our time of glory, but the Romans had prevailed in the end. Piece by piece the whole independent Byzantine world had returned to Roman control, and it was our turn now, Venetia, the westernmost outpost of the fallen realm. Roman barges sailed our canals. A Roman proconsul had come here to live in the Palace of the Doges. Roman soldiers strutted in our streets. Fifty years of bloody civil war, two hundred years of Greek ascendancy

after that, and now it was all nothing but history. We did
not even have an emperor of our own. For a thousand
years, since the time of Constantine, we of the East had
had that. But now we would have to bend our knees to
the Caesars as we did in ancient times. Do you wonder
that I hated Caesar's man on sight, as he proudly made
his entry into our conquered but not humbled city?

Scarcely anything changed at first. They did not recon-
secrate the Temple of Zeus as a temple of Jupiter. Our
fine Byzantine coins, our solidi and miliaresia, continued
to circulate, though I suppose there were Roman sestertii
and denarii among them now. We spoke the language we
had always spoken. Official documents now bore the
Roman date—it was their year 2206—instead of using
the Greek numbering, which ran from the founding of
Constantinopolis. But who among us paid attention to
official documents? For us it was still the year 1123.

We saw Roman officials occasionally in the plaza, or
in the shops of the Rialto, or journeying in gondolas of
state along the main canals, but they were few in number
and they seemed to take care not to intrude on our lives.
The great men of the city, the members of the old aristocracy from whose ranks the Doges once had been drawn,
went about in proper pomp and majesty as usual. There
was no Doge, of course, but there had been none for a
long time.

My own existence was as it had been. As the daughter
of Alexios Phokas and the widow of Heraclios Cantacuzenos I had wealth and privilege. My palace on the
Grand Canal was a center for the high-born and cultured.
My estate to the east in warm and golden Istria yielded a
rich bounty of figs, olives, oats, and wheat, and afforded

me a place of diversion when I wearied of the watery charms of Venetia. For much as I love Venetia I find the city's dank winters and sweltering miasmic summers very much of a burden on my spirit, and must escape from it when those times come.

I had my lovers and my suitors, who were not necessarily the same men. It was generally assumed that I would marry again: I was still only thirty, childless and wealthy and widely hailed for my beauty, and of high family with close connection to the Byzantine imperial dynasty. But although my mourning time was over, I was in no hurry for a new husband. I had been too young when I was married to Heraclios, and had had insufficient experience of the world. The accident that had robbed me of my lord so early had given me the opportunity to make up for my past innocence, and so I had done. Like Penelope, I surrounded myself with suitors who would gladly have taken a daughter of the Phokases to wife, widow that she might be. But while these ambitious grandees, most of them ten years older than I or more, buzzed about me bringing their gifts and murmuring their promises, I amused myself with a succession of less distinguished gentlemen of greater vigor—gondoliers, grooms, musicians, a soldier or two—to the great enhancement of my knowledge of life.

I suppose it was inevitable that I would encounter the Roman proconsul sooner or later. Venetia is a small city; and it was incumbent upon him to ingratiate himself with the local aristocracy. For our part we were obliged to be civil with him: among the Romans all benefits flow downward from the top, and he was the Emperor's man in Venetia. When lands, military rank, lucrative municipal offices became available, it was Quintus Pompeius

Falco who would distribute them, and he could, if he chose, ignore the formerly mighty of the city and raise new men to favor. So it behooved those who had been powerful under the fallen government to court him if they hoped to maintain their high positions. Falco had his suitors just as I had mine. On feast days he was seen at the Temple of Zeus, surrounded by Venetian lords who fawned on him as though he were Zeus himself come to visit. He had the place of honor at many banquets; he was invited to join in the hunt at the estates of the great noblemen; often, as the barges of the wealthy traveled down our canals, there was Pompeius Falco among them on deck, laughing and sipping wine and accepting the flattery of his hosts.

As I say, I could not help but encounter him eventually. From time to time I saw him eyeing me from afar at some grand occasion of state; but I never gave him the satisfaction of returning his glance. And then came an evening when I could no longer avoid direct contact with him.

It was a banquet at the villa of my father's younger brother, Demetrios. With my father dead, Demetrios was the head of our family, and his invitation had the power of a command. What I did not know was that Demetrios, for all his sacks of gold and his many estates in the hinterland, was angling for a political post in the new Roman administration. He wished to become Master of the Cavalry, not a military position at all, for what sort of cavalry could seaborne Venetia have, but simply a sinecure that would entitle him to a share of the city's customs revenues. Therefore he was cultivating the friendship of Pompeius Falco, and had invited him to the banquet. And, to my horror, he had seated me at the proconsul's right hand at the dinner table. Was my uncle willing to play the pimp for the sake of gaining a few extra ducats a year? So it would appear. I was ablaze with fury. But there was nothing I could do now except go through with my part. I had no wish to cause a scandal in my uncle's house.

Falco said to me, "We are companions this evening, it would seem. May I escort you to your seat, Lady Eudoxia?"

He spoke in Greek, and accurate Greek at that, though there was a thick-tongued barbarian undercurrent to his speech. I took his arm. He was taller than I had expected, and very broad through the shoulders. His eyes were alert and penetrating and his smile was a quick, forceful one. From a distance he had seemed quite boyish but I saw now that he was older than I had thought, at least thirty-five, perhaps even more. I detested him for his easy, confident manner, for his proprietorial air, for his command of our language. I even detested him for his beard, thick and black: beards had not been in fashion in the Greek world for several generations now. His was a short, dense fringe, a soldier's beard, that gave him the look of an emperor on one of the old Roman coins. Very likely that was its purpose.

Platters of grilled fish came, and cool wine to go with it. "I love your Venetian wine," he said. "So much more delicate than the heavy stuff of the south. Shall I pour, lady?"

There were servants standing around to do the pouring. But the proconsul of Venetia poured my wine for me, and everyone in the room noticed it.

I was the dutiful niece. I made amiable conversation,

as though Pompeius Falco were a mere guest and not the agent of our conqueror; I pretended that I had utterly accepted the fall of Byzantium and the presence of Roman functionaries among us. Where was he from? Tarraco, he said. That was a city far in the west, he explained: in Hispania. The Emperor Flavius Romulus was from Tarraco also. Ah, and was he related to the Emperor, then? No, said Falco, not at all. But he was a close friend of the Emperor's youngest son, Marcus Quintillius. They had fought side by side in the Cappadocian campaign.

"And are you pleased to have been posted to Venetia?" I asked him, as the wine came around again.

"Oh, yes, yes, lady, very much. What a beautiful little city! So unusual: all these canals, all these bridges. And how civilized it is here, after the frenzy and clamor of Rome."

"Indeed, we are quite civilized," I said.

But I was boiling within, for I knew what he really meant, which was, *How quaint your Venetia is, how sweet, a precious little bauble of a place. And how clever it was of you to build your pretty little town in the sea as you did, so that all the streets are canals and one must get about by gondola instead of by carriage. And what a relief it is for me to spend some time in a placid provincial backwater like this, sipping good wine with handsome ladies while all the local lordlings scurry around me desperately trying to curry my favor, instead of my having to make my way in the cutthroat jungle that surrounds the imperial court in Rome.* And as he went on praising the beauties of the city I came to hate him more and more. It is one thing to be conquered, and quite another to be patronized.

I knew he intended to seduce me. One didn't need the wisdom of Minerva to see that. But I resolved then and there to seduce him first: to seize such little control as I could over this Roman, to humble him and thus to defeat him. Falco was an attractive enough animal, of course. On a sheer animal level there surely was pleasure to be had from him. And also the other pleasure of the conqueror conquered, the pursuer made the pursued: yes, I was eager for that. I was no longer the innocent of seventeen who had been given as bride to the radiant Heraclios Cantacuzenos. I had wiles, now. I was a woman, not a child.

I shifted the conversation to the arts, to literature, to philosophy, to history. I wanted to show him up as the barbarian he was; but he turned out to be unexpectedly well educated, and when I asked if he had been to the theater to see the current play, which was the *Nausicaa* of Sophocles, he said that he had, but that his favorite play of Sophocles was the *Philoctetes*, because it so well defined the conflict between honor and patriotism. "And yet, Lady Eudoxia, I can see why you are partial to the *Nausicaa*, for surely that kind princess must be a woman close to your heart." More flattery, and I loathed him for it; but in truth I had wept at the theater when Nausicaa and Odysseus had loved and parted, and perhaps I did see something of her in myself, or something of myself in her.

At the evening's end he asked me to take the midday meal with him at his palace two days hence. I was prepared for that, and coolly begged a prior engagement. He proposed dinner, then, the first of the week following. Again I invented a reason for declining. He smiled. He understood the nature of the game we had entered into.

"Perhaps another time, then," he said, and gracefully left me for my uncle's company.

I meant to see him again, of course, but at a time and a place of my own choosing. And soon I found the occasion. When traveling troupes of musicians reach Venetia, they find a ready welcome at my home. A concert was to be held; I invited the proconsul. He came, accompanied by a stolid Roman retinue. I gave him the place of honor, naturally. Falco lingered after the performance to praise the quality of the flutes and the poignance of the singer; but he said nothing further about my joining him for dinner. Good: he had abdicated in my favor. From this point on I would define the nature of the chase. I offered him no further invitations either, but allowed him a brief tour of the downstairs rooms of my palace before he left, and he admired the paintings, the sculptures, the cabinet of antiquities, all the fine things that I had inherited from my father and my grandfather.

The next day a Roman soldier arrived with a gift for me from the proconsul: a little statuette in highly polished black stone, showing a woman with the head of a cat. The note from Falco that accompanied it said that he had obtained it while serving in the province of Aiguptos some years ago: it was an image of one of the Aiguptian gods, which he had purchased at a temple in Memphis, and he thought I might find some beauty in it. Indeed it was beautiful, after a fashion, but also it was frightening and strange. In that way it was very much like Quintus Pompeius Falco, I found myself thinking, to my own great surprise. I put the statuette on a shelf in my cabinet—there was nothing like it there; I had never seen anything of its kind—and I resolved to ask Falco to tell me something of Aiguptos the next time I saw him, of its pyramids, its bizarre gods, its torrid sandy wastes.

I sent him a brief note of thanks. Then I waited seven days, and invited him to join me for a holiday at my Istrian estate the following week.

Unfortunately, he replied, that week the cousin of Caesar would be passing through Venetia and would have to be entertained. Could he visit my estate another time?

The rejection caught me off guard. He was a better player of the game than I had suspected; I broke into hot tears of rage. But I had enough sense not to answer immediately. After three days I wrote again, telling him that I regretted being unable to offer him an alternate date at present, but perhaps I would find myself free to entertain him later in the season. It was a risky ploy: certainly it jeopardized my uncle's ambitions. But Falco seemingly took no offense. When our gondolas passed on the canal two days later, he bowed grandly to me and smiled.

I waited what seemed to be the right span of time, and invited him again; and this time he accepted. A ten-man bodyguard came with him: did he think I meant to murder him? But of course the Empire must proclaim its power at every opportunity. I had been warned he would bring an entourage, and I was prepared for it, lodging his soldiers in distant outbuildings and sending for girls of the village to amuse and distract them. Falco himself I installed in the guest suite of my own dwelling.

He had another gift for me: a necklace made from beads of some strange green stone, carved in curious patterns, with a blood-red wedge of stone at its center.

"How lovely," I said, though I thought it frightening and harsh.

"It comes from the land of Mexico," he told me.

"Which is a great kingdom in Nova Roma, far across the sea. They worship mysterious gods there. Their festivals are held atop a great pyramid, where priests cut out the hearts of sacrificial victims until rivers of blood run in the streets of the city."

"And you have been there?"

"Oh, yes, yes. Six years past. Mexico and another land called Peru. I was in the service of Caesar's ambassador to the kingdoms of Nova Roma then."

It stunned me to think that this man had been to Nova Roma. Those two great continents far across the Western Sea—they seemed as remote as the face of the moon to me. But of course in this great time of the Empire under Flavius Romulus the Romans have carried their banners to the most remote parts of the world.

I stroked the stone beads—the green stone was smooth as silk, and seemed to burn with an inner fire—and put the necklace on.

"Aiguptos—Nova Roma—" I shook my head. "And have you been everywhere, then?"

"Yes, very nearly so," he said, laughing. "The men who serve Flavius Caesar grow accustomed to long journeys. My brother has been to Khitai and the islands of Cipangu. My uncle went far south in Africa, beyond Aiguptos, to the lands where the hairy men dwell. It is a golden age, lady. The Empire reaches out boldly to every corner of the world." Then he smiled and leaned close and said, "And you, lady? Have you traveled very much?"

"I have seen Constantinopolis," I said.

"Ah. The great capital, yes. I stopped there on my way to Aiguptos. The races in the Hippodrome—nothing like it, even in Urbs Roma itself! I saw the royal palace: from the outside, of course. They say it has walls of gold. I think not even Caesar's house can equal it."

"I was in it, once, when I was a child. When the Basileus still ruled, I mean. I saw the golden halls. I saw the lions of gold that sit beside the throne and roar and wave their tails, and the jewelled birds on the gold and silver trees in the throne-chamber, who open their beaks and sing. The Basileus gave me a ring. My father was his distant relative, you know. I am of the Phokas family. Later I married a Cantacuzenos: my husband too had royal connections."

"Ah," he said, as though greatly impressed, as though the names of the Byzantine aristocracy might possibly mean something to him.

But in fact I knew he was still condescending to me. A dethroned emperor is no emperor at all; a fallen aristocracy merits little awe.

And what did it matter to him that I had been once to Constantinopolis—he who had been there too, in passing, on his way to fabulous Aiguptos? The one great journey I had taken in my life was a mere stopover to him. His cosmopolitanism humbled me, as I suppose it was meant to do. He had been to other continents: other worlds, really. Aiguptos! Nova Roma! He could find things to praise about our capital, yes, but it was clear from his effusive tone that he really regarded it as inferior to the city of Rome, and inferior perhaps to the cities of Mexico and Peru as well, and other exotic places that he had visited in Caesar's name. The breadth and scope of his travels dazzled me. Here we Greeks were, penned up in our ever-shrinking realm that now had collapsed utterly. Here was I, daughter of one minor city on the periphery of that fallen realm, pathetically proud of my one visit long ago to our formerly mighty capital. But he was a Roman; all the world was open to him. If mighty Constantinopolis of the golden walls was just one more city to him, what was our little Venetia? What was I?

I hated him more violently than ever. I wished I had never invited him.

But he was my guest. I had had a wondrous banquet prepared, with the finest of wines, and delicacies that even a far-traveled Roman might not have met with before. He was obviously pleased. He drank and drank and drank, growing flushed though never losing control, and we talked far into the night.

I must confess that he amazed me with the scope and range of his mind.

He was no mere barbarian. He had had a Greek tutor, as all Romans of good family had had for over a thousand years. A wise old Athenian named Eukleides, he was, who had filled the young Falco's head with poetry and drama and philosophy, and drilled him in the most obscure nuances of our language, and taught him the abstract sciences, at which we Greeks have always excelled. And so this proconsul was at home not just in Roman things like science and engineering and the art of warfare, but also in Plato and Aristoteles, in the playwrights and poets, in the history of my race back to Agamemnon's time—indeed, he was able to discourse on all manner of things that I myself knew more by name than by the inner meaning.

He talked until I had had all the talking I could bear, and then some. And at last—it was the middle hour of the night, and the owls were crying in the darkness—I took him by the hand and led him to my bed, if only to silence that flow of words that came from him like the torrents of Aiguptos's Nile itself.

He lit a taper in the bedchamber. Our clothes dropped away as though they had turned to mist.

He reached for me and drew me down.

I had never been loved by a Roman before. In the last moment before he embraced me I had a sudden fresh burst of fiery contempt for him and all his kind, for I was certain that his innate brutality now would come to the fore, that all his philosophic eloquence had been but a pose and now he would take possession of me the way Romans for fifteen hundred years had taken possession of everything in their path. He would subjugate me; he would colonize me. He would be coarse and violent and clumsy, but he would have his way, as Romans always did, and afterward he would rise and leave without a word.

I was wrong, as I had been wrong about everything else concerning this man.

His touch indeed was Roman, not Greek. That is to say, instead of insinuating himself into me in some devious, cunning, left-handed manner, he was straightforward and direct. But not clumsy, not at all. He knew what to do, and he set about doing it; and where there were things he had to learn, as any man must when it is his first time with a new woman, he knew what they were and he knew how to learn them. I understood now what was meant when women said that Greek men make love like poets and Romans like engineers. What I had never realized until that moment was that engineers have skills that many poets never have, and that an engineer could be capable of writing fine poetry, but would you not think twice about riding across a bridge that had been designed or built by a poet?

We lay together until dawn, laughing and talking when we were not embracing. And then, having had no sleep, we rose in our nakedness and walked through the halls to the bath-chamber, and in great merriment washed ourselves, and, still naked, walked out into the sweet pink dawn. Side by side we stood, saying nothing, watching the sun come up out of Byzantium and begin its day's journey onward toward Roma, toward the lands along the Western Sea, toward Nova Roma, toward far-off Khitai.

We dressed and had a breakfast of wine and cheese and figs, and I called for horses and took him on a tour of the estate. I showed him the olive groves, the fields of wheat, the mill and its stream, the fig trees laden with fruit. The day was warm and beautiful; the birds sang, the sky was clear.

Later, as we took our midday meal on the patio overlooking the garden, he said, "This is a marvelous place. I hope that when I'm old I can retire to a country estate like this."

"Surely there must be one in your family," I said.

"Several. But not, I think, as peaceful as this. We Romans have forgotten how to live peacefully."

"Whereas we, since we are a declining race, can allow ourselves the luxury of a little tranquility?"

He looked at me strangely. "You see yourselves as a declining race?"

"Don't be disingenuous, Quintus Pompeius. There's no need to flatter me now. Of course we are."

"Because you're no longer an imperial power?"

"Of course. Once ambassadors from places like Nova

Roma and Baghdad and Memphis and Khitai came to us. Not here to Venetia, I mean, but to Constantinopolis. Now the ambassadors go only to Roma; what the Greek cities get is tourists. And Roman proconsuls."

"How strange your view of the world is, Eudoxia."

"What do you mean?"

"You equate the loss of the Imperium with being in decline."

"Wouldn't you?"

"If it would happen to Roma, yes. But Byzantium isn't Roma." He was staring at me very seriously now. "The Eastern Empire was a folly, a distraction, a great mistake that somehow endured a thousand years. It should never have been. The burden of ruling the world was given to Roma: we accept it as our duty. There was never any need for an Eastern Empire in the first place."

"It was all some terrible error of Constantine's, you say?"

"Exactly. It was a bad time for Roma, then. Even empires have their fluctuations; even ours. We had overextended ourselves, and everything was shaking. Constantine had political problems at home, and too many troublesome sons. He thought the Empire was unwieldy and impossible to hold together, so he built the eastern capital and let the two halves drift apart. The system worked for a while—no, I admit it, for hundreds of years—but as the East lost sight of the fact that its political system had been set up by Romans and began to remember that it was really Greek, its doom became inevitable. A Greek Imperium is an anomaly that can't sustain itself in the modern world. It couldn't even sustain itself very long in the ancient world. The phrase is a contradiction in terms, a Greek Imperium. Agamemnon had no Imperium; he was only a tribal chief, who could barely make his power felt ten miles from Mycenae. And how long did the Athenian Empire last? How long did Alexander's kingdom hold together, once Alexander had died? No, no, no, Eudoxia, the Greeks are a marvelous people, the whole world is in their debt for any number of great achievements, but building and sustaining governments on a large scale isn't one of their skills. And never has been."

"You think so?" I said, with glee in my voice. "Then why was it that we were able to defeat you in the Civil War? It was Caesar Maximilianus who surrendered to the Basileus Andronicus, is that not so, West yielding to East, and not the other way around. For two hundred years we of the East were supreme in the world, may I remind you."

Falco shrugged. "The gods were teaching Roma a lesson, that's all. It was another fluctuation. We were being punished for having allowed the Empire to be divided in the first place. We needed to be humbled for a little while, so we'd never make the same mistake again. So you Greeks beat us very soundly in Maximilianus's time, and you had a couple of hundred years of being, as you say, supreme, while we discovered what it felt like to be a second-rate power. But it was an impossible situation. The gods *intend* Roma to rule the world. There's simply no doubt of that. It was true in the time of Carthage and it's true today. And so the Greek Empire fell apart without even the need for a second Civil War. And so here we are. A Roman procurator sits in the royal palace at Constantinopolis. And a Roman proconsul in Venetia. Although at the moment he happens to be at the country estate of a lovely Venetian lady."

"You're serious?" I said. "You really believe that you are a chosen people? That Roma holds the Imperium by the will of the gods?"

"Absolutely."

He was altogether sincere.

"The Pax Romana is Zeus's gift to humanity? Jupiter's gift, I should say."

"Yes," he said. "But for us, the world would fall into chaos. Gods, woman, do you think we *want* to spend our lives being administrators and bureaucrats? Don't you think I'd prefer to retire to some estate like this and spend my days hunting and fishing and farming? But we are the race that understands how to rule. And therefore we have the obligation to rule. Oh, Eudoxia, Eudoxia, you think we're simple brutal beasts who go around conquering everybody for the sheer joy of conquest, and you don't realize that this is our task, our burden, our *job*."

"I will weep for you, then."

He smiled. "Am I a simple brutal beast?"

"Of course you are. All Romans are."

He stayed with me for five days. I think we slept perhaps ten hours in all that time. Then he begged leave of me, saying that it was necessary that he return to his tasks in Venetia, and he went away.

I remained behind, with plenty to think about.

I could not, of course, accept his thesis that Greeks were incapable of governing anyone and that Roma had some divine mandate to run the world. The Eastern Empire had spread over great segments of the known world in its first few hundred years—Syria, Arabia, Aiguptos, much of the eastern Europa even as far as Venetia, which is virtually in Roma's back yard—and we had thrived and prospered mightily, as the wealth of the great Byzantine cities still attests. And in later years, when the Romans had begun to find that their Greek cousins were growing uncomfortably powerful and had attempted to reassert the supremacy of the West, we had fought a fifty-year Civil War and had beaten them quite handily. Which had led to two centuries of Byzantine hegemony, hard times for the West while Byzantine merchant-ships traveled to the rich cities of Asia and Africa. I suppose ultimately we had overreached ourselves, as all empires eventually do, or perhaps we simply went soft with too much prosperity, and so the Romans awakened out of their sleep of centuries and shook our empire apart. Maybe they are the great exception: maybe their Imperium really will go on and on and on through the ages to come, as it has done for the last fifteen hundred years, with only minor periods of what Falco would call "fluctuations" to disrupt its unbroken span of command. And therefore our territories have been reduced by the inexorable force of the imperial destiny of Roma to the status of Roman provinces again, as they were in the time of Augustus Caesar. But we had had our time of grandeur. We had ruled the world just as well as the Romans ever did.

Or so I told myself. But even as I thought it, I knew it wasn't so.

We Greeks could understand grandeur, yes. We understand splendor and imperial pomp. But the Romans know how to do the day-by-day work of governing. Maybe Falco was right after all: maybe our pitiful few centuries of Imperium, interrupting the long Roman sway, had been just an anomaly of history. For now the Eastern Empire was only a memory and the Pax Romana was once again in force across thousands of miles, and from his hilltop in Roma the great Caesar Flavius Romulus presided over a realm such as the world had never before known: Romans in remotest Asia, Romans in India, Roman vessels traveling even to the astonishing new continents of the far western hemisphere, strange new inventions coming forth—printed books, weapons that hurl heavy missiles great distances, all sorts of miracles—and we Greeks are reduced to contemplation of past glories as we sit in our conquered cities sipping our wine and reading Homer and Sophocles. For the first time in my life I saw my people as a minor race, elegant, charming, cultivated, unimportant.

How I had despised my handsome proconsul! And how he had revenged himself on me for that!

I stayed in Istria two more days and then I returned to the city. There was a gift waiting for me from Falco: a sleek piece of carved ivory that showed a house of strange design and a woman with delicate features sitting pensively beside a lake under a tree with weeping boughs. The note from him that accompanied it said that it was from Khitai, that he had obtained it in the land of Bactria, on India's borders. He had not told me that he had been to Bactria, too. The thought of his travels on behalf of Roma dizzied me: so many voyages, such strenuous journeys. And I imagined him gathering little treasures such as these wherever he went, and carrying them about with him to bestow on his ladies in other lands. That thought so angered me that I nearly hurled the ivory piece away. But I reconsidered, and put it in my cabinet of curios next to the stone goddess from Aiguptos.

It was his turn now to invite me to dine with him at the

palace of the Doges, and—I assumed—to spend the night in the bed where the Doges and their consorts once had slept. But I waited a week and then a second week, and the invitation did not come. That seemed out of keeping with my new awareness of him as a man of great attainment. But perhaps I had overestimated him. He was, after all, a Roman. He had had what he wanted from me; now he was on to other adventures, other conquests.

I was wrong about that, too.

When my impatience had darkened once again into anger toward him and my fury over having let him use me this way had obliterated all the regard for him that had developed in me during his visit to my estate, I went to my uncle Demetrios and said, "Have you seen this Roman proconsul of ours lately? Has he been ill, do you think?"

"Why, is he of any concern to you, Eudoxia?"

I glowered at him. Having pushed me into Falco's arms to serve his own purposes, Demetrios had no right to mock me now. Sharply I said, "He owes me the courtesy of an invitation to the palace, Uncle. Not that I would accept it—not now. But he should know that he has given offense."

"And I am supposed to tell him that?"

"Tell him nothing. *Nothing!*"

Demetrios gave me a knowing smirk. But I was sure he would keep silent. There was nothing for him to gain in humiliating me in the eyes of Pompeius Falco.

The days went by. And then at last came a note from Falco, in elegant Greek script as all his notes were, asking if he might call on me. My impulse was to refuse. But one did not refuse such requests from a proconsul. And in any case I realized that I wanted to see him again. I wanted very much to see him again.

"I hope you will forgive me, lady, for my inattentiveness," he said. "But I have had a great deal on my mind in these recent weeks."

"I'm certain that you have," I said drily.

Color came to his face. "You have every right to be angry with me, Eudoxia. But this has been a time of unusual circumstances. There have been great upheavals in Roma, do you know? The Emperor has reshuffled his Cabinet. Important men have fallen; others have risen suddenly to glory."

"And how has this concerned you?" I asked him. "Are you one of those who has fallen, or have you risen to glory? Or should I not ask you any of this?"

"One of those who has risen," he said, "is Gaius Julius Flavillus."

The name meant nothing to me.

"Gaius Julius Flavillus, lady, had held the post of Third Flamen. Now he is First Tribune. Which is a considerable elevation, as you may know. It happens that Gaius Flavillus is a man of Tarraco, like the Emperor, like myself. He is my father's cousin. He has been my patron throughout my career. And so—messengers have been going back and forth between Venetia and Roma for all these weeks—I too have been elevated, it seems, by special favor of the new Tribune."

"Elevated," I said hollowly.

"Indeed. I have been transferred to Constantinopolis, where I am to be the new procurator. It is the highest administrative post in the former Eastern Empire." His eyes were glittering with self-satisfaction. But then his expression changed. A kind of sadness came into them, a kind of tenderness. "Lady, you must believe me when I tell you that I greeted the news with a mixture of feelings, not all of them pleasant ones. It is a great honor for me. And yet I would not have left Venetia so quickly of my own choosing. We have barely begun to know each other; and now, to my immense regret, we must part."

He took my hands in his. He seemed almost to be at the edge of tears. His sincerity seemed real; or else he was a better actor than I suspected.

A kind of numbness spread through me.

"When do you leave?" I asked.

"In three days, lady."

"Ah. Three days."

"Three very busy days."

You could always take me with you to Constantinopolis, I found myself thinking. There would surely be room for me somewhere in the vast palace of the former Basileus where you now will make your home.

But of course that could never be. A Roman rising as swiftly as he was would never want to encumber himself with a Byzantine wife. A Byzantine mistress, perhaps. But mistresses of any sort were no longer what he needed. Now was the time for him to make an auspicious marriage and undertake the next stage of his climb. The procurator's seat at Constantinopolis would detain him a little longer than his proconsulship in Venetia had; his path would lead him before very long back to Roma. He would be a flamen, a tribune, perhaps Pontifex Maximus. If he played his cards right he might some day be Emperor. I might be summoned then to Roma to relive old times, perhaps. But I would not see him again before then.

"May I stay this night with you?" he asked, with a

strange new note of uncertainty in his voice, as though
expecting that I might refuse.

But of course I did not refuse. That would have been
crass and petty; and in any case I wanted him. I knew that
this was the last chance.

It was a night of wine and poetry, of tears and laughter,
of ecstasy and exhaustion.

And then he was gone, leaving me mired in my petty
little provincial life while he went on to Constantinopolis
and glory. A grand procession of gondolas followed him
down the canal as he made his way to the sea. A new
Roman proconsul, so they say, will be arriving in Venetia
any day now.

From Falco I had one parting gift: the plays of Aes-
chylus, in a finely bound volume that had been produced
on the printing press, which is one of those new inventions of which they are so proud in Roma. My first reaction was one of scorn, that he should give me this
machine-made thing instead of a manuscript indited by
hand. And then, as I had done so many times in the days
of my involvement with this difficult man, I was forced
to reconsider, to admire what at first sight I had seen as
cheap and vulgar. The book was beautiful, in its way.
More than that: it was a sign of a new age. To deny that
new age, or turn my back on it, would be folly.

And so I have learned at first hand of the power of
Roma and of the insignificance of the formerly great. Our
lovely Venetia was only a way-station for him. Constantinopolis of imperial grandeur will be the same. It was a
powerful lesson: I have been thoroughly educated in the
ways of Roma and the Romans, to my own great cost, for
I see now as I never could have seen before that they are

everything and we, polished and refined as we may be, are nothing at all.

I had underestimated Quintus Pompeius Falco at every turn; I had underestimated his race the same way. As had we all, which is why they once again rule the world, or most of it, and we smile and bow and hope for their favor.

He has written to me several times. So I must have made a strong impression on him. He speaks fondly, if guardedly, of our times together. He says nothing, though, about hoping that I will pay a visit to Constantinopolis to see him.

But perhaps I will, one of these days, nevertheless. Or perhaps not. It all depends on what the new proconsul is like.

We Could Do Worse

Gregory Benford

"We Could Do Worse" appeared in the April 1989 issue of Asimov's, *with an illustration by Robert Shore, one of a string of strong stories that Gregory Benford published in* Asimov's *during the '80s and '90s. Benford is one of the modern giants of the field. His 1980 novel* Timescape *won the Nebula Award, the John W. Campbell Memorial Award, the British Science Fiction Association Award, and the Australian Ditmar Award, and is widely considered to be one of the classic novels of the last two decades. His other novels include* The Stars in Shroud, In the Ocean of Night, Against Infinity, Artifact, *and* Across the Sea of Suns. *His most recent novels are the best-selling* Great Sky River, *and* Tides of Light. *Benford is a professor of physics at the University of California, Irvine.*

Most of Benford's work in the area of Alternate History has been as an editor; he has coedited, with Martin H. Greenberg, several of the core Alternate History anthologies, including the essential What Might Have Been *anthologies, Volumes 1–4—*Alternate Wars, Alternate Empires, Alternate Heroes, *and* Alternate Americas—*and an anthology of alternate World War II stories,* Hitler Victorious. *Every so often, though, he pens one himself, as with* *the chilling story that follows, one depicting an all-too-likely future America that we may have escaped only by the narrowest of margins, and one that shows us that, no matter how bad things are, they could always have been worse . . .*

Everybody in the bar noticed us when we came in. You could see their faces tighten up.

The bartender reached over and put the cover on the free-lunch jar. I caught that even though I was watching the people in the booths.

They knew who we were. You could see the caution come into their eyes. I'm big enough that nobody just glances at me once. You get used to that after a while and then you start to liking it.

"Beer," I said when we got to the mahogany bar. The bartender drew it, looking at me. He let some suds slop over and wiped the glass and stood holding it until I put down a quarter.

"Two," I said. The bartender put the glass in front of me and I pushed it toward Phillips. He let some of the second beer slop out too because he was busy watching my hands. I took the glass with my right and with my left I lifted the cover off the free-lunch jar.

"No," he said.

I took a sandwich out.

"I'm gonna make like I didn't hear that," I said and bit into the sandwich. It was cheese with some mayonnaise and hadn't been made today.

I tossed the sandwich aside. "Got anything better?"

"Not for you," the bartender said.

"You got your license out where I can read it?"

"You guys is federal. Got no call to want my liquor license."

"Lawyer, huh?" Phillips asked slow and steady. He doesn't say much but people always listen.

The bartender was in pretty good shape, a middle-sized guy with big arm muscles, but he made a mistake then. His hand slid under the bar, watching us both, and I reached over and grabbed his wrist. I yanked his hand up and there was a pistol in it. The hammer was already cocked. Phillips got his fingers between the revolver's hammer and the firing pin. We pulled it out of the bartender's hand easy and I tapped him a light one in the snoot, hardly getting off my stool. He staggered back and Phillips put away the revolver in a coat pocket.

"Guys like you shouldn't have guns," Phillips said. "Get hurt that way."

"You just stand there and look pretty," I said.

"It's Garrett, isn't it?" the barkeep muttered.

"Now don't never you mind," Phillips said.

The rest of the bar was quiet and I turned and gave them a look. "What you expect?" I said loud enough so they could all hear. "Man pulls a gun on you, you take care of him."

A peroxide blonde in a back booth called out, "You bastards!"

"There a back alley here?" I asked the whole room.

Their faces were tight and they didn't know whether to tell me the truth or not.

"Hey, yeah," Phillips said, "sure there's a back door. You 'member, the briefing said so."

He's not too bright. So I used a different way to open them up. "Blondie, you want we ask you some questions? Maybe out in that alley?"

Peroxide looked steady at me for a moment and then looked away. She knew what we'd do to her out there if she made any more noise. Women know those things without your saying.

I turned my back to them and said, "My nickel."

The bartender had stopped his nose from bleeding but he wasn't thinking very well. He just blinked at me.

"Change for the beers," I said. "You can turn on that TV, too."

He fumbled getting the nickel. When the last of the Milton Berle hour came on the bar filled with enough sound so anybody coming in from the street wouldn't notice that nobody was talking. They were just watching Phillips and me.

I sipped my beer. Part of our job is to let folks know we're not fooling around any more. Show the flag, kind of.

The Berle show went off and you could smell the tense sweat in the bar. I acted casual, like I didn't care. The government news bulletins were coming on and the bartender started to change channels and I waved him off.

"Time for Lucy," he said. He had gotten some backbone into his voice again.

I smiled at him. "I guess I know what time it is. Let's inform these citizens a li'l."

There was a Schlitz ad with dancing and singing bottles, the king of beers, and then more news. They mentioned the new directives about the state of emergency, but nothing I didn't already know two days ago. Good. No surprises.

"Let's have Lucy!" somebody yelled behind me.

I turned around but nobody said anything more. "You'd maybe like watchin' the convention?" I said.

Nobody spoke. So I grinned and said, "Maybe you patriots could learn somethin' that way."

I laughed a little and gestured to the bartender. He spun the dial and there was the Republican convention, warming up. Cronkite talking over the background noise.

"Somethin', huh?" I said to Phillips. "Not like four years ago."

"Don't matter that much," Phillips said. He watched the door while I kept an eye on the crowd.

"You kiddin'? Why, that goddamn Eisenhower almost took the nomination away from Taft last time. Hadn't been for Nixon deliverin' the California delegation to old man Taft, that pinko general coulda won."

"So?" Phillips sipped his beer. A station break came and I could hear tires hissing by outside in the light rain. My jacket smelled damp. I never wear a raincoat on a job like this. They get in your way. The street lights threw stretched shapes against the bar windows. Phillips watched the passing shadows, waiting calm as anything for one of them to turn and come in the door.

I said, "You think Eisenhower, with that Kraut name, woulda picked our guy for the second spot?"

"Mighta."

"Hell no. Even if he had, Eisenhower didn't drop dead a year later."

"You're right there," Phillips said to humor me. He's not a man for theory.

"I tell you, Taft winnin' and then dyin', it was a godsend. Gave us the man we shoulda had. Never coulda elected him. The Commies, they'd never have let him get in power."

Phillips stiffened. I thought it was what I'd said, but

then a guy came through the doors in a slick black raincoat. He was pale and I saw it was our man. Cheering at the convention came up then and he didn't notice anything funny, not until he got a few steps in and saw the faces.

Garrett's eyes widened as I came at him. He pulled his hands up like he was reaching for something under his coat, or maybe just to protect himself.

I didn't care which. I hit him once in the stomach to take the wind out of him and then gave him two quick overhand punches in the jaw. He went down nice and solid and wasn't going to get back up in a hurry.

Phillips searched him. There was no gun after all. The bar was dead quiet.

A guy in a porkpie hat came up to me all hot and bothered, like he hadn't been paying attention before, and said, "You can't just attack a, a member of the Congress! That's Congressman Garrett there! I don't care—"

The big talk went right out of him when I slammed a fist into his gut. Porkpie was another lawyer, no real fight in him.

I walked back to the bar and drained my beer. The '56 convention was rolling on, nominations just starting, but you knew that was all bull. Only one man was possible, and when the election came there'd be plenty guys like me to fix it so he won.

Just then they put on some footage of the President and I stood there a second, just watching him. There was a knot in my throat when I looked at him, a real American. There were damn few of us, even now. We'd gotten in by accident, maybe, but now we were going to make every day count. Clean up the country. And hell, if the work wasn't done by the time his second term ended in 1961, we might have to diddle the Constitution a little, keep him in power until things worked okay.

Cronkite came on then, babbling about letting Adlai Stevenson out of house arrest, and I went to help Phillips get Garrett to his feet. I sure didn't want to have to haul the guy out to our car.

We got him up with his raincoat all twisted around him. Then the porkpie hat guy was there again, but this time with about a dozen of them behind him. They looked mad and jittery. A bunch like that can be trouble. I wondered if this was such a good idea, taking Garrett in his neighborhood bar. But the chief said we had to show these types we'd go anywhere, anytime.

Porkpie said, "You got no warrant."

"Sure I do." I showed them the paper. These types always think paper is God.

"Sit down," Phillips said, being civil. "You people all sit down."

"That's a congressman you got there. We—"

"Traitor, is what you mean," I said.

Peroxide came up then, screeching. "You think you can just take anybody, you lousy sonsabitches—"

Porkpie took a poke at me then. I caught it and gave him a right cross, pretty as you please. He staggered back. Still, I saw we could really get in a fix here if they all came at us.

Peroxide called out, "Come on, we can—"

She stopped when I pulled out the gun. It's a big steel automatic, just about the right size for a guy like me. Some guys use silencers with them but me, I like the noise.

They all looked at it a while and their faces changed,

closing up, each one of them alone with their thoughts, and then I knew they wouldn't do anything.

"Come on," I said. We carried the traitor out into the night. I was so pumped up he felt light.

Even a year before, we'd have had big trouble bringing in a commie network type like Garrett. He was a big deal on the House Internal Security Committee and had been giving us a lot of grief. Now nailing him was easy. And all because of one man at the top with real courage.

We don't bother with the formalities any more. Phillips opened the trunk of the Pontiac and I dumped Garrett in. Easier and faster than cramming him into the front and I wanted to get out of there.

Garrett was barely conscious and just blinked at me as I slammed down the trunk. They'd wake him up plenty later.

As I came around to get in the driver's side I looked through the window of the bar. Cronkite was interviewing the President now. Ol' Joe looked like he was in good shape, real statesmanlike, but tough, you could see that.

Cronkite was probably asking him why he'd chosen Nixon for the V.P. spot, like there was any other choice. Like I'd tried to tell Phillips, Nixon's delivering California on the delegate issue in '52 had paved the way for the Taft ticket. And old Bob Taft, rest his soul, knew what the country needed when the Vice Presidency nomination came up.

Just like now. Joe, he doesn't forget a debt. So Dick Nixon was a shoo-in. McCarthy and Nixon—good ticket, regional balance, solid anti-commie values. We could do worse. A lot worse.

I got in and gunned the motor a little, feeling good.

The rain had stopped. The meat in the trunk was as good as dead, but we'd deliver it fresh anyway. We took off with a roar into the darkness.

Over There

Mike Resnick

"Over There" appeared in the September 1991 issue of Asimov's, *with an illustration by Laurie Harden. Mike Resnick has become a mainstay of the magazine in the '80s and '90s, publishing a long string of stories here, including the popular Kirinyaga stories about life in a future space colony reshaped in the image of ancient Kenya. He's one of the best-selling authors in science fiction, and one of the most prolific. His many novels include* The Dark Lady, Stalking the Unicorn, Paradise, Santiago, Ivory, Soothsayer Oracle, Lucifer Jones, Purgatory, Inferno, *and* A Miracle of Rare Design. *His award-winning short fiction has been gathered in the collection* Will the Last Person to Leave the Planet Please Turn Off the Sun? *Of late, he has become almost as prolific as an anthologist, producing, as editor,* Inside the Funhouse: 17 SF Stories About SF, Whatdunits, More Whatdunits, *and* Shaggy B.E.M. Stories, *as well as a long string of anthologies coedited with Martin H. Greenberg, and two anthologies coedited with Gardner Dozois,* Future Earths: Under African Skies *and* Future Earths: Under South American Skies. *He won the Hugo Award in 1989 for "Kirinyaga." He won another Hugo Award in 1991 for another story in the Kirinyaga series, "The Manu-*

mouki," and another Hugo and a Nebula in 1995 for his novella Seven Views of Olduvai Gorge. *His most recent books include the novels* The Widowmaker *and* A Hunger in the Soul. *Several of his books are in the process of being turned into big-budget movies.*

In the subgenre of Alternate History, Resnick has perhaps been most influential as an editor, producing, with Martin H. Greenberg, some of the most prominent Alternate History anthologies of the last ten years, including Alternate Presidents, Alternate Kennedys, Alternate Warriors, By Any Other Fame, Alternate Outlaws, *and, most recently,* Alternate Tyrants. *Resnick has written a popular Alternate History series of his own, though, detailing the possible alternate lives of American president Teddy Roosevelt. The story that follows is part of that series, and in it Resnick shows that Alternate History stories don't necessarily have to be concerned with big, sweeping changes in the fate of nations—they can also deal with small private changes in one person's life that may alter that life forever ... as here, in an eloquent story that demonstrates that the difference between a fool and a hero is sometimes in the eye of the beholder.*

I respectfully ask permission to raise two divisions for immediate service at the front under the bill which has just become law, and hold myself ready to raise four divisions, if you so direct. I respectfully refer for details to my last letters to the Secretary of War.

—Theodore Roosevelt
Telegram to President Woodrow
Wilson, May 18, 1917

I very much regret that I cannot comply with the request in your telegram of yesterday. The reasons I have stated in a public statement made this morning, and I need not assure you that my conclusions were based upon imperative considerations of public policy and not upon personal or private choice.

—Woodrow Wilson,
Telegram to Theodore Roosevelt,
May 19, 1917

The date was May 22, 1917.

Woodrow Wilson looked up at the burly man standing impatiently before his desk.

"This will necessarily have to be an extremely brief meeting, Mr. Roosevelt," he said wearily. "I have consented to it only out of respect for the fact that you formerly held the office that I am now privileged to hold."

"I appreciate that, Mr. President," said Theodore Roosevelt, shifting his weight anxiously from one leg to the other.

"Well, then?" said Wilson.

"You know why I'm here," said Roosevelt bluntly. "I want your permission to reassemble my Rough Riders and take them over to Europe."

"As I keep telling you, Mr. Roosevelt—that's out of the question."

"You haven't told *me* anything!" snapped Roosevelt. "And I have no interest in what you tell the press."

"Then I'm telling you now," said Wilson firmly. "I can't just let any man who wants to gather up a regiment go fight in the war. We have procedures, and chains of command, and . . ."

"I'm not just *any* man," said Roosevelt. "And I have every intention of honoring our procedures and chain of command." He glared at the president. "I created many of those procedures myself."

Wilson stared at his visitor for a long moment. "Why are you so anxious to go to war, Mr. Roosevelt? Does violence hold so much fascination for you?"

"I abhor violence and bloodshed," answered Roosevelt. "I believe that war should never be resorted to when it is honorably possible to avoid it. But once war has begun, then the only thing to do is win it as swiftly and decisively as possible. I believe that I can help to accomplish that end."

"Mr. Roosevelt, may I point out that you are fifty-eight years old, and according to my reports you have been in poor health ever since returning from Brazil three years ago."

"Nonsense!" said Roosevelt defensively. "I feel as fit as a bull moose!"

"A one-eyed bull moose," replied Wilson dryly. Roosevelt seemed about to protest, but Wilson raised a hand to silence him. "Yes, Mr. Roosevelt, I know that you lost the vision in your left eye during a boxing match while you were president." He couldn't quite keep the distaste for such juvenile and adventurous escapades out of his voice.

"I'm not here to discuss my health," answered Roosevelt gruffly, "but the reactivation of my commission as a colonel in the United States Army."

Wilson shook his head. "You have my answer. You've told me nothing that might change my mind."

"I'm about to."

"Oh?"

"Let's be perfectly honest, Mr. President. The Republican nomination is mine for the asking, and however the war turns out, the Democrats will be sitting ducks. Half the people hate you for entering the war so late, and the other half hate you for entering it at all." Roosevelt paused. "If you will return me to active duty and allow me to organize my Rough Riders, I will give you my personal pledge that I will neither seek nor accept the Republican nomination in 1920."

"It means that much to you?" asked Wilson, arching a thin eyebrow.

"It does, sir."

"I'm impressed by your passion, and I don't doubt your sincerity, Mr. Roosevelt," said Wilson. "But my answer must still be no. I am serving my second term. I have no intention of running again in 1920, I do not need your political support, and I will not be a party to such a deal."

"Then you are a fool, Mr. President," said Roosevelt. "Because I am going anyway, and you have thrown away your only opportunity, slim as it may be, to keep the Republicans out of the White House."

"I will not reactivate your commission, Mr. Roosevelt."

Roosevelt pulled two neatly folded letters out of his lapel pocket and placed them on the president's desk.

"What are these?" asked Wilson, staring at them as if they might bite him at any moment.

"Letters from the British and the French, offering me commissions in *their* armies." Roosevelt paused. "I am first, foremost, and always an American, Mr. President, and I had entertained no higher hope than leading my men into battle under the Stars and Stripes—but I am going to participate in this war, and you are not going to stop me." And now, for the first time, he displayed the famed Roosevelt grin. "I have some thirty reporters waiting for me on the lawn of the White House. Shall I tell them that I am fighting for the country that I love, or shall I tell them that our European allies are more concerned with winning this damnable war than our own president?"

"This is blackmail, Mr. Roosevelt!" said Wilson, outraged.

"I believe that is the word for it," said Roosevelt, still grinning. "I would like you to direct Captain Frank Mc-Coy to leave his current unit and report to me. I'll handle the rest of the details myself." He paused again. "The press is waiting, Mr. President. What shall I tell them?"

"Tell them anything you want," muttered Wilson furiously. "Only get out of this office!"

"Thank you, sir," said Roosevelt, turning on his heel and marching out with an energetic bounce to his stride.

Wilson waited a moment, then spoke aloud. "You can come in now, Joseph."

Joseph Tummulty, his personal secretary, entered the Oval Office.

"Were you listening?" asked Wilson.

"Yes, sir."

"Is there any way out of it?"

"Not without getting a black eye in the press."

"That's what I was afraid of," said Wilson.

"He's got you over a barrel, Mr. President."

"I wonder what he's really after?" mused Wilson thoughtfully. "He's been a governor, an explorer, a war hero, a police commissioner, an author, a big-game hunter, and a president." He paused, mystified. "What more can he want from life?"

"Personally, sir," said Tummulty, making no attempt to hide the contempt in his voice, "I think that damned cowboy is looking to charge up one more San Juan Hill."

Roosevelt stood before his troops, as motley an assortment of warriors as had been assembled since the last incarnation of the Rough Riders. There were military men and cowboys, professional athletes and adventurers, hunters and ranchers, barroom brawlers and Indians, tennis players and wrestlers, even a trio of Maasai *elmoran* he had met on safari in Africa.

"Some of 'em look a little long in the tooth, Colonel," remarked Frank McCoy, his second-in-command.

"Some of *us* are a little long in the tooth too, Frank," said Roosevelt with a smile.

"And some of 'em haven't started shaving yet," continued McCoy wryly.

"Well, there's nothing like a war to grow them up in a hurry."

Roosevelt turned away from McCoy and faced his men, waiting briefly until he had their attention. He paused for a moment to make sure that the journalists who were traveling with the regiment had their pencils and notebooks out, and then spoke.

"Gentlemen," he said, "we are about to embark upon a great adventure. We are privileged to be present at a crucial point in the history of the world. In the terrible whirlwind of war, all the great nations of the world are facing the supreme test of their courage and dedication. All the alluring but futile theories of the pacifists have vanished at the first sound of gunfire."

Roosevelt paused to clear his throat, then continued in his surprisingly high-pitched voice. "This war is the greatest the world has ever seen. The vast size of the armies, the tremendous slaughter, the loftiness of the heroism shown and the hideous horror of the brutalities committed, the valor of the fighting men and the extraordinary ingenuity of those who have designed and built the fighting machines, the burning patriotism of the peoples who defend their homelands and the far-reaching complexity of the plans of the leaders—all are on a scale so huge that nothing in past history can be compared with them.

"The issues at stake are fundamental. The free people of the world have banded together against tyrannous militarism, and it is not too much to say that the outcome will largely determine, for those of us who love liberty above all else, whether or not life remains worth living."

He paused again, and stared up and down the ranks of his men.

"Against such a vast and complex array of forces, it may seem to you that we will just be another cog in the military machine of the allies, that one regiment cannot possibly make a difference." Roosevelt's chin jutted forward pugnaciously. "I say to you that this is rubbish! We represent a society dedicated to the proposition that every free man makes a difference. And I give you my solemn pledge that the Rough Riders will make a difference in the fighting to come!"

It was possible that his speech wasn't finished, that he

still had more to say . . . but if he did, it was drowned out beneath the wild and raucous cheering of his men.

One hour later they boarded the ship to Europe.

Roosevelt summoned a corporal and handed him a hand-written letter. The man saluted and left, and Roosevelt returned to his chair in front of his tent. He was about to pick up a book when McCoy approached him.

"Your daily dispatch to General Pershing?" he asked dryly.

"Yes," answered Roosevelt. "I can't understand what is wrong with the man! Here we are, primed and ready to fight, and he's kept us well behind the front for the better part of two months!"

"I know, Colonel."

"It just doesn't make any sense! Doesn't he know what the Rough Riders did at San Juan Hill?"

"That was a long time ago, sir," said McCoy.

"I tell you, Frank, these men are the elite—the cream of the crop! They weren't drafted by lottery. Every one of them volunteered, and every one was approved personally by you or by me. Why are we being wasted here? There's a war to be won!"

"Pershing's got a lot to consider, Colonel," said McCoy. "He's got a half million American troops to disperse, he's got to act in concert with the French and the British, he's got to consider his lines of supply, he's . . ."

"Don't patronize me, Frank!" snapped Roosevelt. "We've assembled a brilliant fighting machine here, and he's ignoring us. There *has* to be a reason. I want to know what it is!"

McCoy shrugged helplessly. "I have no answer, sir."

"Well, I'd better get one soon from Pershing!" muttered Roosevelt. "We didn't come all this way to help in some mopping-up operation after the battle's been won." He stared at the horizon. "There's a glorious crusade being fought in the name of liberty, and I plan to be a part of it."

He continued staring off into the distance long after McCoy had left him.

A private approached Roosevelt as the former president was eating lunch with his officers.

"Dispatch from General Pershing, sir," said the private, handing him an envelope with a snappy salute.

"Thank you," said Roosevelt. He opened the envelope, read the message, and frowned.

"Bad news, Colonel?" asked McCoy.

"He says to be patient," replied Roosevelt. "Patient?" he repeated furiously. "By God, I've been patient long enough! Jake—saddle my horse!"

"What are you going to do, Colonel?" asked one of his lieutenants.

"I'm going to go meet face-to-face with Pershing," said Roosevelt, getting to his feet. "This is intolerable!"

"We don't even know where he is, sir."

"I'll find him," replied Roosevelt confidently.

"You're more likely to get lost or shot," said McCoy, the only man who dared to speak to him so bluntly.

"Runs With Deer! Matupu!" shouted Roosevelt. "Saddle your horses!"

A burly Indian and a tall Maasai immediately got to their feet and went to the stable area.

Roosevelt turned back to McCoy. "I'm taking the two best trackers in the regiment. Does that satisfy you, Mr. McCoy?"

"It does not," said McCoy. "I'm going along, too."

Roosevelt shook his head. "You're in command of the regiment in my absence. You're staying here."

"But—"

"That's an order," said Roosevelt firmly.

"Will you at least take along a squad of sharpshooters, Colonel?" persisted McCoy.

"Frank, we're forty miles behind the front, and I'm just going to talk to Pershing, not shoot him."

"We don't even know where the front *is*," said McCoy.

"It's where we're *not*," said Roosevelt grimly. "And that's what I'm going to change."

He left the mess tent without another word.

The first four French villages they passed were deserted, and consisted of nothing but the burnt skeletons of houses and shops. The fifth had two buildings still standing—a manor house and a church—and they had been turned into Allied hospitals. Soldiers with missing limbs, soldiers with faces swathed in filthy bandages, soldiers with gaping holes in their bodies lay on cots and floors, shivering in the cold damp air, while an undermanned and harassed medical team did their best to keep them alive.

Roosevelt stopped long enough to determine General Pershing's whereabouts, then walked among the wounded to offer words of encouragement while trying to ignore the unmistakable stench of gangrene and the stinking scent of disinfectant. Finally he remounted his horse and joined his two trackers.

They passed a number of corpses on their way to the front. Most had been plundered of their weapons, and one, lying upon its back, displayed a gruesome, toothless smile.

"Shameful!" muttered Roosevelt as he looked down at the grinning body.

"Why?" asked Runs With Deer.

"It's obvious that the man had gold teeth, and they have been removed."

"It is honorable to take trophies of the enemy," asserted the Indian.

"The Germans have never advanced this far south," said Roosevelt. "This man's teeth were taken by his companions." He shook his head. "Shameful!"

Matupu the Maasai merely shrugged. "Perhaps this is not an honorable war."

"We are fighting for an honorable principle," stated Roosevelt. "That makes it an honorable war."

"Then it is an honorable war being waged by dishonorable men," said Matupu.

"Do the Maasai not take trophies?" asked Runs With Deer.

"We take cows and goats and women," answered Matupu. "We do not plunder the dead." He paused. "We do not take scalps."

"There was a time when *we* did not, either," said Runs With Deer. "We were taught to, by the French."

"And we are in France now," said Matupu with some satisfaction, as if everything now made sense to him.

They dismounted after two more hours and walked their horses for the rest of the day, then spent the night in a bombed-out farmhouse. The next morning they were mounted and riding again, and they came to General Pershing's field headquarters just before noon. There were thousands of soldiers bustling about, couriers bringing in hourly reports from the trenches, weapons and tanks being dispatched, convoys of trucks filled with food and water slowly working their way into supply lines.

Roosevelt was stopped a few yards into the camp by a young lieutenant.

"May I ask your business here, sir?"

"I'm here to see General Pershing," answered Roosevelt.

"Just like that?" said the soldier with a smile.

"Son," said Roosevelt, taking off his hat and leaning over the lieutenant, "take a good look at my face." He paused for a moment. "Now go tell General Pershing that Teddy Roosevelt is here to see him."

The lieutenant's eyes widened. "By God, you *are* Teddy Roosevelt!" he exclaimed. Suddenly he reached his hand out. "May I shake your hand first, Mr. President? I just want to be able to tell my parents I did it."

Roosevelt grinned and took the young man's hand in his own, then waited astride his horse while the lieutenant went off to Pershing's quarters. He gazed around the camp; there were ramshackle buildings and ramshackle soldiers, each of which had seen too much action and too little glory. The men's faces were haggard, their eyes haunted, their bodies stooped with exhaustion. The main paths through the camp had turned to mud, and the constant drizzle brought rust, rot, and disease with an equal lack of cosmic concern.

The lieutenant approached Roosevelt, his feet sinking inches into the mud with each step.

"If you'll follow me, Mr. President, he'll see you immediately."

"Thank you," said Roosevelt.

"Watch yourself, Mr. President," said the lieutenant as Roosevelt dismounted. "I have a feeling he's not happy about meeting with you."

"He'll be a damned sight less happy when I'm through with him," said Roosevelt firmly. He turned to his companions. "See to the needs of the horses."

"Yes, sir," said Runs With Deer. "We'll be waiting for you right here."

"How is the battle going?" Roosevelt asked as he and the lieutenant began walking through the mud toward Pershing's quarters. "My Rough Riders have been practically incommunicado since we arrived."

The lieutenant shrugged. "Who knows? All we hear are rumors. The enemy is retreating, the enemy is advancing, we've killed thousands of them, they've killed thousands of us. Maybe the general will tell you; he certainly hasn't seen fit to tell *us*."

They reached the entrance to Pershing's quarters.

"I'll wait here for you, sir," said the lieutenant.

"You're sure you don't mind?" asked Roosevelt. "You can find some orderly to escort me back if it will be a problem."

"No, sir," said the young man earnestly. "It'll be an honor, Mr. President."

"Well, thank you, son," said Roosevelt. He shook the lieutenant's hand again, then walked through the doorway and found himself facing General John J. Pershing.

"Good afternoon, Jack," said Roosevelt, extending his hand.

Pershing looked at Roosevelt's outstretched hand for a moment, then took it.

"Have a seat, Mr. President," he said, indicating a chair.

"Thank you," said Roosevelt, pulling up a chair as Pershing seated himself behind a desk that was covered with maps.

"I mean no disrespect, Mr. President," said Pershing, "but exactly who gave you permission to leave your troops and come here?"

"No one," answered Roosevelt.

"Then why did you do it?" asked Pershing. "I'm told you were accompanied only by a red Indian and a black savage. That's hardly a safe way to travel in a war zone."

"I came here to find out why you have consistently refused my requests to have my Rough Riders moved to the front."

Pershing lit a cigar and offered one to Roosevelt, who refused it.

"There are proper channels for such a request," said the general at last. "You yourself helped create them."

"And I have been using them for almost two months, to no avail."

Pershing sighed. "I *have* been a little busy conducting this damned war."

"I'm sure you have," said Roosevelt. "And I have assembled a regiment of the finest fighting men to be found in America, which I am placing at your disposal."

"For which I thank you, Mr. President."

"I don't want you to thank me!" snapped Roosevelt. "I want you to unleash me."

"When the time is right, your Rough Riders will be brought into the conflict," said Pershing.

"When the time is right?" repeated Roosevelt. "Your men are dying like flies! Every village I've passed has become a bombed-out ghost town! You needed us two months ago, Jack!"

"Mr. President, I've got half a million men to maneuver. *I'll* decide when and where I need your regiment."

"When?" persisted Roosevelt.

"You'll be the first to know."

"That's not good enough!"

"It will have to be."

"You listen to me, Jack Pershing!" said Roosevelt heatedly. "I *made* you a general! I think the very least you owe me is an answer. When will my men be brought into the conflict?"

Pershing stared at him from beneath shaggy black eyebrows for a long moment. "What the hell did you have to come here for, anyway?" he said at last.

"I told you: to get an answer."

"I don't mean to my headquarters," said Pershing. "I mean, what is a fifty-eight-year-old man with a blind eye and a game leg doing in the middle of a war?"

"This is the greatest conflict in history, and it's being fought over principles that every free man holds dear. How could I *not* take part in it?"

"You could have just stayed home and made speeches and raised funds."

"And you could have retired after Mexico and spent the rest of your life playing golf," Roosevelt shot back. "But you didn't, and I didn't, because neither of us is that kind of man. Damn it, Jack—I've assembled a regiment the likes of which hasn't been seen in almost twenty years, and if you've any sense at all, you'll make use of us. Our horses and our training give us an enormous advantage on this terrain. We can mobilize and strike at the enemy as easily as this fellow Lawrence seems to be doing in the Arabian desert."

Pershing stared at him for a long moment, then sighed deeply.

"I can't do it, Mr. President," said Pershing.

"Why not?" demanded Roosevelt.

"The truth? Because of *you*, sir."

"What are you talking about?"

"You've made my position damnably awkward," said Pershing bitterly. "You are an authentic American hero, possibly the first one since Abraham Lincoln. You are as close to being worshiped as a man can be." He paused. "You're a goddamned icon, Mr. Roosevelt."

"What has *that* got to do with anything?"

"I am under direct orders not to allow you to participate in any action that might result in your death." He glared at Roosevelt across the desk. "*Now* do you understand? If I move you to the front, I'll have to surround you with at least three divisions to make sure nothing happens to you—and I'm in no position to spare that many men."

"Who issued that order, Jack?"

"My Commander-in-Chief."

"Woodrow Wilson?"

"That's right. And I'd no more disobey him than I would disobey you if you still held that office." He paused, then spoke again more gently: "You're an old man, sir. Not old by your standards, but too damned old to be leading charges against the Germans. You should be home writing your memoirs and giving speeches and rallying the people to our cause, Mr. President."

"I'm not ready to retire to Sagamore Hill and have my

face carved on Mount Rushmore yet," said Roosevelt. "There are battles to be fought and a war to be won."

"Not by you, Mr. President," answered Pershing. "When the enemy is beaten and on the run, I'll bring your regiment up. The press can go crazy photographing you chasing the few German stragglers back to Berlin. But I cannot and will not disobey a direct order from my Commander-in-Chief. Until I can guarantee your safety, you'll stay where you are."

"I see," said Roosevelt, after a moment's silence. "And what if I relinquish my command? Will you utilize my Rough Riders then?"

Pershing shook his head. "I have no use for a bunch of tennis players and college professors who think they can storm across the trenches on their polo ponies," he said firmly. "The only men you have with battle experience are as old as you are." He paused. "Your regiment might be effective if the Apaches ever leave the reservation, but they are ill-prepared for a modern, mechanized war. I hate to be so blunt, but it's the truth, sir."

"You're making a huge mistake, Jack."

"You're the one who made the mistake, sir, by coming here. It's my job to see that you don't die because of it."

"Damn it, Jack, we could make a difference!"

Pershing paused and stared, not without sympathy, at Roosevelt. "War has changed, Mr. President," he said at last. "No one regiment can make a difference any longer. It's been a long time since Achilles fought Hector outside the walls of Troy."

An orderly entered with a dispatch, and Pershing immediately read and initialed it.

"I don't mean to rush you, sir," he said, getting to his feet, "but I have an urgent meeting to attend."

Roosevelt stood up. "I'm sorry to have bothered you, General."

"I'm still Jack to you, Mr. President," said Pershing. "And it's as your friend Jack that I want to give you one final word of advice."

"Yes?"

"Please, for your own sake and the sake of your men, don't do anything rash."

"Why would I do something rash?" asked Roosevelt innocently.

"Because you wouldn't be Teddy Roosevelt if the thought of ignoring your orders hadn't already crossed your mind," said Pershing.

Roosevelt fought back a grin, shook Pershing's hand, and left without saying another word. The young lieutenant was just outside the door, and escorted him back to where Runs With Deer and Matupu were waiting with the horses.

"Bad news?" asked Runs With Deer, as he studied Roosevelt's face.

"No worse than I had expected."

"Where do we go now?" asked the Indian.

"Back to camp," said Roosevelt firmly. "There's a war to be won, and no college professor from New Jersey is going to keep me from helping to win it!"

"Well, that's the story," said Roosevelt to his assembled officers, after he had laid out the situation to them in the large tent he had reserved for strategy sessions. "Even if I resign my commission and return to America, there is no way that General Pershing will allow you to see any action."

"I knew Black Jack Pershing when he was just a captain," growled Buck O'Neill, one of the original Rough Riders. "Just who the hell does he think he is?"

"He's the supreme commander of the American forces," answered Roosevelt wryly.

"What are we going to do, sir?" asked McCoy. "Surely you don't plan to just sit back here and then let Pershing move us up when all the fighting's done with?"

"No, I don't," said Roosevelt.

"Let's hear what you got to say, Teddy," said O'Neill.

"The issues at stake in this war haven't changed since I went to see the General," answered Roosevelt. "I plan to harass and harry the enemy to the best of our ability. If need be we will live off the land while utilizing our superior mobility in a number of tactical strikes, and we will do our valiant best to bring this conflict to a successful conclusion."

He paused and looked around at his officers. "I realize that in doing this I am violating my orders, but there are greater principles at stake here. I am flattered that the president thinks I am indispensable to the American public, but our nation is based on the principle that no one man deserves any rights or privileges not offered to all men." He took a deep breath and cleared his throat. "However, since I *am* contravening a direct order, I believe that not only each one of you, but every one of the men as well, should be given the opportunity to withdraw from the Rough Riders. I will force no man to ride against his conscience and his beliefs. I would like you to go out now and put the question to the men; I will wait here for your answer."

To nobody's great surprise, the regiment voted unanimously to ride to glory with Teddy Roosevelt.

August 3, 1917

My Dearest Edith:

As strange as this may seem to you (and it seems surpassingly strange to me), I will soon be a fugitive from justice, opposed not only by the German army but quite possibly by the U.S. military as well.

My Rough Riders have embarked upon a bold adventure, contrary to both the wishes and the direct orders of the president of the United States. When I think back to the day he finally approved my request to reassemble the regiment, I cringe with chagrin at my innocence and naïveté; he sent us here only so that I would not have access to the press and he would no longer have to listen to my demands. Far from being permitted to play a leading role in this noblest of battles, my men have been held far behind the front, and Jack Pershing is under orders from Wilson himself not to allow any harm to come to us.

When I learned of this, I put a proposition to my men, and I am extremely proud of their response. To a one, they voted to break camp and ride to the front so as to strike at the heart of the German military machine. By doing so, I am disobeying the orders of my Commander-in-Chief, and because of this somewhat peculiar situation, I doubt that I shall be able to send too many more letters to you until I have helped to end this war. At that time, I shall turn myself over to Pershing, or whoever is in charge, and argue my case before whatever tribunal is deemed proper.

However, before that moment occurs, we shall finally see action, bearing the glorious banner of the Stars and Stripes. My men are a finely tuned fighting machine, and I daresay that they will give a splendid account of themselves before the conflict is over. We have not made contact with the enemy yet, nor can I guess where we shall finally meet, but we are primed and eager for our first taste of battle. Our spirit is high, and many of the old-timers spend their hours singing the old battle songs from Cuba. We are all looking forward to a bully battle, and we plan to teach the Hun a lesson he won't soon forget.

Give my love to the children, and when you write to Kermit and Quentin, tell them that their father has every intention of reaching Berlin before they do!

All my love,
Theodore

Roosevelt, who had been busily writing an article on ornithology, looked up from his desk as McCoy entered his tent.

"Well?"

"We think we've found what we've been looking for, Mr. President," said McCoy.

"Excellent!" said Roosevelt, carefully closing his notebook. "Tell me about it."

McCoy spread a map out on the desk.

"Well, the front lines, as you know, are *here*, about fifteen miles to the north of us. The Germans are entrenched *here*, and we haven't been able to move them for almost three weeks." McCoy paused. "The word I get from my old outfit is that the Americans are planning a major push on the German left, right about *here*."

"When?" demanded Roosevelt.

"At sunrise tomorrow morning."

"Bully!" said Roosevelt. He studied the map for a moment, then looked up. "Where is Jack Pershing?"

"Almost ten miles west and eight miles north of us," answered McCoy. "He's dug in, and from what I hear, he came under pretty heavy mortar fire today. He'll have his hands full without worrying about where an extra regiment of American troops came from."

"Better and better," said Roosevelt. "We not only get to fight, but we may even pull Jack's chestnuts out of the fire." He turned his attention back to the map. "All right," he said, "the Americans will advance along this line. What would you say will be their major obstacle?"

"You mean besides the mud and the Germans and the mustard gas?" asked McCoy wryly.

"You know what I mean, Frank."

"Well," said McCoy, "there's a small rise here—I'd hardly call it a hill, certainly not like the one we took in Cuba—but it's manned by four machine guns, and it gives the Germans an excellent view of the territory the Americans have got to cross."

"Then that's our objective," said Roosevelt decisively. "If we can capture that hill and knock out the machine guns, we'll have made a positive contribution to the battle that even that Woodrow Wilson will be forced to acknowledge." The famed Roosevelt grin spread across his face. "We'll show him that the dodo may be dead, but the Rough Riders are very much alive." He paused. "Gather the men, Frank. I want to speak to them before we leave."

McCoy did as he was told, and Roosevelt emerged from his tent some ten minutes later to address the assembled Rough Riders.

"Gentlemen," he said, "tomorrow morning we will meet the enemy on the battlefield."

A cheer arose from the ranks.

"It has been suggested that modern warfare deals only in masses and logistics, that there is no room left for heroism, that the only glory remaining to men of action is upon the sporting fields. I tell you that this is a lie. *We matter!* Honor and courage are not outmoded virtues, but are the very ideals that make us great as individuals and as a nation. Tomorrow we will prove it in terms that our detractors and our enemies will both understand." He paused, and then saluted them. "Saddle up—and may God be with us!"

They reached the outskirts of the battlefield, moving silently with hooves and harnesses muffled, just before sunrise. Even McCoy, who had seen action in Mexico, was unprepared for the sight that awaited them.

The mud was littered with corpses as far as the eye could see in the dim light of the false dawn. The odor of death and decay permeated the moist, cold morning air. Thousands of bodies lay there in the pouring rain, many of them grotesquely swollen. Here and there they had virtually exploded, either when punctured by bullets or when the walls of the abdominal cavities collapsed. Attempts had been made during the previous month to drag them back off the battlefield, but there was simply no place left to put them. There was almost total silence, as the men in both trenches began preparing for another day of bloodletting.

Roosevelt reined his horse to a halt and surveyed the carnage. Still more corpses were hung up on barbed wire, and more than a handful of bodies attached to the wire still moved feebly. The rain pelted down, turning the plain between the enemy trenches into a brown, gooey slop.

"My God, Frank!" murmured Roosevelt.

"It's pretty awful," agreed McCoy.

"This is not what civilized men do to each other," said Roosevelt, stunned by the sight before his eyes. "This isn't war, Frank—it's butchery!"

"It's what war has become."

"How long have these two lines been facing each other?"

"More than a month, sir."

Roosevelt stared, transfixed, at the sea of mud.

"A month to cross a quarter mile of *this*?"

"That's correct, sir."

"How many lives have been lost trying to cross this strip of land?"

McCoy shrugged. "I don't know. Maybe eighty thousand, maybe a little more."

Roosevelt shook his head. "Why, in God's name? Who cares about it? What purpose does it serve?"

McCoy had no answer, and the two men sat in silence for another moment, surveying the battlefield.

"This is madness!" said Roosevelt at last. "Why doesn't Pershing simply march *around* it?"

"That's a question for a general to answer, Mr. President," said McCoy. "Me, I'm just a captain."

"We can't continue to lose American boys for *this*!" said Roosevelt furiously. "Where is that machine gun encampment, Frank?"

McCoy pointed to a small rise about three hundred yards distant.

"And the main German lines?"

"Their first row of trenches is in line with the hill."

"Have we tried to take the hill before?"

"I can't imagine that we haven't, sir," said McCoy. "As long as they control it, they'll mow our men down like sitting ducks in a shooting gallery." He paused. "The problem is the mud. The average infantryman can't reach the hill in less than two minutes, probably closer to three—and until you've seen them in action, you can't believe the damage these guns can do in that amount of time."

"So as long as the hill remains in German hands, this is a war of attrition."

McCoy sighed. "It's been a war of attrition for three years, sir."

Roosevelt sat and stared at the hill for another few minutes, then turned back to McCoy.

"What are our chances, Frank?"

McCoy shrugged. "If it was dry, I'd say we had a chance to take them out. . . ."

"But it's not."

"No, it's not," echoed McCoy.

"Can we do it?"

"I don't know, sir. Certainly not without heavy casualties."

"How heavy?"

"*Very* heavy."

"I need a number," said Roosevelt.

McCoy looked him in the eye. "Ninety percent—if we're lucky."

Roosevelt stared at the hill again. "They predicted fifty percent casualties at San Juan Hill," he said. "We had to charge up a much steeper slope in the face of enemy machine gun fire. Nobody thought we had a chance—but I did it, Frank, and I did it alone. I charged up that hill and knocked out the machine gun nest myself, and then the rest of my men followed me."

"The circumstances were different then, Mr. President," said McCoy. "The terrain offered cover, and solid footing, and you were facing Cuban peasants who had been conscripted into service, not battle-hardened professional German soldiers."

"I know, I know," said Roosevelt. "But if we knock those machine guns out, how many American lives can we save today?"

"I don't know," admitted McCoy. "Maybe ten thousand, maybe none. It's possible that the Germans are dug in so securely that they can beat back any American charge even without the use of those machine guns."

"But at least it would prolong some American lives," persisted Roosevelt.

"By a couple of minutes."

"It would give them a *chance* to reach the German bunkers."

"I don't know."

"More of a chance than if they had to face machine gun fire from the hill."

"What do you want me to say, Mr. President?" asked McCoy. "That if we throw away our lives charging the hill that we'll have done something glorious and affected the outcome of the battle? I just don't know!"

"We came here to help win a war, Frank. Before I send my men into battle, I have to know that it will make a difference."

"I can't give you any guarantees, sir. We came to fight a war, all right. But look around you, Mr. President—*this* isn't the war we came to fight. They've changed the rules on us."

"There are hundreds of thousands of American boys in the trenches who didn't come to fight this kind of war," answered Roosevelt. "In less than an hour, most of them are going to charge across this sea of mud into a barrage of machine gun fire. If we can't shorten the war, then perhaps we can at least lengthen their lives."

"At the cost of our own."

"We are idealists and adventurers, Frank—perhaps the last this world will ever see. We knew what we were coming here to do." He paused. "Those boys are here because of speeches and decisions that politicians have made, myself included. Left to their own devices, they'd go home to be with their families. Left to ours, we'd find another cause to fight for."

"This isn't a cause, Mr. President," said McCoy. "It's a slaughter."

"Then maybe this is where men who want to prevent further slaughter belong," said Roosevelt. He looked up at the sky. "They'll be mobilizing in another half hour, Frank."

"I know, Mr. President."

"If we leave now, if we don't try to take that hill, then Wilson and Pershing were right and I was wrong. The time for heroes is past, and I *am* an anachronism who should be sitting at home in a rocking chair, writing memoirs and exhorting younger men to go to war." He paused, staring at the hill once more. "If we don't do what's required of us this day, we are agreeing with them that we don't matter, that men of courage and ideals can't make a difference. If that's true, there's no sense waiting for a more equitable battle, Frank—we might as well ride south and catch the first boat home."

"That's your decision, Mr. President?" asked McCoy.

"Was there really ever any other option?" replied Roosevelt wryly.

"No, sir," said McCoy. "Not for men like us."

"Thank you for your support, Frank," said Roosevelt, reaching out and laying a heavy hand on McCoy's shoulder. "Prepare the men."

"Yes, sir," said McCoy, saluting and riding back to the main body of the Rough Riders.

"Madness!" muttered Roosevelt, looking out at the bloated corpses. "Utter madness!"

McCoy returned a moment later.

"The men are awaiting your signal, sir," he said.

"Tell them to follow me," said Roosevelt.

"Sir . . ." said McCoy.

"Yes?"

"We would prefer you not lead the charge. The first ranks will face the heaviest bombardment, not only from the hill but also from the cannons behind the bunkers."

"I can't ask my men to do what I myself won't do," said Roosevelt.

"You are too valuable to lose, sir. We plan to attack in three waves. You belong at the back of the third wave, Mr. President."

Roosevelt shook his head. "There's nothing up ahead except bullets, Frank, and I've faced bullets before—in the Dakota Badlands, in Cuba, in Milwaukee. But if I hang back, if I send my men to do a job I was afraid to do, then I'd have to face *myself*—and as any Democrat will tell you, I'm a lot tougher than any bullet ever made."

"You won't reconsider?" asked McCoy.

"Would you have left your unit and joined the Rough Riders if you thought I might?" asked Roosevelt with a smile.

"No, sir," admitted McCoy. "No, sir, I probably wouldn't have."

Roosevelt shook his hand. "You're a good man, Frank."

"Thank you, Mr. President."

"Are the men ready?"

"Yes, sir."

"Then," said Roosevelt, turning his horse toward the small rise, "let's do what must be done."

He pulled his rifle out, unlatched the safety catch, and dug his heels into his horse's sides.

Suddenly he was surrounded by the first wave of his own men, all screaming their various war cries in the face of the enemy.

For just a moment there was no response. Then the machine guns began their sweeping fire across the muddy plain. Buck O'Neill was the first to fall, his body riddled with bullets. An instant later Runs With Deer screamed in agony as his arm was blown away. Horses had their legs shot from under them, men were blown out of their saddles, limbs flew crazily through the wet morning air, and still the charge continued.

Roosevelt had crossed half the distance when Matupu fell directly in front of him, his head smashed to a pulp. He heard McCoy groan as half a dozen bullets thudded home in his chest, but he looked neither right nor left as his horse leaped over the fallen Maasai's bloody body.

Bullets and cannonballs flew to the right and left of him, in front and behind, and yet miraculously he was unscathed as he reached the final hundred yards. He dared a quick glance around, and saw that he was the sole survivor from the first wave, then heard the screams of the second wave as the machine guns turned on them.

Now he was seventy yards away, now fifty. He yelled a challenge to the Germans, and as he looked into the blinking eye of a machine gun, for one brief, final, glorious instant, it was San Juan Hill all over again.

September 18, 1917

Dispatch from General John J. Pershing to Commander-in-Chief, President Woodrow Wilson.

Sir:

I regret to inform you that Theodore Roosevelt died last Tuesday of wounds received in battle. He had disobeyed his orders, and led his men in a futile charge against an entrenched German position. His entire regiment, the so-called "Rough Riders," was lost. His death was almost certainly instantaneous, although it was two days before his body could be retrieved from the battlefield.

I shall keep the news of Mr. Roosevelt's death from the press until receiving instructions from you. It is true that he was an anachronism, that he belonged more to the nineteenth century than the twentieth, and yet it is entirely possible that he was the last authentic hero our country shall ever produce. The charge he led was ill-conceived and foolhardy in the extreme, nor did it diminish the length of the conflict by a single day, yet I cannot help but believe that if I had 50,000 men with his courage and spirit, I could bring this war to a swift and satisfactory conclusion by the end of the year.

That Theodore Roosevelt died the death of a fool is

beyond question, but I am certain in my heart that with his dying breath he felt he was dying the death of a hero. I await your instructions, and will release whatever version of his death you choose upon hearing from you.

                          —Gen. John J. Pershing

September 22, 1917

Dispatch from President Woodrow Wilson to General John J. Pershing, Commander of American Forces in Europe.

John:
    That man continues to harass me from the grave.
    Still, we have had more than enough fools in our history. Therefore, he died a hero.
    Just between you and me, the time for heroes is past. I hope with all my heart that he was our last.

                             —Woodrow Wilson

And he was.

Ink from the New Moon

A. A. Attanasio

"Ink from the New Moon" appeared in the November 1992 issue of Asimov's, *with an illustration by Laurie Harden. Attanasio has sold only a few stories to the magazine to date, but each has been memorable, and we hope to coax more work out of him in the future. Attanasio devotes most of his energy to novels, not to short fiction, and has been successful and prolific as a novelist. His books include the critically acclaimed* Radix Tetrad—*consisting of* Radix, In Other Worlds, Arc of the Dream, *and* The Last Legends of Earth—*as well as* Wyvern, Hunting the Ghost Dancer, *the Arthurian fantasy* Kingdom of the Grail, *and, most recently, the hard SF novel* Solis.

Even in our own reality, the claim that Christopher Columbus discovered the New World has long been challenged, with various historians putting forth Viking warriors, Irish monks, Basque fishermen, Roman explorers, Phoenician traders, and a score of other possibilities as the ones who really discovered it (ignoring the Amerinds, of course, who clearly discovered it millennia before any of these Johnny-come-latelies). In the elegant story that follows, Attanasio gives us a world in which the question of who discovered the New World—and who intends to keep it—has been settled decisively, beyond all possibility of argument . . .

Forgive my long silence, wife. I would have written sooner, had not my journey across the Sandalwood Territories of the Dawn been an experience for me blacker than ink can show. Being so far from the homeland, so far from you, has dulled the heat of my life. Darkness occupies me. Yet, this unremitting gloom brings with it a peculiar knowledge and wisdom all its own—the treasure that the snake guards—the so-called poison cure.

Such is the blood's surprise, my precious one, that even in the serpent's grip of dire sorrow, I would find a clarity greater than any since my failures took me from you.

Here, at the farthest extreme of my journey, in the islands along the eastern shores of the Sandalwood Territories, with all of heaven and earth separating us—here at long last I have found enough strength to pen these words to you. Months of writing official reports, of recording endless observations of irrigation techniques, contour transport canals, factories, prisons, and village schools had quite drained me of the sort of words one writes to one's wife; but, at last, I feel again the place where the world is breathing inside me.

You, of course, will only remember me as you left me—that sour little man for whom being Third Assistant Secretarial Scribe at the Imperial Library was more punishment than privilege; the husband whittled away by shame and envy whom you dutifully bid farewell as he departed in that sorry delegation sent to examine the social structure of the Sandalwood Territories of the Dawn (or rather, the "Unified Sandalwood Autocracies" as the natives have insisted on calling it since their secession from the Kingdom two centuries ago). Yes, I do admit, I was ashamed, most especially in your eyes. Only you, Heart Wing, know me for who I truly am—a storyteller hooked on the bridebait of words, writing by the lamp of lightning. Yet my books, those poor defenseless books written in the lyrical style of a fargone time! Well, as you know too well, there was no livelihood for us on those printed pages. My only success as a writer was that my stories won you for me. After our blunderful attempt to farm in the western provinces, to live the lives of field-and-stream poet-recluses, which defiance of destiny and station cost us your health and the life of our one child, all my pride indeed soured into cynicism and self-pity. I felt obliged to accept the Imperial post because there seemed no other recourse.

From that day eighteen months ago until now, the shadow of night has covered me. I was not there to console you in your grief when our second child fell from your womb before he was strong enough to carry his own breath. By then, the big ship had already taken me to the Isles of the Palm Grove Vow in the middle of the World Sea. There, I sat surrounded by tedious tomes of Imperial chronicles about the Sandalwood Territories, while you suffered alone.

Like you, I never had a taste for the dry magisterial prose of diplomacy and the bitter punctuations of war that is history. What did it matter to me that five centuries ago, during the beginning of our modern era in the Sung Dynasty, the Buddhists, persecuted for adhering to a faith of foreign origin, set sail from the Middle Kingdom and, instead of being devoured by seven hundred dragons or plunging into the Maelstrom of the Great Inane, crossed nine thousand *li* of ocean and discovered a chain of sparsely populated tropical islands? Of what consequence was it to me that these islands, rich in palm, hardwoods, and the fragrant sandalwood beloved of the furniture-makers, soon attracted merchants and the Emperor's soldiers? And that, once again, the Buddhists felt compelled to flee, swearing their famous Palm Grove Vow to sail east until they either faced death together or found a land of their own. And that after crossing another seven thousand *li* of ocean, they arrived at the vast Land of Dawn, from whose easternmost extreme I am writing to you.

Surely, you are pursing your lips now with impatience, wondering why I burden you with so much bothersome history, you, a musician's daughter, who always preferred the beauty of song to the tedium of facts. But stay with me yet, Heart Wing. My discovery, the hardwon clarity gained through my poison cure, will mean less to you without some sharing of what I have learned of this land's history.

We know from our schooldays that the merchants eventually followed the Buddhists to the Land of Dawn, where the gentle monks had already converted many of the aboriginal tribes. Typical of the Buddhists, they did not war with the merchants but retreated farther east, spreading their doctrine among the tribes and gradually opening the frontier to other settlers. Over time, as the Imperialists established cities and trade routes, the monks began preaching the foolishness of obeisance to a Kingdom far across the World Sea. "Here and now!" the monks chanted, the land of our ancestors being too far away and too entrenched in the veil of illusion to be taken seriously anymore. Though the Buddhists themselves never raised a weapon against the Emperor, the merchants and farmers eagerly fought for them, revolting against Imperial taxation. And out of the Sandalwood Territories of Dawn, the settlers founded their own country: the Unified Sandalwood Autocracies.

There are numerous kingdoms here in the USA, each governed by an autocrat elected by the landowners of that kingdom. These separate kingdoms in turn are loosely governed by an overlord whom the autocrats and the landowners elect from among themselves to serve for an interval of no more than fifty moons. It is an alien system that the denizens here call Power of the People, and it is fraught with strife as the conservative Confucians, liberal Buddhists, and radical Taoist-aboriginals continually struggle for dominance. Here, the Mandate of Heaven is not so much granted celestially as taken by wiles, wealth, or force, grasped and clawed for.

I will not trouble you with this nation's paradoxical politics: its abhorrence of monarchs, yet its glorification of leaders; its insistence on separation of government and religion, yet its reliance on oaths, prayers, and moralizing; its passionate patriotism, yet fervent espousal of individual endeavor. There are no slaves here as at home and so there is no dignity for the upper classes, nor even for the lower classes, for all are slaves to money. The commonest street-sweeper can invest his meager earnings to form his own road maintenance company and after years of slavery to his enterprise become as wealthy as nobility. And, likewise, the rich can squander their resources and, without the protection of servants or class privilege, become street beggars. Amitabha! This land has lost entirely the sequence of divine order that regulates our serene sovereignty. And though there are those who profit by this increase of social and economic mobility, it is by and large a country mad with, and subverted by, its own countless ambitions. In many ways, it is, I think, the Middle Kingdom turned upside down.

The rocky west coast, rife with numerous large cities, is the industrial spine of this nation as the east coast is in our land. On the coast, as in our kingdom, refineries, paper mills, textile factories, and shipbuilding yards abound. Inland are the lush agricultural valleys—and then the mountains and beyond them the desert—just as in our country. Where to the north in our homeland the Great Wall marches across mountains for over four thousand *li*, shutting out the Mongol hordes, here an equally immense wall crosses the desert to the south, fending off ferocious tribes of Aztecatl.

Heart Wing, there is even a village on the eastern prairie, beyond the mountains and the red sandstone arches of the desert, that looks very much like the village on the Yellow River where we had our ruinous farm. There, in a bee-filled orchard just like the cherry grove where we buried our daughter, my memory fetched back to when I held her bird-light body in my arms for the last time. I wept. I wanted to write you then, but there were irrigation networks to catalogue, and on the horizons of amber wheat and millet, highways to map hundreds of *li* long, where land boats fly faster than horses, their colorful sails fat with wind.

Beyond the plains lies the Evil East, which is what the Dawn-Settlers call their frontier, because said hinterland is dense with ancient forests no ax has ever touched. Dawn legends claim that the hungry souls of the unhappy dead wander those dense woods. Also, tribes of hostile aboriginals who have fled the settled autocracies of the west shun the Doctrine of the Buddha and the Ethics of Confucius and reign there, as anarchic and wild as any Taoist could imagine.

When our delegation leader sought volunteers to continue the survey into that wilderness, I was among those who offered to go. I'm sorry, Heart Wing, that my love for you was not enough to overcome my shame at the failures that led to our child's death and that took me from you. Wild in my grief, I sought likeness in that primeval forest. I had hoped it would kill me and end my suffering.

It did not. I had somehow imagined or hoped that there might well be ghosts in the Evil East, or at least cannibalistic savages to whom I would be prey, but there were neither. So I survived despite myself, saddened to think that all our chances bleed from us, like wounds that never heal.

The vast expanse of forest was poignantly beautiful even in its darkest vales and fog-hung fens, haunted only with the natural dangers of serpents, bears, and wolves. As for the tribes, when they realized that we had come merely to observe and not to cut their trees or encroach on their land, they greeted us cordially enough, for barbarians. For their hospitality, we traded them toys—bamboo dragonflies, kites, and firecrackers. I knew a simple joy with them, forgetting briefly the handful of chances that had already bled from me with my hope of fading from this world.

On the east coast are Buddhist missions and trading posts overlooking the Storm Sea. By the time we emerged from the wildwoods, a message for me from the west had already arrived at one of the posts by the river routes that the fur traders use. I recognized your father's calligraphy and knew before I read it—that you had left us to join the ancestors.

When the news came, I tried to throw myself from the monastery wall into the sea, but my companions stopped me. I could not hear beyond my heart. We who had once lived as one doubled being had become mysteries again to each other. I shall know no greater enigma.

For days I despaired. My failures had lost all my cherished chances, as a writer and a farmer, as a father and, now, as your mate. With that letter, I became older than the slowest river.

It is likely I would have stayed at the monastery and accepted monkhood had not news come one day announcing the arrival of strangers from across the Storm Sea. Numb, indifferent, I sailed south with the delegation's other volunteers. Autumn had come to the forest. Disheveled oaks and maples mottled the undulant shores. But gradually the hoar-frost thinned from the air, and colossal domes of cumulus rose from the horizon. Shaggy cypress and palm trees tilted above the dunes.

Like a roving, masterless dog, I followed the others from one mission to the next among lovely, verdant islands. Hunger abandoned me, and I ate only when food was pressed on me, not tasting it. In the silence and fire of night, while the others slept, my life seemed an endless web of lies I had spun and you a bird I had caught and crippled. In the mirrors of the sea, I saw faces. Mostly they were your face. And always when I saw you, you smiled at me with an untellable love. I grieved that I had ever left you.

The morning we found the boats that had crossed the

Storm Sea, I greeted the strangers morosely. They were stout men with florid faces, thick beards, and big noses. Their ships were clumsy, worm-riddled boxes without watertight compartments and with ludicrous cloth sails set squarely, leaving them at the mercy of the winds. At first, they attempted to impress us with their cheap merchandise, mostly painted tinware and clay pots filled with sour wine. I do not blame them, for, not wishing to slight the aboriginals, we had approached in a local raft with the tribal leaders of that island.

Soon, however, beckoned by a blue smoke flare, our own ship rounded the headland. The sight of her sleek hull and orange sails with bamboo battens trimmed precisely for maximum speed rocked loose the foreigners' arrogant jaws—for our ship, with her thwartwise staggered masts fore and aft, approached *into* the wind. The Big Noses had never seen the likes of it.

Ostensibly to salute us, though I'm sure with the intent of displaying their might, the Big Noses fired their bulky cannon. The three awkward ships, entirely lacking leeboards, keeled drastically. Our vessel replied with a volley of Bees' Nest rockets that splashed overhead in a fiery display while our ship sailed figure eights among the foreigners' box-boats.

At that, the Big Noses became effusively deferential. The captain, a tall, beardless man with red hair and ghostly pale flesh, removed his hat, bowed, and presented us with one of his treasures, a pathetically crude book printed on coarse paper with a gold-leaf cross pressed into the animal-hide binding. Our leader accepted it graciously.

Fortunately, the Big Noses had on board a man who spoke Chaldean and some Arabic, and two of the linguists in our delegation could understand him slightly. He told us that his captain's name was Christ-bearer the Colonizer and that they had come seeking the Emperor of the Middle Kingdom in the hope of opening trade with him. They actually believed that they were twenty-five thousand *li* to the west, in the spice islands south of the Middle Kingdom! Their ignorance fairly astounded us.

Upon learning their precise location, the Colonizer appeared dismayed and retreated to his cabin. From his second in command, we eventually learned that the Colonizer had expected honor and wealth from his enterprise. Both would be greatly diminished now that it was evident he had discovered neither a route to the world's wealthiest kingdom nor a new world to be colonized by the Big Noses.

Among our delegation was much debate about the implications of the Colonizer's first name—Christ-bearer. For some centuries, Christ-bearers have straggled into the Middle Kingdom, though always they were confined to select districts of coastal cities. Their gruesome religion, in which the flesh and blood of their maimed and tortured god is symbolically consumed, disgusted our Emperor, and their proselytizing zeal rightly concerned him. But here, in the USA, with the Dawn-Settlers' tolerance of diverse views, what will be the consequences when the Christ-bearers establish their missions?

I did not care. Let fat-hearted men scheme and plot in far away temples and kingdoms. Heart Wing! I will never see the jewel of your face again. That thought—that truth—lies before me now, an unexplored wilderness I will spend the rest of my life crossing. But on that day when I first saw the Big Noses, I had not yet grasped this truth. I still believed death was a doorway. I thought perhaps your ghost would cross back and succor my mourning. I had seen your face in the mirrors of the sea, a distraught girl both filled and exhausted with love. I had seen that, and I thought I could cross the threshold of this life and find you again, join with you again, united among the ancestors. I thought that.

For several more days, I walked about in a daze, looking for your ghost, contemplating ways to die. I even prepared a sturdy noose from a silk sash and, one moon-long evening, wandered into the forest to hang myself. As I meandered through the dark avenues of a cypress dell seeking the appropriate bough from which to stretch my shameless neck, I heard voices. Three paces away, on the far side of a bracken screen, the Big Noses were whispering hotly. I dared to peek and spied them hurrying among the trees, crouched over, sabers and guns in hand and awkwardly hauling a longboat among them.

The evil I had wished upon myself had led me to a greater evil, and, without forethought, I followed the Big Noses. They swiftly made their way to the cove where the Imperial ship was moored. I knew then their intent. The entire delegation, along with most of the crew, was ashore at the mission interviewing the aboriginals who had first encountered the Big Noses and drafting a report for the Emperor and the local authorities about the arrival of the Christ-bearer in the USA. The Big Noses would meet little resistance in pirating our ship.

Clouds walked casually away from the moon, and the mission with its serpent pillars and curved roof shone gem-bright high on the bluff—too far away for me to race there in time or even for my cries to reach. Instead, I ducked among the dunes and scurried through the switching salt grass to the water's edge even as the Big Noses pushed their longboat into the slick water and piled in. With a few hardy oarstrokes, they reached the Imperial ship and began clambering aboard unseen by the watch, who was probably in the hold sampling the rice wine.

I stood staring at the ship perched atop the watery moon, knowing what I had to do but hardly believing I had such strength. I, who had iron enough in my blood to strangle my own life, wavered at the thought of defying other men, even the primitive Big Noses. Truly, what a coward I am! I would have stood rooted as a pine and watched the pirates sail our ship into the dark like a happy cloud scudding under the moon—but a scream and a splash jolted me.

The Big Noses had thrown the watch overboard. I saw him swimming hard for shore and imagined I saw fear in his face. His craven face galled me! The watch, flailing strenuously to save his own miserable life, would make no effort to stop barbarians from stealing the life of his own people! For I knew that we would lose nothing less if the Big Noses stole our ship and learned to build vessels that could challenge the USA and even the Middle Kingdom.

I dove into the glossed water and thrashed toward the ship. I am a weak swimmer, as you know, but there was not far to go, and the noise of the watch beating frantically to shore muted my advance. The moorings were cut, and the ship listed under the offshore breeze. The Big Noses, accustomed to climbing along yard-arms to adjust their sails, were unfamiliar with the windlasses and halyards that control from the deck the ribbed sails of our ship, and so there was time for me to clutch onto the hull before the sails unfurled.

After climbing the bulwark, I slipped and fell to the deck right at the feet of the tall, ghost-faced captain! We stared at each other with moonbright eyes for a startled moment, and I swear I saw an avidity in his features as malefic as a temple demon's. I bolted upright even as he shouted. Blessedly, the entire crew was busy trying to control the strange new ship, and I eluded the grasp of the Colonizer and darted across the deck to the gangway.

Death had been my intent from the first. When I plunged into the hold and collapsed among coils of hempen rope, I had but one thought: to reach the weapons bin and ignite the powder. I blundered in the dark, slammed into a bulkhead, tripped over bales of sorghum, and reached the powder bin in a gasping daze. Shouts boomed from the gangway, and the hulking shapes of the Big Noses filled the narrow corridor.

Wildly, I grasped for the flintstriker I knew was somewhere near the bin. Or was it? Perhaps that was too dangerous to keep near the powder. The Big Noses closed in, and I desperately bounded atop the bin and shoved open the hatch that was there. Moonlight gushed over me, and I saw the horrid faces of the barbarians rushing toward me. And there, at my elbow, was a sheaf of matches.

I seized the fire-sticks and rattled them at the Big Noses, but they were not thwarted. The oafs had no idea what these were! They dragged me down, barking furiously. I gaped about in the moonglow, spotted a flintstriker hanging from a beam. Kicking like a madman, I twisted free just long enough to snatch the flintstriker. But I had inspired their fury, and heavy blows knocked me to the planks.

Stunned, I barely had the strength to squeeze the lever of the flintstriker. My feeble effort elicited only the tiniest spark, but that was enough to ignite a match. The sulfurous flare startled my assailants, and they fell back. Immediately, I lurched about and held high the burning pine stick while gesturing at the powder bin behind me. The Big Noses pulled away.

With my free hand, I grabbed a bamboo tube I recognized as a Beard-the-Moon rocket. I lit the fuse and pointed it at the open hatch. In a radiant whoosh, sparks and flames sprayed into the night. The cries of the Big Noses sounded from the deck, and the men who had seized me fled. A laugh actually tore through me as I fired two more Beard-the-Moon rockets. I was going to die, but now death seemed a fate worthy of laughter.

Perhaps the longtime company of Buddhists and Taoists had affected me, for I had no desire to kill the Big Noses. I waited long enough for them to throw themselves into the sea before I ignited the fuses on several heaven-shaking Thunderclap bombs. My last thought, while waiting for the explosion to hurl me into the Great Inane, was of you, Heart Wing. Once I had committed myself to using death as a doorway, your ghost had actually come back for me, to lead me to the ancestors in a way that would serve the Kingdom. I thanked you, and the Thunderclap bombs exploded.

Yet, I did not die—at least, not in an obvious way. Later, when I could think clearly again, I realized that your ghost had not yet done with me. Who else but you could have placed me just where I was so that my body would be hurtled straight upward through the open hatch and into the lustrous night? I remember none of that, however, but the watch, who had made it to shore and been alerted by the showering of the Beard-the-Moon rockets, claims that when the Imperial ship burst into a fireball, he saw me flying, silhouetted against the moon.

He found me unconscious in the shallows, unscathed except that my beard and eyebrows were singed and my clothes torn. Like a meteor, I had fallen back to earth, back to life. I had fallen the way stars fall, from the remote darkness where they have shivered in the cold down into the warm, close darkness of earthly life. That night, I fell from the gloom of my solitary grief into the dark of terrestrial life, where we all suffer together in our unknowing. Slapped alert by the watch, I sat up in the moondappled shallows and saw my forty summers fall away into emptiness. The ship was gone—just as you are gone, Heart Wing, and our daughter gone into that emptiness the Buddhists call *sunyata*, which is really the void of our unknowing, the mystery that bears everything that lives and dies.

How foolish to say all this to *you*, who dwells now in the heart of this emptiness. But I, I have been ignorant, asleep. I needed reminding that time and the things of falling shall not fall into darkness but into a new freedom we cannot name, and so call emptiness. All of reality floats in that vacancy, like the spheres in the void of space, like these words floating in the emptiness of the page. Words try to capture reality, yet what they actually capture are only more words and deeper doubts. Mystery is the preeminent condition of human beings—and yet it is also our freedom to be exactly who we are, free to choose the words our doubts require.

No one in the delegation understood this when I was

taken back to the mission to account for myself. Grateful as they were for my stopping the theft of the Imperial ship, they were sure the explosion had addled me. I think the monks knew what I meant, but they're of the "just-so" sect of Ch'an Buddhism, so they'd be the last to let on.

Be that as it may, I sat there quite agog and amazed, awakened to the knowledge that the freedom to be who I am means, quite simply, that I am alone—without you. For now, it is meant that this be so. For reasons I will never truly understand, death is denied me. So what am I to do with this life, then, and this loneliness? This freedom to *be*, this freedom whose chances bleed from us, creates new imperatives. In the place of my failure and shame waits a gaping emptiness wanting to be filled with what I might yet be.

As I meditated on this, the delegation wrote an official missive admonishing the Big Noses for their attempted thievery and threatening to report them to the Emperor. The Big Noses, all of whom had escaped the explosion and retreated to their ships, replied with a terse letter of half-hearted apology. With no other Imperial vessel anywhere in the vicinity and none of the Autocracies' forces nearby, our host, the monastery's abbot, urged us to accept the apology.

In an effort to both placate and hurry the Colonizer on his way, the delegation decided to load his ships with all the porcelain in the mission, several remarkable landscape paintings, a jade statue of Kwan Yin, goddess of serenity, as well as bales of crops he had never seen before, notably tobacco, peanuts, and potatoes. By then, inspired by my lack of family and career, I had decided to take the poison cure required by my sorrow; I have, dear wife, forsaken my return to the Middle Kingdom to go with the Colonizer on his return voyage across the Storm Sea to his homeland.

Do you admonish me for being foolish? Indeed, the decision was a difficult one, for I had hoped to return to our homeland and administer the rites myself at your gravesite. But if what I have learned of the emptiness is true, then you are no more there than here. The path of the Way is a roadlessness without departure or arrival. I have decided, Heart Wing, to follow the path, to fit the unaccomplished parts of my life to the future and embrace the unknown.

The delegation strove in vain to dissuade me. They fear that I have gone truly mad. But I don't care at all. I know you would understand, Heart Wing, you whom I first won with the bridebait of stories written by the lamp of lightning. So, as absurd as this may be, I sit here now, writing to you on the quarterdeck of a leaky vessel named *Santa Maria*.

I can tell from the way he looks at me that the Colonizer is still angry that I deprived him of his booty, and I know he has only taken me on board with the expectation of getting useful information from me. But for now our ignorance of each other's languages offers me a chance to win the Big Noses' respect by my deeds—and to watch and learn about these barbarians.

In time, I will understand their language. I will inform their emperor of the wonders of the Middle Kingdom, of the achievements of the Unified Sandalwood Autocracies, of the glory of our people. And I will write again from the far side of the world, from so far east it is the west where sun and moon meet. And from there, I will send back to the kingdom and to the USA stories everyone will read, stories of another world, written in ink from the new moon.

Southpaw

Bruce McAllister

"Southpaw" appeared in the August 1993 issue of Asimov's, *with an illustration by Gary Freeman. Bruce McAllister published his first story in 1963, when he was seventeen (it was written at the tender age of fifteen). Since then, with only a handful of stories and a few novels, he has nevertheless managed to establish himself as one of the most respected writers in the business. In addition to* Asimov's, *his short fiction has appeared in* Omni, The Magazine of Fantasy and Science Fiction, In the Field of Fire, Alien Sex, *and elsewhere. His first novel,* Humanity Prime, *was one of the original Ace Specials series. His most recent novel was the critically acclaimed* Dream Baby, *and he is at work on several other novel projects. McAllister lives in Redlands, California, where he is the director of the writing program at the University of Redlands.*

Unlike many Alternate History stories, which are often on the level of "What if Napoleon had a B-52 at Waterloo?" or "Suppose Plato and JFK had formed a rock band and become costumed crime fighters?", the clever story that follows turns on an obscure and little-known point of historical fact. And so this surprising and in-

*triguing scenario actually could have happened, strange
as it may seem . . . and, in fact, it very nearly did.*

> *"Eventually New York Giants' scout Alex Pompez got
> the authorization from their front office to offer
> Castro a contact. After several days of deliberation
> with friends, family, and some of his professors,
> Castro turned down the offer. The Giants' officials
> were stunned. "No one had ever turned us down
> from Latin America before," recalled Pompez. "Castro
> said no, but in his very polite way. He was really a
> very nice kid. . . ."*

> —*J. David Truby,*
> Sports History,
> *November 1988*

Fidel stands on the pitcher's mound, dazed. For an
instant he doesn't know where he is. It *is* a pitcher's
mound. It *is* a baseball diamond, and there is a woman—
the woman he loves—out there in the stands with her
beautiful blonde hair and her very American name
waving to him, because she loves him, too. It is *July*. He
is sure of this. It is '51 or '52. He cannot remember
which. But the crowd is as big as ever and he can smell
the leather of his glove, and he knows he is playing baseball—the way, as a child in the sugarcane fields of Oriente Province, he always dreamed he might.

His fastball is a problem, but he throws one anyway, it
breaks wide and the ump calls the ball. He throws a curve
this time, a *fine* one, and it's a strike—the third. He grins
at Westrum, his catcher, his friend. The next batter's up.
Fidel feels an itching on his face and reaches up to

scratch it. It feels like the beginning of a beard, but that can't be. You keep a clean face in baseball. He tried to tell his father that, in Oriente, the last time he went home, but the old man, as always, had just argued.

He delivers another curve—with *great* control—and smiles when the ball drops off the table and Sterling swings like an idiot. He muscles up on the pitch, blows the batter down with a heater, but Williams gets a double off the next slider, Miller clears the bases with a triple, and they bring Wilhelm in to relieve him at last. The final score is 9 to 4, just like the oddsmakers predicted, and that great centerfielder Mays still won't look at him in the lockers.

Nancy—her name is Nancy—is waiting for him at the back entrance when he's in his street clothes again, the flowered shirt and the white ducks he likes best, and she looks wonderful. She's chewing gum, which drives him crazy, but her skin is like a dream—like moonlight on the Mulano—and he kisses her hard, feeling her tongue between his lips. When they pull away she says: "I really like the way you walked that Negro in the fifth."

He smiles at her. He loves her so much it hurts. She doesn't know a damn thing about the game and nothing about Cuba, but she's doing her best and she loves him too. "I do it for *you*, *chica*," he tells her. "I *always* do it for you."

That night he dreams he's in the mountains of the Sierra Maestra, at a place called La Playa. He has no idea why he's here. He's never dreamt this dream before. He's lying on the ground with a rifle in his hand. He's wearing the fatigues a soldier wears, and doesn't understand why—who the two men lying beside him are, what it means. The clothes he's wearing are rough. His face itches like hell.

When he wakes, she is beside him. The sheet has fallen away from her back, which is to him, and her ass—which is so beautiful, which any man would find beautiful—is there for him and him alone to see. *How can anything be more real than this? How can I be dreaming of such things?* He can hear a song fading but does not know it. There is a bay—a bay with Naval ships—and the song is fading away.

Guantanamera . . . the voice was singing.

Yo soy un hombre sincero, it sang.

I am a truthful man.

Why, Fidel wonders, was it singing this?

After the game with the Cardinals on Saturday, when he pitches six innings before they bring Wilhelm in to relieve him and end up a little better than the oddsmakers had it, a kid comes up to him and wants his autograph. The kid is dark, like the children he played with on the *finca* his father owns—the ones that worked with their families during the cane harvest and sat beside him in the country school at Marcana between harvests. He knows this boy is Cuban, too.

"*¿Señor?*" the kid asks, holding up a baseball card. "*¿Por favor?*"

Fidel doesn't understand. It is a baseball card, sure. But whose? He takes it and sees himself. No one has told him—no one has told him there is a card with his face on it, something else he has always dreamed of. He remembers now. He has been playing for the Giants—this is his first year. The offer was a good one, with a five thousand dollar bonus for signing. Now he's on a baseball card. He tries to read it, but the words are small. Nancy has his glasses and he must squint. The words fill him with awe.

It says nothing about his fastball, and he is grateful. He smiles at the boy, whose eyes are on him. The father hands him a pen. "What's your name, *hijo*?" he asks. "Raul," the boy says. *"Me llamo Raul." To Raul,* he writes. He writes it across his own face because that is where the room is. It is harder than hell writing on a card this small and he must kneel down, writing it on his knee. *May your dreams come true,* he also writes, putting it across his jersey now. He wants to write *And may your fastball be better than mine,* but there isn't any room. He gives the card back and returns the pen. The boy thanks him. The father nods, grinning. Fidel grins back. *"Muy*

FIDEL ALEJANDRO CASTRO RUZ

Pitcher: New York Giants   Home: Queens, New York

Born: August 13, 1926, Biran, Cuba   Eyes: Brown   Hair: Brown

Ht: 6'2"   Wt: 190   Throws: Left   Bats: Right

• Fidel first attracted attention as the star of the University of Havana's baseball team. At Havana in '48 he had 16 wins, 5 losses, and a shutout and no-hitter to his credit. He is known for the great variety of his curveballs.

MAJOR & MINOR LEAGUE PITCHING RECORDS

	G	IP	W	L	R	ER	SO	BB	ERA
'49 Roch.	20	127	7	5	62	58	102	43	4.11
'50 Roch.	35	260	14	9	115	101	182	63	3.50
Min. Lea. Totals	55	387	21	14	177	159	284	106	3.69
'51 Giants	31	209	12	10	98	82	129	51	3.53
Maj. Lea. Totals	31	209	12	10	98	82	129	51	3.53

c T. C. G. • TOPPS BASEBALL • PRTD. IN U.S.A.

guapo," Fidel tells him. The man keeps nodding. "I mean it," Fidel says.

He dreams of a cane field near Allegria del Oio, to the north, of soldiers moving through the cane. He can't breathe. He is lying on the ground, he can't move, can't breathe. He's holding something in his hand—but what? None of it makes sense. There isn't any war in Cuba. Life in Cuba is peaceful, he knows. Fulgencio Batista, the President, is running it, and running it well. After Pirontes, how could he not? Relations with the United States are good. Who could possibly be hiding in the Sierra Maestra? Who could be lying in the cane with rifles in their hands, hiding from soldiers and singing a song about a *truthful man*?

After they have made love, after she has asked him to take her from behind first, then from the front, where they can see each other, after they've reached their most beautiful moment together, he tells her about his dream and she says: "Dreams aren't suppose to make sense, honey."

He can't believe she is a waitress. He cannot, even for a moment, believe that anyone this beautiful, this American in so many ways, is only a waitress. He wants her to stop working. He would rather have her watch television all day in the apartment or shop for nice clothes for herself than walk around in such a dull uniform. But she's going to keep working, she tells him, until he gets his new contract. She *wants* to, she says.

He doesn't have the heart to tell her that he is probably not going to be renewed, that he's probably going to be sent back to work on his strength, which has been getting worse, not better, and how once you go back down it is so very hard to return. Durocher, that crazy man, may love having him, a left-handed Cuban, on his team, may have brought him up just for that, but that just isn't enough now.

He loves her too much to scare her, and there's always a chance—isn't there?—that his fastball will get better, that his arm will become as strong as it needs to be.

All he really needs, he knows, is a break—like the one Koslo got in the Series, Durocher's surprise starter who got to go all the way in that first great game with the Yankees, when they really had them by the balls. His arm would feel the pride, would be strong from it, and maybe then Mays and Irvin would look at him in the fucking lockers.

Nancy loves the "I Love Lucy" television show. Because she does, on her birthday he buys her a new Zenith television set—a big one. One with an antenna big enough to make the picture better. Some day there will be television sets with *colored* pictures—everyone says so—and he knows he'll buy her one of those too when the stores have them. On her days off she watches the show, and every chance he gets he watches it with her. She tells him: "I wish I had red hair like Lucy. Would you like that?" He looks at the black-and-white picture on the television set and does his best to imagine Lucy's hair *in color*. *Sure,* he thinks. *Red hair is amazing. But so is blonde.* "If you want," he says, "but I like your blonde hair, *chica*. You look like an angel to me. You fill this room with light—just like an angel." He wants to sound like a poet; he has always wanted to sound like a poet. He wants never to lose the magic of their lives, and this is possible in America, is it not? Not to lose what you have, what you have dreamed of? If she wants red hair, okay, but not if it's because she thinks she isn't beautiful without it. "You're beautiful, *chica*. You're the most beautiful woman I have ever known," he tells her, and then a face—a woman with dark hair, in the ugly green fatigues a soldier wears—comes to him. He doesn't know her. He doesn't know why this face has come to him, when he is with the woman he loves.

He closes his eyes and the face, like the song, fades.

They watch "I Love Lucy" and "Your Show of Shows" and "You Bet Your Life," and the next week, too—like a date, there in their own living room on the big Zenith he has bought for her birthday—they watch Lucy and her best friend Ethel work on Lucy's crazy plans to get what she wants out of life. They laugh at all the trouble Lucy gets herself into only because she wants to be taken seriously, and also wants to be a good wife. *Is this the struggle of all American women?* he wonders. To be taken seriously, but to be a good wife too?

Nancy isn't laughing, and he knows that look. She isn't happy. Like Lucy, she wants something but isn't sure she can have it. She still wants that *red hair*, he knows. She wants red hair the same way he has always wanted to play pro ball, because in America all things are possible, and so you dream about them, and you aren't happy unless you get them. The tenderness he feels for her suddenly brings tears to his eyes, and he hides them by looking away.

Now she is laughing. She has lost herself again in the television show. She is watching Lucy do her crazy things while Ricky, that amazing drummer—that Cuban dancer all American women are in love with—doesn't know what she's up to, though when he finds out he will indeed forgive her, because he loves her. This is American too, Fidel knows.

The Cuban phones him three days later. The man says only, "I would like the opportunity to meet with you, *Señor*. Would this be possible?" When Fidel asks what it is about, the man says, "Our country." "Cuba?" Fidel asks. "Yes," the man tells him. "I ask only for an hour of your time—at the very most." Fidel feels an uneasiness begin, but says, "Yes." *Why not?* This man is a fellow Cuban, another son of Cuba and Martí, so why should he not? If there is something happening in Cuba that he should know about, what is an hour of his time?

They meet at the coffee shop where Nancy works. Nancy serves them and smiles at them both. The man begins to talk. He is not direct. He talks of many things, but not important ones. The uneasiness grows. What is wrong? What is so wrong in Cuba that a man contacts him like this, talks around things and does not get to the point? "What are you trying to say?" Fidel says.

"Things are happening now," the man says.

"What things?"

"People are not happy, *Señor*."

"What people?"

"The farmers and workers," the man says, and Fidel understands at last.

"You are a *communist*," he says to the man.

"No. I am not," the man answers. "I am a son of Cuba, like you. I am simply *concerned*. And I happen to represent others who are concerned, others who feel that you, a son of Cuba—a celebrity in both countries—might wish to know about these things, to consider them."

"I am a baseball player," Fidel says at last. "I know nothing of politics. We have a president in Cuba and a president in the United States. Except for an American war in Asia, I am not aware of any problems."

The man is quiet for a moment. "Yes," he says, "you are in America now, and you are playing baseball, and so you might not be in a position to hear about things at home, would you agree?"

That is true, Fidel thinks. *A baseball player would not, would he. . . .*

"There is a movement in Oriente Province, your own province," the man tells him, "a movement that is growing. The current administration in Havana is not happy with it, but I must emphasize to you that it is a movement *of the sons of Cuba*, men who are tired of the manner in which Cuba remains a child in the shadow of North America—a child not allowed to grow up, to know what it is like to be a man, to build a life from hard work, to have a family, to feel the pride a *man* should feel. . . ."

The man is looking at him, and Fidel looks away.

"The United States is a good country," Fidel says.

"Yes, I know. It has been good to Cubans like you, *Señor*. But, if you will forgive me, it has not been as good to everyone. Those who work on the *fincas*, in the cities, those who work for a few *kilos* a day to serve the wealthy tourists who come to Havana to play. . . ."

He knows what the man is saying. He knows he is lucky. He remembers the boys and girls from the cane fields and knows where they are now. They do not play on baseball fields in New York. They do not play on tennis courts in California. They do not run hotels in Miami. And only a few will ever have careers in boxing.

He knows what the man is saying, and he feels the shame.

He sighs at last. "What is the United States doing that is so wrong? Please, I would like to know. . . ."

When the man is gone, Fidel sits for a while in the booth with its red upholstery. Nancy comes to give him the check, to smile at him and to purse her lips in a kiss in his direction, so that he will do the same. When he does not, she frowns just like Lucy—as if to say *What's wrong, Ricky?* He gives her what smile he can, so that she will not think he no longer loves her.

He hasn't felt this way since he was a child, he realizes, as he walks from the coffee shop to the blue Chevrolet in the parking lot—since the days he would argue with his father at home and his father would shout, not wanting to hear what he had to say. His father, with that wonderful beard of his, had come from Spain, the poorest part, had begun his life as a soldier sent to fight in Cuba, had become a brickmaster who bought a little land here and there, until eventually he was a *land owner*, a man of the *finca*, a man who had made a life for himself out of *nothing*, who did not want to hear about the poor children his son played with. And why should he? *You should not be playing with them!* his father would shout.

No son wants his father angry with him, Fidel knows.

Even the thought of *love*—even the thought of love of a woman like Nancy, or a fine baseball card with his picture on it—cannot make the feelings go away as he drives toward the Polo Grounds and the double header.

That night he dreams that someone—he himself or someone else—has set fire to his father's cane fields. He wakes from the dream in a sweat. And yet his father was *there*—in the dream. Standing beside the flames and nodding, as if everything were okay, as if he had given his permission. When he falls asleep again, he dreams of a prison on an island of pine trees, a ship that almost sinks, of soldiers asleep (or *dead*) lying beside him under the *paja* of dried cane leaves.

After the game with Brooklyn on Sunday, when he pitches six innings before they call in Hutchinson, he doesn't take Nancy out for black beans or steak. She isn't angry. He goes to bed early. He dreams of the mountains again, and then, right before he wakes, of that same ship, the one full of the soldiers he knew . . . before they died.

It takes him three weeks to get through to Desi Arnaz. He tries calling the studio where the show is filmed, and then the company that makes the show. He writes two letters, certain that neither will get through. When he sends a telegram, it says simply, "A fellow son of Cuba would like to meet with you."

The answer takes four weeks. Arnaz, who lives in a valley north of Hollywood, California, will meet with him if he can be in Los Angeles on the 13th of September at ten in the morning. A driver will be sent to his hotel.

Nancy wants to go, and for a moment he almost says *yes*. Yet he knows what it will be like: He, full of feelings he hasn't felt in so long, needing to talk to a fellow son of Cuba; she, wanting to have fun in the city she has always dreamed of. It would be worse to take her with him, would it not? Worse than telling her *no*? "But *why*?" she asks. She is hurt. He has made a dream come true for her for a moment—the chance to go to Hollywood, maybe even to meet Lucille Ball herself—only to take it away. What has she done? Her body sags, older, and he is afraid: *What am I doing? What am I doing to us?* Suddenly he is angry at the man for telling him about Cuba, for making him feel what he feels, for making him hurt the woman he loves. And for making him *afraid.* "*Señor* Arnaz is a busy man, *chica,*" he tells her gently. "His wife is a busy woman. I will be speaking to him for no more than an hour and then I will come home. It is *political* business. *Cuban* business. If I were going to Hollywood for fun, you would be the only one I would take. But I am not going for fun. I would not be able to have fun without you. Can you understand?"

She does not speak, and when she does, she says: *Maybe another time.* She says: *I understand.* This should make him happy, but it does not. Even this depresses him—that she *understands*, that she is willing to wait for something that may never come again. *Everything is falling apart,* he feels. *Everything is becoming something else—*

A darkness.

The night before he leaves for Hollywood, he dreams he is high up in an airplane, looking down at an island. It is Cuba. Below him he can see things he does not understand. Below, in black and white—like photographs—are buildings, are trucks covered with palm fronds and bushes, things that look like long, thin bullets. He is holding something in his hand—a glove, a camera, a favorite rifle with a telescope on top—but he cannot see it. He is looking down.

Everything is quiet . . . as if the whole world were waiting.

* * *

The chauffeur sent by Arnaz takes him from the ancient hotel on Hollywood Boulevard to the valley, which is over the hills, to a gate, which the driver gets out and opens. At the end of a long driveway stands Lucy and Desi's house, which looks not unlike a *hacienda*. Arnaz is waiting in the hallway for him—with a smile and a manly handshake—and they sit down immediately in a bright white room full of windows and light. A servant brings them drinks—a rum for Fidel and a lemonade for Desi. Lucy does not appear. She is pregnant—everyone knows this—and besides, she is very involved in her Hollywood projects. She will not appear, he knows now. He will not even be able to ask her for an autograph to take back to Nancy.

But he can see the portrait of Lucy—that famous painting by that famous American painter—on the wall above them, in the light. *In color* her hair is indeed remarkable. "I have heard many great things about you, *Señor* Castro," Arnaz says suddenly. He is wearing gabardine slacks, is thinner than Fidel imagined. "I was the only boy in Cuba never to play baseball, I am certain, but I follow the sport avidly—especially when one of its players is a son of Cuba and boasts your gifts."

"Muchas gracias," Fidel says. He is uncomfortable, sitting with the man he has seen so many times on television, and knows he should not be. They are both Cubans. They are both important men. "If I may say so, *Señor* Arnaz, you are the most famous Cuban in America and my girlfriend and I are but two of the many many fans you and your wife have in both countries. . . ."

It is not what he wanted to say. Arnaz smiles, saying

nothing. He is waiting. He is waiting to hear the reason Fidel has come.

He has rehearsed this many times and yet the rehearsals mean nothing. It is like his fastball. All the practice in the world means nothing. He must simply find the courage to say what he has come to say:

"Thank you for agreeing to meet with me, *Señor*. I have asked for this meeting because I am concerned about our country. . . ."

He waits. The face of Arnaz does not change. The smile is there. The eyes look at him respectfully, just as the eyes of the Cuban in the coffee shop looked at him.

And then Arnaz says, "I see," and the smile changes.

Fidel is unable to breathe. All he can see is the frown, faint but there. All he can do, holding his breath, is wonder what it means: *Disappointment,* because Arnaz imagined something different—a Hollywood project, a *baseball* Hollywood project, an event for charity with baseball players and Hollywood people . . . for the poor of Cuba perhaps?

Or is it *anger*?

"To what do you refer?" Arnaz asks, his voice different now. *I do not imagine this,* Fidel tells himself. *It is real. The warmth is gone. . . .*

Even the room looks darker now, Lucy's portrait on the wall dimmer. Fidel takes a breath, exhales, and begins again: "I cannot be sure of the details myself, *Señor*. That is why I wished to see you. Perhaps you know more than I." He takes another breath, exhales it too, and smells suddenly the cane fields of Oriente, their sweetness, and sweet rain. "We are both celebrities, *Señor* Arnaz—myself to a much lesser degree, to be sure—and I believe that celebrities like you and I hold unusual positions in our two countries. We are Cubans, yes, but we are not *ordinary* Cubans. We are famous in two countries and have the power, I believe, and even— if I may be so bold—the responsibility as well, to know what is happening in Cuba, to speak publicly, even to influence matters between those two countries . . . for the sake of the sons and daughters of Martí. . . ."

Arnaz waits.

"Have you," Fidel goes on quickly, "heard of a movement in Oriente Province, in the Sierra Maestra, or of any general unrest in our country, *Señor*? Word of such matters has reached me recently through a fellow Cuban whose credentials I have no reason to question and who I do *not* believe is a communist."

Arnaz looks at him and the silence goes on and on. When the little Cuban finally speaks, it is like wind through pine trees near a sea, like years of walls there. "Forgive me for what I am about to say, *Señor* Castro, but like many men in your profession, you are very naïve. You hear a rumor and from it imagine a *revolution*. You hear the name of José Martí invoked by those who would invoke any name to suit their purposes and from this suddenly imagine that it is your duty to become *involved*.

"It would hurt you seriously, *Señor* Castro," Arnaz continues, "were word of this concern of yours—of our meeting and your very words to me today—to become public. Were that to happen, I assure you, you would find yourself in an unfavorable public light, one that would have consequences for you professionally for many many years, for your family in Cuba, for your girlfriend here. I will not mention your visit to anyone. I trust you will do the same."

Arnaz is getting up. "I would also suggest, *Señor* Castro, that you leave matters of the kind you have been so concerned with to the politicians, to our presidents in Washington and Havana, who have wisdom in such things."

Fidel is nodding, rising too. He can feel the heat of the shame on his face. They are at the door. The chauffeur is standing by the limousine. Arnaz is telling him goodbye, wishing him good luck and a fine baseball season. The gracious smile is there, the manly handshake somehow, and now the limousine is carrying him back down the driveway toward the gate.

The despair that fills him is vast, as vast as the un-cleared forests beyond the sugarcane and tobacco fields of Oriente Province, lifting only when the limousine is free of the gate and he can think of Nancy again—her face, her hair—and can realize that, *yes,* she would look good with red hair, that indeed he would like her hair to be such an amazing red.

The West Is Red

Greg Costikyan

"The West Is Red" appeared in the May 1994 issue of Asimov's, *with an illustration by Steve Cavallo. This was Costikyan's second sale to* Asimov's. *A relatively new writer, Costikyan is the author of two comic fantasy novels,* Another Day, Another Dungeon *and* One Quest, Hold the Dragons. *He lives in New York City.*

In the suspenseful story that follows, he takes us sideways in time for a fast-paced look, full of odd echoes of today's headlines, at a world in crisis . . .

"Parlor pink," I said.

I didn't have much time; the door was unlocked, and people might wander in at any moment. The bar in the ballroom of the Chinese embassy was swamped; apparently, people hadn't discovered this bar yet, which gave me a chance to test the robot behind it. It puzzled me.

One, two, three. . . . There was a time delay before the bartender swung into action. Its brain was in Moscow, or possibly Beijing; but why so long a delay? It mixed me the cocktail: cranberry juice, dark Cuban rum, seltzer, twist of lime. Devilish clever, these Chinese.

I sidled around the bar. The electronics were in a box

held closed by small hex screws. The tools I use to maintain my terminal were in my purse; I had the cover off in seconds. I pulled out a breadboard. Several black chips said РБГ 16И; standard memory chips, probably bought from the Proletarian Electronics plant outside Vladivostok. Sixteen megs a piece; they had cost someone a pretty kopek. What I wanted to know was, how did it communicate with Beijing? There were no obvious cables, but the U.S. had no cellular phone system yet, and . . .

There, that was a radio transmitter. It occurred to me that the Chinese embassy must have a satellite link; that explained the delay. It takes a quarter second or so to bounce data off a satellite; it would take less time to route communications over cable, but America's rickety phone system probably wasn't up to the task.

The door to the room opened. I cursed, crouching behind the bar. I was not entirely comfortable, not in high heels.

"Hello?" said someone in English. I kept down. He muttered something, then made his way to the bartender. "Scotch on the—hello. I thought I saw you come in here." It was that American; handsome fellow. He'd been eying me from across the party.

There I was, on the floor behind the bar, electronics spread out around me. Stupid, stupid; I shouldn't have let curiosity get the better of me. I started shoving things back into the bartender.

"Bloody hell," I said. "I hadn't expected you to follow me."

"Why'd you wink at me, then?" he said.

"Why not?" I said. "Boring party."

"Getting in a little industrial espionage before they serve dinner?"

"Really, no," I said, screwing the plate back onto the box. "Scotch on the rocks," I said experimentally; one, two—the thing seemed to work okay. "That is what you wanted?"

"Yeah," he said, taking the drink.

"I was just curious," I said. "The Chinese are very clever about commercial use of electronics, you know; ahead of us in many ways."

"Sure," he said. "You Russkis spent too much time building killer satellites, and not enough time building color TVs. I'm Frank Mangiara."

"I can read," I said, a little irritably; that's what his nametag said, of course. I glanced behind the bar; no, there didn't seem to be any evidence of my tinkering. I straightened my stockings. Thankfully, Mangiara seemed more interested in my legs than my, um, extralegal activities.

"Look, let's get back to the party before Sam here starts spraying us with vodka, okay?" I said.

"Okay," said Mangiara, and held the door for me.

The noise of the ballroom was a shock. I waved at Ambassador Wan, who waved back. He was drunk, weaving a bit on his feet, and getting drunker by the minute; I had no doubt he was regaling the Americans clustered about him with yet another interminable story about the Long March. I wondered how I was going to ditch Mangiara. Then, I wondered whether I wanted to; the party looked like it was getting duller by the moment.

"I've never met an academician before," Mangiara said, shouting over the mob. He was reading my nametag, of course: Academician Nazarian, that's me. A fully-vested member of the Soviet Academy of Sciences. Really.

"You're a Marxist?" Mangiara asked.

"Isn't everyone?" I said, snagging a dumpling from a

passing waiter. "But no," I said. "Marxism isn't my science. I work with the Big Brain."

"You're in computers?" he asked.

"Yes," I said.

"Why are you in Washington, then? Isn't Moscow the place to be?"

I shrugged. "Fraternal Soviet assistance to aid America in its difficult transition to the modern socialist order," I said. "Central planners need accurate, timely data to manage an economy efficiently—can't have central planning without central processing. Your computers need help. I'm supposed to bring them up to snuff."

"We're decades behind, I suppose," said Mangiara dolorously.

"Of course," I said. "Look, Frank, I'm bored out of my skull. What say we paint the town red?"

He gave me a sudden grin. "I think I can find some drop cloths and brushes."

"Lead on, Macduff," said I.

Mangiara unlocked a nifty little Great Wall roadster, bucket seats and gull-wing doors. It had government plates—well, of course. Mangiara had to have something to do with the U.S. government, or he wouldn't be attending a party at the Chinese embassy.

"How did you wangle this?" I asked, as we slid into the sparse Washington traffic.

"Hmm?"

"Doesn't the U.S. government require its functionaries to drive American cars?"

He gave me a boyish grin. "Those rattletraps?" he said. "I've got a friend in the dispatcher's office. Let them stick someone else with those two-stroke Chevies."

"What do you do, anyway?"

Mangiara spoke absently, concentrating on driving. "Department of Transportation," he said. "Something to do with choo-choo trains. Pretty dull, really."

Well, if even he thought it was dull, I wasn't too interested in talking about it.

Washington was more attractive by night than by day; darkness hid the coal-smoke grime, the despairing faces, the stoop-shouldered men and women clad in badly tailored clothes. As we neared Pennsylvania Avenue, the traffic thickened. Mangiara grunted. "Oops," he said. "Forgot about that."

"About what?"

He pointed through the windshield. At the end of the block, past the motionless cars that blocked our way, were flickering torches. "Demo tonight," he said.

"Who is it?" I said.

"Republicans," he said.

I shivered—fascists. They still had enough influence in the Supreme Court and Senate to block reforms. From time to time, the police would halt the marchers long enough to let a few cars across the street.

"I'm sorry," said Mangiara. "If I'd remembered, I could have taken a different route. We'll just have to wait."

"Nichevo," I told him.

After some time, we reached the end of the block. A very nervous policeman held up a hand to stop us, then waved the marchers past.

They bore burning brands in the darkness, American flags and eagles, portraits of the tyrant Nixon, signs demanding, "No More Nationalizations!" and "Live Free or

Die" and "Death to Radey"—the senator from California, the first member of the CP/USA to be elected to federal office. Many of them were in uniform. Breath puffed white in the cold winter air.

They looked angry; the policemen lining the street, in their riot garb, looked a little scared.

I don't know what set them off; a thrown rock, a curse, rabble-rousing, provocation by the police . . . it hardly matters. Any demonstration is a tinderbox. Suddenly, the marchers were running and shouting. The police line was in motion, tear gas swirled across the avenue. Mangiara swiftly shut the vent on the car's heater, to avoid sucking in the gas.

One man, a hefty blue-collar type, began pounding on the hood of Mangiara's Chinese car, shouting "Buy American!"

"For shame!" I shouted at him. "Where's your international working-class solidarity!"

"Please," Mangiara moaned.

The worker turned puce, found an uprooted No Parking sign, and bashed at the windshield. Cracks spread across the glass, but it held. Mangiara backed up and floored the accelerator; the worker dodged out of the way, only just in time. We drove hesitantly across the street, marchers stumbling into the side of the car as they fled, unable to see for the roiling, noisome gas.

We finally made it across the road. Mangiara sped down the street, getting away from the demo as fast as he could. "Well," he said, "not exactly the start to the evening I had planned."

"Actually, I quite enjoyed it," I said.

He gave me a startled glance.

"Invigorating," I said.

He looked somewhat bemused.

"I'm sorry about your windshield," I said.

"Well," he said, "there are advantages to being part of the motor pool."

We sped down darkened streets, past sleeping bums and hopeless faces, to an area I would have hesitated to visit, unescorted. He led me down a flight of stairs to a basement cabaret.

The lights were low, the room inevitably smoke-filled—the American health authorities have worse things to worry about than smoking. The clientele, to my startlement, was at least half Negro; I had been few places in America where the races mixed freely. At the stage was a jazz band. They were absolutely first rate.

Mangiara ordered us ribs and an American whisky, and we listened attentively.

After a while, the band took a break. "I'm surprised there are places like this in America," I said.

"Not too many," he said. "Jazz doesn't get the audience here it does in Europe; but not too many Negroes have the price of a ticket to Paris, you know."

The next set began, and the ribs came soon after. Mangiara showed me how to eat them: with the fingers, gnawing the meat off the bones, a primitive, somehow satisfying practice. His leg was against mine, under the table.

When we were finished, Mangiara said, "Well, it's getting late."

"You disappoint me, *tovarishch*," I said. "This is your idea of a town painted red?"

He gave me a lopsided smile. He had a nice dimple. "You don't have to work tomorrow?"

"More to the point," I said, "I *can't* work tomorrow."

"Why not?"

I sighed. "The bloody Pentagon won't let me in to take a look at Univac."

"Someone should tell them the Cold War is over."

"That would be nice."

"Still," he said, "they *did* spend fifty years making sure no Reds ever got close to the thing."

"Yes, yes, understandable," I said, "but it's damned debilitating. I didn't come to the U.S. to loaf."

He nodded philosophically, and caught the waitress's eye. He made scribbling motions with his hands. "Feel like dancing?" The waitress brought the check.

"Definitely *da*," I said.

"Cité d'Espace," it said in neon; didn't look like *my* idea of a space station. It had once been a warehouse, all bare brick walls and industrial piping, glittering lights and loud music. The clientele was what passed for the spoiled children of the American elite, teenagers and post-teens clad in tight mylar and European fashions. The headline act was a third-rate German techno band—I imagined the U.S. didn't get first-rate talent—followed by local groups. I was puzzled by the French name— techno originated in Berlin, and its stars are still mainly German—until I recalled the depths of American bitterness at West Germany's withdrawal from NATO and its reunification under a communist regime, the act that precipitated the end to the Western alliance.

Mangiara got me a drink laced with something, and we spent some time on the floor. I enjoyed myself.

Afterward we hit a little pâtisserie for Napoleons and coffee; had a drink in the bar at one of Washington's better hotels, where a piano player sang tunes from old Brecht-Weill musical comedies; and wound up at a rather seedy club that featured vaudeville.

"There's life in America after all," I told Mangiara, happily exhausted, as we sped onward, apparently through the country north of Washington. We'd been so many places, I didn't bother to ask where we were headed; it didn't seem to matter.

"This is nothing," he said. "You should see New York."

"I'd love to," I said.

We arrived at a clapboard house somewhere in Maryland, overlooking a valley filled with crisp, white snow, several miles off the main road. Mangiara told me it belonged to a friend.

He built a fire in the hearth and made the featherbed, piling it high with patchwork quilts. We made love there, for the first time, sinking deep into the mattress's down, amid geometric patterns and the smell of woodsmoke and camphor, a winter wind whistling past the windows and rattling the panes.

A few days later the Pentagon finally gave in, and I was admitted to work on what had been America's deepest military secret. I found myself frantic with activity, working around the clock, sometimes, down there in the bowels of the Pentagon, peering at amber screens under blue fluorescent lights. Actually, it made a pleasant change from sitting around twiddling my thumbs and cursing the military mentality. I'd been looking for a challenge; well, trying to bash the antiquated U.S. computer system into something like modern utility was a challenge of the first order.

I didn't have much time for Mangiara; he took it hard, the poor sod. Whenever I got back to my room at the embassy, there were always little plaintive messages awaiting me. I took pity on him, and we went out several times, but I could tell he was chafing. He wanted more.

But I was determined not to take the relationship too seriously; long-distance romances rarely work out, I knew. Hadn't Irina fallen for the actor—Mischa, was that his name? He had moved to Vladivostok, to join the Soviet cinema on the booming Pacific Coast, and though they had tried to carry on the romance, by phone and electronic mail and supersonic jet, they had gradually drifted away. How much less likely a long-term romance with an American seemed; certainly, I had no intention of staying in Washington forever.

One night, Mangiara asked, "Can I see my rival?"

"Your what?" I said.

"Univac," he said.

"You think of the machine as your rival?"

"Well, you spend more time with it than with me."

I had to laugh. "You're a better conversationalist," I said, "a lot handsomer, and much better in bed. You have nothing to fear."

Mangiara drifted off to sleep; I studied his face affectionately. Still, I told him silently, my work is my life; you don't become an academician by thirty without dedication. You are an amusement, my dear, my handsome American. If you and Univac are rivals, Univac, too, has nothing to fear.

"Strip," I told Mangiara.

He looked uneasily around, at the bare, white walls,

the smell of antiseptic rising from the tiled floor. "You want to screw here?"

"No, pretty boy," I said. "You can't go in to see Univac dressed like that."

He looked down at his charcoal suit. "My tie crooked?" he asked.

I sighed. "Don't be obtuse. Even a mote of dust can endanger the circuitry, get into the drives; we operate under clean-room conditions. Out of those clothes, and into the shower."

He insisted on privacy, which I found rather funny; not like I hadn't seen him in the buff. He met me by the airlock in the uniform of the computer professional: lab smock, hair cap, disposable paper booties over the shoes. We cycled the airlock.

"Is this really necessary?" he asked.

"Yup. The chamber's at positive pressure, to prevent dust infiltration."

The lock's inner door opened onto the elevator. We took it down, down, for long moments.

"Must be a long way down," said Mangiara.

"It's supposed to be able to withstand a direct nuclear hit," I said. "Getting Univac was top priority for the Strategic Rocket Forces, you know."

The elevator opened with a clang. We left for the metal catwalk. Mangiara peered over the railing and down into the Well. Down it stretched, dozens of levels. On each, corridors led off past metal frames holding circuit boards and cables. Lab-coated technicians scurried everywhere, pulling defective boards and replacing them, testing connections, running diagnostics. Against the far wall were the tape and disk drives, bank after bank, alert lights blinking, tape reels whirring away. The whole place thrummed with the air-conditioning, the whirring drives, the fans cooling individual peripherals. It was a cavern, a man-made cavern, the largest man-made structure, by volume, in the world, or so I'd been told—the Big Brain's chamber was smaller, but then, Soviet electronics are more highly miniaturized. I couldn't imagine what the Well had cost, to blast out from the bedrock underneath Washington.

"My God," said Mangiara.

"No reactionary sentiments here, please," I said. "Credit human genius, not some infantile father-myth."

"Just a figure of speech," he muttered. "What is it all *for*?"

I led the way down the walk, shoes clanging against the grating. I pulled a circuit board—multiple redundancy meant I'd do no harm. "Looks like any electronic device," Mangiara said.

"Sure," I said. "Just a breadboard, capacitors and resistors; these big black ones are memory chips. Individually, nothing much; put them together, and it's the second most powerful processor in the solar system."

"These are all memory chips?"

I shrugged. "Memory chips, modulator/demodulators for phone connections, peripheral control devices. Univac's the second most complicated machine ever conceived by the human mind; I'm not sure any single person could tell you what everything in the Well does."

"What's the most complicated—never mind. The Big Brain in Moscow, I assume."

I nodded.

Mangiara shivered. "This is where the FBI keeps its files."

"All the U.S. military and quasi-military agencies. Come on."

We took the elevator several levels down. Mangiara looked a little drawn. We found a terminal, and I signed on.

"Here's your credit record," I said, pulling it up. I studied it for a moment; "Pretty clean."

Mangiara grunted. "Anyone can do that?"

"No," I said. "But I am a big cheese here, you know. I can do just about anything short of shutting Univac down."

"This kind of thing could be abused," he said.

I sighed. "The people's state does not abuse the people's trust."

"Tell that to Stalin," he said.

"A transitional stage to true socialism. And, hum, here's your FBI dossier."

Mangiara turned white, and put his hand over the screen.

"Don't be silly, Frank," I said. "I could read it any time."

"Promise me you won't," he said.

I shrugged. "If you like," I said. But I did later, of course—well, wouldn't you? Dear Frank had a homosexual fling during college, it seems. Fairly petty, as mortal secrets go.

"Is the Big Brain much larger?" Mangiara asked.

I fluttered my hand: *comme ci, comme ça.* "Two orders of magnitude or so."

"A factor of a hundred?" Frank said, sounding impressed.

"Not so much, really," I said. "Two generations of technology; you're at most a decade behind us. And Univac would be larger if it weren't for the civilian machine in Boston, you know; it was foolish for your government to build a separate civilian processor."

He shrugged. "It would have endangered military security to use Univac for civilian ends," he said. "Besides, what's the big deal?"

"Isn't it obvious?" I said. "It all comes down to cost per operation; two separate processors are more than double the expense of one large one. A large one can time-share tasks, and therefore is always busy; small ones spend many cycles idle. And there are economies in programming, in data consistency, in maintenance, in manufacture."

"I see," said Mangiara thoughtfully. "It's like central planning."

I blinked at him. "What?"

"Competing firms duplicate effort; centralization is always efficient. Smoothly increasing economies of scale. Central planners can gather and process information more efficiently than scattered, individual businessmen; a central computer does the same."

"Smoothly increasing economies of scale, yes," I said slowly. "I hadn't seen the parallel, before."

The American government was like a weathervane, twisting this way and that as public opinion moved in its random, Brownian way. President Jackson kept on trying to find a nonexistent "third way" between socialism and the market; the economy continued its decline. I'd been admitted to Univac during one of the warmer moments in U.S./Soviet relations; then, things got chillier again. The military started forcing me to clear every change to Univac's software; and that meant endless, time-wasting obstruction. Work was increasingly frustrating; and so, I began to spend more time with Mangiara.

I wasn't getting much sleep; too many late nights. I found myself napping on the job between compiles. The constant white noise of the air-conditioning was annoyingly soothing. I think some of my co-workers caught me asleep, but were too much in awe of the august Soviet academician to make anything of it.

One night, as Frank was drifting off to sleep, he used the L word.

And I found myself wakeful. I did, I realized, feel an inordinate fondness for him. "You'll know when you're in love," my mother had always said; a blatant lie. A damned slippery thing, love. But I realized I could no longer dismiss our relationship as a fling.

One day, Frank called me at work. "Do you still want to see New York?" he asked.

"You bet," I said.

"I've wangled an assignment there," he said. "Actually it's one I think you can help me with."

He explained.

"Okay," I said. "I'll bring my terminal. Tell them to secure a line to Moscow, and keep it open for our arrival." With America's rickety telephone system, I knew, it might take hours to obtain a connection to the Big Brain otherwise.

Frank got us a private car on the train—"Being in the Department does have its perquisites," he said, somewhat apologetically. I shrugged; might as well take advantage of such bourgeois pleasures while they lasted. It was plush, mahogany and velvet, Negro attendants in crisp white coats, champagne in silver buckets.

It was amazing how much of the land between Washington and New York was unpeopled; forests and fields stretching on forever, pale green with the first growth of spring. America's poverty, the rarity of cars, had at least spared it the curse of suburban sprawl.

Pennsylvania Station was a rococo Gothic structure, obviously decades old, grimy, like every building in coal-burning America, but quite charming, in its way. That was another thing, it occurred to me, America had been spared through its poverty; in the Soviet Union, we had lost so many similar grand old structures, torn down in the name of progress.

The offices of the Pennsylvania Railroad Corporation—how absurdly romantic a name, how amazing that so archaic a thing as a limited liability corporation should still exist!—were in the building, in a warren of offices above the main chamber. We were quickly ushered into the president's office.

It was quite as grand as one might expect; the portrait of some great robber baron, white-haired and mustachioed, several times larger than life, glared down on the desk of his successor. Oriental carpets swept across hardwood floors; the desk itself looked as if it could accommodate a regiment.

"Mr. Mangiara," said the president, rising from a leather armchair. He was balding, in his fifties, clad in a Savile Row suit with collar so tight that flesh bulged out above it. "And—Madame Nazarian, I take it?"

I shook his hand. "Academician Nazarian," I said. "Or 'comrade' will do."

The president's eyebrows danced. "I'll refrain from 'comrade,' if you will," he said. "The Engineers' Union would about die laughing, if they heard me calling any-one 'comrade.' Mr. Mangiara says you have a demonstra-tion for me?"

"Is the line to Moscow open?"

He turned to a secretary, who sat by the desk with a telephone. She nodded. I went to the phone, took my ter-minal out of its case, set it up on the desk, and wired the modulator/demodulator into the phone.

"What is this device?" asked the president.

"A remote terminal," I said absently, as I signed onto the Brain.

"Chinese, I assume?" the president said.

I nodded; the best terminals were still made in the Soviet Union, but the Chinese made perfectly adequate ones. Colored pictures unfurled on the screen.

"Before I start," I said, "I'd like to ask a few questions."

"Certainly," said the president, taking a seat facing the screen.

"On average, what portion of your freight containers are idle?"

He blinked. "At any given time, roughly 40 percent of the total."

I nodded. "And if you have, say, two carloads of steel waiting at Red Hook, one bound for Allentown and another for Newark, how do you determine when they get picked up and how they get switched to the right trains?"

He shook his head. "I've got a corps of engineers sit-ting downstairs with calculators, bashing keys like mad in an effort to figure that out. Figuring how to switch loads around efficiently is the key to profitability, and it's no trivial task."

"You don't use a computer?" Frank asked.

"My good man," said the president. "We are not the government. The Penn may be a profitable road, but we can't afford aircraft carriers, lunar probes, or computers."

"Good," I said. "Here's the Soviet rail net; I'm centering on Moscow."

On the screen appeared a square, a hundred kilometers on a side. Rail lines in blue, moving trains in red. By various stations were blinking lights. I clicked on a light; up sprang a window. "Chimki station," I read. "Three loads grain, one of goods from the Red Star Consumer Electronics factory in Yaroslavl. Let's look at that." I clicked on it; up sprang another window. "Slated for pickup by the fast freight from Leningrad at 06:12 hours; switched at Moscow for the 08:48 to Baku; and then . . ."

"My God," said the president, staring at the screen entranced. "Can I change it, send it to Berlin, say?"

"You could if you were in the Ministry of Transport," I said. "I'm not authorized to do that."

"You can see the whole net?"

I clicked; the screen showed the whole Union, trunk lines in red, width of each line showing the volume of freight in transit at the moment. They pulsed slowly over time. I clicked in on the Pacific coast, Vladivostok and its burgeoning suburbs, the busy lines over the Amur and into thriving China.

"This is an amazing toy," said the president. "But what's the point?"

"This lets you monitor the rail net," I said, "but the net is operated, of course, by the Brain—every switch, every station, every connection. Total container utilization is . . ." I clacked at the keyboard briefly, "93.4 percent at the moment." The final digit flickered up and down; random fluctuations, really, carloads being switched across the whole Soviet network.

"That's impossible," the president said flatly.

"Not at all," I said. "You are trying to solve complex transit-time equations on mechanical calculators; it is absurd. The Big Brain can perform quadrillions of operations a second, more by the day as we add capacity. Optimizing the rail net uses a tiny fraction of its processing time. You could never afford the computing power yourself."

He grunted. "We still won't if we're nationalized," he pointed out.

"No," I said, "but even if Univac is a decade behind the Big Brain in technology, it can do a far better job than people punching buttons."

"Univac—is that possible?" he said, turning to Frank.

Frank nodded. "Of course," he said. "With the Cold War over, it's being turned to civilian use."

The president mulled that over for a moment. "And if, say, the Feds nationalize the Erie road and the New York Central, Univac will optimize their operations. If the Penn stays independent, we—we'll lose our shirts. We'll be out-competed."

"You must not think in those terms," I said. "It is not competition. It is planning. Separate companies duplicate effort; competition itself wastes resources."

To my surprise, he almost snarled at me. "Competition is the American way," he said intensely. "We're a nation built on individualism. Change France from a monarchy to a republic to socialism, it stays France. But what is America without individual rights, without capitalism?"

"We're going to have to find out," Frank said gently.

"There is no alternative. The verdict of history is in, and it says: Central planning works. Capitalism doesn't."

The president took a ragged breath. "I don't have a choice, do I?" he said bitterly. "Either we accept nationalization, or we'll be run into the ground."

Frank sighed. "No," he said reluctantly, "there's no point in running the Pennsylvania Railroad into the ground. If we have to, we'll nationalize it forcibly. But we'd rather have management's cooperation."

The president stared at that looming portrait on the wall for a long time. At last, he said, "If you don't mind, I'd like to ask you to leave. I have a great deal to discuss with the board, and with my subordinates."

I loved New York.

The contrast with Washington was stark. Here, healthy unions, powerful local government, and a strong civil-service ethic had done their best to create local socialism even under the capitalist government that savaged the rest of the nation. The results were everywhere, in the hopeful faces of children departing the city's excellent public schools, in the gleaming corridors of its municipal hospital system, in the pristine streets, even in the tiny, by American standards, rate of crime.

Oh, the city wasn't spared America's misery entirely; there were homeless everywhere, but at least here they were served by the city's first-rate welfare system. And the lack of economic opportunity meant the products of the city's superb educational system were, more often than not, forced to emigrate to find work that befitted their skills. By American standards, the city was well off, but by the standards of the socialist world, it was still quite poor.

Still, even that poverty had a charm. Here, there were the shabby bars, the small neighborhoods with strong sense of community, the comfortable blue-collar feeling I remembered from the Moscow of my youth—a Moscow now much altered by yuppification.

And though New York lagged far behind London as a capital of the Anglophone world's intellectual life, here there was Broadway, publishing, the remnants of America's film industry in flight from collapsing California, first-rate restaurants and museums. It was enormous fun, visiting New York, as a Soviet; with the ruble so strong and the dollar so weak, everything cost practically nothing at all.

It was wonderful seeing the Matisses at the Museum of Modern Art; so many masterpieces had been locked away behind the Iron Curtain for so many years. We hit Broadway every night, seeing things by obscure local playwrights like Neil Simon and George Lucas, as well as the usual Lloyd Webber and Brecht-Weill standards. We browsed for hours in the myriad used bookstores on Fourth Avenue, lunched at the sidewalk cafes among the glitter of Times Square, and even chartered a boat to tour the harbor and the sadly decayed ruins of the Statue of Liberty.

And we ate our way across the city, from Lutèce to sidewalk hot dog carts, from Sweets at the Fulton Fish Market to Sylvia's in Harlem.

On Thursday night, we rode the subway to Astoria, in Queens. The train moved swiftly, silently under the river.

"Amazing that you have such good subways, but can't build a decent car," I told Frank.

He shrugged. "The city has run the subways for

decades," he said. "One of the few planned institutions in a largely chaotic economy."

The Astoria station, in recognition of the ethnic background of the region's inhabitants, was decorated in Greek fashion: Corinthian columns, murals in patterns copied from ancient vases, wide marble steps leading upward.

We walked through busy streets, where children played stickball until their mothers called them in to dinner, to what Frank claimed was the best Greek restaurant in America.

Certainly the bouzouki music was joyful enough; Frank ordered us drinks, pointedly avoiding the retsina. As we waited for the calamari, he said, "I had an idea the other day."

"Is that unusual?" I asked.

"Thank you very much, Academician," he said. "There's a brain behind this pretty face, you know. I was thinking: what if centralized information processing were inefficient?"

"Say what?"

He spread his hands. "It's easy enough to devise a rationale," he said. "Let's suppose that information is best handled locally, that centralizing it simply overloads the people at the top with too much data. Suppose that individual managers, familiar with the problems they face every day, make better decisions than remote managers at headquarters. Suppose that competition works the way the old classical economists thought, to drive down prices and drive out the inefficient; that government monopoly is no better than private. . . ."

"You mean, suppose capitalism works better than Marxism," I said. "Patently, it doesn't. You can't set up controlled experiments in economics, but you can look at what happened in the past, and everything since the end of the Great Patriotic War says socialism is the better way."

"Elementary, my dear Engels," he said. "But just suppose America would have own the Cold War."

"Ah!" I said. "This is an exercise in alternate history. But you're varying natural law, rather than a particular historical event. Interesting. Germany would unify under the Federal Republic, Britain would be an economic laggard instead of a powerhouse, the population of the Soviet Pacific would still be under a million. . . ."

"And that of California would approach thirty million," he said. "Los Angeles, not Vladivostok, would be the film capital of the world."

"Let's not get carried away," I said. "China would be a backwater, and—why not?—Japan the great economic success story of the century."

"Who's getting carried away now?" he said. "What about computers?"

I blinked. "What about them?"

"If local managers work better than central planners, then won't small computers work better than a big central one?"

"You mean, distributed processing would work better than time-sharing," I mused. "The cost-per-MIPS curve would be the opposite of our world; little machines would prevail. There'd be a computer for every company, perhaps several—"

"Or one per person," said Frank.

"Per person?" I said. "That's absurd; a computer on every desk? The average person's bookkeeping needs are pretty minor. What would people use them for?"

"Who knows?" he said. "We don't know what software people would devise for such machines, because we haven't had the need or opportunity."

"The mind boggles," I said. The calamari came, and we ate for a while. "Well," I said, "thank Marx your world is mere fantasy."

"Why?" Frank asked.

"Would you really want capitalism to win out over socialism? The poor ignored, the environment raped, everyone living under a constant barrage of commercial blandishment? I realize times are hard, in the West, but it is all for the best."

Frank said, "Some people aren't too happy that civil liberties must be sacrificed to progress."

I waved my fork. "Can't be helped," I said. "There can be no right to property, because property is theft; no right to free speech, if that means promulgating lies."

We left the subway at Columbus Circle, detouring through Central Park on our way back to the Plaza. We walked hand in hand past fragrant forsythia. The park was almost crowded, other late-night strollers taking in the soft spring air. We passed a policeman, twirling his nightstick as he walked his beat; he beamed at us. "All the world loves lovers," Frank whispered, nuzzling my ear.

"Frank," I said, "have you given any thought to what we'll do when my stint here ends?"

"I've tried not to," he said, kissing a line down my neck.

"Stop it," I said. "I'm serious."

"I'm sure you could get a job here," Frank said. "There's no one in the country who knows what you know."

"No doubt," I said. "But I don't think I could stand Washington for very long."

"What about New York?"

"Better," I admitted. "But I have a career back home, you know. You'd like Moscow, Frank."

Frank scratched an ear. "What could I do there?" he said. "I don't have any particular technical skills, I don't speak the language. . . ."

"At least you'd be a citizen," I said.

There was a pause. "Nadia," he said. "I do believe you've just proposed."

I blinked; I guess I had.

"Ex-tree!" a newsboy shouted. "Airborne occupies Capitol! Reeeeedallabouuuutit!"

The coup had begun.

"I've got to get back to Washington," Frank said.

"I'm coming with you," I said.

"No! Absolutely not. You must go to the Soviet embassy here." There was one in New York, of course, representing the USSR to the United Nations.

"Why shouldn't I come?" I demanded.

"You don't know what will happen," he said grimly. "This might be over tomorrow, or it might be the beginning of a civil war. Either way, Soviet citizens are going to be at risk."

"It's not like I'm KGB," I protested. "I'm just a scientist. Why would—"

"You'll be safer here in New York, and safer still at the embassy. Why would you want to go to Washington, anyway? They won't let you in the Pentagon, you know; you won't be able to do any work."

"I didn't come to America to be safe," I said. "If that's what I wanted, I would have stayed in Moscow."

"This isn't a game, Nadia!" Frank said. "They kill people!"

I had no argument for that; there were at least a dozen dead, in the coup's first hours.

"I'll stay if you stay," I said.

Frank hesitated; "I—I can't," he said.

"Why not?"

He sighed, and said, somewhat self-deprecatingly, "Now is the time for all good men to come to the aid of their country."

I grew alarmed. "What the hell does that mean? What are you going to do?"

"I don't know," he said, spreading his hands. "Maybe nothing; maybe there's nothing to be done. But if they get away with this, it's back into the deep freeze, America digging itself a deeper grave. Do you think Radey will just cave in? And what about the president? I can't imagine the junta has his support."

"I see," I said. "You want the little woman safe so you can go off and play at revolution. The phrase 'sexist pig' springs to mind."

He gave me a lopsided smile. "A man's gotta do what a man's gotta do."

"Stuff it," I said.

We'd still be arguing, there in our room at the Plaza, if I hadn't beaten a tactical retreat. I let him go, letting him think I'd decamp to the embassy. I intended to follow him, on the next available train.

As I was packing, I got a call from Ambassador Vassilikov.

"Academician," he said, "good. I'm glad we caught you still in New York."

"Yes, Ambassador," I said. "What is it?"

"The Soviet government has issued an advisory, urging all Soviet citizens either to leave the country or seek asylum at the embassy. I suggest you go to the embassy in New York; I've informed Ambassador Chernikov that you'll be coming, and they—"

"Thank you for your concern, Ambassador," I said, "but I intend to return to Washington, to witness these historic events first hand."

There was silence on the line, for a while. "Academician," Vassilikov said, "you are a highly educated woman. The government of the Union of Soviet Socialist Republics has invested hundreds of thousands of rubles in your skills."

"And what of it?" I said.

"We have no intention of risking that investment. I am authorized to order you to go to the embassy."

I felt a chill. He had not actually issued the order; if he did, it would become a permanent blot on my record.

"I understand, Ambassador."

"You will go?"

"No."

"Academician Nazarian," he said. "You do not have the right to defy the state. Your duty is to serve the people, not to act on whim."

He was absolutely in the right; there is no place for— for individual liberty, as Frank would have called it—in the socialist order. I was privileged by intelligence and education, and by my very privilege, compelled to serve. I was unable to respond.

"Academician," the ambassador said, "I *am* ordering you to go to the embassy. Do you understand?"

"Yes," I whispered.

"Will you comply?"

"No," I said.

I put the receiver down, feeling sick.

There went my career.

Union Station had become the nerve center of the resistance; Senator Radey ate and slept there, surrounded by half the Congress and a substantial part of Washington's population, rallying in resistance to the fascist regime. From across the country, people came by rail to join them, sleeping in the surrounding streets despite the chill April air. It was a precarious time; not a mile distant, the junta's troops guarded the Capitol and the White House. Among the communists, there were only light weapons; a few rifles, rather more handguns. If the fascists chose to attack, the resistance could be crushed in an afternoon.

But the junta seemed paralyzed, unable to move. They were seemingly surprised at the strength of the resistance; perhaps they had expected general support. Certainly, President Jackson and his half-hearted reforms enjoyed no great popularity; but the junta had misread the nature of the people's discontent. There was no desire for a return to the days of the military-industrial complex, no nostalgia for nuclear terror and gradual decline. To most people, the communist program still seemed too radical; but there was even less support for a military regime.

They might have succeeded, if Jackson had come out

in their support; but he remained silent, a prisoner at Camp David.

Frank was furious when he learned I was there. But I was determined to stay.

My skills even came in handy; I had my terminal, and dialed into Univac. The military was divided; indeed, shortly after I arrived, several tanks from the 7th Cavalry arrived, and took up stations protecting the station. Perhaps Univac's system operators sympathized with the resistance; perhaps, in the confusion, the junta had merely neglected to order restrictions on public access to Univac.

Whatever the case, with my account's privileges, it was a simple matter to hack into the files that recorded the junta's orders and troop movements. We could see what they were doing, virtually as they began to do it.

And we made good use of our intelligence; no doubt, you've seen the footage, people lying down in front of tanks to prevent their entry into Washington, our people haranguing the advancing troops and, not infrequently, persuading them to defect.

It was a tense, glorious time, marred only by the growing rift between Frank and me.

On the afternoon of April 10, Radey decided it was time to make a move. You've seen that speech, I suppose, the senator clambering onto a tank to harangue the crowd—no doubt the most famous image of the April Revolution.

No, the second most famous one.

After the speech, he led the way down Constitution Avenue. Frank was at the van; I had wanted to march with him, but he pointedly refused, insisting I stay at Union Station.

I was not about to do that. Still, we were widely separated in the order of march.

We skirted the troops surrounding the Capitol, and headed west down the Mall, past the brown towers of the Smithsonian. They say a hundred thousand people marched that day; I believe it. It was a sea of humanity, moving across the green, the vast Mall carpeted with human forms.

At the Washington Monument, we turned right, walking through the needle's shadow. We crossed Constitution Avenue again, and walked across the Ellipse— directly toward the White House gate. I could glimpse it only in snatches, through the crowd ahead; I might be fool enough to be here, thought I, but I was not such a fool as to be at the front of what might quickly become a disaster.

At the center of the gate was a Patton tank; and behind the iron fence surrounding the White House were armed soldiers of the 101st, defending what had become the junta's headquarters.

"Halt!" shouted a soldier through a megaphone. "We have orders to defend this gate."

Radey shouted something in response; so far back, I did not hear what he said. Later, I learned he had asked if they would fire on fellow Americans.

There was silence for a moment. Then, "We have our orders," said the soldier.

The crowd was motionless for a long moment. And then, it began to move forward again. Heart in throat, I moved with it.

There are moments frozen in time, instants that can be remembered with perfect clarity. The sky was achingly blue above, the sun bright, still high but moving toward the west. Though the crowd had chanted during the march, now it was curiously silent, the red banners audibly flapping, the soft sound of thousands of feet walking across grass. The breeze was cool, from the southwest, bearing the sweet scent of cherry blossoms from the trees around the Tidal Basin; indeed, the trees were already beginning to shed their petals, and little motes of pink skittered across the grass, driven by the freshening breeze. That breeze was cool on the skin; though the sun was warm, it was April still. Though the human world might be in turmoil, the natural world was calm, serene. So much for Shakespeare.

Those at the front neared the iron bars. It began to appear that the soldiers' threat was a bluff; they seemed almost visibly to dither, unprepared to face such massive defiance. . . .

And then, the quiet was shattered by a submachine-gun's staccato rap.

The crowd gave almost an animal roar; and while there might have been confusion at the front of the mob, the rest surged forward. The iron fence gave way, falling before massed bodies. . . .

And another gun rang out; another and another, explosion after explosion rattling all across the line, panicked soldiers firing wildly into the mob, the noise punctuated by the tank cannon's boom.

If there are moments that are frozen in time, so there are moments that are shattered into a thousand jangling images. People screaming, fleeing in all directions; blood spraying across space, wounded dragging themselves desperately away, the slow or unwary trampled under foot, grass churned to mud, screams of terror and moans of agony. I fell and was trod upon, but suffered no worse than bruises. I fled, I don't know why, down through West Potomac Park.

Encroaching night found me squatting under Lincoln's massive feet, shivering more from remembered terror than the cold.

At last, I rose and walked to the Soviet embassy on 16th. A jeepful of soldiers sped past me on the way, but apparently decided that a single, haggard woman violating curfew was not worth bothering.

Seven hundred people died that day; the casualties were in the thousands. The following morning, the TV showed helicopter footage of the Ellipse and the White House lawn, bodies still lying everywhere, black gouges in the turf where tanks had passed.

A thin tendril of smoke rose from the East Wing, which the demonstrators had set afire; but the flames had soon been suppressed.

I called Frank's number again and again, but there was no reply.

It was days before I learned: Frank was among the dead. He had taken a bullet in the gut, and had bled to death there on the lawn. Washington's ambulance corps had, with few exceptions, been too craven to rescue the wounded. With help, he might have lived.

The storming of the White House was, they say, the turning point, the moment when the junta realized the scantiness of its support, when public opinion crystalized against them. When President Jackson was released, he condemned them thoroughly, and that was the coup's end.

* * *

And I; well, the state has forgiven me. Ambassador Vassilikov wept when he learned about Frank; he muttered something about "the Slavic soul," and told me that love is sufficient reason to defy the state—an unorthodox opinion. "I shall remove any mention of the incident from your record," he said, "if you agree to tell your story for publication." And so I shall.

My sojourn in America has descended by degrees, from high spirits to agony; if life in Moscow was missing something, if it was too smooth, too easy, well, the lack has been remedied, to excess. I am looking forward to return.

But I am not wholly in despair.

America has years of desolation to endure, and possibly rivers of blood still to shed; even in Western Europe, the transition to socialism has proven more difficult than expected, and here, the market's last bastion, it will be more difficult still.

I never saw Frank's corpse, not until it rested, features composed, in a coffin; but I have an image of it lying there on the White House lawn, atop the black cast-iron bars of the fallen fence, blank eyes staring wildly, blood pooling on the ground. The sun shines, the sky is blue, the breeze scatters pink cherry blossoms across the unknowing form. The Japanese who gave those trees would understand, I think; how very Oriental, to see beauty in death.

Frank didn't die in vain. The red flags rise across America. The specter of nuclear oblivion haunts the world no longer; socialism's triumph promises a better life for all. Beyond these times of trouble, we can glimpse a future of peace, and prosperity.

As Marx foretold, the victory of the proletariat is fore-ordained. But oh, it is we who suffer, ground in history's inexorable wheels.

And yet, and yet, it is all worthwhile.

The West is Red; and Frank Mangiara's blood helped to dye it so.

The Forest of Time

Michael F. Flynn

Michael F. Flynn is not only one of the most skilled new writers of the last few years, but that singular anomaly, a hard science fiction writer whose work, at least until recently, was set almost entirely in the past, present, or very near future. Here he shows us an alternate world in which the thirteen American Colonies failed to unify themselves—but that's just the beginning. If you pursue the full implications of a new universe being created every time a choice is made, you get not just a fork, or even a tree, but a veritable forest of time. Now, if you're a lost traveler from another branch of that tree, how could you prove it—or find your way home?

It was the autumn of the year and the trees were already showing their death-colors. Splashes of orange and red and gold rustled in the canopy overhead. Oberleutnant Rudolf Knecht, Chief Scout of the Army of the Kittatinny, wore the same hues mottled for his uniform as he rode through the forest. A scout's badge, carefully rusted to dullness, was pinned to his battered campaign cap.

Knecht swayed easily to the rhythm of his horse's gait

as he picked his way up the trail toward Fox Gap Fortress. He kept a wary eye on the surrounding forest. Periodically, he twisted in the saddle and gazed thoughtfully at the trail where it switchbacked below. There had been no sign of pursuit so far. Knecht believed his presence had gone undetected; but even this close to home, it paid to be careful. The list of those who wanted Knecht dead was a long one; and here, north of the Mountain, it was open season on Pennsylvanians.

There were few leaves on the forest floor, but the wind gathered them up and hurled them in mad dances. The brown, dry, crisp leaves of death. Forerunners of what was to be. Knecht bowed his head and pulled the jacket collar tighter about his neck.

Knecht felt the autumn. It was in his heart and in his bones. It was in the news he carried homeward. Bad news even in the best of times, which these were not. Two knick regiments had moved out of the Hudson Valley into the Poconos. They were camped with the yankees. Brothers-in-arms, as if last spring's fighting had never happened. General Schneider's fear: New York and Wyoming had settled their quarrel and made common cause.

Common cause. Knecht chewed on his drooping moustache, now more grey than brown. No need to ask the cause. There was little enough that yanks and knicks could agree on, but killing Pennsylvanians was one.

He remembered that General Schneider was inspecting the fortress line and would probably be waiting for him at Fox Gap. He did not feel the pleasure he usually felt on such occasions. *Na, Konrad, meiner Alt*, he thought. What will you do now? What a burden I must lay upon your shoulders. God help the Commonwealth of Pennsylvania.

He pulled in on the reins. There was a break in the trees here and through it he could see the flank of Kittatinny Mountain. A giant's wall, the ridge ran away, straight and true, becoming bluer and hazier as its forested slopes faded into the distance. Spots of color decorated the sheer face of the Mountain. Fox Gap, directly above him, was hidden by the forest canopy; but Knecht thought he could just make out the fortresses at Wind Gap and Tott Gap.

As always, the view comforted him. There was no way across the Kittatinny, save through the Gaps. And there was no way through the Gaps.

Twenty years since anyone has tried, he thought. He kicked at the horse and they resumed their slow progress up the trail. Twenty years ago; and we blew the knick riverboats off the water.

That had been at Delaware Gap, during the Piney War. Knecht sighed. The Piney War. It seemed such a long time ago. A different world; more innocent, somehow. Or perhaps he had only been younger. He remembered how he had marched away, his uniform new and sharply creased. Adventure was ahead of him, and his father's anger behind. I am too old for such games, he told himself. I should be sitting by the fire, smoking my pipe, telling stories to my grandchildren.

He chewed again on his moustache hairs and spit them out. There had never been any children; and now, there never would be. He felt suddenly alone.

Just as well, he thought. The stories I have to tell are not for the ears of youngsters. What were the stories, really? A crowd of men charged from the trench. Later, some of them came back. What more was there to say? Once, a long time ago, war had been glamorous, with pageantry and uniforms to shame a peacock. Now it was only necessary, and the uniforms were the color of mud.

There was a sudden noise in the forest to his right. Snapping limbs and a muffled grunt. Knecht started, and chastised himself. A surprised scout is often a dead one as well. He pulled a large bore pistol from his holster and dismounted. The horse, well-trained, held still. Knecht stepped into the forest and crouched behind a tall birch tree. He listened.

The noise continued. Too much noise, he decided. Perhaps an animal?

Then he saw the silhouette of a man thrashing through the underbrush, making no attempt at silence. Knecht watched over his gunsight as the man blundered into a stickerbush. Cursing, the other stopped and pulled the burrs from his trousers.

The complete lack of caution puzzled Knecht. The no-man's-land between Pennsylvania and the Wyoming was no place for carelessness. The other was either very foolish or very confident.

The fear ran through him like the rush of an icy mountain stream. Perhaps the bait in a trap; something to hold his attention? He jerked round suddenly, looking behind him, straining for the slightest sign.

But there was nothing save the startled birds and the evening wind.

Knecht blew his breath out in a gust. His heart was pounding. *I am getting too old for this.* He felt foolish and his cheeks burned, even though there was no one to see.

The stranger had reached the trail and stood there brushing himself off. He was short and dark complexioned. On his back he wore a rucksack, connected by wires to a device on his belt. Knecht estimated his age at thirty, but the unkempt hair and beard made him look older.

He watched the man pull a paper from his baggy canvas jacket. Even from where he crouched, Knecht could see it was a map, handsomely done in many colors. A stranger with a map on the trail below Fox Gap. Knecht made a decision and stepped forth, cocking his pistol.

The stranger spun and saw Knecht. Closer up, Knecht could see the eyes bloodshot with fatigue. After a nervous glance at the scout's pistol, the stranger smiled and pointed to the map. "Would you believe it?" he asked in English. "I think I'm lost."

Knecht snorted. "I would not believe it," he answered in the same language. "Put in the air your hands up."

The stranger complied without hesitation. Knecht reached out and snatched the map from his hand.

"That's a Pennsylvania Dutch accent, isn't it?" asked his prisoner. "It sure is good to hear English again."

Knecht looked at him. He did not understand why that should be good. His own policy when north of the Mountain was to shoot at English-speaking voices. He gave quick glances to the map while considering what to do.

"Are you hunting? I didn't know it was hunting season."

The scout saw no reason to answer that, either. In a way, he *was* hunting, but he doubted the prisoner had meant it that way.

"At least you can tell me where in the damn world I am!"

Knecht was surprised at the angry outburst. Considering who held the pistol on whom, it seemed a rash act at best. He grinned and held up the map. "Naturally, you know where in the damn world you are. While you have this map, it gives only one possibility. You are the spy, *nicht wahr?* But, to humor you . . ." He pointed northward with his chin. "Downtrail is the Wyoming, where your Wilkes-Barre masters your report in vain will await. Uptrail is *Festung* Fox Gap . . . and your cell."

The prisoner's shoulders slumped. Knecht looked at the sun. With the prisoner afoot, they should still reach the fort before nightfall. He decided to take the man in for questioning. That would be safer than interrogating him on the spot, Knecht glanced at the map once more. Then he frowned and looked more closely. "United States Geological Survey?" he asked the prisoner. "What are the United States?"

He did not understand why the prisoner wept.

There was a storm brewing in the northwest and the wind whipped through Fox Gap, tearing at the uniform blouses of the sentries, making them grab for their caps. In the dark, amid the rain and lightning, at least one man's grab was too late and his fellows laughed coarsely as he trotted red-faced to retrieve it. It was a small diversion in an otherwise cheerless duty.

What annoyed Festungskommandant Vonderberge was not that Scout Knecht chose to watch the chase also, but that he chose to do so while halfway through the act of entering Vonderberge's office. The wind blew a blizzard of paper around the room and Vonderberge's curses brought Knecht fully into the office, closing the door behind him.

Knecht surveyed the destruction. Vonderberge shook his head. He looked at Knecht. "These bits of paper," he said. "These orders and memoranda and requisitions, they are the nerve messages of the Army. A thousand messages a day cross my desk, Rudi; and not a one of them but deals with matters of the greatest military import." He clucked sadly. "Our enemies need not defeat us in the field. They need only sabotage our filing system and we are lost." He rose from his desk and knelt, gathering up papers. "Come, Rudi, quickly. Let us set things aright, else the Commonwealth is lost!"

Knecht snorted. Vonderberge was mocking him with this elaborate ridicule. In his short time at Fox Gap, Knecht had encountered the Kommandant's strange humor several times. Someone had once told him that Vonderberge had always dreamed of becoming a scientist, but that his father had pressured him into following the family's military tradition. As a result, his command style was, well, unorthodox.

Na, *we all arrive by different paths,* Knecht thought. *I joined to* spite *my father.* It startled him to recall that his father had been dead for many years and that they had never become reconciled.

Knecht stooped and helped collect the scattered documents. Because he was a scout, however, he glanced at their contents as he did so; and as he absorbed their meaning, he read more and collected less.

One sheet in particular held his attention. When he looked up from it, he saw Vonderberge waiting patiently behind his desk. He was leaning back in a swivel chair, his arms crossed over his chest. There was a knowing smile on the Kommandant's thin aristocratic face.

"Is this all . . ." Knecht began.

"Ach, nein," the Kommandant answered. "There is much, much more. However," he added pointedly, "it is no longer in order."

"But, this is from the prisoner, Nando Kelly?"

"Hernando is the name; not Herr Nando. It is Spanish, I believe." Vonderberge clucked sadly over the documents and began setting them in order.

Knecht stood over the desk. "But this is crazy stuff!" He waved the sheet in his hand. Vonderberge grabbed for it vainly. Knecht did not notice. "The man must be crazy!" he said.

Vonderberge paused and cocked an eyebrow at him. "Crazy?" he repeated. "So says the Hexmajor. He can support his opinion with many fine words and a degree from Franklin University. I am but a simple soldier, a servant of the Commonwealth, and cannot state my own diagnosis in so impressive a manner. On what basis, Rudi, do *you* say he is crazy?"

Knecht sputtered. "If it is not crazy to believe in countries that do not exist, I do not know what is. I have looked on all our world maps and have found no United States, not even in deepest Asia."

Vonderberge smiled broadly. He leaned back again, clasping his hands behind his neck. "Oh, I know where the United States are," he announced smugly.

Knecht made a face. "Tell me then, O Servant of the Commonwealth. Where are they?"

Vonderberge chuckled. "If you can possibly remember so far back as your childhood history lessons, you may recall something of the Fourth Pennamite War."

Knecht groaned. The Pennamite Wars. He could never remember which was which. Both Connecticut and Pennsylvania had claimed the Wyoming Valley and had fought over it several times, a consequence of the English king's cavalier attitude toward land titles. The fourth one? Let's see . . . 1769, 1771, 1775 . . .

"No," he said finally. "I know nothing at all of the time between 1784 and 1792. I never heard of Brigadier Wadsworth and the Siege of Forty-Fort, or how General Washington and his Virginia militia were mowed down in the crossfire."

"Then you must also be ignorant," continued the Kommandant, "of the fact that the same Congress that sent the General to stop the fighting was also working on a plan to unify the thirteen independent states. Now what do you suppose the name of that union was to be?"

Knecht snorted. "I would be a great fool if I did not say 'The United States.' "

Vonderberge clapped. "Right, indeed, Rudi. Right, indeed. Dickinson was president of the Congress, you know."

Knecht was surprised. "Dickinson? John Dickinson, our first Chancellor?"

"The very same. Being a Pennsylvanian, I suppose the yankee settlers thought he was plotting something by dispatching the supposedly neutral Virginians. . . . Well, of course, with Washington dead, and old Franklin incapacitated by a stroke at the news, the whole thing fell apart. Maryland never did sign the Articles of Confederation; and as the fighting among the states grew worse—over the Wyoming, over Vermont, over Chesapeake fishing rights, over the western lands—the others seceded also. All that Adams and the radicals salvaged was their New England Confederation; and even that was almost lost during Shay's Rebellion and General Lincoln's coup. . . ."

Knecht interrupted. "So this almost-was United States

was nothing more than a wartime alliance to throw the English out. It was stillborn in the 1780s. Yet Kelly's map is dated this year."

"*Ja*, the map," mused Vonderberge, as if to himself. "It is finely drawn, is it not? And the physical details—the mountains and streams—are astonishingly accurate. Only the man-made details are bizarre. Roads and dams that are not there. A great open space called an 'airport.' Towns that are three times their actual size. Did you see how large Easton is shown to be?"

Knecht shrugged. "A hoax."

"Such an elaborate hoax? To what purpose?"

"To fool us. He is a spy. If messages can be coded, why not maps?"

"Ah. You say he is a spy. The Hexmajor says he is mad and the map is the complex working out of a system of delusions. I say . . ." He picked up a sheaf of papers from his desk and handed them to Knecht. "I say you should read Kelly's notebook."

The scout glanced at the typewritten pages. "These are transcripts," he pointed out. "They were done on the machine in your office. I recognize the broken stem on the r's." He made it a statement.

Vonderberge threw his head back and laughed, slapping the arm of the chair. "Subtlety does not become you, Rudi," he said looking at him. "Yes, they are transcripts. General Schneider has the originals. When I showed the journal to him, he wanted to read it himself. I made copies of the more interesting entries."

Knecht kept his face neutral. "You, and the General, and the Hexmajor. *Ach!* Kelly is *my* prisoner. I have yet to interview him. I gave you his possessions for safe-keeping, not for distribution."

"Oh, don't be so official, Rudi. What are we, Prussians? You were resting, I was bored, and the journal was here. Go ahead. Read it now." Vonderberge waved an inviting hand.

Knecht frowned and picked up the stack. The first few pages were filled with equations. Strange formulae full of inverted A's and backward E's. Knecht formed the words under his breath. ". . . twelve dimensional open manifold . . . Janatpour hypospace . . . oscillatory time . . ." He shook his head. "Nonsense," he muttered.

He turned the page and came to a text:

I am embarking on a great adventure. Does that sound grandiose? Very well, let it. Grandiose ideas deserve grandiose expression. Tomorrow, I make my first long range Jump. Sharon claims that it is too soon for such a field test, but she is too cautious. I've engineered the equipment. I know what it can do. Triple redundancy on critical circuits. Molecular foam memory. I *am* a certified reliability engineer, after all. The short Jumps were all successful. So what could go wrong?

Rosa could answer that. Sweet Rosa. She is not an engineer. She only sees that it is dangerous. And what can I say? It is dangerous. But when has anything perfectly safe been worth doing? The equipment is as safe as I can make it. I tried to explain about probabilities and hazard analysis to Rosa last night, but she only cried and held me tighter.

She promised to be in the lab a week from tomorrow when I make my return Jump. A week away from Rosa. A week to study a whole new universe. *Madre de Dios!* A week can be both a moment and an eternity.

Knecht chewed his moustache. The next page was titled "Jump #1" followed by a string of twelve "coordinate settings." Then there were many pages which Knecht skimmed, detailing a world that never was. In it, the prehistoric Indians had not exterminated the Ice Age big game. Instead, they had tamed the horse, the elephant, and the camel and used the animal power to keep pace technologically with the Old World. Great civilizations arose in the river valleys of the Colorado and Rio Grande, and mighty empires spread across the Caribbean. Vikings were in Vinland at the same time the Iroquois were discovering Ireland. By the present day there were colonies on Mars.

Knecht shook his head. "Not only do we have a United States," he muttered.

The next entry was briefer and contained the first hint of trouble. It was headed "Jump #2." Except for the reversal of plus and minus signs, the coordinate settings were identical with the first set.

A slight miscalculation. I should be back in the lab with Rosa, but I'm in somebody's apartment, instead. It's still Philly out the window—though a shabbier, more run-down Philly than I remember. I must be close to my home timeline because I can recognize most of the University buildings. There's a flag that looks like the stars and stripes on the flagpole in front of College Hall. There's something or other black hanging from the lamppost, but I can't make it out.

Well, work first; tourism later. I bet I'll need a vernier control. There must be a slight asymmetry in the coordinates.

Knecht skipped several lines of equations and picked up the narrative once more.

I must leave immediately! That black thing on the lamppost kept nagging at the back of my mind. So I got out my binoculars and studied it. It was a nun in a black habit, hanging in a noose. Hanging a long time, too, by the looks of it. Farther along the avenue, I could see bodies on all the lampposts. Then the wind caught the flag by College Hall and I understood. In place of the stars there was a swastika . . .

Jump #3. Coordinates . . .
Wrong again. I was too hasty in leaving the Nazi world. The settings were not quite right, but I think I know what went wrong now. The very act of my Jumping has created new branches in time and changed the oscillatory time-distance between them. On the shorter Jumps it didn't matter much, but on the longer ones . . .
I think I finally have the calculations right. This is a pleasant world where I am, and—thanks to Goodman deVeres and his wife—I've had the time to think the problem through. It seems the Angevin kings still rule in this world and my host has described what seems like scientific magic. Superstition? Mass delusion? I'd like to stay and study this world, but I'm already a week overdue. Darling Rosa must be frantic with worry. I think of her often.

The next page was headed "Jump #4" with settings but no narrative entry. This was followed by . . .

Jump #5. Coordinates unknown.

Damn! It didn't work out right and I was almost killed. This isn't an experiment any more. Armored samurai in a medieval Philadelphia? Am I getting closer to or farther from Home? I barely escaped them. I rode north on a stolen horse and Jumped as soon as my charge built up. Just in time, too—my heart is still pounding. No time for calculations. I don't even know what the settings were.

Note: the horse Jumped with me. The field must be wider than I thought. A clue to my dilemma? I need peace and quiet to think this out. I could find it with Goodman deVeres. I have the coordinates for his world. But his world isn't where I left it. When I Jumped, I moved it. Archimedes had nothing on me. Haha. That's a joke. Why am I bothering with this stupid journal?

I dreamed of Rosa last night. She was looking for me. I was right beside her but she couldn't see me. When I awoke, it was still dark. Off to the north there was a glow behind the crest of the hills. City lights? If that is South Mountain, it would be Allentown or Bethlehem on the other side—or their analogs in this world. I should know by next night. So far I haven't seen anyone; but I must be cautious.

I've plenty of solitude here and now. That slag heap I saw from the mountain must have been Bethlehem, wiped out by a single bomb. The epicenter looked to be about where the steelworks once stood. It happened a long time ago, by the looks of things. Nothing living in the valley but a few scrub plants, insects, and birds.

I rode out as fast as I could to put that awful sight behind me. I didn't dare eat anything. My horse did and is dead for it. Who knows what sort of adaptations have fit the grass for a radioactive environment? I may already have stayed too long. I must Jump, but I daren't materialize inside a big city. I'll hike up into the northern hills before I Jump again.

Knecht turned to the last page. Jump #6. Settings, but no notes. There was a long silence while Knecht digested what he had read. Vonderberge was watching him. Outside, the wind rattled the windows. A nearby lightning strike caused the lights to flicker.

"Herr Festungskommandant . . ."

"His last Jump landed him right in your lap out on the Wyoming Trail."

"Herr Festungskommandant . . ."

"And instead of the solitude he sought, he's gotten solitude of another sort."

"You don't believe . . ."

"Believe?" Vonderberge slammed his palm down on the desk with unexpected violence. He stood abruptly and walked three quick paces to the window, where he gazed out at the storm. His fingers locked tightly behind his back. "Why not believe?" he whispered, his back to the room. "Somewhere there is a world where Heinrich Vonderberge is not trapped in a border fort on the edge of a war with the lives of others heavy on his back. He is in a laboratory, experimenting with electrical science, and he is happy."

He turned and faced Knecht, self-possessed once more.

"What if," he said. "What if the Pennamite Wars had not turned so vicious? If compromise had been possible? Had they lived, might not Washington and Franklin have forged a strong union, with the General as king and the

Doctor as prime minister? Might not such a union have spread west, crushing Sequoyah and Tecumseh and their new Indian states before the British had gotten them properly started? Can you imagine a single government ruling the entire continent?"

Knecht said, "No," but Vonderberge continued without hearing him.

"Suppose," he said, pacing the room, "every time an event happens, several worlds are created. One for each outcome." He paused and smiled at Knecht. "Suppose Pennsylvania had not intervened in the Partition of New Jersey? No Piney War. New York and Virginia cut us off from the sea. Konrad Schneider does not become a great general, nor Rudi Knecht a famous spy. Somewhere there is such a world. Somewhere . . . close.

"Now suppose further that on one of these . . . these *moeglichwelten* a man discovers how to cross from one to another. He tests his equipment, makes many notes, then tries to return. But he fails!"

A crash of thunder punctuated the Kommandant's words. Knecht jumped.

"He fails," Vonderberge continued, "because in the act of jumping he has somehow changed the 'distance.' So, on his return, he undershoots. At first, he is not worried. He makes a minor adjustment and tries again. And misses again. And again, and again, and again."

Vonderberge perched on the corner of his desk, his face serious. "Even if there is only one event each year, and each event had but two outcomes, why then in ten years do you know how many worlds there would have to be?"

Knecht shook his head dumbly.

"A thousand, Rudi, and more. And in another ten

years, a thousand for each of those. Time is like a tree; a forest of trees. Always branching. One event a year? Two possible outcomes? *Ach!* I am a piker! In all of time, how many, many worlds there must be. How to find a single twig in such a forest?"

Knecht could think of nothing to say. In the quiet of the office, the storm without seemed louder and more menacing.

In the morning, of course, with the dark storm only muddy puddles, Knecht could dismiss the Kommandant's remarks as a bad joke. "What if?" was a game for children; a way of regretting the past. Knecht's alert eye had not missed the row of technofiction books in Vonderberge's office. "What if?" was a common theme in that genre, Knecht understood.

When he came to Kelly's cell to interrogate the prisoner, he found that others had preceded him. The guard at the cell door came to attention, but favored Knecht with a conspiratorial wink. From within the cell came the sound of angry voices. Knecht listened closely, his ear to the thick, iron door; but he could make out none of the words. He straightened and looked a question at the guard. The latter rolled his eyes heavenward with a look of resigned suffering. Knecht grinned.

"So, Johann," he said. "How long has this been going on?"

"Since sun-up," was the reply. "The Kommandant came in early to talk to the prisoner. He'd been in there an hour when the Hexmajor arrived. Then there was thunder-weather, believe me, sir." Johann smiled at the thought of two officers bickering.

Knecht pulled two cigars from his pocket humidor and

offered one to the guard. "Do you suppose it is safe to leave them both locked in together?" He laughed. "We may as well relax while we wait. That is, if you are permitted . . ."

The guard took the cigar. "The Kommandant is more concerned that we are experts in how to shoot our rifles than in how to sneak a smoke." There was a pause while Knecht lit his cigar. He puffed a moment, then remarked, "This is good leaf. Kingdom of Carolina?"

Knecht nodded. He blew out a great cloud of acrid smoke. "You know you should not have allowed either of them in to see the prisoner before me."

"Well, sir. You know that and I know that; but the Hexmajor and the Kommandant, they make their own rules." The argument in the cell reached a crescendo. Johann flinched. "Unfortunately, they do not make the *same* rules."

"Hmph. Is your Kommandant always so . . . impetuous?" He wanted to know Heinrich Vonderberge better; and one way to do that was to question the men who followed him.

The guard frowned. "Sir, things may be different in the Scout Corps, but the Kommandant is no fool, in spite of his ways. He always has a reason for what he does. Why, no more than two months ago—this was before you were assigned here—he had us counting the number of pigeons flying north. He plotted it on a daily chart." Johann laughed at the memory. "Then he sent us out to intercept a raiding party from the Nations. You see, you know how the sachems still allow private war parties? Well . . ."

There was a banging at the cell door and Johann broke off whatever yarn he had been about to spin and opened it. Vonderberge stalked out.

"We will see about that!" he snapped over his shoulder, and pushed past Knecht without seeing him. Knecht took his cigar from his mouth and looked from the Kommandant to the doorway. Hexmajor Ochsenfuss stood there, glaring at the Kommandant's retreating form. "Fool," the doctor muttered through clenched teeth. Then he noticed Knecht.

"And what do *you* want? My patient is highly agitated. He cannot undergo another grilling."

Knecht smiled pleasantly. "Why, Herr Doctor. He is not your patient until I say so. Until then, he is my prisoner. I found him north of the Mountain. It is my function to interview him."

"He is a sick man, not one of your spies."

"The men I interview are never *my* spies. I will decide if he is . . . sick."

"That is a medical decision, not a military one. Have you read his journal? It is the product of a deluded mind."

"If it is what it appears to be. It could also be the product of a clever mind. Madness as a cover for espionage? Kelly would not be the first spy with an outrageous cover."

He walked past the doctor into the cell. Ochsenfuss followed him. Kelly looked up from his cot. He sat on the edge, hands clasped tightly, leaning on his knees. A night's sleep had not refreshed him. He pointed at Knecht.

"I remember you," he said. "You're the guy that caught me."

The Hexmajor forestalled Knecht's reply. "*Bitte,* Herr Leutnant," he said in Pennsylvaanish. "You must speak in our own tongue."

"Warum?" Knecht answered, with a glance at Kelly. "The prisoner speaks English, *nicht wahr?*"

"Ah, but he must understand German, at least a little. Either our own dialect or the European. Look at him. He is not from the West, despite his Spanish forename. Their skin color is much darker. Nor is he from Columbia, Cumberland, or the Carolina Kingdom. Their accents are most distinctive. And no white man from Virginia on north could be ignorant of the national tongue of Pennsylvania."

"Nor could any European," finished Knecht. "Not since 1917, at any rate. I cannot fault your logic, Herr Doctor; but then, why . . ."

"Because for some reason he has suppressed his knowledge of German. He has retreated from reality, built himself fantasy worlds. If we communicate only in Pennsylvaanish as we are doing now, his own desire to communicate will eventually overcome his 'block' (as we call it); and the process of drawing him back to the real world will have begun."

Knecht glanced again at the prisoner. "On the other hand, it is my duty to obtain information. If the prisoner will speak in English, then so will I."

"But . . ."

"And I must be alone." Knecht tapped his lapel insignia meaningfully. The double-X of the Scout Corps.

Ochsenfuss pursed his lips. Knecht thought he would argue further, but instead, he shrugged. "Have it your way, then; but remember to treat him carefully. If I am right, he could easily fall into complete withdrawal." He nodded curtly to Knecht and left.

Knecht stared at the closed door. He disliked people who "communicated." Nor did he think Vonderberge was a fool like Ochsenfuss had said. Still, he reminded himself, the Hexmajor had an impressive list of cures to his credit. Especially of battle fatigue and torture cases. Ochsenfuss was no fool, either.

He stuck his cigar back between his teeth. Let's get this over with, he thought. But he knew it would not be that easy.

Within an hour Knecht knew why the others had quarreled. Kelly could describe his fantasy world and the branching timelines very convincingly. But he had convinced Vonderberge that he was telling the truth and Ochsenfuss that he was mad. The conclusions were incompatible; the mixture, explosive.

Kelly spoke freely in response to Knecht's questions. He held nothing back. At least, the scout reminded himself, he *appeared* to hold nothing back. But who knew better than Knecht how deceptive such appearances could be?

Knecht tried all the tricks of the interrogator's trade. He came at the same question time after time, from different directions. He hopscotched from question to question. He piled detail on detail. No lie could be perfectly consistent. Contradictions would soon reveal themselves. He was friendly. He was harsh. He put his own words in the prisoner's mouth to see their effect.

None of it worked.

If Kelly's answers were contradictory, Knecht could not say. When the entire story is fantasy, who can find the errors? It was of a piece with the nature of Kelly's cover. If two facts contradict each other, which is true? Answer: both, but in two different worlds.

Frustrated, Knecht decided to let the prisoner simply

talk. Silence, too, was an effective tactic. Many a prisoner had said too much simply to fill an awkward silence. He removed fresh cigars from his pocket humidor and offered one to the prisoner, who accepted it gratefully. Knecht clipped the ends and lit them. When they were both burning evenly, he leaned back in the chair. Nothing like a friendly smoke to set the mind at ease. And off-guard.

"So, tell me in your own words, then, how you on the Wyoming Trail were found."

Kelly grunted. "I wouldn't expect the military mind to understand, or even be interested."

Knecht flushed, but he kept his temper under control. "But I am interested, Herr Kelly. You have a strange story to tell. You come from another world. It is not a story I have often encountered."

Kelly looked at him, startled, and unexpectedly laughed. "No, not very often, I would imagine."

"*Ach,* that is the very problem. Just what *would* you imagine? Your story is true, or it is false; and if it is false, it is either deliberately so or not. I must know which, so I can take the proper action."

Kelly ran a hand through his hair. "Look. All I want is to get out of here, away from you . . . military men. Back to Rosa."

"That does not tell me anything. Spy, traveler, or madman, you would say the same."

The prisoner scowled. Knecht waited.

"All right," said Kelly at last. "I got lost. It's that simple. Sharon tried to tell me that a field trip was premature, but I was so much smarter then. Who would think that the distance from B to A was different than the distance from A to B?"

Who indeed? Knecht thought, but he kept the thought to himself. Another contradiction. Except, grant the premise and it wasn't a contradiction at all.

"Sure," the prisoner's voice was bitter. "Action requires a force; and action causes reaction. It's not nice to forget Uncle Isaac." He looked Knecht square in the eye. "You see, when I Jumped, my world moved, too. Action, reaction. I created multiple versions of it. In one, my equipment worked. In others, it malfunctioned in various ways. Each was slightly displaced from the original location." He laughed again. "How many people can say they've misplaced an entire world?"

"I don't understand," said Knecht. "Why not two versions of *all* worlds? When you, ah, Jumped, you could for many different destinations have gone; and in each one, you either arrived, or you did not."

His prisoner looked puzzled. "But that's not topologically relevant. The Jump occurs in the metacontinuum of the polyverse, so . . . Ah, hell! Why should I try to convince you?"

Knecht sat back and puffed his cigar. Offhand, he could think of several reasons why Kelly should try to convince him.

"You see," the prisoner continued, "there is not an infinity of possible worlds."

Knecht had never thought there was more than one, so he said nothing. Even the idea that there were two would be staggering.

"And they are not all different in the same way. Each moment grows out of the past. Oh, say . . ." He looked at his cigar and smiled. He held it out at arm's length. "Take this cigar, for instance. If I drop it, it'll fall to the floor. That is deterministic. So are the rate, the falling time, and the energy of impact. But, I may or may not choose to drop it. That is probabilistic. It is the choice that creates worlds. We are now at a cusp, a bifurcation point on the Thom manifold." He paused and looked at the cigar. Knecht waited patiently. Then Kelly clamped it firmly between his teeth. "It is far too good a smoke to waste. I chose not to drop it; but there was a small probability that I would have."

Knecht pulled on his moustache, thinking of Vonder-berge's speculations of the previous night. Before he had spoken with Kelly. "So you say that . . . somewhere . . . there is a world in which you did?"

"Right. It's a small world, because the probability was small. Temporal cross-section is proportional to *a priori* probability. But it's there, close by. It's a convergent world."

"Convergent."

"Yes. Except for our two memories and some ash on the floor, it is indistinguishable from this world. The differences damp out. Convergent worlds form a 'rope' of intertwined timelines. We can Jump back and forth among them easily, inadvertently. The energy needed is low. We could change places with our alternate selves and never notice. The only difference may be the number of grains of sand on Mars. Tomorrow you may find that I remember dropping the cigar; or I might find that you do. We may even argue the point."

"Unconvincingly," said Knecht sardonically.

Kelly chuckled. "True. How could you *know* what I remember? Still, it happens all the time. The courts are full of people who sincerely remember different versions of reality."

"Or perhaps it is the mind that plays tricks, not the reality."

Kelly flushed and looked away. "That happens, too."

After a moment, Knecht asked, "What has this to do with your becoming lost?"

"What? Oh. Simple, really. The number of possible worlds is large, but it's not infinite. That's important to remember," he continued to himself. "Finite. I haven't checked into Hotel Infinity. I can still find my own room, or at least the right floor." He stood abruptly and paced the room. Knecht followed him with his eyes.

"I don't have to worry about worlds where Washington and Jefferson instituted a pharaonic monarchy with a divine god-king. Every moment grows out of the previous moment, remember? For that to happen, so much previous history would have had to be different that Washington and Jefferson would never have been born." He stopped pacing and faced Knecht.

"And I don't have to worry about convergent worlds. If I find the right 'rope,' I'll be all right. Even a parallel world would be fine, as long as it would have Rosa in it." He frowned. "But it mightn't. And if it did, she mightn't know me."

"Parallel?" asked Knecht.

Kelly walked to the window and gazed through the bars. "Sure. Change can be convergent, parallel, or divergent. Suppose, oh suppose Isabella hadn't funded Columbus, but the other Genoese, Giovanni Caboto, who was also pushing for a voyage west. Or Juan de la Cosa. Or the two brothers who captained the Niña and the Pinta. There was no shortage of bold navigators. What practical difference would it have made? A few names are changed in the history books, is all. The script is the same, but different actors play the parts. The differences stay constant."

He turned around. "You or I may have no counterpart in those worlds. They are different 'ropes.' Even so, we could spontaneously Jump to one nearby. Benjamin Bathurst, the man who walked behind a horse in plain sight and was never seen again. No one took his place. Judge Crater. Ambrose Bierce. Amelia Earhart. Jimmy Hoffa. The Legion II Augusta. Who knows? Some of them may have Jumped."

Kelly inspected his cigar. "Then there are the cascades. For want of a nail, the shoe was lost. The differences accumulate. The worlds diverge. That was my mistake. Jumping to a cascade world." His voice was bitter, self-mocking. "Oh, it'll be simple to find my way back. All I have to do is find the nail."

"The nail?"

"Sure. The snowflake that started the avalanche. What could be simpler?" He took three quick steps along the wall, turned, stepped back, and jammed his cigar out in the ashtray. He sat backward, landing on his cot. He put his face in his hands.

Knecht listened to his harsh breathing. He remembered what Ochsenfuss had said. If I push him too hard, he could crack. A spy cracks one way; a madman, another.

After a while, Kelly looked up again. He smiled. "It's not that hard, really," he said more calmly. "I can approximate it closely enough with history texts and logical calculus. That should be good enough to get me back to my own rope. Or at least a nearby one. As long as Rosa is there, it doesn't matter." He hesitated and glanced at Knecht. "You've confiscated my personal effects," he said, "but I would like to have her photograph. It was in my wallet. Along with my identification papers," he added pointedly.

Knecht smiled. "I have seen your papers, Herr 'Professor Doctor' Kelly. They are very good."

"But . . ."

"But I have drawn others myself just as good."

Kelly shrugged and grinned. "It was worth a try," he said.

Knecht chuckled. He was beginning to like this man. "I suppose it can do no harm," he said, thinking out loud, "to give you a history text. Surely there gives one here in the fortress. If nothing else, it can keep you amused during the long days. And perhaps it can reacquaint you with reality."

"That's what the shrink said before."

"The shrink? What . . . ? Oh, I see. The Hexmajor." He laughed. Then he remembered how Ochsenfuss and Vonderberge had quarreled over this man and he looked at him more soberly. "You understand that you must here stay. Until we know who or what you are. There are three possibilities and only one is to your benefit." He hesitated a moment, then added, "It gives some here who your story believe, and some not."

Kelly nodded. "I know. Do you believe me?"

"Me? I am a scout. I look. I listen. I try to fit pieces together so they make a picture. I take no direct action. No, Herr Kelly. I do not believe you; but neither do I disbelieve you."

Kelly nodded. "Fair enough."

"Do not thank me yet, Herr Kelly. In our first five minutes of talking it is clear to me you know nothing of value of the Wyoming, or the Nations, or anything. In such a case, my official interest in you comes to an end."

"But unofficially . . ." prompted the other.

"*Ja.*" Knecht rose and walked to the door. "Others begin to have strong opinions about you, for whatever reasons of their own I do not know. Such are the seeds, and I do not like what may sprout. Perhaps this . . ." He jabbed his cigar at Kelly, suddenly accusing. "You know more than you show. You play-act the hinkle-dreck *Quatschkopf*. And this, the sowing of discord, may be the very reason for your coming."

He stepped back and considered the prisoner. He gestured broadly, his cigar leaving curlicues of smoke. "I see grave philosophical problems with you, Herr Kelly. We Germans, even we Pennsylvaanish Germans, are a very philosophical people. From what you say there are many worlds, some only trivially different. I do not know why we with infinitely many Kellys are not deluged, each coming from a world *almost* like your own!"

Kelly gasped in surprise. He stood abruptly and turned to the wall, his back to Knecht. "Of course," he said. "Stupid, stupid, stupid! The transformation isn't homeomorphic. The topology of the inverse sheaf must not be Hausdorff after all. It may only be a Harris proximity." He turned to Knecht. "Please, may I have my calculator, the small box with the numbered buttons . . . No, damn!" He smacked a fist into his left hand. "I ran the batteries down when I was with Goodman deVeres. Some pencils and paper, then?" He looked eager and excited.

Knecht grunted in satisfaction. Something he had said had set Kelly thinking. It remained to be seen along which lines those thoughts would run.

* * *

Rumors flew over the next few days. A small border fort is their natural breeding ground, and Fox Gap was no exception. Knecht heard through the grapevine that Vonderberge had had the Hexmajor barred from Kelly's cell; that Ochsenfuss had telegraphed his superiors in Medical Corps and had Vonderberge overruled. Now there was talk that General Schneider himself had entered the dispute, on which side no one knew; but the General had already postponed his scheduled departure for Wind Gap Fortress and a packet bearing his seal had gone by special courier to Oberkommando Pennsylvaanish in Philadelphia City. A serious matter if the General did not trust the security of the military telegraph.

The General himself was not talking, not even to Knecht. That saddened the scout more than he had realized it could. Since his talk with the prisoner, Knecht had thought more than once how slender was the chain of chance that had brought Schneider and himself together, the team of scout and strategist that had shepherded the Commonwealth through two major wars and countless border skirmishes.

He had dined with the General shortly after submitting his report on Kelly. Dinner was a hearty fare of *shnitz un' knepp*, with *deutsch*-baked corn, followed by shoofly pie. Afterwards, cigars and brandy wine. Talk had turned, as it often did, to the Piney War. Schneider had deprecated his own role.

"What could I do, Rudi?" he asked. "A stray cannon shot and both Kutz and Rittenhouse were dead. I felt the ball go by me, felt the wind on my face. A foot the other way would have deprived this very brandy of being so thoroughly enjoyed today. Suddenly, I was Commander of the Army of the Delaware, with my forces scattered among the Wachtungs. Rittenhouse had always been the tight-lipped sort. I had no idea what his plans had been. So I studied his dispositions and our intelligence on Enemy's dispositions, and . . ." A shrug. "I improvised."

Knecht lifted his glass in salute. "Brilliantly, as always."

Schneider grinned through his bushy white mutton-chop whiskers. "We mustn't forget who secured that intelligence for me. Brilliance cannot improvise on faulty data. You have never failed me."

Knecht flushed. "Once I did."

"Tcha!" The General waved his hand in dismissal. "The nine hundred ninety-nine other times make me forget the once. Only you constantly remember."

Knecht remembered how once he had misplaced an entire regiment of Virginia Foot. It was not where he had left it, but somewhere else entirely. General Schneider, except that he had been Brigadier Schneider, had salvaged the situation and had protected him from Alois Kutz's anger. He had learned something about Konrad Schneider then: The General never let the short-term interfere with the long-term. He would not sacrifice the future on the whim of the moment. It had been such a simple error. He had improperly identified the terrain. The Appalachian Mountains of western Virginia looked much the same from ridge to ridge.

Or was it so simple? He recalled his discussion with the prisoner, Kelly. *Ich biete Ihre Entschuldigung, Herr Brigadier,* he imagined himself saying, *but I must have slipped over into a parallel universe. In my timeline, the Rappahannock Guards were on the north side of the river, not the south.*

No, it wouldn't work. To believe it meant chaos: A

world without facts. A world where lies hid among multiple truths. And what did the General think? What did Konrad Schneider make of Kelly's tale?

Knecht swirled the brandy in his snifter. He watched his reflection dance on the blood-red liquid. "Tell me, Konrad, have you read my report on the prisoner?"

"*Ja,* I have."

"And what did you think?"

"It was a fine report, Rudi. As always."

"No. I meant what did you think of the prisoner's story?"

The General lifted his glass to his lips and sipped his brandy. Knecht had seen many men try to avoid answers and recognized all the tactics. Knecht frowned and waited for an answer he knew he could not trust. For as long as Knecht could remember Schneider had been his leader. From the day he had left his father's house, he had followed Colonel, then Brigadier, then General Schneider, and never before had he been led astray. There was an emptiness in him now. He bit the inside of his cheek so that he could feel something, even pain.

Schneider finished his slow, careful sip and set his glass down. He shrugged broadly, palms up. "How could I know? Vonderberge tells me one thing; Ochsenfuss, another. You, in your report, tell me nothing."

Knecht bristled. "There is not enough data to reach a conclusion," he protested.

Schneider shook his head. "No, no. I meant no criticism. You are correct, as always. Yet, our friends *have* reached conclusions. Different conclusions, to be sure, but we don't know which is correct." He paused. "Of course, he *might* be a spy."

"If he is, he is either a very bad one, or a very, very good one."

"And all we know is . . . What? He loves Rosa and does not love the military. He has some peculiar documents and artifacts and he believes he comes from another world, full of marvelous gadgets. . . ."

"Correction, Herr General. He *says* he believes he came from another world. There is a difference."

"Hmph. *Ja,* you are right again. What is it you always say? The map is not the territory. The testimony is not the fact. Sometimes I envy our friends their ability to reach such strong convictions on so little reflection. You and I, Rudi, we are always beset by doubts, eh?"

Knecht made a face. "If so, Konrad, your doubts have never kept you from acting."

The General stared at him a moment. Then he roared with laughter, slapping his thigh. "Oh, yes, you are right, Rudi. What should I do without you? You know me better than I know myself. There are two kinds of doubts, *nicht wahr?* One says: What is the right thing to do? The other says: Have I done the right thing? But, to command means to decide. I have never fought a battle but that a better strategy has come to mind a day or two later. But where would we be had I waited? Eh, Rudi? The second sort of doubt, Rudi. That is the sort of doubt a commander must have. Never the first sort. And never certainty. Both are disasters."

"And what of Kelly?"

The General reached for his brandy once more. "I will have both the Hexmajor and the Kommandant interview him. Naturally, each will be biased, but in different ways. Between them, we may learn the truth of it." He paused thoughtfully, pursing his lips. "Sooner or later, one will concede the matter. We need not be hasty. No, not hasty at all." He drank the last of his brandy.

"And myself?"

Schneider looked at him. He smiled. "You cannot spend so much time on only one man, one who is almost surely not an enemy agent. You have your spies, scouts, and rangers to supervise. Intelligence to collate. Tell me, Rudi, what those fat knick patroons are planning up in Albany. Have the Iroquois joined them, too? Are they dickering with the Lee brothers to make it a two-front war? I must know these things if I am to . . . improvise. Our situation is grave. Forget Kelly. He is not important."

After he left the General, Knecht took a stroll around the parapet, exchanging greetings with the sentries. Schneider could not have announced more clearly that Kelly was important. But why? And why keep him out of it?

Fox Gap was a star-fort and Knecht's wanderings had taken him to one of the points of the star. From there, defensive fire could enfilade any attacking force. He leaned his elbows on a gun port and gazed out at the nighttime forest farther down the slope of the mountain. The sky was crisp and clear as only autumn skies could be, and the stars were brilliantly close.

The forest was a dark mass, a deeper black against the black of night. The wind soughed through the maple and elm and birch. The sound reached him, a dry whisper, like crumpling paper. Soon it would be the Fall. The leaves were dead; all the life had been sucked out of them.

He sighed. General Schneider had just as clearly ordered him away from Kelly. He had never disobeyed an order. Angrily, he threw a shard of masonry from the parapet wall. It crashed among the treetops below and a sentry turned sharply and shouted a challenge. Embarrassed, Knecht turned and left the parapet.

Once back in his own quarters, Knecht pondered the dilemma of Kelly. His room was spartan. Not much more comfortable, he thought, than Kelly's cell. A simple bed, a desk and chair, a trunk. Woodcuts on the wall: heroic details of long-forgotten battles. An anonymous room, suitable for a roving scout. Next month, maybe, a different room at a different fort.

So what was Kelly? Knecht couldn't see but three possibilities. A clever spy, a madman, or the most pitiful refugee ever. But, as a spy he was not credible; his story was unbelievable, and he simply did not talk like a madman.

And where does that leave us, Rudi? Nowhere. Was there a fourth possibility? It didn't seem so.

Knecht decided it was time for a pipe. Cigars were for talk; pipes for reflection. He stepped to the window of his room as he lit it. The pipe was very old. It had belonged to his grandfather, and a century of tobacco had burned its flavor into the bowl. His grandfather had given it to him the night before he had left home forever, when he had confided his plans to the old man, confident of his approval. He had been, Knecht remembered, about Kelly's age at the time. An age steeped in certainties.

Spy, madman, or refugee? If the first, good for me; because I caught him. If the second, good for him; because he will be cared for. He puffed. For two of the three possibilities, custody was the best answer; the only remaining question being what sort of custody. And those two choices were like the two sides of a coin: they used up all probability between them. Heads I win, Herr Kelly, and tails you lose. It is a cell for you either way. That is obvious.

So then, why am I pacing this room in the middle of the night, burning my best leaf and tasting nothing?

Because, Rudi, there is just the chance that the coin could land on its edge. If Kelly's outrageous tale were true, custody would not be the best answer. It would be no answer at all.

Ridiculous. It could not be true. He took the pipe from his mouth. The warmth of the bowl in his hand comforted him. Knecht had concluded tentatively that Kelly was no spy. That meant Ochsenfuss was right. Knecht could see that. It had been his own first reaction on reading the notebook. But he could also see why Vonderberge believed otherwise. The man's outlook and Kelly's amiable and sincere demeanor had combined to produce belief.

It was Schneider that bothered him. Schneider had *not* decided. Knecht was certain of that. And that meant ... What? With madness so obvious, Schneider saw something else. Knecht had decided nothing because he was only interested in spies. Beyond that, what Kelly was or was not meant nothing.

Even if his tale is true, he thought, it is none of my concern. My task is done. I have taken in a suspicious stranger under suspicious circumstances. It is for higher authorities to puzzle it out. Why should I care what the answer is?

Because, Rudi, it was you who brought him here.

Knecht learned from Johann the guard that Vonderberge spent the mornings with Kelly, and Ochsenfuss, the afternoons. So when Knecht brought the history book to the cell a few days later, he did so at noon, when no one else was about. He had made it a habit to stop by for a few minutes each day.

He nodded to Johann as he walked down the cell block corridor. "I was never here, soldier," he said. Johann's face took on a look of obligingly amiable unawareness.

Kelly was eating lunch, a bowl of thick rivel soup. He had been provided with a table, which was now littered with scribbled pages. Knecht recognized the odd equations of Kelly's "logical calculus." He handed the prisoner the text: "The History of North America." Kelly seized it eagerly and leafed through it.

"Thanks, lieutenant," he said. "The shrink brought me one, too; but it's in German and I couldn't make sense of it."

"Pennsylvaanish," Knecht corrected him absently. He was looking at the other book. It was thick and scholarly. A good part of each page consisted of footnotes. He shuddered and put it down.

"What?"

"Pennsylvaanish," he repeated. "It is a German dialect, but it is not *Hochdeutsch*. It is Swabian with some English mixed in. The spelling makes it different sometimes. A visitor from the Second Reich would find it nearly unintelligible, but . . ." An elaborate shrug. "What can one expect from a Prussian?"

Kelly laughed. He put his soup bowl aside, finished. "How did that happen?" he asked. "I mean, you folks speaking, ah, Pennsylvaanish?"

Knecht raised an eyebrow. "Because we are Pennsylvanians."

"So were Franklin, Dickinson, and Tom Penn."

"Ah, I see what you are asking. It is simple. Even so far back as the War Against the English the majority of Pennsylvanians were *Deutsch*, German-speakers. So high was the feeling against the English—outside of Philadelphia City, that is—that the Assembly German the official language made. Later, after the Revolution in Europe, many more from Germany came. They were fleeing the Prussians and Austrians."

"And from nowhere else? No Irish? No Poles, Italians, Russian Jews? 'I lift my lamp beside the golden door.' What happened to all of that?"

"I don't understand. *Ja,* some came from other countries. There were Welsh and Scots-Irish here even before the War. Others came later. A few, not many. Ranger Oswoski's grandparents were Polish. But, when they come here, then Pennsylvaanish they must learn."

"I suppose with America so balkanized, it never seemed such a land of opportunity."

"I don't understand that, either. What is 'balkanized'?"

Kelly tapped with his pencil on the table. "No," he said slowly, "I suppose you wouldn't." He aimed the pencil at the history book. "Let me read this. Maybe I'll be able to explain things better."

"I hope you find in it what you need."

Kelly grinned, all teeth. "An appropriately ambiguous wish, lieutenant. 'What I need.' That could mean anything. But, thank you. I think I will." He hesitated a moment. "And, uh, thanks for the book, too. You've been a big help. You're the only one who comes here and listens to me. I mean, *really* listens."

Knecht smiled. He opened the door, but turned before leaving. "But, Herr Kelly," he said. "It is my job to listen."

* * *

Knecht's work absorbed him for several days. Scraps of information filtered in from several quarters. He spent long hours in his office going over them, separating rumor from fact from possible fact. Sometimes, he sent a man out to see for himself and waited in nervous uncertainty until the pigeons flew back. Each night, he threw himself into his rack exhausted. Each morning, there was a new stack of messages.

He moved pins about in his wall map. Formations whose bivouac had been verified. Twice he telegraphed the Southern Command using his personal code to discover what the scouts down along the Monongahela had learned. Slowly, the spaces filled in. The pins told a story. Encirclement.

Schneider came in late one evening. He stood before the map and studied it for long minutes in silence. Knecht sipped his coffee, watching. The General drew his forefinger along the northwestern frontier. There were no pins located in Long House territory. "Curious," he said aloud, as if to himself. Knecht smiled. Five rangers were already out trying to fill in that gap. Schneider would have his answer soon enough.

Knecht had almost forgotten Kelly. There had been no more time for his noontime visits. Then, one morning he heard that Vonderberge and Ochsenfuss had fought in the officers' club. Words had been exchanged, then blows. Not many, because the Chief Engineer had stopped them. It wasn't clear who had started it, or even how it had started. It had gotten as far as it had only because the other officers present had been taken by surprise. Neither man had been known to brawl before.

Knecht was not surprised by the fight. He knew the tension between the two over Kelly. What did surprise him was that Schneider took no official notice of the fight.

Something was happening. Knecht did not know what it was, but he was determined to find out. He decided to do a little intramural spy work of his own.

Knecht found the Hexmajor later that evening. He was sitting alone at a table in the officers' club, sipping an after-dinner liqueur from a thin glass, something Knecht found vaguely effeminate. He realized he was taking a strong personal dislike to the man. Compared to Vonderberge, Ochsenfuss was haughty and cold. Elegant, Knecht thought, watching the man drink. That was the word: elegant. Knecht himself liked plain, blunt-spoken men. But scouts, he told himself firmly, must observe what is, not what they wish to see. The bar orderly handed him a beer stein and he strolled casually to Ochsenfuss' table.

"Ah, Herr Doctor," he said smiling. "How goes it with the prisoner?"

"It goes," said Ochsenfuss, "but slowly."

Knecht sat without awaiting an invitation. He thought he saw a brief glimmer of surprise in the other's face, but the Hexmajor quickly recovered his wooden expression. Knecht was aware that Vonderberge, at a corner table, had paused in his conversation with the Chief Engineer and was watching them narrowly.

"A shame the treatment cannot go speedier," he told Ochsenfuss.

A shrug. "Under such circumstances, the mind must heal itself."

"I remember your work with Ranger Harrison after we rescued him from the Senecas."

Ochsenfuss sipped his drink. "I recall the case. His

condition was grave. Torture does things to a man's mind; worse in many ways than what it does to his body."

"May I ask how you are treating Kelly?"

"You may."

There was a long silence. Then Knecht said, "How are you treating him?" He could not detect the slightest hint of a smile on the doctor's face. He was surprised. Ochsenfuss had not seemed inclined to humor of any sort.

"I am mesmerizing him," he said. "Then I allow him to talk about his fantasies. In English," he admitted grudgingly. "I ply him for details. Then, when he is in this highly suggestible state, I point out the contradictions in his thinking."

"Contradictions . . ." Knecht let the word hang in the air.

"Oh, many things. Heavier-than-air flying machines: a mathematical impossibility. Radio, communication without connecting wires: That is action at a distance, also impossible. Then there is his notion that a single government rules the continent, from Columbia to New England and from Pontiac to Texas. Why, the distances and geographical barriers make the idea laughable.

"I tell him these things while he is mesmerized. My suggestions lodge in what we call the subconscious and gradually make his fantasies less credible to his waking mind. Eventually he will again make contact with reality."

"Tell me something, Herr Doctor."

They both turned at the sound of the new voice. It was Vonderberge. He stood belligerently, his thumbs hooked in his belt. He swayed slightly and Knecht could smell alcohol on his breath. Knecht frowned unhappily.

Ochsenfuss blinked. "Yes, Kommandant," he said blandly. "What is it?"

"I have read that by mesmerization one can also implant false ideas."

Ochsenfuss smiled. "I have heard that at carnival sideshows, the mesmerist may cause members of the audience to believe that they are ducks or some such thing."

"I was thinking of something more subtle than that."

The Hexmajor's smile did not fade, but it seemed to freeze. "Could you be more specific."

Vonderberge leaned towards them. "I mean," he said lowly, "the obliteration of true memories and their replacement with false ones."

Ochsenfuss tensed. "No reputable hexdoctor would do such a thing."

Vonderberge raised a palm. "I never suggested such a thing, either. I only asked if it were possible."

Ochsenfuss paused before answering. "It is. But the false memories would inevitably conflict with a thousand others and, most importantly, with the evidence of the patient's own senses. The end would be psychosis. The obliteration of *false* memories, however . . ."

Vonderberge nodded several times, as if the Hexmajor had confirmed a long-standing belief. "I see. Thank you, Doctor." He turned and looked at Knecht. He touched the bill of his cap. "Rudi," he said in salutation, then turned and left.

Ochsenfuss watched him go. "There is a man who could benefit from therapy. He would reject reality if he could."

Knecht remembered Vonderberge's outburst in his office during the storm. He remembered too, the map in his own office. "So might we all," he said. "Reality is none too pleasant these days. General Schneider believes . . ."

"General Schneider," interrupted Ochsenfuss, "believes what he wants to believe. But truth is not always what we want, is it?" He looked away, his eyes focused on the far wall. "Nor always what we need." He took another sip of his liqueur and set the glass down. "I am not such a fool as he seems to think. For all that he primes me with questions to put to Kelly, and the interest he shows in my reports, he still has not decided what to do with my patient. He should be in hospital, in Philadelphia."

For the briefest moment, Knecht thought he meant Schneider should be in hospital. When he realized the confusion, he laughed. Ochsenfuss looked at him oddly and Knecht took a pull on his mug to hide his embarrassment.

"If I could use mescal or peyote to heighten his suggestibility," Ochsenfuss continued to no one in particular. "Or if I could keep our friend the Kommandant away from my patient. . . ." He studied his drink in silence, then abruptly tossed it off. He looked at his watch and waved off a hovering orderly. "Well, things cannot go on as they are. Something must break." He laughed and rose from the table. "At least there are a few of us who take a hard-headed and practical view of the world, eh, Leutnant?" He patted Knecht on the arm and left.

Knecht watched him go. He took another drink of beer and wiped the foam from his lips with his sleeve, thinking about what the Hexmajor had said.

A few days later, a carrier pigeon arrived and Knecht rode out to meet its sender at a secret rendezvous deep inside Wyoming. Such meetings were always risky, but his agent had spent many years working her way into a position of trust. It was a mask that would be dropped if she tried to leave the country. Knecht wondered what the information was. Obviously more than could be entrusted to a pigeon.

But she never came to the rendezvous. Knecht waited, then left a sign on a certain tree that he had been there and gone. He wondered what had happened. Perhaps she had not been able to get away after all. Or perhaps she had been unmasked and quietly executed. Like many of the old-style Quakers, Abigail Fox had learned English at her mother's knee and spoke without an accent; but one never knew what trivial detail would prove fatal.

Knecht chewed on his moustache as he rode homeward. He had not seen Abby for a long time. Now he didn't know if he would ever see her again. The worst part would be never knowing what had happened. Knecht hated not knowing things. That's why he was a good scout. Even bad news was better than no news.

Well, perhaps another pigeon would arrive, explaining everything, arranging another rendezvous. *But how could you be sure, Rudi, that it really came from her?* Spies have been broken before, and codes with them. One day, he knew, he would ride out to a meeting and not come back. He felt cold and empty. He slapped his horse on the rump and she broke into a trot. He was afraid of death, but he would not send others to do what he would not.

It had been two weeks to rendezvous and back and Schneider was still at Fox Gap when Knecht returned. The rumors had grown up thick for harvesting. Between the front gate and the stables five soldiers and two officers asked him if a command shake-up were coming. His friendship with the General was well-known, and why else would Schneider stay on?

Why else, indeed. Kelly. Knecht was certain of it, but the why still eluded him.

Catching up on his paperwork kept Knecht at his desk until well after dark. When he had finished, he made his way to Vonderberge's quarters. Knecht's thought was to pay a "social call" and guide the conversation around to the subject of Kelly. Once he arrived, however, he found himself with some other officers, drinking dark beer and singing badly to the accompaniment of the Chief Engineer's equally bad piano playing. It was, he discovered, a weekly ritual among the permanent fortress staff.

Ochsenfuss was not there, but that did not surprise him.

He was reluctant to bring up the business of the prisoner in front of the other officers, so he planned to be the last to leave. But Vonderberge and the Fortress Staff proved to have a respectable capacity for drinking and singing and Knecht outlasted them only by cleverly passing out in the corner, where he was overlooked when Vonderberge ushered the others out.

"Good morning, Rudi."

Knecht opened his eyes. The light seared his eyes and the top of his head fell off and shattered on the floor. "Ow," he said.

"Very eloquent, Rudi." Vonderberge leaned over him, looking impossibly cheerful. "That must be some hangover."

Knecht winced. "You can't get hangovers from beer."

Vonderberge shrugged. "Have it your way." He held out a tall glass. "Here, drink this."

He sniffed the drink warily. It was dark and red and pungent. "What is it?" he asked suspiciously.

"Grandmother Vonderberge's Perfect Cure for Everything. It never fails."

"But what's in it?"

"If I told you, you wouldn't drink it. Go ahead. Grandmother was a wise old bird. She outlasted three husbands."

Knecht drank. He shuddered and sweat broke out on his forehead. "Small wonder," he gasped. "She probably fed them this."

Vonderberge chuckled and took the glass back. "You were in fine form last night. Fine form. Who is Abby?"

Knecht looked at him. "Why?"

"You kept drinking toasts to her."

He looked away, into the distance. "She was ... someone I knew."

"Like that, eh?" Vonderberge grinned. Knecht did not bother to correct him.

"You should socialize more often, Rudi," continued the Kommandant. "You'll find we're not such bad sorts. You have a good baritone. It gave the staff a fuller sound." Vonderberge gestured broadly to show how full the sound had been. "We need the higher registers, though. I've thought of having Heinz and Zuckerman gelded. What do you think?"

Knecht considered the question. "Where do they stand on the promotion list?"

Vonderberge looked at him sharply. He grinned. "You are beginning to show a sense of humor, Rudi. A sense of humor."

Knecht snorted. He was easily twenty years the Kommandant's senior. He knew jokes that had been old and wrinkled before Vonderberge had been born. He recalled suddenly that Abigail Fox had been an alto. There were other memories, too; and some empty places where there could have been memories, but weren't. *Ach*, for what might have been! It wasn't right for spymaster and spy to be too close. He wondered if Kelly had a world somewhere where everything was different.

Vonderberge had his batman serve breakfast in rather than go to the mess. He invited Knecht to stay and they talked over eggs, scrapple, and coffee. Knecht did not have to lead into the subject of Kelly because Vonderberge raised it himself. He unrolled a sheet of paper onto the table after the batman had cleared it, using the salt and pepper mills to hold down the curled ends.

"Let me show you," he said, "what bothers me about Kelly's world."

A great many things about Kelly's world bothered Knecht, not the least of which was the fact that there was no evidence it even existed; but he put on a polite face and listened attentively. Was Vonderberge beginning to have doubts?

The Kommandant pointed to the sheet. Knecht saw that it was a table of inventions, with dates and inventors. Some of the inventions had two dates and two inventors, in parallel columns.

"Next to each invention," said Vonderberge, "I've written when and by whom it was invented. The first column is our world; the second, Kelly's, as nearly as he can remember. Do you notice anything?"

Knecht glanced at the list. "Several things," he replied casually. "There are more entries in the second column, most of the dates are earlier, and a few names appear in both columns."

Vonderberge blinked and looked at him. Knecht kept his face composed.

"You're showing off, aren't you, Rudi?"

"I've spent a lifetime noticing details on documents."

"But do you see the significance? The inventions came earlier and faster in Kelly's world. Look how they *gush* forth after 1870! Why? How could they have been so much more creative? In the early part of the list, many of the same men are mentioned in both columns, so it is not individual genius. Look . . ." His forefinger searched the first column. "The electrical telegraph was invented, when? In 1875, by Edison. In Kelly's world, it was invented in the 1830s, by a man named Morse."

"The painter?"

"Apparently the same man. Why didn't he invent it here? And see what Edison did in Kelly's world: The electrical light, the moving picture projector, dozens of things we never saw until the 1930s."

Knecht pointed to an entry. "Plastics," he said. "We discovered them first." He wondered what "first" meant in this context.

"That is the exception that proves the rule. There are others. Daguerre's photographic camera, Foucault's gyroscope. They are the same in both worlds. But overall there is a pattern. Not an occasional marvel, every now and then; but a multitude, every year! By 1920, in Kelly's world, steamships, *heavier*-than-air craft, railroads, *voice* telegraphy with *and without* wires, horseless carriages, they were old hat. Here, they are still wonders. Or wondered about."

Inventions and gadgets, decided Knecht. Those were Vonderberge's secret passion, and Kelly had described a technological faerieland. No wonder the Kommandant was entranced. Knecht was less in awe, himself. He had seen the proud ranks of the 18th New York mowed down like corn by the Pennsylvaanish machine guns at the Battle of the Raritan. And he had not forgotten what Kelly had written in his notebook: There were bombs that destroyed whole cities.

Vonderberge sighed and rolled up his list. He tied a cord around it. "It is difficult, Rudi," he said. "Very difficult. Your General, he only wants to hear about the inventions. He does not wonder why there are so many. Yet, I feel that this is an important question."

"Can't Kelly answer it?"

"He might. He has come close to it on several occasions; but he is . . . confused. Ochsenfuss sees to that."

Knecht noticed how Vonderberge's jaw set. The Kommandant's usual bantering tone was missing.

Vonderberge pulled a watch from his right pants pocket and studied its face. "It is time for my appointment with Kelly. Why don't you come with me. I'd like your opinion on something."

"On what?"

"On Kelly."

Knecht sat backward on a chair in the corner of the cell, leaning his arms on the back. A cigar was clamped tightly between his teeth. It had gone out, but he had not bothered to relight it. He watched the proceedings between Kelly and Vonderberge. So far, he did not like what he had seen.

Kelly spoke hesitantly. He seemed distracted and lapsed into frequent, uncomfortable silences. The papers spread out on his table were blank. No new equations. Just doodles of flowers. Roses, they looked like.

"Think, Kelly," Vonderberge pleaded. "We were talking of this only yesterday."

Kelly pursed his lips and frowned. "Were we? *Ja,* you're right. I think we did. I thought it was a dream."

"It was not a dream. It was real. You said you thought the Victorian Age was the key. What was the Victorian Age?"

Kelly looked puzzled. "Victorian Age? Are you sure?"

"Yes. You mentioned Queen Victoria . . ."

"She was never Queen, though."

Vonderberge clucked impatiently. "That was in this world," he said. "In your world it must have been different."

"In my world . . ." It was half a statement, half a question. Kelly closed his eyes, hard. "I have such headaches, these days. It's hard to remember things. It's all confused."

Vonderberge turned to Knecht. "You see the problem?"

Knecht removed his cigar. "The problem," he said judiciously, "is the source of his confusion."

Vonderberge turned back to Kelly. "I think we both know who that is."

Kelly was losing touch, Knecht thought. That was certain. But was he losing touch with reality, or with fantasy?

"Wait!" Kelly's eyes were still closed but his hand shot out and gripped Vonderberge's wrist. "The Victorian Age. That was the time from the War Between the States to World War I." He opened his eyes and looked at Vonderberge. "Am I right?"

"Vonderberge threw his hands up. "Tchah! Why are you asking *me*?"

Knecht chewed thoughtfully on his cigar. *World* wars? And they were *numbered*?

"What has this 'Victorian Age' to do with your world's inventiveness?"

Kelly stared at a space in the air between them. He

rapped rhythmically on the table with his knuckles. "Don't push it," he said. "I might lose the . . . Yes. I can hear Tom's voice explaining it." The eyes were unfocused. Knecht wondered what sort of mind heard voices talking to it. "What an odd apartment. We were just BS'ing. Sharon, Tom, and . . . a girl, and I. The subject came up, but in a different context."

They waited patiently for Kelly to remember.

"Critical mass!" he said suddenly. "That was it. The rate at which new ideas are generated depends in part on the accumulation of past ideas. The more there are, the more ways they can be combined and modified. Then, boom," he gestured with his hands. "An explosion." He laughed shrilly; sobered instantly. "That's what happened during the Victorian Age. That's what's happening now, but slower."

A slow explosion? The idea amused Knecht. "Why slower?" he asked.

"Because of the barriers! Ideas must circulate freely if they're to trigger new ones. The velocity of ideas is as important to culture and technology as, as the velocity of money is to the economy. The United States would have been the largest free trade zone in the world. The second largest was England. Not even the United Kingdom, just England. Can you imagine? Paying a toll or a tariff every few miles?"

"What has commerce to do with ideas?" asked Vonderberge.

"It's the traveling people who carry ideas from place to place. The merchants, sailors, soldiers. At least until an international postal system is established. And radio. And tourism."

"I see . . ."

"But look at the barriers we have to deal with! The largest nation on the Atlantic seaboard is what? The Carolina Kingdom. Some of the Indian states are larger, but they don't have many people. How far can you travel before you pay a tariff? Or run into a foreign language like English or Choctaw or French? Or into a military patrol that shoots first and asks questions later? No wonder we're so far behind!"

Knecht pulled the cigar from his mouth. "We?" he asked. Vonderberge turned and gave him an anxious glance, so he, too, had noticed the shift in Kelly's personal pronoun.

The prisoner was flustered. "You," he said. "I meant 'you.' Your rate of progress is slower. I . . ."

Knecht forestalled further comment. "No, never mind. A slip of the tongue, *ja*?" He smiled to show he had dismissed the slip. He knew it was important; though in what way he was not yet sure. He took a long puff on his cigar. "Personally, I have never thought our progress slow. The horseless carriage was invented, what? 1920-something, in Dusseldorf. In less than fifty years you could find some in all the major cities. Last year, two nearly collided on the streets of Philadelphia! Soon every well-to-do family will have one."

The prisoner laughed. It was a great belly laugh that shook him and shook him until it turned imperceptibly into a sob. He squeezed his eyes tight.

"There was a man," he said distantly. "Back in my hometown of Longmont, Colorado." He opened his eyes and looked at them. "That would be in Nuevo Aztlan, if it existed, which it doesn't and never has . . ." He paused and shook his head, once, sharply, as if to clear it. "Old Mr. Brand. I was just a kid, but I remember when the newspapers and TV came around. When Old Brand was a youngster, he watched his dad drive a stagecoach. Before he died, he watched his son fly a space shuttle." He looked intently at Knecht. "And you think it is wonderful that a few rich people have hand-built cars after half a century?"

He laughed again; but this time the laugh was brittle. They watched him for a moment, and the laugh went on and on. Then Vonderberge leaned forward and slapped him sharply, twice.

Knecht chewed his moustache. What the prisoner said made some sense. He could see how technological progress—and social change with it—was coupled with free trade and the free exchange of ideas. Yet, he wasn't at all sure that it was necessarily a good thing. There was a lot to be said for stability and continuity. He blew a smoke ring. He wondered if Kelly were a social radical, driven mad by his inability to instigate change, who had built himself a fantasy world in which change ran amok. That made sense, too.

He glanced at his cigar, automatically timing the ash. A good cigar should burn at least five minutes before the ash needed knocking off.

Suddenly, he felt a tingling in his spine. He looked at the cigar as if it had come alive in his hand. It had gone out—he remembered that clearly. Now, it was burning, and he could not recall relighting it. He looked at the ashtray. Yes, a spent match. *I relit it, of course. It was such an automatic action that I paid it no mind.* That was one explanation. It was his memory playing tricks, not his reality. But the tingling in his spine did not stop.

He looked at Kelly, then he carefully laid his cigar in the ashtray to burn itself out.

"You just wait, though," Kelly was saying to Vonderberge. "Our curve is starting up, too. It took us longer, but we'll be reaching critical mass soon. We're maybe a hundred years off the pace. About where the other . . . where my world was just before the world wars."

That simple pronouncement filled Knecht with a formless dread. He watched the smoke from his smoldering cigar and saw how it rose, straight and true, until it reached a breaking point. There, it changed abruptly into a chaos of turbulent streamers, swirling at random in the motionless air. Then we could do the same, he thought. Fight worldwide wars.

Afterwards, Knecht and Vonderberge spoke briefly as they crossed the parade ground. The sun was high in the sky, but the air held the coolness of autumn. Knecht was thoughtful, his mind on his cigar, on alternate realities, on the suddenness with which stability could turn to chaos.

"You saw it, didn't you?" asked Vonderberge.

For a moment he thought the Kommandant meant his mysteriously relit cigar. "Saw what?" he replied.

"Kelly. He has difficulty remembering his own world. He becomes confused, disoriented, melancholy."

"Is he always so?"

"Today was better than most. Sometimes I cannot stop his weeping."

"I have never heard him talk so long without mentioning his Rosa."

"Ah, you noticed that, too. But three days ago he was completely lucid and calculated columns of figures. Settings, he said, for his machine. They take into account, ah . . . 'many-valued inverse functions.' " Vonderberge smiled. "Whatever that means. And, if he ever sees his machine again."

"His machine," said Knecht. "Has anyone handled it?"

"No," said Vonderberge. "Ochsenfuss doesn't think it matters. It's just a collection of knobs and wires."

"And you?"

"Me?" Vonderberge looked at him. "I'm afraid to."

"Yet, its study could be most rewarding."

"A true scout. But if we try, four things could happen and none of them good."

Knecht tugged on his moustache. "We could open it up and find that it is an obvious fake, that it couldn't possibly work."

"Could we? How would it be obvious? We would still wonder whether the science were so advanced that we simply did not understand how it did work. Like a savage with a steam engine." The Kommandant was silent for a moment.

"That's one. You said four things could happen."

"The other three assume the machine works." He held up his fingers to count off his points. "Two: In our ignorance, we damage it irreparably, marooning Kelly forever. Three: We injure ourselves by some sort of shock or explosion."

"And four?"

"Four: We transport ourselves unwittingly to another world."

"A slim possibility, that."

Vonderberge shrugged. "Perhaps. But the penalty for being wrong is . . ."

"Excessive," agreed Knecht dryly.

"I *did* examine his 'calculator,' you know."

Knecht smiled to himself. He had wondered if the Kommandant had done that, too. Knecht had learned little from it, himself.

"It was fine work: the molded plastic, the tiny buttons, the intricate circuits and parts."

"Not beyond the capabilities of any competent electrosmith."

"What! Did you see how small the batteries were? And the, what did he call them? The chips? How can you say that?"

"I didn't mean we could build a calculating engine so small. But, is it a calculating engine? Did you see it function? No. Kelly says the batteries have gone dead. Which is convenient for him. Our regimental electrosmith could easily construct a copy that does the same thing: mainly, nothing."

Vonderberge stopped and held him by the arm. "Tell me, Rudi. Do you believe Kelly or not?"

"I . . ." Well, did he? The business with the cigar was too pat. It seemed important only because of Kelly's toying with another cigar a few weeks before. Otherwise, he would never have noticed, or thought nothing even if he had. Like the prophetic dream: It seems to be more than it is because we only remember them when they come true. "I . . . have no convincing evidence."

"Evidence?" asked Vonderberge harshly. "What more evidence do you need?"

"Something solid," Knecht snapped back. *Something more than that I like the prisoner and the Kommandant and I dislike the Hexmajor.* "Something more than a prisoner's tale," he said, "that becomes more confused as time goes on."

"That is Ochsenfuss' bungling!"

"Or his success! Have you thought that perhaps the Hexmajor is *curing* Kelly of a long-standing delusion?"

Vonderberge turned to go. "No."

Knecht stopped him. "Heinrich," he said.

"What?"

Knecht looked past the Kommandant. He could see the sentries where they paced the walls, and the cannon in their redoubts, and the gangways to the underground tunnels that led to the big guns fortified into the mountainside. "Real or fantasy, you've learned a lot about the prisoner's technology."

"Enough to want to learn more."

"Tell me, Heinrich. Do you *want* to learn to make nuclear bombs?"

Vonderberge followed Knecht's gaze. A troubled look crossed his face and he bit his lower lip. "No, I do not. But the same force can produce electricity. And the medical science that produces the miracle drugs can tailor-make horrible plagues. The jets that fly bombs can just as easily fly people or food or trade goods." He sighed. "What can I say, Rudi. It is not the tool, but the tool-user who creates the problems. Nature keeps no secrets. If something can be done, someone will find a way to do it."

Knecht made no reply. He didn't know if a reply was even possible. Certainly none that Vonderberge would understand.

When Ranger O Brien brought the news from the Nations, General Schneider was away from the fortress, inspecting the outposts on the forward slope. Knecht received O Brien's report, ordered the man to take some rest, and decided the General should see it immediately. He telegraphed Outpost Three that he was coming and rode out.

The crest of Kittatinny Mountain and all the forward slope had been clear-cut the distance of a cannon shot. Beyond that was wilderness. Ridge and valley alternated into the distant north, dense with trees, before rising once more into the Pocono range, where Wyoming had her own fortress line. Legally, the border ran somewhere through the no-man's-land between, but the main armies were entrenched in more easily defended terrain.

Knecht reined in at the crest of the Mountain and looked back. The valley of the Lehigh was checkerboarded with broad farms. Farther away, he could discern the smoke plumes of cities at the canal and rail heads. There was a speck in the air, most likely an airship sailing south.

When he turned, the contrast with the land north of the Mountain was jarring. He must have gazed upon that vista thousands of times over the years. Now, for just an instant, it looked *wrong*. It was said to be fertile land. Certainly, enough blood had manured it. And some said there was coal beneath it. He imagined the land filled with farms, mills, and mines.

At that moment of *frisson* he knew, irrationally, that Kelly had been telling the truth all along. Somewhere the barbed wire was used only to keep the *milch* cows safe.

And the bombs and missiles? What if it were a rain of death from the other side of the world that we feared, and not a party of Mohawk bucks out to prove themselves to their elders? A slow explosion, Kelly had said. The inventions would come. Nature kept no secrets. The discoveries would be made and be given to the petty rulers of petty, quarreling states. Men with dreams of conquest, or revenge.

Knecht clucked to his horse and started downslope to the picket line. Give Konrad Schneider that, he thought. His only dream is survival, not conquest. Yet he is desperate; and desperate men do desperate things, not always wise things.

"Hah! Rudi!" General Schneider waved to him when he saw him coming. He was standing on the glacis of the outpost along with the Feldwebel and his men. The General's staff was as large as the platoon stationed there, so the area seemed ludicrously crowded. The General stood in their midst, a portly, barrel-chested man with a large curved pipe clenched firmly in his teeth. He pointed.

"Do you think the field of fire is clear enough and wide enough?"

Knecht tethered his horse and walked to where the General stood. He had never known Schneider to ask an idle question. He decided the real question was whether Vonderberge was reliable. He gave the cleared area careful scrutiny. Not so much as a blade of grass. No force large enough to take the outpost could approach unseen. "It seems adequate," he said.

"Hmph. High praise from you, Rudi." The General sucked on his pipe, staring downslope, imagining ranks of yankees and knickerbockers charging up. "It had better be. But you did not ride out here from Fox Gap only to answer an old man's foolish questions."

"No, General."

Schneider stared at him and the smile died on his face.

He put his arm around Knecht's shoulder and led him off to the side. The others eyed them nervously. When scouts and generals talked the result was often trouble.

"What is it?"

"Friedrich O Brien has returned from the Nations."

"And?"

"The League has voted six to two to join the alliance against us."

They paced together in silence. Then Schneider said, "So, who held out?"

"Huron and Wyandot."

The General nodded. He released Knecht's shoulder and walked off by himself. He turned and gave a hollow laugh. "Well, at least some of our money was well spent. In the old days, it would have been enough. League votes would have had to be unanimous. Do you think they will fight? The two holdouts, I mean."

"Do you think they will split the League, General, over Pennsylvania?"

"Hmph. No. You are right again. They will go with the majority. But, perhaps, the fighting on the west will be less, what? Enthusiastic?"

"At least it is too late in the year for an offensive."

"Perhaps, Rudi. But the crops are in. If they think they can knock us out in a lightning-war before the snows, they may try anyway. How long can they hold their alliance together? It is unnatural. Yankees and knicks and long-housers side by side? Pfah! It cannot last. No, they must strike while they have Virginia with them, as well. What do you think? A holding action along the Fortress Line while the Lees strike up the Susquehannah and Shenandoah?"

"Will Virginia bleed for New York's benefit?"

Schneider nodded. "A two-front war, then." He rubbed his hands together briskly. "Well, our strategy is clear. We must stir up problems behind them. In New England or Carolina or Pontiac. And perhaps we have a few surprises of our own."

Knecht looked at him sharply. Schneider was smiling. It was a small smile, but it was a real one, not forced. "What are you talking about?"

Schneider pointed to the wires running from the outpost to the Fortress. "Suppose there were no wires to be cut or tapped. Suppose there were voices in the air, undetectable, sent from anywhere a man could carry an instrument. We would not need messengers or pigeons, either. Think how quickly we could learn of enemy formations and mobilize our own forces to meet them. The right force in the right time and place is worth regiments a mile away and a day late. Or airplanes, darting among the airships with machine guns and bombs. We could carry the fighting all the way to Wilkes-Barre and Painted Post."

"Kelly."

"*Ja.*" The General chuckled. "Vonderberge tells me of these gadgets, like radio. Crazy notions. But I wonder. What if it were true? Kelly's waking mind does not remember the details of the sort of, hmph, primitive inventions we could hope to copy. And from your report I suspect he would not help us willingly. Oh, he is friendly enough; but he does not like the military and would not help us prepare for war. Especially a war none of his concern. A problem. So, I seize the moment." He clenched his fist and waved it.

"You pass along the information to Ochsenfuss and

ask him to find the details by prying in his unconscious mind."

Schneider looked at him. "You knew?"

"I guessed."

"You never guess. You're offended."

"No."

"You are. But I had to leave you out. You would have cut to the truth too quickly. I knew you. If you found that Kelly was mad, well, no harm done; but I was speculating that he was just what he said he was. If that were the case, I could not allow you to prove it."

"Why not?"

"Ochsenfuss, that old plodder. He will not mesmerize except for medical reasons. If you had proven Kelly was, well, Kelly, our friend the Hexmajor would have bowed out and Kelly's secrets would have remained secret. No. I needed Ochsenfuss' skill at mesmerizing. I needed Vonderberge's enthusiasm for technofiction, so he would know what questions to ask. And, for it to work, I needed Kelly's status to remain ambiguous."

"Then the Hexmajor does not know."

"No. He is our protective plumage. I read his reports and send them to a secret team of scientists that OKP has assembled at Franklin University. Only a few people at OKP know anything. Only I, and now you, know everything."

Knecht grunted. Ochsenfuss *did* know. At least he knew something. His remarks at the officers' club had made that clear.

"Vonderberge said we lack the tools to make the tools to make the things Kelly described."

"Then Vonderberge is short-sighted. Pfah! I am no fool. I don't ask for the sophisticated developments.

Those are years ahead. Decades. But the original, basic inventions, those are different. As Kelly described it, they came about in a world much like our own. And, Rudi?"

"*Ja*, Herr General?"

"This morning I received word from Franklin. They have sent telegraphic messages *without wires* between Germantown and Philadelphia. They used a special kind of crystal. The pulses travel through the air itself." He grinned like a child with a new toy.

Knecht wondered how much difference such things would make in the coming war. There wasn't time to make enough of them and learn how to use them. He also remembered what Ochsenfuss had said in the officers' club. Something had to break. The question was what. Or who.

Knecht took a deep breath. "It's over, then. You've learned how to make radio messages. Ochsenfuss can stop treating him."

Schneider would not meet his eyes. "The mesmerization must continue. There are other inventions. We need to know about airframes. The details are sketchy yet. And napalm. And . . ."

"Between Ochsenfuss and Vonderberge, Kelly's personality is being destroyed. He hardly remembers who he is, or which world is real."

"This is war. In war there are casualties. Even innocent ones."

"It is not Kelly's war."

"No. But it is yours."

Knecht's mouth set in a grim line. "*Ja*, Herr General."

"You make it look so easy," said Vonderberge.

"Shh," hissed Knecht. He twisted his probe once more

and felt the bolt slide back. "These old-style locks are easy, and I've had much practice." He pulled the storeroom door open and they stepped inside.

"Schneider will know you did it. Who else has your skill with locks?"

Knecht scowled. "Every scout and ranger in the Corps. But, yes, Schneider will know it was me."

Vonderberge began searching the shelves. "Does that bother you?"

Knecht shrugged. "I don't know. It should. The General has been . . . like a father to me."

"Here it is," said Vonderberge. He stepped back, Kelly's rucksack in his hands. He looked inside. "Yes, the bell controls are here also. I don't think anyone has touched it. Schneider has the only key."

"Do you suppose it still works?"

Vonderberge's hands clenched around the straps. "It must."

They crossed the parade ground to the brig. It was dark. Knecht felt that he should dart from cover to cover; but that was silly. They were officers and they belonged here. They took salutes from three passing soldiers. Everything was normal.

The night guard in the cell block shook his head sadly when he saw them coming. "In the middle of the night, sir?" he said to Vonderberge. "Hasn't the poor bastard spilled his guts yet? Who is he, anyway?"

"As you said, soldier," Vonderberge answered. "Some poor bastard."

While the guard unlocked the cell door, Vonderberge hefted the rucksack, getting a better grip. He stroked the canvas nervously. Knecht could see beads of perspiration on his forehead.

Well, he's risking his career, too, he thought.

"We will never have a better chance, Rudi," Vonderberge whispered. "Kelly was very clear this morning when I told him what we proposed to do. He had already calculated settings several days ago, using his new 'formula.' He only needed to update them. I arranged a diversion to keep Ochsenfuss away from him, so he has not been mesmerized in the meantime. Tomorrow and he may relapse into confusion once more."

"As you say," said Knecht shortly. He was not happy about this. For Knecht, his career was his life. He had been army since his teens. A scout, and a good one; perhaps the best. Now it was on the line. A scout observes and listens and pieces things together. He does not initiate action. How many times had he said that over the years? He had said it to Kelly. Why should he break his code now, for a man he hardly knew?

Knecht didn't know. He only knew that it would be worse to leave Kelly where he was. An obligation? Because I brought him here? Because of what we might learn from him?

Perhaps I could have argued Konrad into this, he thought. And perhaps not. And if not, there would have been a guard on that storeroom door, and restricted access to the prisoner, and so I have to do this by night and by stealth.

The guard came suddenly to attention. Knecht looked around and saw Ochsenfuss entering the corridor from the guardroom. Vonderberge, already stepping inside the cell, saw him, too. He grabbed Knecht's shoulder. "Talk to him. Keep him out until it's too late."

Knecht nodded and Vonderberge pulled the door shut. Knecht had a momentary glimpse of Kelly, rising from his cot fully dressed. Then the door closed and Ochsenfuss was at his side. The guard looked at them and pretended to be somewhere else. Knecht wondered what he would say to the Hexmajor that would keep him out.

"Up late, *Herr Doctor*," he said. *Clever, Rudi. Very clever.*

"Insomnia," was the reply. "A common malady, it seems. You might ask who is *not* up late, whiling away the hours in the guardhouse. Do you have a cigar?"

The request caught Knecht by surprise. Dumbly, he took out his pocket humidor. Ochsenfuss made a great show of selecting one of the cigars inside. Knecht took one also and offered one to the guard, who refused.

"Fire?" Ochsenfuss struck a match for Knecht, then lit his own. After a moment or two, he blew a perfect smoke ring. "I had an interesting experience today."

"Oh?" Knecht glanced at the guard, who decided this would be a good time to patrol the outside of the building.

"*Ja.* I had a message from Outpost 10. The farthest one. One of the men was behaving oddly. Confinement mania, perhaps. But when I arrived, no one knew about the message. Or, more precisely, no one *acknowledged* knowing about the message. Odd, don't you think?"

"A hoax." Dimly, through the door, Knecht could hear a low-pitched hum. The floor seemed to be vibrating, ever so slightly. He thought he could detect a faint whiff of ozone in the air. He studied the doctor's face, but saw no sign of awareness.

"Certainly a hoax. That was obvious. But to what purpose? Simply to laugh at the foolish doctor? Perhaps. But perhaps more. I could see but two possibilities, logically. The message was to make me do something or to prevent me from doing something."

Knecht nodded. "That does seem logical." The night air was cool, but he could feel the sweat running down his back, staining his shirt. The humming rose in pitch.

"Logic is a useful tool," Ochsenfuss agreed inanely. "As nearly as I could tell, the only thing the message made me do was to ride down the Mountain and back up. That did not seem to benefit anyone."

"Is there a point to this, *Herr Doctor*?" Knecht felt jumpy. Abruptly, the humming rose sharply in pitch and dropped in volume, sounding oddly like the whistle of a railroad train approaching and receding at the same time. Then it was gone. Knecht suppressed the urge to turn around. He swallowed a sigh of relief.

"What remains?" Ochsenfuss continued. "What was I prevented from doing? Why treating Kelly, of course. And who has been my opponent in the treatment? The Festungskommandant. So, since my return, I have been watching."

Knecht took the cigar from his mouth and stared. "*You* spied on *me*?"

Ochsenfuss laughed. A great bellow. He slapped Knecht's shoulder. "No, I pay you a high compliment. No one could watch you for long without you becoming aware of the fact. A sense shared by all scouts who survive. No, I followed Vonderberge. When you met him at the storeroom, I retired. It was obvious what you intended to do."

Knecht flushed. "And you told no one?"

Ochsenfuss sucked on his cigar. "No. Should I have?" He paused and pointed the stub of his cigar at the cell door. "He's not coming out, you know."

"What? Who?"

"Your friend, Vonderberge. He's not coming out. He's gone."

Knecht turned and stared at the door. "You mean he took the equipment and left Kelly behind?"

"No, no. They left together. If they stayed close, if they hugged, they would both be inside the field."

"Guard!" bellowed Knecht. "Open this door!" The guard came pounding down the corridor. He unlocked the door and he and Knecht crowded inside. The cell was empty. Knecht saw that Ochsenfuss had not bothered to look. The guard gave a cry of astonishment and ran to fetch the watch-sergeant. Knecht stepped out and looked at the doctor.

The doctor shrugged. "I told you he would reject reality if he could."

"Explain that!" Knecht pointed to the empty cell.

Ochsenfuss blew another smoke ring. "He ran from reality." With a sudden motion, he kicked the cell door. It swung back and banged against the wall. "This is reality," he said harshly. "Vonderberge has fled it. How else can I say it?"

"Obviously, the other worlds are no less real. The evidence is there, now."

"What of it? It is the flight that matters, not the destination. What if the next world fails to please him? Will he reject that reality as well?"

A squad of soldiers came pelting from the guardroom. They pushed past Knecht and Ochsenfuss and crowded into the cell. Their sergeant followed at a more majestic pace.

"How long have you known," Knecht asked Ochsenfuss, "that the other worlds were real?"

Ochsenfuss shrugged. "Long enough." He laughed.

"Poor, dull-witted Ochsenfuss! He cannot see a fact if it bit him on the nose." The Hexmajor's lips thinned. "Granted, I am no physical scientist, but what Kelly said went against everything I had ever read or heard. Later, I came to know I was wrong." Another shrug. "Well, we grow too soon old and too late smart. But I ask you, why did Vonderberge believe? He was correct from the beginning, but he believed before he had any real proof. He believed because he *wanted* to believe. And that, too, is madness."

"And Schneider?"

"Schneider never believed. He was making a bet. Just in case it was true. *He was playing games with my patient!*"

Knecht could see genuine anger now. The first real emotion he had ever seen in the Hexmajor. He saw the General for a moment through the doctor's eyes. It was a side of Konrad he did not care for.

They spoke in an island of calm. Around them soldiers were searching, looking for tunnels. Schneider would be coming soon, Knecht realized. Perhaps it was time to leave, to postpone the inevitable. He and the doctor walked to the front of the guardhouse but they went no further than the wooden portico facing the parade ground. There was really no point in postponement.

Knecht leaned on the railing, looking out over the parade ground. A squad of soldiers marched past in the dusk: full kit, double-time. Their sergeant barked a cadence at them. Idly, Knecht wondered what infraction they had committed. Across the quadrangle, the Visiting Officers' Quarters were dark.

"So why, after you knew, did you continue to treat him?" He looked over his shoulder at the doctor.

Ochsenfuss waved his hands. The glowing tip of his cigar wove a complex pattern in the dark. "You read his journal. Do you really suppose he has found his way home this time? No, he goes deeper into the forest of time, hopelessly lost. And Vonderberge with him. Six worlds he had visited already and in what? In three of them, he was in danger. The next world may kill him."

"But . . ."

"Tchah! Isn't it obvious? He was driven to try. He had friends, family. His darling Rosa. Left behind forever. He could not bear the thought that he would never, ever see her again. How could he not try? How could he not fail? With me he had a chance. I saw it and I took it. If I could make him accept *this* world as the only reality, forget the other, then he might have adjusted. It was a daring thing to try."

Knecht looked back out at the parade ground. There had been a fourth possibility, after all. A refugee, but one slowly going mad. Lightning bugs flashed in the evening air. "It was daring," he agreed, "and it failed."

"Yes, it failed. His senses worked for me: everything Kelly saw and heard told him this world was real; but in the end there were too many memories. I could not tie them all off. Some would remain, buried under the false ones, disturbing him, surfacing in his dreams, eventually emerging as psychoses. I restored his memories, then. I could do no more to help him, so I made no effort to stop you."

Knecht's mind was a jumble. Every possible action was wrong. Whether Kelly had been the person he claimed to be, or a madman, Schneider had done the wrong thing. Ochsenfuss had been wrong to try and obliterate the man's true memories. As for himself, all he and Vonderberge had accomplished was to turn him out into a trackless jungle. Oh, we all had our reasons. Schneider wanted defense. Ochsenfuss wanted to heal. Vonderberge wanted escape. And I . . . Knecht wasn't sure what he had wanted.

"We could have kept him here, without your treatment," he told Ochsenfuss. "So the General could have learned more." Knecht was curious why the doctor had not done that.

As if on cue, the door of the VOQ burst open. Knecht could see Schneider, dressed in pants and undershirt, framed in its light. Schneider strode toward the guardhouse, his face white with rage and astonishment.

Ochsenfuss smiled. "Kelly would have lost what sanity he had left. If we have not given him the way home, we have at least given him hope. And . . ." He looked in Schneider's direction. "While I am a logical man, I, too, have feelings. Your General thought to make me the fool. So, I made a medical decision in my patient's best interest."

Knecht could not help smiling also. "Perhaps I can buy you a drink tomorrow, in the officers' club. If we are both still in the army by then." His cigar had gone out. He looked at it. "I wonder what world they are in now."

"We will never know," replied Ochsenfuss. "Even if they try to come back and tell us, this world is a twig in an infinite forest. They will never find us again. It will be bad for you, Rudi, if you cannot bear not knowing."

Knecht threw his cigar away. He was a scout. It would be bad for him, not knowing.

Aristotle and the Gun

L. Sprague de Camp

Suppose you could visualize an alternate history that would lead to a present you'd like better than the one you live in, and you had a way to change the past to create that alternate history. Would you do it? The time traveler in this tale by L. Sprague de Camp, who has had one of the longest and most distinguished careers in science fiction, finds that decision easy. After careful consideration, he figures out exactly what to change to replace his own world's history by an alternate that, at least to him, is clearly better. Unfortunately, it's very difficult to foresee all the long-term consequences of any action. De Camp's time traveler gets an alternate history, all right, but not quite the one he had in mind. What he does get gives a whole new meaning to "the shot heard round the world . . ."

FROM: Sherman Weaver, Librarian
       The Palace
       Paumanok, Sewanhaki
       Sachimate of Lenape
       Flower Moon 3, 3097

TO: Messire Markos Koukidas
      Consulate of the Balkan Commonwealth
      Kataapa, Muskhogian Federation

My dear Consul:

You have no doubt heard of our glorious victory at
Ptaksit, when our noble Sachim destroyed the armored
chivalry of the Mengwe by the brilliant use of pikemen
and archery. (I suggested it to him years ago, but never
mind.) Sagoyewatha and most of his Senecas fell, and
the Oneidas broke before our countercharge. The envoys
from the Grand Council of the Long House arrive tomorrow for a peace-pauwau. The roads to the south are
open again, so I send you my long-promised account
of the events that brought me from my own world into
this one.

If you could have stayed longer on your last visit, I
think I could have made the matter clear, despite the
language-difficulty and my hardness of hearing. But perhaps if I give you a simple narrative, in the order in
which things happened to me, truth will transpire.

Know, then, that I was born into a world that looks like
this one on the map, but is very different as regards
human affairs. I tried to tell you of some of the triumphs
of our natural philosophers, of our machines and discoveries. No doubt you thought me a first-class liar, though
you were too polite to say so.

None the less, my tale is true, though for reasons that
will appear I cannot prove it. I was one of those natural
philosophers. I commanded a group of younger philosophers, engaged in a task called a *project*, at a center of
learning named Brookhaven, on the south shore of
Sewanhaki twenty parasangs east of Paumanok. Pau-

manok itself was known as Brooklyn, and formed part of an even larger city called New York.

My project had to do with the study of space-time. (Never mind what that means but read on.) At this center we had learned to get vast amounts of power from sea water by what we called a fusion process. By this process we could concentrate so much power in a small space that we could warp the entity called space-time and cause things to travel in time as our other machines traveled in space.

When our calculations showed that we could theoretically hurl an object back in time, we began to build a machine for testing this hypothesis. First we built a small pilot model. In this we sent small objects back in time for short periods. We began with inanimate objects, and then found that a rabbit or rat could also be projected without harm. The time-translation would not be permanent; rather it acted like one of these rubber balls the Hesperians play games with. The object would stay in the desired time for a period determined by the power used to project it and its own mass, and would then return spontaneously to the time and place from which it started.

We had reported our progress regularly, but my chief had other matters on his mind and did not read our reports for many months. When he got a report saying that we were completing a machine to hurl human beings back in time, however, he awoke to what was going on, read our previous reports, and called me in.

"Sherm," he said, "I've been discussing this project with Washington, and I'm afraid they take a dim view of it."

"Why?" said I, astonished.

"Two reasons. For one thing, they think you've gone off the reservation. They're much more interested in the Antarctic Reclamation Project and want to concentrate all our appropriations and brain power on it.

"For another, they're frankly scared of this time machine of yours. Suppose you went back, say, to the time of Alexander the Great and shot Alexander before he got started? That would change all later history, and we'd go out like candles."

"Ridiculous," I said.

"Well, what *would* happen?"

"Our equations are not conclusive, but there are several possibilities. As you will see if you read Report No. 9, it depends on whether space-time has a positive or negative curvature. If positive, any disturbance in the past tends to be ironed out in subsequent history, so that things become more and more nearly identical with what they would have been anyway. If negative, then events will diverge more and more from their original pattern with time.

"Now, as I showed in this report, the chances are overwhelmingly in favor of a positive curvature. However, we intend to take every precaution and make our first tests for short periods, with a minimum—"

"That's enough," said my superior, holding up a hand. "It's very interesting, but the decision has already been made."

"What do you mean?"

"I mean Project A-257 is to be closed down and a final report written at once. The machines are to be dismantled, and the group will be put to work on another project."

"What?" I shouted. "But you can't stop us just when we're on the verge—"

"I'm sorry, Sherm, but I can. That's what the AEC decided at yesterday's meeting. It hasn't been officially announced, but they gave me positive orders to kill the project as soon as I got back here."

"Of all the lousy, arbitrary, benighted—"

"I know how you feel, but I have no choice."

I lost my temper and defied him, threatening to go ahead with the project anyway. It was ridiculous, because he could easily dismiss me for insubordination. However, I knew he valued my ability and counted on his wanting to keep me for that reason. But he was clever enough to have his cake and eat it.

"If that's how you feel," he said, "the section is abolished here and now. Your group will be broken up and assigned to other projects. You'll be kept on at your present rating with the title of consultant. Then when you're willing to talk sense, perhaps we can find you a suitable job."

I stamped out of his office and went home to brood. I ought now to tell you something of myself. I am old enough to be objective, I hope, and as I have but a few years left there is no point in pretense.

I have always been a solitary, misanthropic man. I had little interest in or liking of my fellow man, who naturally paid me back in the same coin. I was awkward and ill at ease in company. I had a genius for saying the wrong thing and making a fool of myself. I never understood people. Even when I watched and planned my own actions with the greatest care, I never could tell how others would react to them. To me men were and are an unpredictable, irrational, and dangerous species of hair-less ape. While I could avoid some of my worst gaffes by keeping my own counsel and watching my every word, they did not like that either. They considered me a cold, stiff, unfriendly sort of person when I was only trying to be polite and avoid offending them.

I never married, and at the time of which I speak I was verging on middle age without a single close friend and no more acquaintances than my professional work required. I could justify my attitude by telling about the vices and follies of mankind, but I will not because you are, I think, familiar enough with these things already.

My only interest outside my work was a hobby of the history of science. Unlike most of my fellow-philosophers, I was historically minded, with a good smattering of a Classical education. I belonged to the History of Science Society and wrote papers on the history of science for the periodical *Isis*.

I went back to my little rented house, feeling like Galileo. He was a scientist persecuted for his astronomi-cal theories by the religious authorities of my world sev-eral centuries before my time, as Georg Schwartzhorn was a few years ago in this world's Europe.

I felt I had been born too soon. If only the world were scientifically more advanced, my genius would be appre-ciated and my personal difficulties solved.

Well, I thought, why is the world not scientifically more advanced? I reviewed the early growth of science. Why had not your fellow-countrymen, when they made a start towards a scientific age two thousand to twenty-five hundred years ago, kept at it until they made science the self-supporting, self-accelerating thing it at last became—in my world, that is.

I knew the answer that historians of science had worked out. One was the effect of slavery, which made work disgraceful to a free man and therefore made experiment and invention unattractive because they looked like work. Another was the primitive state of the mechanical arts: things like making clear glass and accurate measuring devices. Another was the Hellenes' fondness for spinning cosmic theories without enough facts to go on, the result of which was that most of their theories were wildly wrong.

Well, thought I, could a man go back to this period and, by applying a stimulus at the right time and place, give the necessary push to set the whole trend rolling off in the right direction?

People had written fantastic stories about a man's going back in time and overawing the natives by a display of the discoveries of his own later era. More often than not, such a time-traveling hero came to a bad end. The people of the earlier time killed him as a witch, or he met with an accident, or something happened to keep him from changing history. But, knowing these dangers, I could forestall them by careful planning.

It would do little or no good to take back some major invention, like a printing press or an automobile, and turn it over to the ancients in the hope of grafting it on their culture. I could not teach them to work it in a reasonable time, and if it broke down or ran out of supplies there would be no way to get it running again.

What I had to do was to find a key mind and implant in it an appreciation of sound scientific method. He would have to be somebody who would have been important in any event, or I could not count on his influence spreading far and wide.

After study of Sarton and other historians of science, I picked Aristotle. You have heard of him, have you not? He existed in your world just as he did in mine. In fact, up to Aristotle's time our worlds were one and the same.

Aristotle was one of the greatest minds of all time. In my world, he was the first encyclopedist; the first man who tried to know everything, write down everything, and explain everything. He did much good original scientific work, too, mostly in biology.

However, Aristotle tried to cover so much ground, and accepted so many fables as facts, that he did much harm to science as well as good. For, when a man of such colossal intellect goes wrong, he carries with him whole generations of weaker minds who cite him as an infallible authority. Like his colleagues, Aristotle never appreciated the need for constant verification. Thus, though he was married twice, he said that men have more teeth than women. He never thought to ask either of his wives to open her mouth for a count. He never grasped the need for invention and experiment.

Now, if I could catch Aristotle at the right period of his career, perhaps I could give him a push in the right direction.

When would that be? Normally, one would take him as a young man. But Aristotle's entire youth, from seventeen to thirty-seven, was spent in Athens listening to Plato's lectures. I did not wish to compete with Plato, an overpowering personality who could argue rings around anybody. His viewpoint was mystical and antiscientific, the very thing I wanted to steer Aristotle away from.

Many of Aristotle's intellectual vices can be traced back to Plato's influence.

I did not think it wise to present myself in Athens either during Aristotle's early period, when he was a student under Plato, or later, when he headed his own school. I could not pass myself off as a Hellene, and the Hellenes of that time had a contempt for all non-Hellenes, whom they called "barbarians." Aristotle was one of the worst offenders in this respect. Of course this is a universal human failing, but it was particularly virulent among Athenian intellectuals. In his later Athenian period, too, Aristotle's ideas would probably be too set with age to change.

I concluded that my best chance would be to catch Aristotle while he was tutoring young Alexander the Great at the court of Philip the Second of Macedon. He would have regarded Macedon as a backward country, even though the court spoke Attic Greek. Perhaps he would be bored with bluff Macedonian stag-hunting squires and lonesome for intellectual company. As he would regard the Macedonians as the next thing to *barbaroi*, another barbarian would not appear at such a disadvantage there as at Athens.

Of course, whatever I accomplished with Aristotle, the results would depend on the curvature of space-time. I had not been wholly frank with my superior. While the equations tended to favor the hypothesis of a positive curvature, the probability was not overwhelming. Perhaps my efforts would have little effect on history, or perhaps the effect would grow and widen like ripples in a pool. In the latter case the existing world would, as my superior said, be snuffed out.

Well, at that moment I hated the existing world and

would not give a snap of my fingers for its destruction. I was going to create a much better one and come back from ancient times to enjoy it.

Our previous experiments showed that I could project myself back to ancient Macedon with an accuracy of about two months temporally and a half-parasang spatially. The machine included controls for positioning the time-traveler anywhere on the globe, and safety devices for locating him above the surface of the earth, not in a place already occupied by a solid object. The equations showed that I should stay in Macedon about nine weeks before being snapped back to the present.

Once I had made up my mind, I worked as fast as I could. I telephoned my superior—you remember what a telephone is?—and made my peace. I said:

"I know I was a hotheaded fool, Fred, but this thing was my baby; my one chance to be a great and famous scientist. I might have got a Nobel prize out of it."

"Sure, I know, Sherm," he said. "When are you coming back to the lab?"

"Well . . . uh . . . what about my group?"

"I held up the papers on that, in case you might change your mind. So if you come back, all will go on organization-wise as before."

"You want that final report on A-257, don't you?" I said, trying to keep my voice level.

"Sure."

"Then don't let the mechanics start to dismantle the machines until I've written the report."

"No; I've had the place locked up since yesterday."

"O.K. I want to shut myself in with the apparatus and

the data-sheets for a while and bat out the report without being bothered."

"That'll be fine," he said.

My first step in getting ready for my journey was to buy a suit of Classical traveler's clothing from a theatrical costume company. This comprised a knee-length pull-over tunic or chiton, a short horseman's cloak or chlamys, knitted buskins, sandals, a broad-brimmed black felt hat, and a staff. I stopped shaving, though I did not have time to raise a respectable beard.

My auxiliary equipment included a purse of coinage of the time, mostly golden Macedonian staters. Some of these coins were genuine, bought from a numismatic supply house, but most were copies I cast myself in the laboratory at night. I made sure of being rich enough to live decently for longer than my nine weeks' stay. This was not hard, as the purchasing power of precious metals was more than fifty times greater in the Classical world than in mine.

I wore the purse attached to a heavy belt next to my skin. From this belt also hung a missile-weapon called a *gun*, which I have told you about. This was a small gun, called a pistol or revolver. I did not mean to shoot anybody, or expose the gun at all if I could help it. It was there as a last resort.

I also took several small devices of our science to impress Aristotle: a pocket microscope and a magnifying glass, a small telescope, a compass, my timepiece, a flashlight, a small camera, and some medicines. I intended to show these things to people of ancient times only with the greatest caution. By the time I had slung all these objects in their pouches and cases from my belt, I had a heavy load. Another belt over the tunic supported a small purse for day-to-day buying and an all-purpose knife.

I already had a good reading knowledge of Classical Greek, which I tried to polish by practice with the spoken language and listening to it on my talking machine. I knew I should arrive speaking with an accent, but we had no way of knowing exactly what Attic Greek sounded like.

I decided, therefore, to pass myself off as a traveler from India. Nobody would believe I was a Hellene. If I said I came from the north or west, no Hellene would listen to me, as they regarded Europeans as warlike but half-witted savages. If I said I was from some well-known civilized country like Carthage, Egypt, Babylonia, or Persia, I should be in danger of meeting someone who knew those countries and of being exposed as a fraud. To tell the truth of my origin, save under extraordinary circumstances, would be most imprudent. It would lead to my being considered a lunatic or a liar, as I can guess that your good self has more than once suspected me of being.

An Indian, however, should be acceptable. At this time, the Hellenes knew about that land only a few wild rumors and the account of Ktesias of Knidos, who made a book of the tales he picked up about India at the Persian court. The Hellenes had heard that India harbored philosophers. Therefore thinking Greeks might be willing to consider Indians as almost as civilized as themselves.

What should I call myself? I took a common Indian name, Chandra, and Hellenized it to Zandras. That, I knew, was what the Hellenes would do anyway, as they had no "tch" sound and insisted on putting Greek inflectional endings on foreign names. I would not try to use my own name, which is not even remotely Greek or

Indian-sounding. (Some day I must explain the blunders in my world that led to Hesperians being called "Indians.")

The newness and cleanliness of my costume bothered me. It did not look worn, and I could hardly break it in around Brookhaven without attracting attention. I decided that if the question came up, I should say: yes, I bought it when I entered Greece, so as not to be conspicuous in my native garb.

During the day, when not scouring New York for equipment, I was locked in the room with the machine. While my colleagues thought I was either writing my report or dismantling the apparatus, I was getting ready for my trip.

Two weeks went by thus. One day a memorandum came down from my superior, saying: "How is that final report coming?"

I knew then I had better put my plan into execution at once. I sent back a memorandum: "Almost ready for the writing machine."

That night I came back to the laboratory. As I had been doing this often, the guards took no notice. I went to the time-machine room, locked the door from the inside, and got out my equipment and costume.

I adjusted the machine to set me down near Pella, the capital of Macedon, in the spring of the year 340 before Christ in our system of reckoning (976 Algonkian). I set the auto-actuator, climbed inside, and closed the door.

The feeling of being projected through time really cannot be described. There is a sharp pain, agonizing but too short to let the victim even cry out. At the same time there is the feeling of terrific acceleration, as if one were being shot from a catapult, but in no particular direction.

Then the seat in the passenger-compartment dropped away from under me. There was a crunch, and a lot of sharp things jabbed me. I had fallen into the top of a tree.

I grabbed a couple of branches to save myself. The mechanism that positioned me in Macedon, detecting solid matter at the point where I was going to materialize, had raised me up above the treetops and then let go. It was an old oak, just putting out its spring leaves.

In clutching for branches I dropped my staff, which slithered down through the foliage and thumped the ground below. At least it thumped something. There was a startled yell.

Classical costume is impractical for tree-climbing. Branches kept knocking off my hat, or snagging my cloak, or poking me in tender places not protected by trousers. I ended my climb with a slide and a fall of several feet, tumbling into the dirt.

As I looked up, the first thing I saw was a burly, black-bearded man in a dirty tunic, standing with a knife in his hand. Near him stood a pair of oxen yoked to a wooden plow. At his feet stood a water jug.

The plowman had evidently finished a furrow and lain down to rest himself and his beasts when the fall of my staff on him and then my arrival in person aroused him.

Around me stretched the broad Emathian Plain, ringed by ranges of stony hills and craggy mountains. As the sky was overcast, and I did not dare consult my compass, I had no sure way of orienting myself, or even telling what time of day it was. I assumed that the biggest mountain in sight was Mount Bermion, which ought to be to the west. To the north I could see a trace of water. This would be

Lake Ludias. Beyond the lake rose a range of low hills. A discoloration on the nearest spur of these hills might be a city, though my sight was not keen enough to make out details, and I had to do without my eyeglasses. The gently rolling plain was cut up into fields and pastures with occasional trees and patches of marsh. Dry brown grasses left over from winter nodded in the wind.

My realization of all this took but a flash. Then my attention was brought back to the plowman, who spoke. I could not understand a word. But then, he would speak Macedonian. Though this can be deemed a Greek dialect, it differed so from Attic Greek as to be unintelligible.

No doubt the man wanted to know what I was doing in his tree. I put on my best smile and said in my slow fumbling Attic: "Rejoice! I am lost, and climbed your tree to find my way."

He spoke again. When I did not respond he repeated his words more loudly, waving his knife.

We exchanged more words and gestures, but it was evident that neither had the faintest notion of what the other was trying to say. The plowman began shouting, as ignorant people will when faced by the linguistic barrier.

At last I pointed to the distant headland overlooking the lake, on which there appeared a discoloration that might be the city. Slowly and carefully I said:

"Is that Pella?"

"*Nai, Pella!*" The man's mien became less threatening.

"I am going to Pella. Where can I find the philosopher Aristotle?" I repeated the name.

He was off again with more gibberish, but I gathered from his expression that he had never heard of any Aristotles. So I picked up my hat and stick, felt through my tunic to make sure my gear was all in place, tossed the rustic a final *"Chaire!"* and set off.

By the time I had crossed the muddy field and come out on a cart track, the problem of looking like a seasoned traveler had solved itself. There were green and brown stains on my clothes from the scramble down the tree; the cloak was torn; the branches had scratched my limbs and face; my feet and lower legs were covered with mud. I also became aware that, to one who has lived all his life with his loins decently swathed in trousers and underdrawers, Classical costume is excessively drafty.

I glanced back to see the plowman still standing with one hand on his plow, looking at me in puzzled fashion. The poor fellow had never been able to decide what, if anything, to do about me.

When I found a road, it was hardly more than a heavily used cart track, with a pair of deep ruts and the space between them alternating stones, mud, and long grass.

I walked towards the lake and passed a few people on the road. To one used to the teeming traffic of my world, Macedon seemed dead and deserted. I spoke to some of the people, but ran into the same barrier of language as with the plowman.

Finally a two-horse chariot came along, driven by a stout man wearing a headband, a kind of kilt, and high-laced boots. He pulled up at my hail.

"What is it?" he said, in Attic not much better than mine.

"I seek the philosopher, Aristoteles of Stageira. Where can I find him?"

"He lives in Mieza."

"Where is that?"

The man waved. "You are going the wrong way. Follow this road back the way you came. At the ford across the Bottiais, take the right-hand fork, which will bring you to Mieza and Kition. Do you understand?"

"I think so," I said. "How far is it?"

"About two hundred stadia."

My heart sank to my sandals. This meant five parasangs, or a good two-days' walk. I thought of trying to buy a horse or a chariot, but I had never ridden or driven a horse and saw no prospect of learning how soon enough to do any good. I had read about Mieza as Aristotle's home in Macedon but, as none of my maps had shown it, I had assumed it to be a suburb of Pella.

I thanked the man, who trotted off, and set out after him. The details of my journey need not detain you. I was benighted far from shelter through not knowing where the villages were, attacked by watchdogs, eaten alive by mosquitoes, and invaded by vermin when I did find a place to sleep the second night. The road skirted the huge marshes that spread over the Emathian Plain west of Lake Ludias. Several small streams came down from Mount Bermion and lost themselves in this marsh.

At last I neared Mieza, which stands on one of the spurs of Mount Bermion. I was trudging wearily up the long rise to the village when six youths on little Greek horses clattered down the road. I stepped to one side, but instead of cantering past they pulled up and faced me in a semicircle.

"Who are you?" asked one, a smallish youth of about fifteen, in fluent Attic. He was blond and would have been noticeably handsome without his pimples.

"I am Zandras of Pataliputra," I said, giving the ancient name for Patna on the Ganges. "I seek the philosopher Aristoteles."

"Oh, a barbarian!" cried Pimples. "We know what the Aristoteles thinks of these, eh, boys?"

The others joined in, shouting noncompliments and bragging about all the barbarians they would some day kill or enslave.

I made the mistake of letting them see I was getting angry. I knew it was unwise, but I could not help myself. "If you do not wish to help me, then let me pass," I said.

"Not only a barbarian, but an insolent one!" cried one of the group, making his horse dance uncomfortably close to me.

"Stand aside, children!" I demanded.

"We must teach you a lesson," said Pimples. The others giggled.

"You had better let me alone," I said, gripping my staff in both hands.

A tall handsome adolescent reached over and knocked my hat off. "That for you, cowardly Asiatic!" he yelled.

Without stopping to think, I shouted an English epithet and swung my staff. Either the young man leaned out of the way or his horse shied, for my blow missed him. The momentum carried the staff past my target and the end struck the nose of one of the other horses.

The pony squealed and reared. Having no stirrups, the rider slid off the animal's rump into the dirt. The horse galloped off.

All six youths began screaming. The blond one, who had a particularly piercing voice, mouthed some threat. The next thing I knew, his horse bounded directly at me.

Before I could dodge, the animal's shoulder knocked me head over heels and the beast leaped over me as I rolled. Luckily, horses' dislike of stepping on anything squashy saved me from being trampled. I scrambled up as another horse bore down upon me. By a frantic leap I got out of its way, but I saw that the other boys were jockeying their mounts to do likewise.

A few paces away rose a big pine. I dodged in among its lower branches as the other horses ran at me. The youths could not force their mounts in among these branches, so they galloped round and round and yelled. Most of their talk I could not understand, but I caught a sentence from Pimples:

"Ptolemaios! Ride back to the house and fetch bows or javelins!"

Hoofbeats receded. I could not see clearly through the pine needles, but I inferred what was happening. The youths would not try to rush me on foot, first because they liked being on horseback, and if they dismounted they might lose their horses or have trouble remounting; second, because as long as I kept my back to the tree they would have a hard time getting at me through the tangle of branches, and I could hit and poke them with my stick as I came. Though not an unusually tall man in my own world, I was much bigger than any of these boys.

But this was a minor consideration. I recognized the name "Ptolemaios" as that of one of Alexander's companions, who in my world became King Ptolemy of Egypt and founded a famous dynasty. Young Pimples, then, must be Alexander himself. I was in a real predicament. If I stayed where I was, Ptolemaios would bring back missiles for target practice with me as the target. I could, of course, shoot some of the boys with my gun, which would save me for the time being. But in an absolute monarchy, killing the crown prince's friends, let alone the crown prince himself, is no way to achieve a peaceful old age, regardless of the provocation.

While I was thinking of these matters and listening to my attackers, a stone swished through the branches and bounced off the trunk. The small dark youth who had fallen off his horse had thrown the rock and was urging his friends to do likewise. I caught glimpses of Pimples and the rest dismounting and scurrying around for stones, a commodity with which Greece and Macedon are notoriously well supplied. More stones came through the needles, caroming from the branches. One the size of my fist struck me lightly in the shin.

The boys came closer so that their aim got better. I wormed my way around the trunk to put it between me and them, but they saw the movement and spread out around the tree. A stone grazed my scalp, dizzying me and drawing blood. I thought of climbing, but as the tree became thinner with height, I should be more exposed the higher I got, as well as being less able to dodge while perched in the branches than while I was on solid ground.

That is how things stood when I heard hoofbeats again. This is the moment of decision, I thought. Ptolemaios is coming back with missile weapons. If I used my gun I might doom myself in the long run, but it would be ridiculous to stand there and let them riddle me while I had an unused weapon.

I fumbled under my tunic and unsnapped the safety strap that kept the pistol in its holster. I pulled the weapon out and checked its projectiles.

* * *

A deep voice broke into the bickering. I caught phrases: ". . . Insulting an unoffending traveler . . . how do you know he is not a prince in his own country? The king shall hear of this. . . . Like newly freed slaves, not like princes and gentlemen . . ."

I pushed towards the outer limits of the screen of pine needles. A heavy-set brown-bearded man on a horse was haranguing the youths, who had dropped their stones. Pimples said:

"We were only having a little sport."

I stepped out from the branches, walked over to where my battered hat lay, and put it on. Then I said to the new-comer: "Rejoice! I am glad you came before your boys' play got too rough." I grinned, determined to act cheerful if it killed me. Only iron self-control would get me through this difficulty.

The man grunted. "Who are you?"

"Zandras of Pataliputra, a city in India. I seek Aristoteles the philosopher."

"He insulted us—" began one of the youths, but Brownbeard ignored him. He said:

"I am sorry you have had so rude an introduction to our royal house. This mass of youthful insolence"—he indicated Pimples—"is the Alexandros Philippou, heir to the throne of Makedonia." He introduced the others: Hephaistion, who had knocked my hat off and was now holding the others' horses; Nearchos, who had lost his horse; Ptolemaios, who had gone for weapons; and Harpalos and Philotas. He continued:

"When the Ptolemaios dashed into the house I inquired the reason for his haste, learned of their quarrel with you, and came out forthwith. They have misapplied their master's teachings. They should not behave thus even to a barbarian like yourself, for in so doing they lower themselves to the barbarian's level. I am returning to the house of Aristoteles. You may follow."

The man turned his horse and started walking it back towards Mieza. The six boys busied themselves with catching Nearchos' horse.

I walked after him, though I had to dogtrot now and then to keep up. As it was uphill, I was soon breathing hard. I panted:

"Who . . . my lord . . . are you?"

The man's beard came round and he raised an eyebrow. "I thought you would know. I am Antipatros, regent of Makedonia."

Before we reached the village proper, Antipatros turned off through a kind of park, with statues and benches. This, I supposed, was the Precinct of the Nymphs which Aristotle used as a school ground. We went through the park and stopped at a mansion on the other side. Antipatros tossed the reins to a groom and slid off his horse.

"Aristoteles!" roared Antipatros. "A man wishes to see you."

A man of about my own age—the early forties—came out. He was of medium height and slender build, with a thin-lipped, severe-looking face and a pepper-and-salt beard cut short. He was wrapped in a billowing himation, or large cloak, with a colorful scroll-patterned border. He wore golden rings on several fingers.

Antipatros made a fumbling introduction: "Old fellow, this is . . . ah . . . what's-his-name from . . . ah . . . some place in India." He told of rescuing me from Alexander and his fellow-delinquents, adding: "If you do not beat some manners into your pack of cubs soon, it will be too late."

Aristotle looked at me sharply. "It ith always a pleasure to meet men from afar. What brings you here, my friend?"

I gave my name and said: "Being accounted something of a philosopher in my own land, I thought my visit to the West would be incomplete without speaking to the greatest Western philosopher. And when I asked who he was, everyone told me to seek out Aristoteles Nikomachou."

Aristotle purred. "It ith good of them to thay tho. Ahem. Come in and join me in a drop of wine. Can you tell me of the wonders of India?"

"Yes indeed, but you must tell me in turn of your discoveries, which to me are much more wonderful."

"Come, come, then. Perhapth you could thtay over a few days. I shall have many, many things to athk you."

That is how I met Aristotle. He and I hit it off, as we said in my world, from the start. We had much in common. Some people would not like Aristotle's lisp, or his fussy, pedantic ways, or his fondness for worrying any topic of conversation to death. But he and I got along fine. That afternoon, in the house that King Philip had built for Aristotle to use as the royal school, he handed me a cup of resinated wine and asked:

"Tell me about the elephant, that great beast we have heard of with a tail at both ends. Does it truly exist?"

"Indeed it does," I said, and went on to tell what I knew of elephants, while Aristotle scribbled notes on a piece of papyrus.

"What do they call the elephant in India?" he asked.

The question caught me by surprise, for it had never occurred to me to learn ancient Hindustani along with all the other things I had to know for this expedition. I sipped the wine to give me time to think. I have never cared for alcoholic liquors, and this stuff tasted awful to me, but for the sake of my objective I had to pretend to like it. No doubt I should have to make up some kind of gibberish—but then a mental broad jump carried me back to the stories of Kipling I had read as a boy.

"We call it a *hathi*," I said. "Though of course there are many languages in India."

"How about that Indian wild ath of which Ktesias thpeakth, with a horn in the middle of itth forehead?"

"You had better call it a nose-horn—*rhinokeros*—for that is where its horn really is, and it is more like a gigantic pig than an ass . . ."

As dinner-time neared, I made some artful remarks about going out to find accommodations in Mieza, but Aristotle—to my joy—would have none of it. I should stay right there at the school; my polite protestations of unworthiness he waved aside.

"You muth plan to thtop here for months," he said. "I shall never, never have such a chance to collect data on India again. Do not worry about expense; the king pays all. You are . . . ahem . . . the first barbarian I have known with a decent intellect, and I get lonethome for good tholid talk. Theophrastos has gone to Athens, and my other friends come to these backlands but theldom."

"How about the Macedonians?"

"*Aiboi!* Thome like my friend Antipatros are good fellows, but most are as lackwitted as a Persian grandee. And now tell me of Patal . . . what is your city's name?"

Presently Alexander and his friends came in. They

seemed taken aback at seeing me closeted with their master. I put on a brisk smile and said: "Rejoice, my friends!" as if nothing untoward had happened. The boys glowered and whispered among themselves, but did not attempt any more disturbance at that time.

When they gathered for their lecture next morning, Aristotle told them: "I am too busy with the gentleman from India to waste time pounding unwanted wisdom into your miserable little thouls. Go shoot some rabbitth or catch some fish for dinner, but in any cathe begone!"

The boys grinned. Alexander said: "It seems the barbarian has his uses after all. I hope you stay with us forever, good barbarian!"

After they had gone, Antipatros came in to say goodby to Aristotle. He asked me with gruff good will how I was doing and went out to ride back to Pella.

The weeks passed unnoticed and the flowers of spring came out while I visited Aristotle. Day after day we strolled about the Precinct of the Nymphs, talking, or sat indoors when it rained. Sometimes the boys followed us, listening; at other times we talked alone. They played a couple of practical jokes on me, but, by pretending to be amused when I was really furious, I avoided serious trouble with them.

I learned that Aristotle had a wife and a little daughter in another part of the big house, but he never let me meet the lady. I only caught glimpses of them from a distance.

I carefully shifted the subject of our daily discourse from the marvels of India to the more basic questions of science. We argued over the nature of matter and the shape of the solar system. I gave out that the Indians were well on the road to the modern concepts—modern in my world, that is—of astronomy, physics, and so forth. I told of the discoveries of those eminent Pataliputran philosophers: Kopernikos in astronomy, Neuton in physics, Darben in evolution, and Mendeles in genetics. (I forgot; these names mean nothing to you, though an educated man of my world would recognize them at once through their Greek disguise.)

Always I stressed *method*: the need for experiment and invention and for checking each theory back against the facts. Though an opinionated and argumentative man, Aristotle had a mind like a sponge, eagerly absorbing any new fact, surmise, or opinion, whether he agreed with it or not.

I tried to find a workable compromise between what I knew science could do on one hand and the limits of Aristotle's credulity on the other. Therefore I said nothing about flying machines, guns, buildings a thousand feet high, and other technical wonders of my world. Nevertheless, I caught Aristotle looking at me sharply out of those small black eyes one day.

"Do you doubt me, Aristoteles?" I said.

"N-no, no," he said thoughtfully. "But it does theem to me that, were your Indian inventors as wonderful as you make out, they would have fabricated you wings like those of Daidalos in the legend. Then you could have flown to Makedonia directly, without the trials of crothing Persia by camel."

"That has been tried, but men's muscles do not have enough strength in proportion to their weight."

"Ahem. Did you bring anything from India to show the thkills of your people?"

I grinned, for I had been hoping for such a question. "I did fetch a few small devices," said I, reaching into my tunic and bringing out the magnifying glass. I demonstrated its use.

Aristotle shook his head. "Why did you not show me this before? It would have quieted my doubtth."

"People have met with misfortune by trying too suddenly to change the ideas of those around them. Like your teacher's teacher, Sokrates."

"That is true, true. What other devices did you bring?"

I had intended to show my devices at intervals, gradually, but Aristotle was so insistent on seeing them all that I gave in to him before he got angry. The little telescope was not powerful enough to show the moons of Jupiter or the rings of Saturn, but it showed enough to convince Aristotle of its power. If he could not see these astronomical phenomena himself, he was almost willing to take my word that they could be seen with the larger telescopes we had in India.

One day a light-armed soldier galloped up to us in the midst of our discussions in the Precinct of Nymphs. Ignoring the rest of us, the fellow said to Alexander: "Hail, O Prince! The king, your father, will be here before sunset."

Everybody rushed around cleaning up the place. We were all lined up in front of the big house when King Philip and his entourage arrived on horseback with a jingle and a clatter, in crested helmets and flowing mantles. I knew Philip by his one eye. He was a big powerful man, much scarred, with a thick curly black beard going gray. He dismounted, embraced his son, gave Aristotle a brief greeting, and said to Alexander:

"How would you like to attend a siege?"

Alexander whooped.

"Thrace is subdued," said the king, "but Byzantion and

Perinthos have declared against me, thanks to Athenian intrigue. I shall give the Perintheans something to think about besides the bribes of the Great King. It is time you smelled blood, youngster; would you like to come?"

"Yes, yes! Can my friends come too?"

"If they like and their fathers let them."

"O King!" said Aristotle.

"What is it, spindle-shanks?"

"I trust thith ith not the end of the prince's education. He has much yet to learn."

"No, no; I will send him back when the town falls. But he nears the age when he must learn by doing, not merely by listening to your rarefied wisdom. Who is this?" Philip turned his one eye on me.

"Zandras of India, a barbarian philothopher."

Philip grinned in a friendly way and clapped me on the shoulder. "Rejoice! Come to Pella and tell my generals about India. Who knows? A Macedonian foot may tread there yet."

"It would be more to the point to find out about Persia," said one of Philip's officers, a handsome fellow with a reddish-brown beard. "This man must have just come through there. How about it, man? Is the bloody Artaxerxes still solid on his throne?"

"I know little of such matters," I said, my heart beginning to pound at the threat of exposure. "I skirted the northernmost parts of the Great King's dominions and saw little of the big cities. I know nothing of their politics."

"Is that so?" said Redbeard, giving me a queer look. "We must talk of this again."

They all trooped into the big house, where the cook and the serving-wenches were scurrying about. During dinner I found myself between Nearchos, Alexander's little Cretan friend, and a man-at-arms who spoke no Attic. So I did not get much conversation, nor could I follow much of the chatter that went on among the group at the head of the tables. I gathered that they were discussing politics. I asked Nearchos who the generals were.

"The big one at the king's right is the Parmenion," he said, "and the one with the red beard is the Attalos."

When the food was taken away and the drinking had begun, Attalos came over to me. The man-at-arms gave him his place. Attalos had drunk a lot of wine already, but if it made him a little unsteady it did not divert him.

"How did you come through the Great King's domain?" he asked. "What route did you follow?"

"I told you, to the north," I said.

"Then you must have gone through Orchoe."

"I—" I began, then stopped. Attalos might be laying a trap for me. What if I said "yes" and Orchoe was really in the south? Or suppose he had been there and knew all about the place? Many Greeks and Macedonians served the Great King as mercenaries.

"I passed through many places whose names I never got straight," I said. "I do not remember if Orchoe was among them."

Attalos gave me a sinister smile through his beard. "Your journey will profit you little, if you cannot remember where you have been. Come, tell me if you heard of unrest among the northern provinces."

I evaded the question, taking a long pull on my wine to cover my hesitation. I did this again and again until Attalos said: "Very well, perhaps you are really as ignorant of Persia as you profess. Then tell me about India."

"What about it?" I hiccuped; the wine was beginning to affect me, too.

"As a soldier, I should like to know of the Indian art of war. What is this about training elephants to fight?"

"Oh, we do much better than that."

"How so?"

"We have found that the flesh-and-blood elephant, despite its size, is an untrustworthy war-beast because it often takes fright and stampedes back through its own troops. So the philosophers of Pataliputra make artificial elephants of steel with rapid-fire catapults on their backs."

I was thinking in a confused way of the armored war-vehicles of my own world. I don't know what made me tell Attalos such ridiculous lies. Partly it was to keep him off the subject of Persia.

Partly it was a natural antipathy between us. According to history, Attalos was not a bad man, though at times a reckless and foolish one. But it annoyed me that he thought he could pump me by subtle questions, when he was about as subtle as a ton of bricks. His voice and manner said as plainly as words: I am a shrewd, sharp fellow; watch out for me, everybody. He was the kind of man who, if told to spy on the enemy, would don an obviously false beard, wrap himself in a long black cloak, and go slinking about the enemy's places in broad daylight, leering and winking and attracting as much attention as possible. No doubt, too, he had prejudiced me against him by his alarming curiosity about my past.

But the main cause for my rash behavior was the strong wine I had drunk. In my own world I drank very little and so was not used to these carousals.

Attalos was all eyes and ears at my tale of mechanical elephants. "You do not say!"

"Yes, and we do even better than that. If the enemy's ground forces resist the charge of our iron elephants, we send flying chariots, drawn by gryphons, to drop darts on the foe from above." It seems to me that never had my imagination been so brilliant.

Attalos gave an audible gasp. "What else?"

"Well ... ah ... we also have a powerful navy, you know, which controls the lower Ganges and the adjacent ocean. Our ships move by machinery, without oars or sails."

"Do the other Indians have these marvels, too?"

"Some, but none is so advanced as the Pataliputrans. When we are outnumbered on the sea, we have a force of tame Tritons who swim under the enemy's ships and bore holes in their bottoms."

Attalos frowned. "Tell me, barbarian, how it is that, with such mighty instruments of war, the Palalal ... the Patapata ... the people of your city have not conquered the whole world?"

I gave a shout of drunken laughter and slapped Attalos on the back. "We *have*, old boy, we have! You Macedonians have just not yet found out that you are our subjects!"

Attalos digested this, then scowled blackly. "I think you have been making a fool of me! Of *me*! By Herakles, I ought—"

He rose and swung a fist back to clout me. I jerked an arm up to guard my face.

There came a roar of "Attalos!" from the head of the table. King Philip had been watching us.

Attalos dropped his fist, muttered something like

"Flying chariots and tame Tritons, forsooth!" and stumbled back to his own crowd.

This man, I remembered, did not have a happy future in store. He was destined to marry his niece to Philip, whose first wife Olympias would have the girl and her baby killed after Philip's assassination. Soon afterwards, Attalos would be murdered by Alexander's orders. It was on the tip of my tongue to give him a veiled warning, but I forebore, I had attracted enough hostile attention already.

Later, when the drinking got heavy, Aristotle came over and shooed his boys off to bed. He said to me: "Let uth walk outthide to clear our heads, Zandras, and then go to bed, too. These Makedones drink like thponges. I cannot keep up with them."

Outside, he said: "The Attalos thinkth you are a Persian thpy."

"A spy? Me? In Hera's name, why?" Silently I cursed my folly in making an enemy without any need. Would I never learn to deal with this human species?

Aristotle said: "He thays nobody could path through a country and remain as ignorant of it as you theem to be. Ergo, you know more of the Persian Empire than you pretend, but wish uth to think you have nothing to do with it. And why should you do that, unleth you are your-thelf a Persian? And being a Persian, why should you hide the fact unleth you are on thome hothtile mission?"

"A Persian might fear anti-Persian prejudice among the Hellenes. Not that I am one," I hastily added.

"He need not. Many Persians live in Hellas without molethtation. Take Artabazos and his sons, who live in Pella, refugees from their own king."

Then the obvious alibi came to me, long after it should

have. "The fact is I went even farther north than I said. I went around the northern ends of the Caspian and Euxine Seas, and so did not cross the Great King's domains save through the Bactrian deserts."

"You did? Then why did you not thay tho? If that is true, you have thettled one of our hottest geographical dithputes: whether the Cathpian is a closed thea or a bay of the Northern Ocean."

"I feared nobody would believe me."

"I am not sure what to believe, Zandras. You are a thtrange man. I do not think you are a Persian, for no Persian was ever a philothopher. It is good for you that you are not."

"Why?"

"Because I *hate* Persia!" he hissed.

"You do?"

"Yeth. I could list the wrongs done by the Great Kings, but it ith enough that they theized my beloved father-in-law by treachery and tortured and crucified him. People like Isokrates talk of uniting the Hellenes to conquer Persia, and Philippos may try it if he lives. I hope he does. However," he went on in a different tone, "I hope he does it without dragging the cities of Hellas into it, for the repositories of civilization have no busineth getting into a brawl between tyrants."

"In India," said I sententiously, "we are taught that a man's nationality means nothing and his personal qualities everything. Men of all nations come good, bad, and indifferent."

Aristotle shrugged. "I have known virtuouth Persians, too, but that monstrouth, bloated empire. . . . No thtate can be truly civilized with more than a few thousand citizens."

There was no use telling him that large states, however monstrous and bloated he thought them, would be a permanent feature of the landscape from then on. I was trying to reform, not Aristotle's narrow view of international affairs, but his scientific methodology.

Next morning King Philip and his men and Aristotle's six pupils galloped off towards Pella, followed by a train of baggage mules and the boys' personal slaves. Aristotle said:

"Let uth hope no chance thlingthtone dashes out Alexandros' brains before he has a chance to show his mettle. The boy has talent, and may go far, though managing him is like trying to plow with a wild bull. Now, let uth take up the question of atoms again, my dear Zandras, about which you have been talking thuch utter rubbish. First, you must admit that if a thing exists, partth of it must also exist. Therefore there is no thuch thing as an indivisible particle . . ."

Three days later, while we were still hammering at the question of atoms, we looked up at the clatter of hoofs. Here came Attalos and a whole troop of horsemen. Beside Attalos rode a tall swarthy man with a long gray beard. This man's appearance startled me into thinking he must be another time-traveler from my own time, for he wore a hat, coat, and pants. The mere sight of these familiar garments filled me with homesickness for my own world, however much I hated it when I lived in it.

Actually, the man's garb was not that of one from my world. The hat was a cylindrical felt cap with ear flaps. The coat was a brown knee-length garment with trousers to match. Over the coat the man wore a yellow vest embroidered with faded red and blue flowers. The whole outfit looked old and threadbare, with patches showing. He was a big craggy-looking fellow, with a great hooked nose, wide cheek bones, and deep-set eyes under bushy beetling brows.

They all dismounted, and a couple of grooms went around collecting the bridles to keep the horses from running off. The soldiers leaned on their spears, with their bronze bucklers slung on their backs, in a circle around us. These spears were the ordinary six-foot jabbing pikes of the Greek hoplite, not the twelve- or fifteen-foot *sarissai* of the phalanx.

Attalos said: "I should like to ask your guest some more philosophical questions, O Aristoteles."

"Athk away."

Attalos turned, not to me, but to the tall graybeard. He said something I did not catch, and then the man in trousers spoke to me in a language I did not know.

"I do not understand," I said.

The graybeard spoke again, in what sounded like a different tongue. He did this several times, using a different-sounding speech each time, but each time I had to confess ignorance.

"Now you see," said Attalos. "He pretends not to know Persian, Median, Armenian, or Aramaic. He could not have traversed the Great King's dominions from east to west without learning at least one of these."

"Who are you, my dear sir?" I asked Graybeard.

The old man gave me a small dignified smile and spoke in Attic with a guttural accent. "I am Artavazda, or Artabazos as the Hellenes say, once governor of Phrygia but now a poor pensioner of King Philippos."

This, then, was the eminent Persian refugee of whom Aristotle had spoken.

"I warrant he does not even speak Indian," said Attalos.

"Certainly," I said, and started off in English: *"Now is the time for all good men to come to the aid of the party. Four score and seven years ago our fathers brought forth . . ."*

"What would you call that?" Attalos asked Artavazda. The Persian spread his hands. "I never heard the like. But then, India is a vast country of many tongues."

"I was not—" I began, but Attalos kept on:

"What race would you say he belonged to?"

"I do not know. The Indians I have seen were much darker, but there might be light-skinned Indians for all I know."

"If you will listen, General, I will explain," I said. "For most of the journey I was not even in the Persian Empire. I crossed through Bactria and went around the north of the Caspian and Euxine Seas."

"Oh, so now you tell another story?" said Attalos. "Any educated man knows the Caspian is but a deep bay opening into the Ocean River to the north. Therefore you could not go around it. So in trying to escape, you but mire yourself deeper in your own lies."

"Look here," said Aristotle. "You have proved nothing of the sort, O Attalos. Ever thince Herodotos there have been those who think the Cathpian a closed thea—"

"Hold your tongue, professor," said Attalos. "This is a matter of national security. There is something queer about this alleged Indian, and I mean to find out what it is."

"It is not queer that one who comes from unknown dithtant lands should tell a thingular tale of his journey."

"No, there is more to it than that. I have learned that he

first appeared in a treetop on the farm of the freeholder Diktys Pisandrou. Diktys remembers looking up into the tree for crows before he cast himself down under it to rest. If the Zandras had been in the tree, Diktys would have seen him, as it was not yet fully in leaf. The next instant there was the crash of a body falling into the branches, and Zandras' staff smote Diktys on the head. Normal mortal men do not fall out of the sky into trees."

"Perhapth he flew from India. They have marvelous mechanisms there, he tells me," said Aristotle.

"If he survives our interrogation in Pella, perhaps he can make me a pair of wings," said Attalos. "Or better yet, a pair for my horse, so he shall emulate Pegasos. Meanwhile, seize and bind him, men!"

The soldiers moved. I did not dare submit for fear they would take my gun and leave me defenseless. I snatched up the hem of my tunic to get at my pistol. It took precious seconds to unsnap the safety strap, but I got the gun out before anybody laid a hand on me.

"Stand back or I will blast you with lightning!" I shouted, raising the gun.

Men of my own world, knowing how deadly such a weapon can be, would have given ground at the sight of it. But the Macedonians, never having seen one, merely stared at the device and came on. Attalos was one of the nearest.

I fired at him, then whirled and shot another soldier who was reaching out to seize me. The discharge of the gun produces a lightning-like flash and a sharp sound like a close clap of thunder. The Macedonians cried out, and Attalos fell with a wound in his thigh.

I turned again, looking for a way out of the circle of

soldiers, while confused thoughts of taking one of their horses flashed through my head. A heavy blow in the flank staggered me. One of the soldiers had jabbed me with his spear, but my belt kept the weapon from piercing me. I shot at the man but missed him in my haste.

"Do not kill him!" screamed Aristotle.

Some of the soldiers backed up as if to flee; others poised their spears. They hesitated for the wink of an eye, either for fear of me or because Aristotle's command confused them. Ordinarily they would have ignored the philosopher and listened for their general's orders, but Attalos was down on the grass and looking in amazement at the hole in his leg.

As one soldier dropped his spear and started to run, a blow on the head sent a flash of light through my skull and hurled me to the ground, nearly unconscious. A man behind me had swung his spear like a club and struck me on the pate with the shaft.

Before I could recover, they were all over me, raining kicks and blows. One wrenched the gun from my hand. I must have lost consciousness, for the next thing I remember is lying in the dirt while the soldiers tore off my tunic. Attalos stood over me with a bloody bandage around his leg, leaning on a soldier. He looked pale and frightened but resolute. The second man I had shot lay still.

"So that is where he keeps his infernal devices!" said Attalos, indicating my belt. "Take it off, men."

The soldiers struggled with the clasp of the belt until one impatiently sawed through the straps with his dagger. The gold in my money pouch brought cries of delight.

I struggled to get up, but a pair of soldiers knelt on my

arms to keep me down. There was a continuous mumble of talk. Attalos, looking over the belt, said:

"He is too dangerous to live. Even stripped as he is, who knows but what he will soar into the air and escape by magic?"

"Do not kill him!" said Aristotle. "He has much valuable knowledge to impart."

"No knowledge is worth the safety of the kingdom."

"But the kingdom can benefit from his knowledge. Do you not agree?" Aristotle asked the Persian.

"Do not drag me into this, pray," said Artavazda. "It is no concern of mine."

"If he is a danger to Makedonia, he should be destroyed at once," said Attalos.

"There is but little chance of his doing harm now," said Aristotle, "and an excellent chance of his doing us good."

"Any chance of his doing harm is too much," said Attalos. "You philosophers can afford to be tolerant of interesting strangers, but if they carry disaster in their baggage it is on us poor soldiers that the brunt will fall. Is it not so, Artabazos?"

"I have done what you asked and will say no more," said Artavazda. "I am but a simple-minded Persian nobleman who does not understand your Greek subtleties."

"I can increase the might of your armies, General!" I cried to Attalos.

"No doubt, and no doubt you can also turn men to stone with an incantation, as the Gorgons did with their glance." He drew his sword and felt the edge with his thumb.

"You will thlay him for mere thuperstition!" wailed

Aristotle, wringing his hands. "At least let the king judge the matter."

"Not superstition," said Attalos, "murder." He pointed to the dead soldier.

"I come from another world! Another age!" I yelled, but Attalos was not to be diverted.

"Let us get this over with," he said. "Set him on his knees, men. Take my sword, Glaukos; I am too unsteady to wield it. Now bow your head, my dear barbarian, and—"

In the middle of Attalos' sentence, he and the others and all my surroundings vanished. Again there came that sharp pain and sense of being jerked by a monstrous catapult. . . .

I found myself lying in leaf-mold with the pearl-gray trunks of poplars all around me. A brisk breeze was making the poplar-leaves flutter and show their silvery bottoms. It was too cool for a man who was naked save for sandals and socks.

I had snapped back to the year 1981 of the calendar of my world, which I had set out from. But where was I? I should be near the site of the Brookhaven National Laboratories in a vastly improved super-scientific world. But there was no sign of super-science here; nothing but poplar trees.

I got up, groaning, and looked around. I was covered with bruises and bleeding from nose and mouth.

The only way I had of orienting myself was the boom of a distant surf. Shivering, I hobbled towards the sound. After a few hundred paces I came out of the forest on a beach. This beach could be the shore of Sewanhaki, or Long Island as we called it, but there was no good way of telling. There was no sign of human life; just the beach curving into the distance and disappearing around headlands, with the poplar forest on one side and the ocean on the other.

What, I wondered, had happened? Had science advanced so fast as a result of my intervention that man had already exterminated himself by scientific warfare? Thinkers of my world had concerned themselves with this possibility, but I had never taken it seriously.

It began to rain. In despair I cast myself down on the sand and beat it with my fists. I may have lost consciousness again.

At any rate, the next thing I knew was the now-familiar sound of hoofs. When I looked up, the horseman was almost upon me, for the sand had muffled the animal's hoofbeats until it was quite close.

I blinked with incredulity. For an instant I thought I must be back in the Classical era still. The man was a warrior armed and armored in a style much like that of ancient times. At first he seemed to be wearing a helmet of Classical Hellenic type. When he came closer I saw that this was not quite true, for the crest was made of feathers instead of horsehair. The nasal and cheek-plates hid most of his face, but he seemed dark and beardless. He wore a shirt of scalemail, long leather trousers, and low shoes. He had a bow and a small shield hung from his saddle and a slender lance slung across his back by a strap. I saw that this could not be ancient times because the horse was fitted with a large, well-molded saddle and stirrups.

As I watched the man stupidly, he whisked the lance out of his boot. He spoke in an unknown language.

I got up, holding my hands over my head in surrender.

The man kept repeating his question, louder and louder, and making jabbing motions. All I could say was "I don't understand" in the languages I knew, none of which seemed familiar to him.

Finally he maneuvered his horse around to the other side of me, barked a command, pointed along the beach the way he had come, and prodded me with the butt of the lance. Off I limped, with rain, blood, and tears running down my hide.

You know the rest, more or less. Since I could not give an intelligible account of myself, the Sachim of Lenape, Wayotan the Fat, claimed me as a slave. For fourteen years I labored on his estate at such occupations as feeding hogs and chopping kindling. When Wayotan died and the present Sachim was elected, he decided I was too old for that kind of work, especially as I was half crippled from the beatings of Wayotan and his overseers. Learning that I had some knowledge of letters—for I had picked up spoken and written Algonkian in spite of my wretched lot—he freed me and made me official librarian.

In theory I can travel about as I like, but I have done little of it. I am too old and weak for the rigors of travel in this world, and most other places are, as nearly as I can determine, about as barbarous as this one. Besides, a few Lenapes come to hear me lecture on the nature of man and the universe and the virtues of the scientific method. Perhaps I can light a small spark here after I failed in the year 340 B.C.

When I went to work in the library, my first thought was to find out what had happened to bring the world to its present pass.

Wayotan's predecessor had collected a considerable library which Wayotan had neglected, so that some of the books had been chewed by rats and others ruined by dampness. Still, there was enough to give me a good sampling of the literature of this world, from ancient to modern times. There were even Herodotos' history and Plato's dialogues, identical with the versions that existed in my own world.

I had to struggle against more language barriers, as the European languages of this world are different from, though related to, those of my own world. The English of today, for instance, is more like the Dutch of my own world, as a result of England's never having been conquered by the Normans. I also had the difficulty of reading without eyeglasses. Luckily most of these manuscript books are written in a large, clear hand. A couple of years ago I did get a pair of glasses, imported from China, where the invention of the printing press has stimulated their manufacture. But, as they are a recent invention in this world, they are not so effective as those of mine.

I rushed through all the history books to find out when and how your history diverged from mine. I found that differences appeared quite early. Alexander still marched to the Indus but failed to die at thirty-two on his return. In fact he lived fifteen years longer and fell at last in battle with the Sarmatians in the Caucasus Mountains. I do not know why that brief contact with me enabled him to avoid the malaria-mosquito that slew him in my world. Maybe I aroused in him a keener interest in India than he would otherwise have had, leading him to stay there longer so that all his subsequent schedules were changed.

His empire held together for most of a century instead of breaking up right after his death as it did in my world.

The Romans still conquered the whole Mediterranean, but the course of their conquests and the names of the prominent Romans were all different. Two of the chief religions of my world, Christianity and Islam, never appeared at all. Instead we have Mithraism, Odinism, and Soterism, the last an Egypto-Hellenic synthesis founded by that fiery Egyptian prophet whose followers call him by the Greek word for "savior."

Still, Classical history followed the same *general* course that it had in my world, even though the actors bore other names. The Roman Empire broke up, as it did in my world, though the details are all different, with a Hunnish emperor ruling in Rome and a Gothic one in Antioch.

It is after the fall of the Roman Empire that profound differences appear. In my world there was a revival of learning that began about nine hundred years ago, followed by a scientific revolution beginning four centuries later. In your history the revival of learning was centuries later, and the scientific revolution has hardly begun. Failure to develop the compass and the full-rigged ship resulted in North America's—I mean Hesperia's—being discovered and settled via the northern route, by way of Iceland, and more slowly than in my world. Failure to invent the gun meant that the natives of Hesperia were not swept aside by the invading Europeans, but held their own against them and gradually learned their arts of iron-working, weaving, cereal-growing, and the like. Now most of the European settlements have been assimilated, though the ruling families of the Abnakis and Mohegans frequently have blue eyes and still call themselves by names like "Sven" and "Eric."

I was eager to get hold of a work by Aristotle, to see what effect I had had on him and to try to relate the effect to the subsequent course of history. From allusions in some of the works in this library I gathered that many of his writings had come down to modern times, though the titles all seemed different from those of his surviving works in my world. The only actual samples of his writings in the library were three essays, "Of Justice," "On Education," and "Of Passions and Anger." None of these showed my influence.

I had struggled through most of the Sachim's collection when I found the key I was looking for. This was an Iberic translation of "Lives of the Great Philosophers," by one Diomedes of Mazaka. I never heard of Diomedes in the literary history of my own world, and perhaps he never existed. Anyway, he had a long chapter on Aristotle, in which appears the following section:

Now Aristotle, during his sojourn at Mitylene, had been an assiduous student of natural sciences. He had planned, according to Timotheus, a series of works which should correct the errors of Empedokles, Demokritos, and others of his predecessors. But after he had removed to Macedonia and busied himself with the education of Alexander, there one day appeared before him a traveler Sandos of Palibothra, a mighty philosopher of India. The Indian ridiculed Aristotle's attempts at scientific research, saying that in his land these investigations had gone far beyond anything the Hellenes had attempted, and the Indians were still a long way from arriving at satisfactory explanations of the universe. Moreover he asserted that no real progress could be made in natural philosophy unless the Hellenes abandoned their disdain for physical labor and undertook exhaustive experiments with mechanical devices of the sort which cunning Egyptian and Asiatic craftsmen make.

King Philip, hearing of the presence of this stranger in his land and fearing lest he be a spy sent by some foreign power to harm or corrupt the young prince, came with soldiers to arrest him. But when he demanded that Sandos accompany him back to Pella, the latter struck dead with thunderbolts all the king's soldiers that were with him. Then, it is said, mounting into his chariot drawn by winged gryphons, he flew off in the direction of India. But other authorities say that the man who came to arrest Sandos was Antipatros, the regent, and that Sandos cast darkness before the eyes of Antipatros and Aristotle, and when they recovered he had vanished.

Aristotle, reproached by the king for harboring so dangerous a visitor and shocked by the sanguinary ending of the Indian's visit, resolved to have no more to do with the sciences. For, as he explains in his celebrated treatise "On the Folly of Natural Science," there are three reasons why no good Hellene should trouble his mind with such matters. One is that the number of facts which must be mastered before sound theories are possible is so vast that if all the Hellenes did nothing else for centuries, they would still not gather the amount of data required. The task is therefore futile. Secondly, experiments and mechanical inventions are necessary to progress in science, and such work, though all very well for slavish Asiatics, who have a natural bent for it, is beneath the dignity of a Hellenic gentleman. And lastly, some of the barbarians have already surpassed the Hellenes in this activity, wherefore it ill becomes the Hellenes to compete with their inferiors in skills at which the latter have an inborn advantage. They should rather cultivate personal rectitude, patriotic valor, political rationality, and aesthetic sensitivity, leaving to the barbarians such artificial aids to the good and virtuous life as are provided by scientific discoveries.

This was it, all right. The author had gotten some of his facts wrong, but that was to be expected from an ancient historian.

So! My teachings had been too successful. I had so well shattered the naïve self-confidence of the Hellenic philosophers as to discourage them from going on with science at all. I should have remembered that glittering theories and sweeping generalizations, even when wrong, are the frosting on the cake; they are the carrot that makes the donkey go. The possibility of pronouncing such universals is the stimulus that keeps many scientists grinding away, year after year, at the accumulation of facts, even seemingly dull and trivial facts. If ancient scientists had realized how much laborious factfinding lay ahead of them before sound theories would become possible, they would have been so appalled as to drop science altogether. And that is just what happened.

The sharpest irony of all was that I had placed myself where I could not undo my handiwork. If I had ended up in a scientifically advanced world, and did not like what I found, I might have built another time machine, gone back, and somehow warned myself of the mistake lying in wait for me. But such a project is out of the question in a backward world like this one, where seamless columbium tubing, for instance, is not even thought of. All I proved by my disastrous adventure is that space-time has a negative curvature, and who in this world cares about that?

You recall, when you were last here, asking me the meaning of a motto in my native language on the wall of my cell. I said I would tell you in connection with my whole fantastic story. The motto says: "Leave Well Enough Alone," and I wish I had.

Cordially yours,
Sherman Weaver

How I Lost the Second World War and Helped Turn Back the German Invasion

Gene Wolfe

In this short story, Gene Wolfe, perhaps best known for his complex and richly crafted novels, has fun with an alternate path our last few decades might have followed. No tinkering by time travelers here; just another turn we might have taken. The key is a radically different kind of conquest—or maybe, come to think of it, not that different after all...

1 April 1938
Dear Editor:

As a subscriber of some years standing—ever since taking up residence in Britain, in point of fact—I have often noted with pleasure that in addition to dealing with the details of the various *All New and Logical, Original Games* designed by your readers, you have sometimes welcomed to your columns vignettes of city and rural life, and especially those having to do with games. Thus I hope that an account of a gamesing adventure which lately befell me, and which enabled me to rub elbows (as it were) not only with Mr. W. L. S. Churchill—the man who, as you will doubtless know, was dismissed from the position of First Lord of the Admiralty during the Great War for his sponsorship of the ill-fated Dardanelles Expedition, and is thus a person of particular interest to all those of us who (like myself) are concerned with Military Boardgames—but also with no less a celebrity than the present *Reichschancellor* of Germany, Herr Adolf Hitler.

All this, as you will already have guessed, took place in connection with the great Bath Exposition; but before I begin my account of the extraordinary events there (events observed—or so I flatter myself—by few from as advantageous a position as was mine), I must explain, at least in generalities (for the details are exceedingly complex) the game of *World War*, as conceived by my friend Lansbury and myself. Like many others we employ a large world map as our board; we have found it convenient to mount this with wallpaper paste upon a sheet of deal four feet by six, and to shellac the surface; laid flat upon a commodious table in my study this serves us admirably. The nations siding with each combatant are determined by the casting of lots; and naval, land, and air units of all sorts are represented symbolically by tacks with heads of various colors; but in determining the *nature* of these units we have introduced a new principle— one not found, or so we believe, in any other game. It is that either contestant may at any time propose a new form of ship, firearm, or other weapon; if he shall urge its probability (not necessarily its utility, please note—if it prove not useful the loss is his only) with sufficient force to convince his opponent, he is allowed to convert such of his units as he desires to the new mode, and to have the exclusive use of it for three moves, after which his opponent may convert as well if he so chooses. Thus a player of *World War*, as we conceive it, must excel not only in the strategic faculty, but in inventive and argumentative facility as well.

Now as it happened Lansbury and I had spent most of the winter now past in setting up the game and settling the rules for the movement of units. Both of us have had considerable experience with games of this sort, and knowing the confusion and ill feeling often bred by a rulebook treating inadequately of (what may once have appeared to be) obscure contingencies, we wrote ours with great thoroughness. On February 17th (Lansbury and I caucus weekly) we held the drawing: it allotted Germany, Italy, Austria, Bulgaria, and Japan to me; Britain, France, China, and the Low Countries to Lansbury. I confess that these alignments appear improbable—the literal-minded man might well object that Japan and Italy, having sided with Britain in the Great War, would be unlikely to change their coats in a second conflict. But a close scrutiny of history will reveal even less probable reversals (as when France, during the Sixteenth Century, sided with Turkey in what has been called the Unholy Alliance) and Lansbury and I decided to abide by the luck of the draw. On the 24th we were to make our first moves.

On the 20th, as it happened, I was pondering my strategy when, paging casually through the *Guardian*, my eye was drawn to an announcement of the opening of the Exposition; and it at once occurred to me that among the representatives of the many nations exhibiting I might find someone whose ideas would be of value to me. In any event I had nothing better to do, and so—little knowing that I was to become a witness to history—I thrust a small memorandum book in my pocket and I was off to the fair!

I suppose I need not describe the spacious grounds to the readers of this magazine. Suffice it to say that they were, as everyone has heard, surrounded by an oval hippodrome nearly seven miles in length, and dominated by the Dirigible Tower that formed a most impressive part of the German exhibit, and by the vast silver bulk of the airship *Graf Spee*, which, having brought the chief functionary of the German *Reich* to Britain, now waited, a slave of the lamp of *Kultur* (save the Mark!) to bear him away again. This was, in fact, the very day that *Reichschancellor* Hitler—for whom the Exposition itself had opened early—was to unveil the "People's Car" exhibit. Banners stretched from poles and even across the main entry carried such legends as:

WHICH PEOPLE SHOULD HAVE A "PEOPLE'S CAR"?????
THE ENGLISH PEOPLE!!

and

GERMAN CRAFTSMANSHIP
BRITISH LOVE OF FINE MACHINES

and even

IN SPIRIT THEY ARE AS BRITISH
AS THE ROYAL FAMILY

Recollecting that Germany was the most powerful of the nations that had fallen to my lot in our game, I made for the German exhibit.

There the crowd grew dense; there was a holiday atmosphere, but within it a note of sober calculation—one heard workingmen discussing the mechanical merits (real and supposed) of the German machines, and their extreme cheapness and the interest-free loans available from the *Reichshauptkasse*. Vendors sold pretzels, *Lebkuchen*, and Bavarian creams in paper cups, shouting their wares in raucous Cockney voices. Around the great showroom where, within the hour, the *Reichschancellor* himself was to begin the "People's Car" invasion of Britain by demonstrating the vehicle to a chosen circle of celebrities, the crowd was now ten deep, though the building (as I learned subsequently) had long been full, and no more spectators were being admitted.

The Germans did not have the field entirely to themselves, however. Dodging through the crowd were driverless model cars only slightly smaller (or at least so it seemed) than the German "People's Cars." These "toys," if I may so style something so elaborate and yet inherently frivolous, flew the rising sun banner of the Japanese Empire from their aerials, and recited through speakers, in ceremonious hisses, the virtues of that industrious nation's products, particularly the gramophones, wirelesses, and so on employing those recently invented wonders, transistors.

Like others I spent a few minutes sightseeing—or rather, as I should say, craning myself upon my toes in an attempt to sightsee. But my business was no more with the "People's Car" and the German *Reichschancellor* than with the Japanese marionette motorcars, and I soon turned my attention to searching for someone who might aid me in the coming struggle with Lansbury. Here I was fortunate indeed, for I had no sooner looked around than I beheld a portly man in the uniform of an officer of the *Flugzeugmeisterei* buying a handful of Germanic confections from a hawker. I crossed to him at once, bowed, and after apologizing for having ventured to address him without an introduction made bold to congratulate him upon the great airship floating above us.

"Ah!" he said. "So you like that" (it was almost "dot") "fat sailor up there? Well, he is a fine ship, and no mistake." He puffed himself up in the good-natured German way as he said this and popped a sweet into his mouth, and I could see that he was pleased. I was about to ask him if he had ever given any consideration to the military aspects of aviation when I noticed the decorations on his uniform jacket. Seeing the direction of my gaze he asked, "You know what those are?"

"I certainly do," I replied. "I was never in combat myself, but I would have given anything to have been a flier. I was about to ask you, Herr—"

"Goering."

"Herr Goering, how you feel the employment of aircraft would differ if—I realize this may sound absurd—the Great War were to take place now?"

I saw from a certain light in his eyes that I had found a kindred soul. "That is a good question," he said, and for a moment he stood staring at me, looking for all the world like a Dutch schoolmaster about to give a favorite pupil's inquiry the deep consideration it deserved. "And I will tell you this—what we had then was nothing. Kites, with guns. If war was to come again now . . ." He paused.

"It is unthinkable, of course."

"*Ja*. Today the *Vaterland*, that could not conquer Europe with bayonets in that war, conquers all the world with money and our little cars. With those things our leader has brought down the enemies of the party, and all the industry of Poland, of Austria, is ours. The people say, 'Our company, our bank,' but now the shares are in Berlin."

I knew all this, of course, as every well-informed person does; and I was about to steer the conversation back toward new military techniques, but it was unnecessary. "But you," Goering continued, his mood suddenly lightening, "and I, my friend, what do we care? That is for the financial people, *nicht wahr?* Do you know what I" (he thumped his broad chest) "would do when the war came? I would build *Stutzkampfbombers*."

"*Stutzkampfbombers?*"

"Each to carry one bomb! Only one, but a big one. Fast planes—" he stooped and made a diving motion with his right hand, at the last moment "pulling out" and releasing a Bavarian cream in such a way that it struck my shoe. "Fast planes. I would put my tanks—you know tanks?"

I nodded and said, "A little."

"—in columns. The *Stutzkampfbombers* ahead of the tanks, the storm troops behind. Fast tanks too—not so much armor, but fast, with big guns."

"Brilliant . . . a lightning war."

"*Ja, blitzkrieg;* but listen, my friend. I must go now and wait upon our *Führer*, but there is someone here you should meet. You like tanks—this man is their father—he was in the navy here in the war, and when the army would not do it he did it from the navy, and they told the newspapers they were making water tanks. You use that silly name still, and when you stand on the outside talk about decks on it because of him. He is in there—" He jerked a finger at the huge pavilion where the *Reichschancellor* was shortly to demonstrate the "People's Cars" to a delighted British public.

I told him I could not possibly get in there—the place was packed already, and the crowd twenty deep outside now.

"You watch. With Hermann you will get in. You come with me, and look like you might be from the newspaper."

Docilely I followed the big, blond German as he bulled his way—as much by his bulk and loud voice as by his imposing uniform—through the crowd. At the door the guard (in *lederhosen*) saluted him and made no effort to prevent my entering at all.

In a moment I found myself in an immense hall, the work of the same Germanic engineering genius that had recently stunned the world with the *Autobahn*. A vaulted metallic ceiling as bright as a mirror reflected with lustrous distortion every detail below. In it one saw the tiled floor, and the tiles, each nearly a foot on a side, formed an enormous image of the small car that had made German industry preeminent over half the world. By an artistry hardly less impressive than the wealth and power which had caused this great building to be erected on the exposition grounds in a matter of weeks, the face of the driver of this car could be seen through the windshield— not plainly, but dimly, as one might actually see the features of a driver about to run down the observer; it was, of course, the face of Herr Hitler.

At one side of this building, on a dais, sat the "customers," those carefully selected social and political notables whose good fortune it would be to have the "People's Car" demonstrated personally to them by no less a person than the German nation's leader. To the right of this, upon a much lower dais, sat the representatives of the press, identifiable by their cameras and notepads, and their jaunty, sometimes slightly shabby, clothing. It was toward this group that Herr Goering boldly conducted me, and I soon identified (I believe I might truthfully say, "before we were halfway there") the man he had mentioned when we were outside.

He sat in the last row, and somehow seemed to sit higher than the rest; his chin was upon his hands, which in turn were folded on the handle of his stick. His remarkable face, broad and rubicund, seemed to suggest both the infant and the bulldog. One sensed here an innocence, an unspoiled delight in life, coupled with that courage to which surrender is not, in the ordinary conversational sense "unthinkable," but is actually never thought. His clothes were expensive and worn, so that I would have imagined he might be a valet save that they fit him so perfectly, and that something about him forbade his ever having been anyone's servant save, perhaps, the King's.

"Herr Churchill," said Goering, "I have brought you a friend."

His head lifted from his stick and he regarded me with keen blue eyes. "Yours," he asked, "or mine?"

"He is big enough to share," Goering answered easily. "But for now I leave him with you."

The man on Churchill's left moved to one side and I sat down.

"You are neither a journalist nor a panderer," Churchill rumbled. "Not a journalist because I know them all, and the panderers all seem to know me—or say they do. But since I have never known that man to like anyone who wasn't one of the second or be civil to anyone except one of the first, I am forced to ask how the devil you did it."

I began to describe our game, but I was interrupted after five minutes or so by the man sitting in front of me, who without looking around nudged me with his elbow and said, "Here he comes."

The *Reichschancellor* had entered the building, and, between rows of *Sturmsachbearbeiters* (as the elite sales force was known), was walking stiffly and briskly toward the center of the room; from a balcony fifty feet above our heads a band launched into *Deutschland, Deutschland uber alles* with enough verve to bring the place down, while an American announcer nearby me screamed to our compatriots on the far side of the Atlantic that Herr Hitler was *here*, that he was even now, with commendable German punctuality, nearing the place where he was supposed to be.

Unexpectedly a thin, hooting sound cut through the music—and as it did the music halted as abruptly as though a bell jar had been dropped over the band. The hooting sounded again, and the crowd of onlookers began to part like tall grass through which an approaching animal, still unseen, was making its way. Another hoot, and the last of the crowd, the lucky persons who stood at the very edge of the cordoned-off area in which the *Reichschancellor* would make his demonstrations, parted, and we could see that the "animal" was a small, canary-yellow "People's Car"; as the *Reichschancellor* approached the appointed spot from one side, so did this car approach him from the other, its slow, straight course and bright color combining to give the impression of a personality at once docile and pert, a pleasing and fundamentally obedient insouciance.

Directly in front of the notables' dais they met and halted. The "People's Car" sounded its horn again, three measured notes, and the *Reichschancellor* leaned forward, smiled (almost a charming smile because it was so unexpected), and patted its hood; the door opened and a blond German girl in a pretty peasant costume emerged; she was quite tall, yet she had—as everyone had seen—been comfortably seated in the car a moment before. She blew a kiss to the notables, curtsied to Hitler, and withdrew; the show proper was about to begin.

I will not bore the readers of this magazine by rehearsing yet again those details they have already read so often, not only in the society pages of the *Times* and other papers but in several national magazines as well. That Lady Woolberry was cheered for her skill in backing completely around the demonstration area is a fact already, perhaps, too well known. That it was discovered that Sir Henry Braithewaite could not drive only after he had taken the wheel is a fact hardly less famous. Suffice it to say that things went well for Germany; the notables were impressed, and the press and the crowd attentive. Little did anyone present realize that only after the last of the scheduled demonstrations was History herself to wrest the pen from Tattle. It was then that Herr Hitler made one of the unexpected and indeed utterly unforeseeable intuitive decisions for which he is famous. (The order, issued from Berchtesgaden at a time when nothing of the kind was in the least expected, and, indeed, when every commentator believed that Germany would be content, at least for a time, to exploit the economic suzerainty she had already gained in Eastern Europe and elsewhere, by which every "People's Car" sold during May, June, and July would be equipped with Nordic Sidewalls at no extra cost comes at once to mind.) Having exhausted the numbers, if not the interest, of the nobility, Herr Hitler turned toward the press dais and offered a demonstration to any journalist who would step forward.

The offer, as I have said, was made to the dais at large; but there was no doubt—there could be no doubt—for whom it was actually intended; those eyes, bright with fanatic energy and the pride natural to one who commands a mighty industrial organization, were locked upon a single placid countenance. That man rose and slowly, without speaking a word until he was face to face with the most powerful man in Europe, went to accept the challenge; I shall always remember the way in which he exhaled the smoke of his cigar as he said: "I believe this is an automobile?"

Herr Hitler nodded. "And you," he said, "I think once were of the high command of this country. You are Herr Churchill?"

Churchill nodded. "During the Great War," he said softly, "I had the honor—for a time—of filling a post in the Admiralty."

"During that time," said the German leader, "I myself was a corporal in the Kaiser's army. I would not have expected to find you working now at a newspaper."

"I was a journalist before I ever commenced being a politician," Churchill informed him calmly. "In fact, I covered the Boer War as a correspondent with a roving commission. Now I have returned to my old trade, as a politician out of office should."

"But you do not like my car?"

"I fear," Churchill said imperturbably, "that I am hopelessly prejudiced in favor of democratically produced products—at least, for the people of the democracies. We British also manufacture a small car, you know—the Centurion."

"I have heard of it. You put water in it."

By this time the daises were empty. We were, to the last man and woman, and not only the journalists but the notables as well, clustered about the two (I say, intentionally, *two,* for greatness remains greatness even when stripped of power) giants. It was a nervous moment, and might have become more so had not the tension been broken by an unexpected interruption. Before Churchill could reply we heard the sibilant syllables of a Japanese voice, and one of the toy automobiles from Imperial Nippon came scooting across the floor, made as though to go under the yellow "People's Car" (which it was much too large to do), then veered to the left and vanished in the crowd of onlookers again. Whether it was madness that seized me at the sight of the speeding little car, or inspiration, I do not know—but I shouted, "Why not have a race?"

And Churchill, without an instant's delay, seconded me: "Yes, what's this we hear about this German machine? Don't you call it the race master?"

Hitler nodded. "*Ja,* it is very fast, for so small and economical a one. Yes, we will race with you, if you wish." It was said with what seemed to be perfect poise; but I noted, as I believe many others did, that he had nearly lapsed into German.

There was an excited murmur of comment at the *Reichschancellor*'s reply, but Churchill silenced it by raising his cigar. "I have a thought," he said. "Our cars, after all, were not constructed for racing."

"You withdraw?" Hitler asked. He smiled, and at that moment I hated him.

"I was about to say," Churchill continued, "that vehicles of this size are intended as practical urban and suburban transportation. By which I mean for parking and driving in traffic—the gallant, unheralded effort by which the average Englishman earns his bread. I propose that upon the circular track which surrounds these exposition grounds we erect a course which will duplicate the actual driving conditions the British citizen faces—and that in the race the competing drivers be required to park every hundred yards or so. Half the course might duplicate central London's normal traffic snarl, while the other half simulated a residential neighborhood; I believe we might persuade the Japanese to supply us with the traffic using their driverless cars."

"Agreed!" Hitler said immediately. "But you have made all the rules. Now we Germans will make a rule. Driving is on the right."

"Here in Britain," Churchill said, "we drive on the left. Surely you know that."

"My Germans drive on the right and would be at a disadvantage driving on the left."

"Actually," Churchill said slowly, "I had given that some consideration before I spoke. Here is what I propose. One side of the course must, for verisimilitude, be lined with shops and parked lorries and charabancs. Let the other remain unencumbered for spectators. Your Germans, driving on the right, will go clockwise around the track, while the British drivers, on the left—"

"Go the other direction," Hitler exclaimed. "And in the middle—*Zerstorend Gewalt!*"

"Traffic jam," Churchill interpreted coolly. "You are not afraid?"

The date was soon set—precisely a fortnight from the day upon which the challenge was given and accepted. The Japanese consented to supply traffic with their drone cars, and the exposition officials to cooperate in setting up an artificial street on the course surrounding the grounds. I need not say that excitement was intense; an American firm, Movietone News, sent not less than three crews to film the race, and there were several British newsreel companies as well. On the appointed day excitement was at a fever pitch, and it was estimated that more than three million pounds had been laid with the bookmakers, who were giving three to two on the Germans.

Since the regulations (written, largely, by Mr. Churchill) governing the race and the operation of the unmanned Japanese cars were of importance, and will, in any event, be of interest to those concerned with logical games, allow me to give them in summary before proceeding further. It was explained to the Japanese operators that their task would be to simulate actual traffic. Ten radio-controlled cars were assigned (initially) to the "suburban" half of the course (the start for the Germans, the homestretch for the British team), while fifty were to operate in the "urban" section. Eighty parking positions were distributed at random along the track, and the operators—who could see the entire course from a vantage point on one of the observation decks of the dirigible tower—were instructed to park their cars in these for fifteen seconds, then move onto the course once more and proceed to the next unoccupied position according to the following formula: if a parking space were in the urban sector it was to be assigned a "distance value" equal to its actual distance from the operator's machine, as determined by counting the green "distance lines" with which the course was striped at five-yard intervals—but if a parking position were in the suburban section of the track, its distance value was to be the counted distance plus two. Thus the "traffic" was biased—if I may use the expression—toward the urban sector. The participating German and English drivers, unlike the Japanese, were required to park in every position along the route, but could leave each as soon as they had entered it. The spaces between positions were filled with immobile vehicles loaned for the occasion by dealers and the public, and a number of London concerns had erected mock buildings similar to stage flats along the *parking* side of the course.

I am afraid I must tell you that I did not scruple to make use of my slight acquaintance with Mr. Churchill to gain admission to the paddock (as it were) on the day of the race. It was a brilliant day, one of those fine early spring days of which the west of England justly boasts, and I was feeling remarkably fit, and pleased with myself as well. The truth is that my game with Lansbury was going very satisfactorily indeed; putting into operation the suggestions I had received from Herr Goering I had overrun one of Lansbury's most powerful domains (France) in just four moves, and I felt that only stubbornness was preventing him from conceding the match. It will be understood then that when I beheld Mr. Churchill hurrying in my direction, his cigar clamped between his teeth and his old Homburg pulled almost about his ears, I gave him my broadest smile.

He pulled up short, and said, "You're Goering's friend, aren't you—I see you've heard about our drivers."

I told him I had heard nothing.

"I brought five drivers with me—racing chaps who had volunteered. But the Huns have protested them. They said their own drivers were going to have to be *Sturmsachbearbeiters*, and it wasn't sporting to run professionals against them; the exposition committee has sided with them, and now I'm going to have to get up a scratch team to drive for England. All amateurs—I can offer them nothing but blood, toil, tears, and sweat, and those blasted SS are nearly professional caliber. I've got three men but I'm still one short even if I drive myself . . ."

For a moment we looked at one another; then I said: "I have never raced, but my friends all tell me I drive too fast, and I have survived a number of accidents; I hope you don't think my acquaintance with Herr Goering would tempt me to abandon fair play if I were enlisted for Britain."

"Of course not." Churchill puffed out his cheeks. "So you drive, do you? May I ask what marque?"

I told him I owned a Centurion, the model the British team would field; something in the way he looked at me and drew on his cigar told me that he knew I was lying— and that he approved.

I wish that my stumbling pen could do justice to the race itself, but it cannot. With four others—one of whom was Mr. Churchill—I waited with throbbing engine at the British starting line. Behind us, their backs toward us, were the five German *Sturmsachbearbeiters* in their "People's Cars." Ahead of us stretched a weirdly accurate imitation of a London street, wherein the miniature Japanese cars already dodged back and forth in increasing disorder.

The starting gun sounded and every car shot forward; as I jockeyed my little vehicle into its first park I was acutely aware that the Germans, having entered at the suburban end of the course, would be making two or three positions to our one. Fenders crumpled and tempers flared, and I—all of us—drove and parked, drove and parked, until it seemed that we had been doing it forever. Sweat had long since wilted my shirt collar, and I could feel the blisters growing on my hands; then I saw, about thirty yards in front of me, a tree in a tub—and a flat painted to resemble, not a city shop but a suburban villa. It dawned on me then—it was as though I had been handed a glass of cold champagne—that *we had not yet met the Germans*. We had not yet met them, and the demarcation was just ahead, the halfway point. I knew then that we had won.

Of the rest of the race, what is there to say? We were two hundred yards into the suburban sector before we saw the slanted muzzle of the first "People's Car." My own car finished dead last—among the British team—but fifth in the race when the field was taken as a whole, which is only to say that the British entries ran away with everything. We were lionized (even I); and when *Reichschancellor* Hitler himself ran out onto the course to berate one of his drivers and was knocked off his feet by a Japanese toy, there was simply no hope for the German "People's Car" in the English-speaking world. Individuals who had already taken dealerships filed suits to have their money returned, and the first ships carrying "People's Cars" to reach London (Hitler had ordered them to sail well in advance of the race, hoping to exploit the success he expected with such confidence) simply never unloaded. (I understand their cargo was later sold cheaply in Morocco.)

All this, I realize, is already well known to the public; but I believe I am in a position to add a postscript which will be of special interest to those whose hobby is games.

I had, as I have mentioned, explained the game Lansbury and I had developed to Mr. Churchill while we were waiting for the demonstrations of the "People's Car" to begin, and had even promised to show him how we played if he cared to come to my rooms; and come he did, though it was several weeks after the race. I showed him our board (the map shellacked over) and regretted that I could not also show him a game in progress, explaining that we had just completed our first, which (because we counted the Great War as *one*) we called World War Two.

"I take it you were victorious," he said.

"No, I lost—but since I was Germany that won't discomfort you, and anyway I would rather have won that race against the real Germans than all the games Lansbury and I may ever play."

"Yes," he said. "Never have so many owed so much to you—at least, I suppose not."

Something in his smile raised my suspicions; I remembered having seen a similar expression on Lansbury's face (which I really only noticed afterward) when he persuaded me that he intended to make his invasion of Europe by way of Greece; and at last I blurted out: "Was that race really fair? I mean to say—we did surprisingly well."

"Even you," Churchill remarked, "beat the best of the German drivers."

"I know," I said. "That's what bothers me."

He seated himself in my most comfortable armchair and lit a fresh cigar. "The idea struck me," he said, "when that devilish Japanese machine came scooting out while I was talking to Hitler. Do you remember that?"

"Certainly. You mean the idea of using the Japanese cars as traffic?"

"Not only that. A recent invention, the transistor, makes those things possible. Are you by any chance familiar with the operating principle of the transistor?"

I said that I had read that in its simplest form it was merely a tiny chip or flake of material which was conductive in one direction only.

"Precisely so." Churchill puffed his cigar. "Which is only to say that electrons can move through the stuff more readily in one direction than in another. Doesn't that seem remarkable? Do you know how it is done?"

I admitted that I did not.

"Well, neither did I before I read an article in *Nature* about it, a week or two before I met Herr Hitler. What the sharp lads who make these things do is to take a material called germanium—or silicon will do as well, though the transistor ends up acting somewhat differently—in a very pure state, and then add some impurities to it. They are very careful about what they put in, of course. For example, if they add a little bit of antimony the stuff they get has more electrons in it than there are places for them to go, so that some are wandering about loose all the time. Then there's other kinds of rubbish—boron is one of them—that makes the material have more spots for electrons than electrons to occupy them. The experts call the spots 'holes', but I would call them 'parking places', and the way you make your transistor is to put the two sorts of stuff up against each other."

"Do you mean that our track was . . ."

Churchill nodded. "Barring a little terminological inexactitude, yes I do. It was a large transistor—primitive if you like, but big. Take a real transistor now. What happens at the junction point where the two sorts of material come together? Well, a lot of electrons from the side that has them move over into the side that doesn't—there's so much more space there for them, you see."

"You mean that if a car—I mean an electron—tries to go the other way, from the side where there are a great many parking places—"

"It has a difficult time. Don't ask me why, I'm not an electrical engineer, but some aspects of the thing can't be missed by anyone, even a simple political journalist like myself. One is that the electron you just mentioned is swimming upstream, as it were."

"And we were driving downstream," I said. "That is, if you don't mind my no longer talking about electrons."

"Not at all. I pass with relief from the tossing sea of cause and theory to the firm ground of result and fact. Yes, we were driving with the current, so to speak; perhaps it has also occurred to you that our coming in at the urban end, where most of the Japanese cars were, set up a wave that went ahead of us; we were taking up the spaces, and so they were drawn toward the Germans when they tried to find some, and of course a wave of that sort travels much faster than the individuals in it. I suppose a transistor expert would say that by having like charges we repelled them."

"But eventually they would pile up between the teams—I remember that the going did get awfully thick just about when we passed through the Germans."

"Correct. And when that happened there was no further reason for them to keep running ahead of us—the Jerries were repelling them too by then, if you want to put it that way—and then the rules (my famous distance formula, if you recall) pulled them back into the urban area, where the poor Huns had to struggle with them some more while we breezed home."

We sat silent for a time; then I said, "I don't suppose it was particularly honest; but I'm glad you did it."

"Dishonesty," Churchill said easily, "consists in violating rules to which one has—at least by implication—agreed. I simply proposed rules I felt would be advantageous, which is diplomacy. Don't you do that when you set up your game?" He looked down at the world map on the table. "By the way, you've burnt your board."

"Oh, there," I said. "Some coals fell from Lansbury's pipe toward the end of the game—they cost us a pair of cities in south Japan, I'm afraid."

"You'd better be careful you don't burn up the whole board next time. But speaking of the Japanese, have you heard that they are bringing out an automobile of their own? They received so much attention in the press in connection with the race that they're giving it a name the public will associate with the toy motorcars they had here."

I asked if he thought that that would mean Britain would have to beat off a Japanese invasion eventually, and he said that he supposed it did, but that we Americans would have to deal with them first—he had heard that the first Japanese-made cars were already being unloaded in Pearl Harbor. He left shortly after that, and I doubt that I will ever have the pleasure of his company again, much though I should like it.

But my story is not yet finished. Readers of this magazine will be glad to learn that Lansbury and I are about to begin another game, necessarily to be prosecuted by mail, since I will soon be leaving England. In our new struggle the United States, Britain, and China will oppose the Union of Soviet Socialist Republics, Poland, Romania, and a number of other Eastern European states. Since Germany should have a part in any proper war, and Lansbury would not agree to my having her again, we have divided her between us. I shall try to keep Mr. Churchill's warning in mind, but my opponent and I are both heavy smokers.

Sincerely,
"Unknown Soldier"

Editor's Note. While we have no desire to tear aside the veil of the *nom de guerre* with which "Unknown Soldier" concluded his agreeable communication, we feel we are yet keeping faith when we disclose that he is an American officer of Germanic descent, no longer young (quite) and yet too young to have seen action in the Great War, though we are told he came very near. At present "Unknown Soldier" is attached to the American embassy in London, but we understand that, as he feels it unlikely his country will ever again have need of military force within his lifetime, he intends to give up his commission and return to his native Kansas, where he will operate an agency for Buick motorcars. Best of luck, Dwight.